Forever Man

FOREVER MAN

by A.J. DeWall

interlude press

ISBN 978-1-941530-00-9

Published by Interlude Press
http://interludepress.com

Book design by Lex Huffman
Cover Art by Buckeyegrrl Designs
Cover Art Photography ©Depositphotos.com/mettus/yekophotostudio/
vilaxlt

As ever, for my girl.

No star is ever lost we once have seen,
We always may be what we might have been.

ADELAIDE ANNE PROCTER

Chapter 1

Ren Warner is not a fan of New Mexico—all of that brown, and tan and more brown. And the heat. And those ubiquitous yellow chamisa bushes that assail his sinuses the moment he leaves the confines of the Albuquerque airport. And the miles and miles of endless space. And nature.

"At least it's not Texas," he says, slipping on his Dior sunglasses, hand in the air as though he's hailing a cab. Pushing six feet in his brown Tom Ford shoes, Ren is all legs, his short blond hair and hazel eyes as out of place here in New Mexico as they are back in New York. He's kept up his daily swim practice in the decade since his last school meet and it shows.

From his black Range Rover, idling four doors down, Antonio spots him and smiles. He's used to Ren's big city ways.

Antonio pulls up to the curb, gets out and greets Ren with a quick hug. "Welcome back."

"Hello, Antonio," Ren says, smiling for the first time in hours. He takes in Antonio's appearance. He looks handsome in his new buzz cut, his lemon-yellow button-down a nice complement to his olive skin.

"New boots?"

Antonio looks down at his brand-new steel-toed, midnight blue cowboy boots and nods sheepishly. He gets a lot of grief from his family about being so tall—*Did your mama step out on your dad with a basketball player, or hook up with an alien?*—but that doesn't stop him from wearing his boots. He may skip the requisite cowboy hat, but the boots stay.

"What did your wife say?" Ren asks, giving him the once-over.

"Um..."

Ren smirks. "She likes the boots, doesn't she?"

Antonio nods again. "A lot."

"Told you."

Ever the gentleman, Antonio holds open the front passenger door for Ren and, after he's seated, loads all five of his bags into the back. When he slips into the driver's seat, he notices Ren is already engrossed in his Blackberry; so he turns on KBAC radio and keeps quiet.

"It's obnoxiously hot," Ren whines, ten minutes into their fifty-minute drive up to Santa Fe.

"That it is." Antonio turns up the air conditioner.

"How do you stand it? Seriously. *God.*"

"I'm used to it."

"I've been back exactly thirty-four minutes and I already want to go home," Ren grumbles, texting a reply to a design client with yet another care question about his new upholstered walls.

"So, what's on the agenda this trip?" Antonio asks.

"Doors. Doors and rugs, and so help me, if they haven't finished painting the damn kitchen, I'm going to hurt somebody."

Antonio laughs. After four trips, he knows Ren is all bark and very little bite. They've spent hours together in this very car picking up samples, rounding up laborers, trying to track down obscure artists and muralists and carvers to satisfy the whims of their mutual clients, Clint and Deidre Alexander. He knows Ren hates coming here. Maybe this visit he'll let Antonio take him around, show him *his* New Mexico.

"Doors and rugs, huh?" Antonio says.

"And tile. Always tile. Will she ever just pick a tile?"

Antonio laughs again and speeds up now that they're outside the city limits. "Where's Mr. James? Will we see him around?"

"Stop trying to dodge the question. Did the painters show up, or not?"

"Don't know, actually."

"But you *live* in the same neighborhood..."

"Not quite. Look, Ren. I've been up at the Galisteo ranch for the better part of the week at the beck and call of Clint's German colleagues, and before that I spent five weeks out at the San Antonio place. I don't have time to keep up with painters for Wife Number Four's kitchen."

Ren exhales. "I know, sorry. I really should have hired that project manager, the one from Taos. But Deidre would have *killed* him, Antonio.

She would have pierced his poor little heat-swollen heart and eaten it for breakfast."

This time, there is no laughter; they both know it's only a slight exaggeration.

They're at the base of La Bajada when Antonio asks again. "So—no Mr. James this trip?"

"No. No Mr. James," Ren replies, eyes on his Blackberry. "And stop calling him that."

"Two weeks is a long time to be away from your boyfriend," Antonio says.

"Husband. Almost," Ren says, flashing the ring on his left hand while still looking at his phone.

"Right."

"And not really," Ren continues. "Paul travels even more than I do. We're used to it."

"Oh, okay," Antonio replies, thinking about Sarah, his wife, and the early days of their marriage, when he would sleep on the couch whenever she visited her parents in Boulder. It was only ever for the weekend, but missing her killed him every single time.

"In fact," Ren says, glancing up to look at Antonio for the first time since he got in the car, "it took us four months to go on three dates because we were both crazy busy. I don't know how we ever managed to get engaged."

"When's the big day?"

"Next May. Or June. We're trying to move a few things around... you know how it is."

"Sure," Antonio says, but he really doesn't. He hears a Joni Mitchell cover on the radio. Can't place the artist, but he likes it. So he turns it up.

Ren looks at him, raises one eyebrow and says, "Really, Antonio?"

"What? I can't like Joni Mitchell?"

Ren giggles and the two of them lapse into an easy silence. His texts and emails answered, Ren stares out the window. The flat, piñon-dotted landscape gives way to high desert as they approach the outskirts of Santa Fe.

On his first trip, Antonio pointed out landmarks and places of interest, but the only information Ren retained was the bit about the mountains. "You can see four mountain ranges from Santa Fe," Antonio had said, with the pride of a fifth-generation local. "The Sandias in Albuquerque, the Jemez up by the Lab, the Ortiz over on the Turquoise Trail and the Sangre de Cristos, which bump up right against Santa Fe."

Ren smiles at the memory; these are the kinds of facts his father would love to learn. Erik Warner would want to memorize the names of the mountain ranges so he could tell them to his customers, or the guys in his long-suffering bowling league. Sometimes Ren memorized facts for him:

"Brooklyn was America's first suburb. Did you know that, Dad? It was all farmland, until they built the Brooklyn Bridge."

"Dad, I went to Seattle with Paul. Did you know they have a bridge that floats on the water?"

"Paris is amazing, Dad. Did you know that the Eiffel Tower was only supposed to be a temporary construction?"

"No kidding?" his dad would say, committing the facts to memory.

Except, he hasn't shared any facts with his dad lately. Not for months, maybe longer. Ren thinks about calling him—he has a good thirty minutes before they reach the hotel—but decides he'll wait and call him later that evening.

Ren sighs. He never got over missing his dad. Most of his friends spend as little time as possible with their parents, but even at (almost) thirty Ren still feels the pull of family. It's been at least a year since he made it back to Minnesota. Ren's brother Sean and his wife Erin are expecting their second, a boy, and their daughter Meg is growing so fast, he's embarrassed to admit he has no idea whom she counts as her best friends.

I really should know the names of Meg's friends. I should know more than her size and color preferences; princess dresses and vintage accessories shipped in 'brown paper packages' are a poor substitute for face time.

Ren picks up his phone and scrolls through his calendar, looking for three, even two days he could take off and sneak back home for a visit. "Nothing for months," he mutters.

"I didn't catch that," Antonio says. "Do you need something?"

"No, thanks. Just thinking out loud."

Do you need something?

Antonio's question hangs in the air for a moment and then lands in the pit of Ren's stomach. He shifts in his seat. He's been feeling out of sorts lately, as if something were off, but he can't figure out *why*.

If he were honest with himself, he would admit he really hasn't tried that hard to figure it out. He's simply pushed on, filling his days with work and his nights with cocktails and openings and fundraisers. He'd told himself that there was a perfectly reasonable explanation for his irritability: aging. It was the big 3-0 pressing down on his spine, waking him up at 2:15 a.m. with the feeling that he'd left something behind, twisting his thoughts into knots he could never begin to untie. He'd ignored the voice that kept haranguing him with annoying little questions: *Is this what you really want? Are you happy? Are you even sure you know what happy feels like? What if there's more, so much more—and what if it's too late to find it?*

Ren shakes it off. His life is everything his little gay-boy-in-Minnesota heart could have hoped for, and more.

Do I need something? No. I'm amazing. Everything is amazing. Why would I need anything?

"Almost there," Antonio announces. "Will you have time for some fun this trip?"

"Maybe. I hadn't really thought about it."

"Next week is Fiesta, it's a pretty big deal around here. And there's a benefit concert out at the Santa Fe Opera on Saturday," Antonio offers. "Everyone's excited about seeing Alegra."

"Alegra? Really? In Santa Fe?"

"It's a benefit for Alex Marin House," Antonio explains. "The people on the board have a lot of connections in the entertainment industry. Most of them are retired producers or agents or writers. Some of them are still in the business. This guy Mitch—he's on the board—he's recording with her right now."

"God, I *loved* Alegra in high school. I saw her in concert in New York, maybe three years ago. She's still amazing," Ren exclaims. "Alex Marin House. You told me about that place, right? It's a community center for GLBT youth."

"A shelter. For runaways. Most of them are gay, yeah."

"And your wife works there. Sarah?"

Antonio's entire face lights up at the mention of his wife's name. "Yes. She's the executive director."

"Wow. Very impressive, Antonio."

"She impresses me every day. I still can't believe my luck."

Ren smiles, thinking of his fiancé. Impressive is a word most people would use when describing Paul James, too. A brilliant political strategist. *New York Times* bestselling author. Former development director of the Human Rights Campaign. One of President Landry's confidants. Ren couldn't believe his luck, either.

Do you need something?

Antonio's question echoes in Ren's mind, interrupting his thoughts again. "What the fuck?" Ren whispers, hoping Antonio thinks he's just cursing at an email on his phone.

"Would you like to go? To the benefit, I mean?" Antonio asks. "I can ask my wife for an extra ticket."

Ren sits up straight in his seat and claps his hands. "Oh my God, I just totally clapped my hands like a five-year-old. I would love to! Oh! What will I wear? You're all so dressed down, here."

"Yeah. Dressing up is black jeans, instead of blue. Nice shirt. Nice boots. But I've seen some folks wearing suits to these things, so just do your thing."

"Okay. Thanks."

Ren's phone buzzes. He gives Antonio an apologetic look and answers it on the second ring. "Deidre. Yes, I'm here. Yes, he was on time. We're almost there. Tomorrow, yes. First thing. I'll send photos after lunch. No. I'll walk over after dinner tonight. Yes. No, I don't mind walking. Deidre, really, are you sure you're a New Yorker? It's barely ten blocks. Yes. Fine. Of course, darling. I'll phone you later."

Antonio grimaces. "She's a piece of work. I'm not sure how Clint can stand her."

"He can't. I do it for him," Ren says, turning his phone on vibrate and slipping it into his front pocket. "Why do you think they have so many houses? It keeps her occupied. Clint relies on all of us—the designers, the stylists, the art buyers, the fucking dog groomers—to keep her out of his hair."

"I'm just grateful I only answer to him."

Sitting at a stoplight at the edge of downtown, Antonio glances at the Eldorado Hotel, Ren's home for the next two weeks. One of only two structures for which developers have defied the city's building ordinance, the faux-adobe looks down on its three-storied neighbors. He would have chosen something more authentic for Ren—the Loretto, maybe—but he knows his efforts would be lost on the fashionable man who just wants to get in, get done and get the hell out of Dodge.

Antonio pulls up in front of the impressive hotel and nods to the bellhops, who begin unloading Ren's bags. "Sure you don't want me to drive you over to the house tonight?"

"No. Go home to your wife. I like walking. That's why I chose this hotel over staying up at that Waves place."

"Ten Thousand Waves. She wanted you to stay up there?"

"Yes. Something about 'divine Japanese architecture' and 'master masseurs.' I don't have time for all that."

"It is pretty awesome. Sarah and I go up there every so often. Wooden tubs. Hot stone massage. Shooting stars—"

"Sounds lovely. And it's so not happening. I want to spend all my time working on the house. I need this trip to be my last. No offense."

Antonio laughs and hands Ren the keys to the Alexander house. "If the kitchen isn't done, don't do anything crazy. Just call me. I'll handle it."

"Whatever." Ren flashes Antonio one of his genuine smiles. "Pick me up at ten o'clock? Doors tomorrow, rugs on Thursday."

Antonio offers Ren a mock salute and then, after sliding into the front seat, lowers his window and shouts, "I'm serious. Nothing crazy!"

Ren waves him off and marches into the building, a sandy-haired bellhop trailing behind him.

Once in his room, he orders steak salad and goes over his schedule for the next two weeks. He could finish the project this trip, but it will be a miracle if Deidre gives him her final approval. Still, going over his notes is sure to calm the uneasy feeling conjured up by Antonio's unintentionally disconcerting question.

It doesn't.

He hangs up his clothes and considers calling Paul, but decides against it. He knows he won't answer; Ren can't possibly compete with the fight for marriage equality. *National* marriage equality. Every state. Finally.

Elected to his second term the year before, President Landry wants it done like, yesterday, which means Ren hasn't seen much of Paul these past few months.

Paul is making history. He doesn't have time for travel check-ins or idle conversation.

People often ask Ren if he minds, if he's lonely without Paul, if he's frustrated or angry at the situation, but he isn't any of those things. He's ridiculously proud of Paul. And though he does love him, and is excited to spend the rest of his life with him, he doesn't need him. Not like Sean needs Erin. Not the way his parents need each other. Which is why, in his opinion, he and Paul are perfect for each other.

"What I *need* is a drink," Ren announces to the empty room.

He leaves his travel jeans on and changes into a robin's egg-blue, tailored button-down shirt. Then he heads down to the bar. The Agave Lounge is swank Santa Fe style, small plates and a room full of East Coast tourists and locals who wish they lived on the East Coast.

He's just starting on his mojito, trying not to think about Paul, or Deidre's unpainted kitchen, or anything at all, when he notices his phone vibrating on the table. When he sees the name on the text, he nearly drops his phone.

Cole: Hey, Ren.

Cole McKnight.

Holy hell.

Ren: Hey, yourself. To what do I owe the pleasure of your text?

Cole: I know. It's been a while. I'm glad you still have the same number.

Ren: Of course I do. Why would I change it?

Cole: I don't know. Bad breakup? Creepy stalker?

Ren: Old friend I haven't seen in five years?

Cole: Four. And don't get on my case. I called you last year. New Year's.

Ren: You're such a good friend. Seriously, are you just bored and thumbing through your contact list?

Cole: Nope.

Ren: Drunk texting? Because that would be so like you.

We're doing it again. God, how do we always get back here so fast?

Ren feels that old familiar buzz in his body, as if he can't wait to see what happens next. It's been nearly twelve years since they graduated from Saint Benedict's and damn it, Cole still has this effect on him.

This is what we do. We've always done this.

Ren can't help but smile, thinking about the early days of their bizarre, intense friendship, when he and Cole would circle around each other, tease each other, flirt shamelessly with each other, but never land. All those years and they never *got* to anything.

Ren thumbs over Cole's last text. It seems as if they've had this unspoken "thing" forever. It's still fun. It may be the most fun he's ever had.

Cole: I'm not drunk.

Ren: What, then?

Cole: I guess I miss you.

Ren: Stop. You do not.

Cole: I really do.

Ren: What exactly do you miss about me?

Cole: Your simple, demure, self-effacing ways.

Ren laughs, actually laughs out loud. Oh, this *is* fun. Maybe this round of texting will last a few days and he'll barely notice he's stuck in guacamole land, catering to the tacky whims of a bleached-blonde trophy wife.

Ren: I miss THIS.

Cole: All caps. You must be starved for a good texting.

Ren: Are you for real? That's just... bad.

Cole: How's Paul?

Ren: Excellent. And yours?

Cole: You can't remember his name, can you?

Ren: Lyle?

Cole: No.

Ren: Luke?

Cole: No.

Ren: Come on. Give me a hint.

Cole: No.

Ren: It starts with L. I know his name starts with L.

Cole: Liam. His name is Liam Hill.

Ren: How's it going with LIAM?

Cole: We're happy. It's nice.

Ren ignores the tiny pangs of jealousy and reminds himself that they are just friends. Weird, flirty, slightly inappropriate friends; but friends—*just friends*. And he has Paul. Paul James. Wonderful, doting, fabulous change-agent-for-good Paul James. Cole has Liam and he has Paul. Lovely Paul.

Ren: I'm getting married.

Cole: I heard.

Ren: Ash told you?

Cole: Jeremy. I ran into him in L.A. last month.

Ren: Oh.

Oh? Oh? That's all you can say? Can't you come up with some witty remark? Something heartfelt, maybe? Can't you give him a clue—?

Cole: Am I invited?

Cole: Ren?

Ren gulps down half of his mojito and stares his phone.

Cole: You still there?

Ren: Yes. Sorry. Why not? Just don't embarrass me in your toast.
      I run in very respectable circles now, McKnight.

Cole: Bor-ing.

Ren thinks about how they got to this place where Cole wasn't the first person he called with his engagement news, where he didn't call Cole at all. He did think of him. He just didn't call him. He had thought of Cole almost right away, in fact. But the realization that he had thought of his old crush just moments after accepting Paul's proposal unnerved him to the point that he *couldn't* call him.

Ren realizes he doesn't even know where Cole is living now. *Is he still in Europe? Did he move to L.A. with Liam? A lot could happen in a year.*

There was a time when they couldn't go one day without talking, or Skyping, or texting, or seeing each other, let alone one entire year. But that was before they grew up and moved on and went after "everything they always wanted." That was before his hand slipped out of Cole's grip one last time. That was before Ren decided to be fucking great at this life, this other life.

Though they rarely saw each other after their sophomore year of college, they remained good friends until graduation, Ren at Pratt in Brooklyn, Cole at Berklee College of Music in Boston. But after Cole took the internship at a recording studio in London and Ren started an apprenticeship at Blue, a design firm in SoHo, they talked less and less. There were boyfriends, and long hours, and new friends and never enough time to get beyond catching up. There was also a relief of sorts, a relief that somehow made the distance bearable. There was all of that, widening the gap and taking the bridge apart brick by brick.

Except there was also this: this back and forth. They held that "thing" between them up to the light and played with it, kept it close, private, almost sacred.

And this: this tension, this teasing. They dared to think about it. Usually over text, sometimes over email, occasionally over the phone. They indulged in innuendo that anyone else would see as a precursor to sex, so much so that Ren felt compelled to delete Cole's texts and emails whenever one of their banter sessions coincided with Ren having a semi-serious boyfriend.

And above all, this: this abiding love. Their connection, forged in that bright, hopeful time of adolescence, could not be tempered by time, or distance, or updates on their everyday lives.

There was this. There was always this.

Do you need something?

The hair on the back of Ren's neck stands on end and goosebumps pop up on his arms. It's as though Antonio is whispering his stupid question in Ren's ear like Tinkerbelle's psycho, evil twin, and he just can't do this now. He's too vulnerable. He'll go too far with it. He might say something true.

Ren: I should go. I have an errand to run.

Cole: So text while you run it.

Ren: I need to focus. Sorry. Text me later?

Cole: Did I offend you? You're so far from boring.

Ren: Not offended. I really have to be somewhere. Text me later if you want.

Cole: One more thing.

Ren: ??

Cole: I like your jeans.

Ren: Thanks.

Ren: Wait, what?

Cole: Turn around.

Ren: No way.

Cole: Yes, way.

Ren is seconds away from full on freaking out. Cole is here. In Santa Fe. In this hotel. In this bar.

"Holy fuck," he whispers. His phone buzzes.

Cole: You're not going to turn around?

Ren wants to look, *has* to look, but he can't make himself do it. He stares at his phone, wondering if Cole is behind him and to the right, or behind him and to the left.

Has he been watching me this whole time? Why is he here? Is Liam with him? Oh my God, do something! You probably look like a nervous teenager. Turn around!

Suddenly, Ren senses someone standing behind him. He would know that earthy, slightly citrusy smell of Cole's cologne anywhere. He wants to reach out and grab him, pull him close and tell him how much he's missed his dear, dear friend, but he can't; he's frozen in his seat.

"Ren." Cole's voice is soft. He places a firm hand on his shoulder.

And there it is: sparks. Sparks and electricity and butterflies and dear lord, *why, why, why*? Yup. *That's* why he's scared to turn around. Texts are safe, emails are easy and this is going to be both dangerous and really, really hard.

He decides to play it off.

Ren: I'm scared to turn around because I'm worried you're not pretty anymore.
      Do you still have your hair?

He hears Cole's phone buzz, and then his hand is gone, and then Cole is laughing and then he's just *there* in front of Ren, a smile lighting up his whole face. He grabs Ren in a patented Cole McKnight Hug and plops down in the chair opposite Ren, sets his phone on the table and presents his head for inspection.

"See? No bald spots," he teases, and it's everything Ren can do not to reach out and run his fingers through Cole's thick chestnut hair. "We're not *that* old, Ren. We're only thirty."

"*You're* only thirty. I'm still in my twenties."

"Barely. For a few more months."

"Still."

Cole reaches across the table to grab Ren's hand and squeezes. Ren squeezes back and flashes him a genuine smile. Cole, still an overgrown boy teeming with excitement, finally looks older, as though he could at least buy cigarettes without being carded. They're roughly the same height, but Cole is bigger than Ren remembers—broader in the shoulders, wider in the chest, his biceps, once impressive, now barely contained in his designer T-shirt made to look downtown-thrift. His jacket is clearly tailored, his hands manicured: the last vestiges of careful breeding and a private education. He looks happy, lit up, as if he just found out he's won a much-lauded prize.

Cole is beautiful.

"It's amazing to see you, Ren."

"Thanks. You too."

"So what are you doing in Santa Fe? How long are you staying? Are you staying here at the Eldorado?"

"Excited, much?"

"Come on! Can you blame me? This is Santa Fe, Ren. Santa Fe. It's not the last place I ever thought I'd see you but—"

"That would be a swamp somewhere in Alabama—"

"Or a blinker town in Texas—"

"Ugh. Texas."

"But Ren, this is bizarre. Bizarre and awesome."

Ren gives Cole an affectionate smile. "I'm here in the hotel for two weeks. I'm redecorating a home for Deidre and Clint Alexander," Ren explains.

"Should I know them?" Cole asks.

"Not unless you read *Page Six*," Ren quips.

"Wow. Just, wow. I can't get over it. I saw you walk in and—" Cole hesitates, looks almost sad for a moment, then recovers and winks. "Of all the gin joints in all the towns—"

"Oh, no. Not the *Casablanca* line."

"What? It's a great, classic film."

"True. But that line is cheesy and overdone. And no matter how hard you try, you're no Humphrey Bogart."

"Not since I stopped using product in my hair."

"More like not since ever," Ren says. And then, "It's... good. Your hair. You look good."

"Well, you look stunning. Really. Sometimes I forget how gorgeous you are."

Ren looks down at his drink, rubs his thumb along the condensation on his glass and wills himself not to blush. Blatant, earnest flattery; this is new.

"Best last line of a movie, though," Cole says.

"Huh?"

"*Casablanca.* 'I think this is the beginning of a beautiful friendship.' Best last line."

"I'm partial to the last line of *You've Got Mail.*"

"Meg Ryan over Ingrid Bergman? Say it isn't so!"

"Of course not. Ingrid all the way. Ingrid forever. But it is my favorite last line of a movie."

Just as the words are out of his mouth, he regrets saying them. Because now he has to recite the line. And it shouldn't matter; it doesn't *mean* anything. But it would sound as if it might mean something, or maybe once did, and Ren can't say it.

"I don't remember it. How does it go?" Cole asks.

"No! *Some Kind of Wonderful.* 'You look good wearing my future.' Best last line. Or, almost-last line."

"That is pretty good."

"It's right after Eric Stoltz stands up to the bullies, ditches Lea Thompson and gives Mary Stuart Masterson the diamond stud earrings."

"Wow. You remember all that?"

"We only watched that movie thirty-nine times."

From its perch on the table, Ren's phone lights up with a new message. It's nearly midnight on the East Coast, but it could be Paul, so he checks it. "Sorry." Cole waves his hand to show he doesn't mind, and sits back in his chair.

Paul: Just got out of a 6-hour meeting with Javanovich and Wilder. No movement yet. Back at it tomorrow. You get in okay?

Ren: Yes. Fine.

Paul: Awake enough to talk? I miss you.

Ren: Miss you too. Okay if we talk tomorrow?

Ren knows he probably should excuse himself to talk to Paul, and he probably should text, *You'll never guess who I ran into.* But he doesn't feel like talking and he doesn't feel like explaining.

Paul: No problem. Call me when you wake up. Love you.

Ren: Love you. Goodnight.

"Paul," Ren explains, tucking his phone away in his pocket.

"Oh, right. Want me to give you a few minutes?"

"No, it's fine. We'll talk tomorrow."

Cole tilts his head a bit and searches Ren's face.

"What?" Ren asks.

"I thought you said you were getting married."

"I am."

"Nothing romantic about a goodnight text," Cole teases.

"Maybe not if it's coming from you."

"Hey! I've gotten better!"

"*Really?*"

"Really. I'm so much better at it now. I'm practically a romantic savant."

Ren raises one eyebrow. "Practically?"

"Stop. I'm not totally inept."

"If you say so."

Ren smiles and Cole's eyes are dancing, and Ren thinks this is just the right amount of tension and playfulness to be fun but not enough to ruin his entire life. He can totally handle this. It's just a game, a game they've been playing since they were kids and it always ends the same way, so why worry? Why not just have fun with it?

"You haven't told me why you're here," Ren says.

"You didn't ask."

"Sorry. I guess I'm still a bit surprised to see you."

"We've been here a couple of weeks, recording in a studio out in Galisteo."

"Galisteo? The Alexanders have a ranch out there, but I've only seen it at night."

"It's very John Wayne," Cole says, smiling again. "The studio is amazing. She stays out there, in the main house."

"Who's she?"

"Oh, I thought you knew."

"Knew what?"

"I'm working on Alegra's new album."

"What? Seriously?"

"Yeah, I uh, well, you know I was working for Sound Off in London, and she came in to listen to her friend record, and well, that's how it started. I've been working with her for about nine months now."

"That's amazing! I'm so proud of you!"

He *is* proud of Cole, but he's also a bit sad. Why didn't Cole tell him? Why didn't he call him first thing? They listened to her first two albums in the dorm so many times they could sing her songs in their sleep. This was big news, and yet Ren seemed to be the last to know.

"Thanks. I'm still not over it, you know? I think I'm always going to feel like a stowaway in my own life."

"I feel that way sometimes. About Paul. And New York. And just, all of it."

"Good. I'm happy for you. You deserve an amazing, epic life, Ren."

"Of course I do," Ren agrees. "Are you singing?"

"No. Producing."

"No singing? Cole—"

"Are you making stuff?"

"You know I'm not. That subject is done and buried." He knows he shouldn't push Cole about this, but he does it anyway. "What about writing? Did you write any of her songs?"

Cole looks away from Ren. "No. I produce, play a little here and there."

"But that's not what you said you wanted. Cole—"

"Another round?" the waiter asks, as if they've been sitting together all night.

Ren shakes his head. "Not for me."

"I left my drink over there," Cole says, pointing to the secluded booths in the back of the bar. "I should probably go get it."

"Do you want another?" the waiter asks again.

"No. Thanks. But let me pick up the tab for the group I was with in the back, and for this gentleman as well," Cole says, handing the waiter his credit card.

"That's not necessary."

"I know," Cole says, again with the all-over smile. "Give me a minute?"

"Sure."

Cole stands and pushes back his chair. "Don't go anywhere!"

Ren nods and smiles, takes a sip of his drink. He turns and watches Cole walk toward a smallish group of loud, happy people who get louder as he approaches. A stout blond man says something Ren can't quite make out and Cole reaches over and places his hand over the man's mouth to stop him. Everyone at the table erupts in laughter. Cole is smooth, friendly, magnetic. Ren can't take his eyes off of him.

Cole says something to his friends, salutes them and turns before Ren can look away. He watches Cole come back to him, all smiles. *Does he have a daily quota for smiles or something?* When he catches Ren's eye he mouths, "musicians," and shrugs his shoulders. And then he's back at the table, drink in hand.

Do you need something?

"Hey," Cole says, looking down at Ren.

"Hey. I should go."

"Go? But we just started—"

"No, I meant it. The text. I have an errand."

"At this time of night?"

"It's not that late. And it's not far."

"Shit, Ren, we haven't seen each other in ages, and now you're just walking out after fifteen minutes? This is... it's just so awesome to run into you like this. Could we at least have lunch tomorrow? Or breakfast? Or coffee? How about coffee?"

There's something about the eager tone in Cole's voice that makes him do it, even when he knows he absolutely shouldn't, not tonight. This much, he knows. He should wait to spend time with Cole until he's had a good night's sleep, until Antonio's stupid question leaves his brain, until he talks to Paul and feels rooted again.

He should wait, but he doesn't.

"You could come with me," Ren says softly.

"Yeah?"

"Sure. Why not?"

"Let's go, then."

They pick up their glasses and down what's left of their drinks in one gulp. And then they giggle. It's another moment when they say nothing and yet know everything, and Ren thinks maybe they *can* do this in person. Maybe the boundaries will stay firmly in place, even though there's no Paul or Liam or gaggle of obnoxious Saint Benedict's alums to remind them who they are and who they never will be.

"Lead on," Cole says, following Ren out of the bar. They walk out the main entrance into the cool night air. Even after four trips to Santa Fe,

Ren often forgets he's in the high desert at seven thousand feet, where the temperatures drop considerably at night.

They make their way up San Francisco Street toward the Plaza. The streets are quiet, just a few tourists milling about, peering in shop windows. Several blocks ahead the Saint Francis Cathedral looms, its round arches and rose window lit by artfully-placed floodlights.

"So where are we going?" Cole asks.

"The Alexander house. It's just a few blocks off Marcy."

"This is the house you're decorating?"

"Yes. I have to check on the progress," Ren explains.

"You seem to know the city well."

"Not really. Just here, around downtown."

Cole glances down a side street and says, "It kind of looks like a movie set, or Disneyworld. Everything adobe, even the Starbucks. I like it."

"It's fine for a weekend getaway, but I've had quite enough of the chile wreaths and earth tones, thank you very much. And Cole, have you not noticed all the women wear the same thing? Matchstick skirts in hideous colors, wide belts and turquoise and silver squash-blossom necklaces. It's like a fucking uniform."

"Like I said... Disneyworld."

They catch up, and volley, and, for more than two blocks, walk a little too closely. They pass the independent bookstore where Ren spent hours poring over photography books, looking for a gift for Paul; and the jewelry store where he found black pearl earrings for his mother's birthday; and the little folk art shop where he seriously considered buying a Day of the Dead nativity scene for himself, but decided against it when he realized he might be the only one who would appreciate the irony of skeletal Mary and Joseph in Mexican hats.

After they cut across the charming central Plaza, Cole stops to read a sign outside the Palace of the Governors, and Ren takes him in again: cuffed jeans covering his still-tight ass, T-shirt hugging his still-amazing arms, a light stubble gracing his still-gorgeous, wrinkle-free face. And just like that, the goosebumps are back, along with that old familiar want that took up residence at the base of his pelvic bone when he was sixteen and stayed there until he forced himself to get on with his life.

Cole catches Ren looking at him and smirks.

"What?" Ren asks, trying for innocent.

"You can look. I don't mind."

"I was just thinking, I forgot how short you are. You seem so much taller in your texts."

Cole places both hands over his heart and steps back. "I die by your wit, Mr. Warner."

"Whatever." Ren laughs, marching off toward Marcy Street.

They walk in comfortable silence for two blocks, and then Ren stops in front of a long, tall adobe wall rising into a high curve at the entrance. "This is it," he says, pushing open a blue-painted wooden door. They walk into the hidden courtyard and follow a slate pathway to the front door of a large, traditional adobe home.

"It's historic, which basically means I have to wait for fucking ever to get permits," Ren says. He digs in his leather satchel for the keys and opens the front door. "I'm replacing this door first thing tomorrow."

Ren flips on lights in the foyer and the great room. Cole walks around slowly, mouth agape. Somehow, Ren's managed to create a clean, modern, sophisticated design while keeping the integrity of the Spanish and Native American cultural influences. "Ren, did you *do* this. I mean, this is, how did you do this?"

"It's not rocket science," Ren says, heading for the kitchen. "Just get rid of the kitsch, keep the palette simple and work with wonderful craftspeople and artists to—"

Ren walks into the kitchen, finds it still unpainted and—"Fuck! Fuck, fuck, fuck, fuck, fuck!"

Cole runs to the kitchen. "Are you okay? What—?"

Instantly exhausted and defeated, Ren sits down on the kitchen floor and bangs the back of his head against charcoal-gray cabinets.

"Um... Ren?"

"They didn't." Bang. "Paint." Bang. "The kitchen." Bang.

Cole drops to the floor and sits, his legs outstretched and just an inch away.

Ren is wound tight. He feels as if he's about to explode. This could set him back a week.

Cole runs his thumb along the inside of Ren's wrist to calm him; Ren relaxes his shoulders almost instantly. It's a familiar gesture, one that takes him back to a time when Cole was the only person who could truly find him under the panic, the only boy who could see him, and reflect that back to him to prove that he truly was okay.

He's torn between pulling his hand away and leaning in closer when Cole says, "A friend of Alegra's wanted to send her his piano to use for this album, don't ask me why. The friend lives up in Taos, so Gretchen—she's Alegra's assistant—scheduled movers to pick it up from his house and deliver it to the ranch."

Ren pushes back against the cabinet, his breath slowly evening out.

"So while Gretchen is scheduling the movers, Mary, the girl who runs the office at the studio, she's looking over at Gretchen, kind of nervous. When Gretchen hangs up the phone Mary says, 'Call two more moving companies and schedule a pick-up for the same time, same day.' Gretchen looks at her like she's crazy," Cole says, still rubbing Ren's wrist.

"Then Mary explains that if we want the piano moved that day, we'll have to call at least three companies so that we can get one to show up. She says it's *mañana*, which means—"

"Tomorrow."

"Right. Tomorrow. Everything is tomorrow. It's the way they do things here."

Ren turns his head to look at Cole. "I noticed."

"You probably get more done in one day than most people here get done in a month. It must drive you crazy."

"You have no idea."

Ren looks at Cole, so open, so happy to see him, so willing to be here on this kitchen floor, and he can't stop himself. He rests his head on Cole's shoulder and exhales. They're quiet for a moment, Cole still rubbing Ren's wrist. It feels natural, as if they've been doing this all their lives, and yet odd, as if they are out of time, living in some alternate adobe universe.

"We're sitting on the kitchen floor of a four million-dollar home in Santa Fe, talking about Alegra's piano," Ren says.

Cole laughs. "It's an aerial moment."

"Explain, please," Ren says, trying *not* to nuzzle Cole's neck.

"You know, the moments when you suddenly see yourself from above, usually when you're doing something absurd, or embarrassing, or... unbelievably, unexpectedly... wonderful."

"Oh."

Compliments. Cuddling. Serious sentiment. What the hell is going on with Cole?

Ren decides a change of subject is for the best. "So what happened with the piano?"

"Oh, well, Mary was right. The day of the move, only one company showed up, and they were two hours late."

"*Mañana.*"

Cole is quiet for a few moments and then asks, "Ren, you never did tell me... what's the last line in *You've Got Mail*?"

Ren sucks in his breath. He wants to stand up and shake off Cole's soft voice and the press of his thumb, clear his head and find his bearings. But that would be too obvious. Cole would figure out that the words *do* have meaning, or did at one time, and they don't do that. They don't get that close to the truth. He could pretend he doesn't remember, but Cole would simply look it up on his phone, and that would be just as awkward.

"Tom Hanks says, 'Don't cry, Shopgirl. Don't cry.' And Meg Ryan says, 'I wanted it to be you. I wanted it to be you so badly.'"

Cole's thumb stops but doesn't leave Ren's wrist. After a moment he places his hand flat against Ren's, palm to palm, fingers lined up perfectly. "Yeah. That's a good one."

Chapter 2

"Invite him. I want to meet him," Alegra says, twirling her long, jet-black hair around one finger. It's her "happy" habit, his favorite of her little tics. When she's in a good mood she winds her trademark hair tightly around her fingers and then lets it fall onto her shoulder, over and over again.

"It's not a good idea."

"Barry says he's a stunner." She pokes him in the side.

"Never trust drummers." He pauses, looks at her sheepishly and then adds, "But yeah, he is."

Alegra folds her tiny frame in half, her knees up to her chin, and smiles. Brown eyes dancing, she wants to play; he can tell.

"Angel said you were flirting with him." Testing the waters.

"Never trust guitar players either."

"You're the most untrustworthy of all," she teases.

"Am not!"

"Bring him 'round, then."

"No."

"Gretchen said after you spotted him, you were fucking mute for ten full minutes."

"For that matter, never trust assistants. Or anyone you know. Ever. I was not *mute*. And it was *not* ten minutes. I was just surprised," Cole says.

"Let me ring him. He'll probably piss his pants—"

"Not Ren. He's unflappable."

"Ask him. I'll sing all of the old stuff you used to moon over in between studies." She's full-on teasing him now; Cole can't help but smile.

"Alegra, *please*. I really shouldn't."

"Ah, so that's how it is. You want to, but you shouldn't, so you won't," she says, getting up from the couch. "In a bit of a mess then, are you?"

"What? Because of Liam?"

"You said it, not me."

"It's nothing to do with Liam. Ren and I, we have... unfinished business."

"A *big* mess, then."

"It's just better if we meet for coffee, or something," Cole says.

"So that's how it is? You can't trust yourself around this stunner of yours?"

"I can. I do. I just... it's better this way."

"What did you get up to last night, then? A bit of—?" Alegra makes a bizarrely crude gesture with one hand while shaking her hips. It's always startling to him—her raunchy personality juxtaposed with her childlike appearance. Barely five feet tall, with perfect skin and a playful demeanor, even at forty-two she looks like one of the Saint Margaret's girls who boarded across the highway from Saint Ben's—more specifically, like one of the Saint Margaret's girls who snuck over to the boys' campus to smoke.

"Stop. No. Of course not. He showed me this house he's renovated for a client, and then we walked back to the hotel. Simple."

Except it wasn't simple. They'd been doing their thing, and it was kind of delicious the way they slipped back into it as if no time had passed since their last meeting. They were catching up and teasing each other, and Cole was super excited about spending as much time with his friend as possible. But then Ren shifted closer to him, rested his head on Cole's shoulder and suddenly everything became very complicated.

At the mere memory of Ren's soft exhalation, of their fingertips pressing together like leaves under glass, Cole feels the ache. The ache almost killed him twelve years ago, as he watched Ren go off to New York with so much left unsaid. He'd been able to keep the ache at bay for years, talk himself out of it, had moved across oceans to avoid it, but it had never really left him. The ache remained, dulled over time, but ever-present. And last night, in Ren's presence, away from the familiar and the shared, the ache had taken over and spread through his entire body, leaving him frustrated beyond belief.

So no, inviting Ren to an exclusive performance in a private room, in a tiny nightclub, thousands of miles away from Liam, and reason, and the promises he'd made to his boyfriend in earnest, was *not* a good idea.

"It's not a good idea," Cole insists.

"Don't care." Alegra pecks him on the cheek and hands him her sheet music. "Invite him. I just want to meet him. I'll keep watch, don't worry. I won't let you do anything I would do."

"Gee, thanks." Cole watches her bound out of the studio in search of lunch.

They've been at it all morning, laying down tracks for what Cole hopes will be her first single, "So New." She's writing about love again, but this time it's about her loving husband, not some "rat bastard." She's writing happy these days, and that's why she chose Cole to produce. He's talented, smart, earnest and good. And she chose him because, for the most part, he's a positive guy. Even with the ache, quiet and awful, pressing hard into his spine, he's happy—or as happy as he hoped to be. And he's good at it. Which is why he's recording with Alegra. In this happy, contented, settled life of hers, Cole fits.

If you were to ask his friends (namely, Ash and Dean), they'd say he was *pathologically* happy, that it wasn't real; that underneath his eternal optimism was a desperate need to please, to be polite and that, in seeming happy all the time, Cole was just doing what was expected of him. Could he really blame his whole approach to life on good manners?

"I could blame a lot on good manners," Cole mumbles.

Ren, for instance. He could blame his relationship with Ren on good manners. The day he met him—found him, really, out by the chapel—he couldn't help but offer him kindness, dry his tears. The daily prayers were bad enough, but Ren had been done in by the stress of Wednesday confession and escaped down the long path past the lake to the chapel in the woods. Cole found him, crying behind the back entrance, dirt on his uniform and fear in his eyes.

Cole knew that fear well; you couldn't be a gay boy boarding at a Catholic prep school in Minnesota and *not* be afraid of judgment and condemnation from the monks and harassment and rejection from the legions of homophobic assholes who made up their student body. But

Cole had friends. Good friends. Friends who accepted him for who he was. And they would accept Ren, too.

That day, he held out his hand for Ren to take. He can still see Ren's tearstained face looking up at him in confusion and, seconds later, determination, as he slipped his hand into Cole's and let himself be helped up off of the ground.

That had been the beginning, a beginning he could have avoided if he had simply been less polite, if he had kept walking, or run and got Brother Sam to help. Yet despite how things turned out for the two of them, he wouldn't change a thing about that day.

Later, after Ren entered his bloodstream and staked a claim on his heart, his need for decorum would keep him from doing anything about it. Because it wasn't just his heart. Oh, no. It was something powerful and raw and needy that kept him up at night, trying to ease the pain of want until he was so sore he wanted to cry. He could never risk his friendship with Ren just to satisfy his teenage hormones. He knew Ren felt something similar, or had at one time, but they never found the right moment. *He* never found the right moment.

Midway through college, he convinced himself it just wasn't meant to be. And even if they did get together, they were still so young. It wouldn't, *couldn't* last. But their friendship would stay pure and it *would* last. It would *outlast* the boyfriends, and the distance, and maybe even a husband.

Except their friendship didn't last, not really, not in the way he wanted it to. The want between them grew into its own thing, and then it became *their* thing, and soon they couldn't interact without the teasing and the "what if" looks and the "you know you want it" subtext. And when the ache became unbearable, Cole began to drift. And when Cole began to drift, Ren began to pull away. And they both went on to find other confidants and friends. Every once in a while, they took the want out for a ride with the help of modern technology. And it was fine... mostly because they hadn't really been alone together in years.

He could have avoided Ren last night. They were in the back, Alegra's musicians and Mitch's engineers and Gretchen. He could have just watched Ren from afar, never said a word, and let it be one of those movie moments, two friends who keep missing each other—sometimes by chance, sometimes by choice. He could have continued to watch him, let the ache come alive at the sight of him, wind its way up, vertebra by vertebra, until it burned hot at the back of his neck.

He could have let him go again. But he couldn't help himself.

Besides, he had better manners than that.

"Could you line them up next to each other so I can compare them?" Ren asks the frustrated, sweaty workers at Santa Fe Entrance. His request earns him a series of groans before a tall-ish worker calls for an extra pair of hands to help out.

Ren watches as four men move three giant, hand-carved doors to lean against a wall. He's done with doors, absolutely *done*, having spent the better part of the day roaming around the massive outdoor showroom looking for the perfect front door for Deidre's perfect adobe home. He is in no mood. He's hot, he's dusty and he forgot his sunscreen. And he may be just a little bit annoyed with himself for his behavior with Cole last night. Just a little.

"It's not as if I slept with him, or even kissed him," Ren mutters, staring at the doors. Still, he *did* let his guard down. He let Cole in. Just a bit. Not too much, but enough that he can't stop thinking about him when should be thinking about doors and rugs and unpainted kitchens and guest lists and honeymoon plans and Paul.

After Ren gave Cole a tour of the rest of the Alexander house, they simply walked back to the hotel and said goodnight, promising to get together again at some point in the coming week. It was innocent. Polite. Friendly. "Call me. I'm in room 415," Ren said, regretting it almost instantly.

Why did you tell him your room number? He has your cell. Now he probably thinks you want him to—

"Can we eat yet? It's almost two-thirty," Antonio interrupts Ren's internal rant.

"Thank goodness you're back. I have to get out of the sun. I need air conditioning, and liquid something and food."

"Definitely food," Antonio agrees.

"Let me just take one last picture of all three lined up together," Ren says, motioning for the workers to step out of the way. Two of the men glare at him; the new helper just stares and the tall-ish one surprises him with a wink.

"Really, now?" Ren says just loud enough for Antonio to hear. "Didn't peg him for family."

"New Mexicans are never what they seem," Antonio says, smiling.

"As lovely as you all are, and I do appreciate you so very *much*, I need you to move. Step away from the doors. Yes. Just like that. A little bit farther. Little bit... farther. There! Thank you!" Ren snaps one more photo and then turns on his heels to go back to the car.

"He'll call you." Antonio nods to the group of men, spent from their day attending to the demanding Ren Warner.

Antonio turns to leave and then turns back, adding, "About the doors. He'll call you *about* the *doors.*" The tall-ish man frowns and kicks up dust with his boots.

As he gets in to his Range Rover, Antonio chuckles. "You could have worked that to your advantage." He starts the car. "Maybe you could get free delivery or something."

"What are you talking about?"

"The tall one. He likes you."

"So?"

"Oh, I see. You're so used to being an object of interest, it bores you."

Ren laughs. "I like that. 'Object of interest.' It makes me sound like a spy."

"Maria's, or that soup place you like?" Antonio pulls out into lazy midday traffic.

"Maria's. I need a drink."

"Maria's it is."

It's only two miles to the restaurant. They sit in silence while Ren sends dozens of photos of doors to Deidre. It's nearly six o'clock in New York, and he knows she's busy getting dressed for this event or that fundraiser, so he doesn't expect a prompt reply. She won't want any of the options he sends her anyway. He'll probably spend another long, hot day hunting for just the right door, dripping in sweat and covered in desert. Just the thought of it makes him want to guzzle tequila like a college freshman.

Maria's is quiet, its yellow vinyl tablecloths wiped clean and shiny. The sign near the entrance warns, "The Chile is HOT today," the word "HOT" filled in with white chalk. They're settled into a nondescript booth, margaritas ordered, Antonio shoving chips and spicy homemade salsa into his mouth, when he asks, "What's with all this housewife stuff?"

"Speak English, Antonio."

"Drinking in the middle of the afternoon."

"Since when is that the domain of housewives?"

"I don't know. Sarah watches that show. They all drink in the afternoon, before their kids get home from school."

"Charming," Ren says, sipping his water.

"*Real Housewives* of something."

"Right. Which city are they tarnishing now? Des Moines? Saskatoon? Somewhere on Guam?"

"Hell if I know. So why the need for alcohol, my friend?"

"I might have... run into someone last night who makes me feel... uncomfortable."

Antonio sits up taller in the booth, his expression serious. "Somebody giving you a hard time?"

"No, no. Nothing like that. I just ran into an old friend at the Agave."

"Small world."

"Isn't it just?"

"Okay, fill in the blanks. I'm no good at guessing," Antonio urges.

"We're friends, right? You and me?"

"Well, you've said 'no' to every dinner invitation..."

Ren frowns. He has turned Antonio down in favor of pushing on with work, or hiding out in his hotel room, pretending he's on East Coast time. "I know I haven't been social, but—"

"Shit, I'm just teasing. Of course we're friends."

"I didn't mean to assume—"

Antonio fixes him with a stern gaze. "I let you pick out my boots. Boots are sacred, man."

"Right. So we're friends, and you wouldn't betray a friend's confidence, even if said friend wasn't technically doing anything wrong but still didn't want anyone to know about it?"

"I work for Clint Alexander, Ren. Friend or no friend, I'm fucking Fort Knox."

"Got it. Good. Okay, I might have, at one point in time, harbored unrequited *feelings* for this friend, and may have, over the years, indulged in a bit of... flirting with him, nothing major, nothing untoward, but still very... intense. And he may have, from time to time, flirted back. And it's been five years since we saw each other and even longer since we were alone together... in the same room... until last night, when I *may have* had a fit on Deidre's kitchen floor and then possibly... rested my head on him for comfort. Literally."

"Huh."

"Huh? That's your only response? Huh?"

"I'm not used to 'Nervous Ren.' You're not telling me something."

"No, I—"

Ren is cut off by the arrival of their gigantic margaritas. Ren thanks the waitress and sucks at least half of his down as if it's his first drink in months.

"Yeah. You are definitely leaving something out," Antonio says.

"I'm not."

"Give."

"There's nothing more to it, really."

Antonio raises one eyebrow and folds his arms, not willing to budge.

"Okay, fine! I was in love with him when we were kids and I'm not anymore, I'm *not*. But he's insanely gorgeous and so charismatic—I mean really, he's *magnetic*—and he knows me, and we get each other and it's kind of... he just *does* something to me..."

"Something no one else does?"

Ren looks directly at Antonio, then down at his hands, unable to admit it to his face. "Yes. And it's just a bit dangerous to be here, with *him* here, and our boyfriends *not here*. You know?"

"Fiancé. You have a fiancé."

"That's what I said."

Antonio chooses to ignore Ren's slip and takes another sip of his margarita. "Don't be so hard on yourself. You love Paul, right?"

"I do, yes."

"And this guy—"

"Cole. His name is Cole."

Antonio doesn't miss the way Ren's eyes twinkle and the corners of his mouth turn up when he answers, his voice soft and reverent.

"And this guy Cole, he has a boyfriend or someone he loves?"

"He does."

"So don't worry about it. We all have old flames and people we were once crazy for who pop up every now and again. It's part of this complicated life we live. You never pursued more than friendship before. Why would you cross the line now?"

"I wouldn't."

"Right, so stop worrying." Antonio reaches over to pat his hand, and Ren downs the rest of his drink. He motions to the waitress to bring him another.

"You're right. I know you're right. We're friends. We're just good friends."

Ren turns to look out the window, but not before Antonio sees the look in Ren's eyes. He knows that look.

Antonio relaxes his shoulders and sinks into the booth. "So what's up with this Cole guy? Is he in town on business?"

"Oh, you'll love this. It proves your small world theory."

"It's not really *my* theory, it's pretty much agreed upon by the masses," Antonio interrupts.

"Must you?"

"Sorry."

"He's producing Alegra's new album at a studio out in Galisteo. How's that for a coincidence?" Ren is so excited he's bouncing in his seat.

"That's Mitch's studio. He's on the board at Alex Marin House, remember?"

"See! Small world!"

"Or something."

"Explain."

Antonio doesn't want to explain. He doesn't want to tell Ren what he knows to be true, knows in his bones: Ren will never marry Paul, because this Cole guy, he's the one. He's Ren's Sarah. Antonio could see it all in that one moment. He saw the longing, the truth, the entirety of it all in that one fleeting look, the look Ren didn't want him to see.

The look is never wrong.

That, and Ren just lied to him for the first time. And Ren never lies.

Antonio has a knack for spotting what he calls "soul-love." His friends give him shit about it, tell him he let too many of Sarah's new-agey woo-woo friends "freak his mind." But he's always been able to see it, *the look*, since he was a child. His grandmother, the one with Tewa blood, told him it was a gift passed down from her family.

So he knows. He knows Ren and this Cole guy are tethered to each other, and no other love, no matter how right or good or seemingly perfect, can break it. But he won't explain this to Ren, because though he and Cole are tethered to one another, it doesn't mean they will ever accept it. Being tethered doesn't outweigh free will.

So instead of telling Ren all he knows, he simply says, "Maybe it's fate."

Ren turns back to him, very interested, yet trying to pretend he's anything but. "Fate? Try coincidence."

"No. It's fate."

"Antonio, really. What the hell are you talking about?" Ren demands. "If it's fate that Cole and I meet here in this tumbleweed hellhole, what, pray tell, is the purpose?"

"No, no. I'm not telling you your whole life. You've got to figure some of this shit out on your own. If I tell you, you'll just toss it aside. But if you figure it out yourself, you'll believe it."

"You're seriously freaking me out, Antonio."

"Sorry. Wanna split some tableside guac?"

"Absolutely not."

"Okay." Antonio smiles at Ren and then looks down at his menu. "How about spicy shrimp? Will you split that? Then I'll get the bean burrito with *posole*."

"What? Are you seriously changing the subject?"

"We can talk about it, if you want, but it won't change anything."

Ren stares at Antonio, mouth open. He wants to say something, anything, to refute Antonio's confident yet totally ludicrous (ludicrous!) proclamations about fate, but words fail him. He doesn't believe in fate any more than he believes in God, or angels or the fucking tooth fairy. But then again, he has no reason *not* to believe.

"I can see you working it out," Antonio says. "Good."

Ren's phone buzzes on the table.

Cole: Come out tonight. Alegra is giving a private concert at The Pink Adobe.

"It's from Cole. He's invited me to a thing with Alegra."

"At The Pink?" Antonio asks.

"The Pink Adobe."

"Locals call it 'The Pink.' You should go."

"How do you know about it?"

"Mitch invited us."

"The coincidences are really starting to stack up, aren't they?" Ren stares at his phone.

"Concentric circles, man. Concentric circles."

"I'm not even going to ask what that means," Ren says. Antonio laughs and waves the waitress over to take their order.

Cole: Please come. Alegra wants to meet you.

Ren: I'm saving this text forever.

Cole: So you'll come? She's sort of being annoying about it.

Ren: I'll meet you there. What time?

Cole: Ten-ish. I'll put you on the list.

Ren: This is all a bit New York for the land of shitkickers and ten-gallon hats, isn't it?

Cole: You just said shitkickers. I'm saving this text forever.

Cole: And you're a snob.

"I ordered you the *chile rellenos*," Antonio says. "Ren?"

"What? Oh, sure. Yes. Thank you."

Antonio grins and goes back to attacking the chips and salsa.

Ren: I accept that about myself.

Cole: AND I haven't seen that many cowboy hats, actually. We're not in Texas.

Ren: Thank heaven for small mercies.

Cole: You don't believe in heaven.

Ren: Touché.

Cole: What is it with you and Texas?

Ren: If Louise didn't want Thelma to take a shortcut through Texas, she must have had a good reason.

Ren: Also, George W.

Cole: And that's a good reason to avoid an entire state? Austin is pretty fantastic, Ren.

Ren: If you say so.

Cole: Gotta run. See you later?

Ren: Yes. Thank you for thinking of me.

Ren holds on to his phone, wondering if Cole will respond. He feels a bit silly waiting, as if he's sixteen again.

"Are you done?" Antonio says, a playful smirk at his lips.

"Stop. It's nothing."

"Oh, it's something, all right."

Chapter 3

Cole loves Santa Fe. He loves the way the light descending on the Sangre de Cristo Mountains reminds him of "America the Beautiful." He loves the chile, and the tortilla soup and the *sopapillas*, drizzled with honey. He loves the miles of art galleries. And the people.

He adores the people.

Half the town is focused on personal transformation, tearing themselves down and putting themselves back together again through Bikram yoga, aura cleansing, sage burning, astrological readings, meditation, rebirthing, labyrinth walking, Chinese medicine and channeling. The rest of the town is steeped in history, married to the desert and the big sky above it, passing down ancient traditions and paying no mind to the hustle of modern society. And all of these people, every single one of them, are damn entertaining to watch.

The Pink Adobe is Cole's favorite bar in town. The Pink, a locals' hangout on the Santa Fe Trail, is an institution long on every traveler's "must do" list. The drinks are always doubles and the rooms are dark and comforting. Cole's crew has been in Santa Fe for a few weeks now and has hosted several impromptu private performances for local friends in the back room. Alegra loves the bar because no one really seems terribly impressed that she's there; she can just do her thing, play with new music and blow off some steam.

Cole is actively loving Santa Fe, nursing a vodka tonic and listening to Alegra sing "So New," the song they recorded this morning, when he notices Ren. He's standing across the room, next to a tall man in cowboy boots who looks Hispanic and a strikingly beautiful, short blonde woman who does not. Ren hasn't spotted him yet, so Cole takes a moment to admire Ren's slender frame, the way his jeans hug his perfect, perfect ass, the way his elegant fingers clutch the tall man's arm when he laughs.

Why didn't I see him come in? Why does he have to look so fucking amazing?

Wait. Who is this guy he's touching?

Cole walks over to the trio, a bright smile plastered on his face. "You came." He locks eyes with Ren.

"Of course I did. I mean, really. It's Alegra. Have you met Antonio and Sarah Ortiz?"

"Not yet, no. Cole McKnight," he offers, extending his hand to Antonio.

"Nice to put a face to the name." Antonio shakes Cole's hand.

As Cole leans in to kiss Sarah's cheeks, Ren says, "They're Mitch's guests. He's on the board at Alex Marin House, and Sarah is the executive director."

"Really? That's awesome. I've been meaning to ask someone—you, I guess—if I could come over and meet some of the kids, maybe bring my guitar and play a little," Cole says.

"That would be amazing, Cole. The kids would love it," Sarah says, beaming.

"Alegra is really excited about the benefit," Cole adds. He's trying not to stare at Ren and Antonio, trying not to size them up, trying not to let his irritation show. *Are they involved? Did they just meet? Does Ren fool around on Paul?*

"*She's* excited? We're beside ourselves!" Sarah says.

"So, how do you know each other?" Cole asks in his best casual voice.

"Antonio carts me around New Mexico. He's my personal slave." Ren bumps shoulders with the taller man.

"Keep dreaming," Antonio says.

Cole brings back the smile and just stares. He sees genuine affection between them and he doesn't like it, not one bit. This guy is so tall it's embarrassing.

"We both work for the Alexanders," Antonio explains. "I manage Clint's Southwest properties."

"And I manage Clint's wife," Ren says, giving Antonio a wink.

"Oh," Cole says. *Exactly when did these two start fucking?*

An uncomfortable silence settles in between them before Antonio steps into Sarah's space, places an arm over her shoulder and says, "And this is *my* wife."

"Oh. Oh!" Cole lets out a sigh of relief before he thinks better of it.

"Cole, you *didn't*," Ren looks horrified.

"Didn't what?"

"You didn't honestly think that I would—"

"Do you want drinks? Let me get you drinks," Cole interrupts.

"Ah, sure. I'll just have a beer," Antonio says.

"Margarita, rocks, no salt," Sarah says.

"Ren?"

Ren scowls at Cole, ignores his question and walks over to the bar. Cole throws an apologetic smile at Antonio and Sarah and then trails after Ren.

"God, Cole. You're such an idiot sometimes."

"I know, I know. Sorry."

"I'm *engaged*."

"I know. Believe me, I know."

"What's that supposed to mean?"

"Nothing, just... nothing."

"What can I get for ya?" a forty-something redhead asks from behind the bar. Ren stares at her beehive hairdo, the Cleopatra-esque cat-eye makeup and pink T-shirt stretched tight across her ample breasts. He must like what he sees, because he's beaming.

"How do your margaritas stand up to Maria's?" Ren asks.

"Ours are stronger, which means they're better."

"One margarita please, no salt. I love your hair."

"Thanks. Most people think it's too much."

"Oh it is, but that's why I love it. I'm Ren, by the way. Ren Warner."

"Ren—like Kevin Bacon in *Footloose*?"

Ren points at her and says, "*You* get a big tip, missy. Most people don't make that connection. My mother was obsessed with that movie, made us learn the whole closing dance sequence."

"Missy, huh? At my age I'll take that as my tip," she winks and holds out her hand to shake. "June Merryfeather."

"Stop! That is not your name," Ren says, delighted.

"I might have made it up, but it is my name." She turns to Cole. "And you? What are you having?"

Cole orders drinks for Antonio and Sarah, then perches on a stool to watch Ren and June interact while she makes the drinks. Ren loves people who are "too much." It's a pleasure to watch him connect with another member of the "fabulous" species. He's not friendly the way Cole is; he doesn't feel comfortable talking to anyone and everyone. But whenever he runs across someone who, like him, exemplifies the extraordinary, he's quick to make friends.

"So you just stayed here? But what about your apartment? What about your stuff?" Ren asks, and Cole realizes he's missed a key part of the conversation.

"Ren, what fun is reinvention if you have to lug your old life around like a ball and chain?"

"So you've basically been on a seven-year vacation," Ren says and sips his drink.

"No. This is my home. I don't plan on going back to Seattle. I knew it the moment I pulled into town," June replies as she pops the cap off of Antonio's beer.

"I don't get it. I mean, no offense, but New Mexico really isn't my cup of tea."

"Maybe not, but you can't escape it." She looks at Ren intently, and Cole quashes the urge to step away and let them have a private moment in favor of hearing the conversation play out.

"Escape what, exactly?" Ren asks.

"You know."

"I... what? I know what?" He looks nervous, as if he's afraid she's about to give him really, really bad news.

"You *know*."

"I really don't. What can't I escape?"

"Who you really are. This place reminds you, one way or another." June pats his arm. She takes two steps back, gives them both a big, toothy smile and then walks over to serve a customer at the other end of the bar.

Ren is silent, staring after her.

"You okay?" Cole asks.

"Hmm? Of course. Yes. She's something, right?"

"For sure."

"I love it here."

"You love it everywhere," Ren taunts.

"True. Hey, let's get these drinks back to your friends."

"But we didn't pay."

"Mitch is picking up the tab tonight." Cole slips a twenty onto the bar. "Her tip."

"Always the gentleman."

"You can take the boy out of Saint Ben's, but you can't take Saint Ben's out of the boy," Cole says, walking back to Antonio and Sarah.

Half an hour later they're sitting around a large rectangular table, all four of them focused on Alegra. She's silly tonight, singing loads of covers, playing with new music, avoiding her standards; she'll have to sing enough of them on Saturday for the benefit. After she finishes a bouncy version of an 80s classic, Alegra thanks the room and walks off the stage, making a beeline for Cole. Ren, at his right, sits up a bit taller when he sees her.

Antonio stands and pulls out a chair for her.

"Thanks, darling!" Alegra elbows Cole and then takes a sip of Cole's drink; he can tell she's looking for an extra bit of fun. *Please don't say anything—*

"Alegra, thank you so much for inviting us," Sarah says. "I was captivated by you."

"Captivated? Haven't heard that one yet." Alegra takes Sarah's hands in her own and smiles. "Sarah, right? I'm so happy you came. Mitch adores you, and I'm right behind the work you do, you know?"

"Thanks. That means so much. You remember my husband, Antonio?"

"The tall handsome local boy, yes."

"Nice to see you again," Antonio says, blushing.

Alegra looks straight at Ren. "And *you,* dearest, you have to tell me everything about this one." Alegra points at Cole. "He claims to be a total bore, but I have my theories."

"Ren Warner," he says, offering his hand. "And I'm happy to dish all night about Cole if it means I can sit next to you."

"A stunner and a charmer." Alegra winks at Cole. "Mess, mess, mess."

"Sorry?" Ren says.

"It's nothing. Just a bit of an inside joke. That's rude of me. Sorry," Alegra says. "So Ren, we can't get Cole to record one of his own songs. Any idea why?"

"Wow. You cut right to it, don't you?" Cole says, unable to mask his irritation.

"Record a song? Cole, I thought you weren't singing. Or writing," Ren says.

"Oh, do you sing too, Cole?" Sarah asks.

"I used to."

"He's been writing and singing songs since we were kids. On weekends he would hole up in his dorm room and play his guitar for hours, singing away," Ren explains, eyes fond. "Sometimes he played for me... I mean, with me in the room. But even with his door shut, we could hear him in the dorm."

Alegra is half off her seat now, excited to get any tidbit about Cole's past. "Tell me more. Tell me everything."

Cole groans and sinks into his chair as Ren answers Alegra's questions, coloring in his past in broad, practiced strokes. His drink almost gone, Ren's a bit tipsy, and so he's in full-on storyteller mode. He has the whole table laughing, begging for more, and soon Gretchen and a few of the others are hovering around them, too.

When Ren starts telling them about Hell Weekend, the Saint Ben's party to end all Saint Ben's parties, Cole grabs Ren's glass and his own and goes to the bar before he has to hear Ren tell everyone about his nearly-naked rendition of "Pour Some Sugar On Me." *Lovely.*

"Hey, June. Two more, please," Cole says, turning to watch his dearest friend hold court. He stares as Ren leans in, says something in a low voice—and the whole table erupts in laughter. They all look over at Cole, some smirking, some with hands over their mouths, some giving him the thumbs-up. Cole waves and smiles.

"Here ya be." June slides the drinks across the bar.

He knows he should bring Ren his drink, should rejoin his friends; but his feet feel as though they're encased in cement, so he stays.

"Thanks, June. I'm Cole, by the way."

"You're his, huh?" She nods in Ren's direction.

"Who? Ren? No. He's... I'm not his."

"Are you sure about that?"

"One hundred percent." He chugs his drink.

"No. I'm right. There's something there," June presses.

"Are you one of those self-described clairvoyants? Because there's a lot of them running around this town," Cole says.

"Aren't there, though? No, I'm not one of 'em. I just, you know, size people up. It's kind of a hobby."

"Try knitting," Cole barks. He's being mean now, on purpose, and he's not mean. Ever. "Sorry, sorry. That was uncalled for. I'm just a little tense. But that's no excuse. So again, I apologize—"

"One apology is enough. And it's no problem. I get it. You don't want to want him, but you really, really *do* want him. I'd be tense, too."

Who is this woman? Jesus! Doesn't she know that we don't talk about this? Doesn't she get that I will never talk about it, and he will never talk about it, and we will never, ever, ever do anything *about it?*

Because that's the deal. That's the agreement, forged years ago in heavy silences, in the space between. They can't go back. He can never go back in time, fuck his fears and sense of propriety and go after what he wants.

Cole turns to look back at the group. Ren and Alegra are deep in their own private conversation now; Cole wonders what she's telling Ren, what he's telling her. The last drink creeps up on Cole as if it's his seventh or eighth. He feels it wrap around his brain and fill him with fuzzy bravado. He wants to tell June that she's wrong. He and Ren are friends, friends who don't see each other, friends who don't act much like friends anymore.

He tells her the whole truth instead.

"I do want him. I've always wanted him. But we're about a decade past that now and we chose different lives. I love someone else. Someone good. So that's it."

June looks across the room at Ren and says, "Maybe."

She pats him on the shoulder and does that walking-backwards-smile thing again before she turns and exits through a door marked "PINK STAFF ONLY." He shakes his head and tries to shrug off his exchange with June and thinks instead about how Ren would get a kick out of that sign, how he'd likely want to hang it on his office door or something.

When he turns back to the table again, Alegra is gone, and so are many of his nosy friends. He turns toward the stage and sees they're getting ready for another set, so he picks up Ren's drink and what's left of his own and walks back to the table.

"I didn't tell them anything truly horrifying," Ren says with a smirk.

"Of course you didn't, because that would involve telling stories about you, too," Cole teases.

"Just what exactly are you getting at, Cole McKnight?" Ren teases right back.

"I know things. I know lots of things." Cole looks right at Ren, smile fading. His eyes wander to Ren's neck and linger, old fantasies kicking in. He's staring just a bit too long, and he knows it. But he can't help it.

Ren shifts a bit in his seat, and then forces himself to look away. "You're not playing tonight?"

"Nope. Wanted to spend time with you."

Alegra starts in on "Forever Man," the new torch song they haven't quite perfected yet. Antonio takes that as his cue and silently offers his hand to his wife. Sarah beams up at him, her green eyes wide and happy, and they make their way to the dance floor, now dotted with couples moving to the soulful rasp of Alegra's voice.

Cole is too drunk to smooth over the tension with his trademark moves, so it hangs in the air as they watch the scene before them. It seems as though it takes Ren hours to finally ask, "Did you have a bad day? You seem so... surly."

"No, I'm fine."

"But you're upset about something," Ren presses.

"I'm not."

"Do you miss Liam? Is that it?"

"Of course I miss him. He's my boyfriend."

"You haven't said much about him. I just wondered—"

"I didn't think it was appropriate," Cole interrupts.

"To talk to me about Liam? Why not? I'm your friend—"

"It's private." Cole stares at the dance floor, the wall, his glass, anything but Ren.

"Okay. Just... could you just tell me if you're all right? Is he treating you well?"

"Of course."

"Good. That's good. So if it's not Liam, then why are you so edgy tonight?"

Cole looks up at Ren, exhales, lets the ache wander around to his chest, fill up his lungs, take hold of his teeth, his jaw, his tongue.

"I might... I might not be able to keep this up," Cole says.

"Keep what up?"

Cole stares at him, emotions bare and real and maybe too much. He can't hear it over the music, but he can *see* Ren gasp. He's at the precipice, and he's losing his will to stay put.

"Cole, what—?"

Cole hears the opening bars of that old familiar song, "How We Loved"—Alegra's first big hit. It's another torch song, haunting and epic, showcasing her powerhouse voice: a song about reconnecting with the one who got away, about second chances, and nostalgia, and passion and regret—the song may as well have been written for them, it's so on-point.

Before he can change his mind, Cole takes Ren's hand and pulls him up out of his chair. "Remember this? You used to play this on repeat in your car."

"You have me confused with Jeremy. The R.A. banned that song from the dorm after he played it for six hours nonstop."

"Don't rewrite history." Cole gives Ren his first real smile of the night.

Ren smiles back, squeezing Cole's hand. "I wouldn't dream of it."

They exchange a look that lasts a few seconds too long, but before Ren can pull away, Cole tugs on his hand. "Dance with me?"

"Seriously? This song is so sad—"

"This is one of those moments you'll regret saying no to. Can't we...? Let's just dance to this song we loved when we were kids, okay?"

Ren nods. "Okay."

Cole takes Ren by the hand, winding between tables, leading him to the dance floor. He looks up at Alegra sitting on her stool. She looks right at them; she doesn't smile, doesn't break concentration, but somehow Cole knows she's singing for him—for them.

Cole stops at the darkest spot on the dance floor and turns to face Ren. He lets go of Ren's hand, then, and places both of his hands on Ren's slim waist, pulling him close.

Ren looks at him, a question in his eyes, then exhales and leans into Cole, resting his head on Cole's shoulder. They're barely dancing, just swaying and leaning and pressing into each other like two teenagers learning how to do... everything.

Ren snakes his hands around Cole's waist and up over his shoulder blades, pressing in. It feels like no hug Ren's ever given him before. Ren shivers and burrows his head into Cole's neck, as he had the night before. Within moments, their nerves give way to that unspoken thing, and they let it take over. They'll leave it here on the dance floor anyway, never speak of it again, but for the few measures of this song, for this brief moment in time, they'll give in.

Cole tightens his hold on Ren's waist. They're so close now that it's hard to tell where one ends and the other begins.

Ren brings one of his hands around to the front, placing it on Cole's chest. He slowly moves it higher, higher, pressing softly into Cole's shirt. He stops at the collar, fingers close but not touching Cole's skin.

Cole knows what Ren wants. He can feel the yearning buzzing around them, through them, in them. His hand is over Ren's now, moving it, placing Ren's fingers on his own neck. He can feel Ren smile into his neck as he thumbs Cole's collarbone.

They're lost in it now, so Cole allows his hands to move down low on Ren's back, resting just above the curve of his ass. He can feel the strength in Ren's thighs, his back, his hands.

He wills the song to go on forever.

Cole tilts his head, his mouth close to Ren's ear, and sings softly. *"If I could go back, if I could hang on, if I could be brave, if could I choose right instead of left."*

Ren melts into him, listening with his whole body. He wraps his hand around the back of Cole's neck and somehow manages to pull him even closer. Cole moves his hands back to Ren's hips, digging in this time. He wants to leave marks, marks he'll never see because this is all they'll ever have; marks Ren *will* see in the mirror tonight, tomorrow morning, the next day.

"In the crowd I see a boy who looks like you and I follow, I follow for miles, I follow for days, my friend," Cole sings, his voice catching on the last note.

Ren lifts his head and suddenly they're staring into each other's eyes. Alegra's voice washes over them and wraps them up in the moment, protecting them from consequences and regret. Ren licks his lips, and Cole parts his own in response, moving closer. They're breathing heavily now, barely moving, faces just inches apart.

"Double dare," Ren whispers.

Suddenly Ren's mouth is on his and they're *kissing*. Oh God. This is everything. Cole's whole body gives over to the kiss: lips warm, tongue skating across teeth, hands wrapped in the hair at the base of Ren's neck.

Ren wraps both of his hands around Cole's neck, winds his fingers up into his curls and tugs. Cole hisses, loving the pain; Ren does it again. And again. His lips are strong and insistent, and Cole knew it, he knew Ren would kiss him just exactly like this. Cole nips at Ren's bottom lip, and then Ren's hands are on his hips, and his mouth is at his neck, and Cole can't help but moan into Ren's ear.

The song is like a spell, and Cole feels it coming to an end, so he pulls Ren off of his neck. Ren looks confused, almost hurt, but then Cole takes Ren's face in his hands and gives him a soft, chaste kiss, the kind he should have given him that day by the chapel.

He wants to give him all of the missed kisses now, the sweet, innocent, hopeful kisses he should have given him in the hallways at Saint Benedict, in empty classrooms, under stairs. Cole kisses Ren's forehead, his cheeks. He nuzzles his nose, and then runs his tongue over Ren's bottom lip as he should have done that day in Ren's bedroom when Ren told him he was accepted to Pratt and promised to visit him every month in Boston. He kisses him deeply now, a bit desperately, as he should have done in the backseat of Ren's car every damn Saturday night for years.

He knows he should kiss Ren as though this is another missed kiss, as though this is goodbye, but instead he gives him everything, as he should have done all along; as he should have done every time this perfect man graced him with his presence.

"Cole... Cole—"

Ren whispers into his mouth, and then Cole realizes he's crying, salty tears falling down his cheeks and into their mouths. Ren kisses Cole's tears, returns to his lips, desperate. Ren pulls his mouth away and replaces it with his thumb, rubbing along Cole's top lip, then the bottom. He can tell Ren wants to say something, maybe even the truth, but holds it in. He senses the room now, all eyes on them as Alegra winds the song down, and he knows he'll never get another chance to just tell Ren what he should have told him all along. Even though they can never be, even though it might ruin their friendship, Ren deserves the truth.

"Ren... I've always wanted... you."

Ren's tears flow freely now, too. He kisses Cole one last time and then turns and walks away.

Cole watches Ren slip into the men's room and he stands there, alone on the dance floor, frozen until the piano offers up the last notes of the song. And then he's moving fast through the crowd to the men's room, pushing open the door.

He finds Ren leaning up against the wall, sobbing. He doesn't think. He doesn't ask. He can't. He crosses to Ren and wraps him up in his arms, pulls him in for another kiss. Ren gives in with him, and they claw at each other, lining up their hips, gasping as they feel each other for the first time, hard and hot and wonderful.

Cole nips at Ren's jaw, holding Ren's hips steady as he thrusts up. Ren tugs at the waistband of Cole's jeans and he's gone. He'll do anything Ren asks. Anything. Ren slips his fingers under Cole's shirt, pressing his fingers into his stomach muscles, skating down, down, down and then... nothing. Ren freezes.

"I can't. We can't do this," Ren says, chest heaving.

Cole groans into Ren's neck, trying to keep still. They stay like that for what seems like forever, and then Ren gently pushes Cole away.

"I have to go now or I'll never leave." Ren turns the door handle. He doesn't look at Cole before he goes. There are no final stolen kisses, no tender caresses of his cheek. He's just gone.

Cole waits a few minutes, enough time for Ren to say his goodbyes and get out the door, and goes back into the room. Alegra is singing again, but when she spots him she looks worried. He smiles at her reassuringly. She'll feel badly about this tomorrow, as if she caused it with her pushing and her singing of words that ring true over miles and decades apart. But he'll always be grateful.

He wants to run after Ren. He wants to lift him up and take him down and lose himself in Ren, Ren, Ren.

But Ren said no, and Cole is a gentleman.

Fuck manners.

It's too much. Too *much*. The walk back to the Eldorado did nothing to calm him, and Ren will do anything to stop the deafening roar of want in his brain. He rummages through his toiletry bag, finds the travel-sized bottle of lube and within seconds he's on the bed, jeans and briefs in a pile next to him on the floor. He's so desperate to get off he doesn't even bother to take off his shirt.

I've always wanted... you.

Cole's confession echoes so loudly he can feel the words in his body, coursing through his veins, whispering in his ear, pulsing in his heart. He was moments—mere seconds—away from wrecking everything, and he knows there's a good chance he wouldn't even care if he had.

We were caught up in the song, that's all. It was a long time coming and now it's over. I'll just stay far away from Cole, finish this damn house and get on with my life.

His hands feel punishing on his cock, too rough and too fast, but he deserves it. He deserves pain with pleasure, his boyfriend—*fiancé*—far away, ever-faithful, fighting for their rights, for their marriage. He just needs to get off as quickly as possible and be done with it. No dragging it out. No fantasizing about Cole's hot mouth on his skin, Cole's hands intertwined with his as he fucks Ren—

"Oh God—"

Ren scoots his ass down for easier access, lubes up two fingers and then works one, then the other inside, welcoming the burn. He tries to imagine Paul's long, elegant, practiced fingers working him open, but his mind keeps going back to Cole. Cole. Cole.

Cole.

"It's just a... a...*fuck*... a fantasy. It doesn't count. It doesn't count."

Ren gives in, bucking up as he imagines Cole's callused fingers pressing, pressing, pressing into him. He fucks down on his own fingers, adding a third, and groans loudly, thankful for the hotel's soundproof walls. He's used this fantasy to get off before, many times. But he's never gone right to it just minutes after *seeing* Cole. And he's never done it just minutes after Cole confessed he wanted him. Because Cole had always made him wonder, left that "thing" hanging between them as if he wanted the banter and the tension to go on forever.

I've always wanted... you.

Do you need something?

Sweat at his temples, Ren whines in frustration. It's too much and it's not enough. It's the honesty without the follow-through: agony. His orgasm builds and he's so close, so close, but he just can't get there. He *needs* to come. He'll do *anything* to come. But he can't. He works himself over as if it's the last time, little beads of sweat dripping down the side of his face. He's tried every surefire move, but it's not enough.

Ren pulls his fingers out in defeat and slides to the floor. He holds his head in his hands and, for the second time tonight, he cries. Ass throbbing, cock softening, fingers cramping, he pulls his knees up to his chest and sobs. He's never cried from sexual frustration before.

"It's so much more—" Ren mumbles, between sobs. He can still feel Cole's hands on his biceps, gripping him, his eyes black with longing. *Longing.*

Ren knows it's about more than sex. It's everything. No one, *no one* had ever kissed him like that. He felt it in his bones. Cole's kisses were reverent, passionate, demanding, sweet. It can't be about more than sex, though, or he'll run after him. He'll do something foolish like call things off with Paul and fly to London and tell Cole he'll wait for him, wait for him to be done with Liam and come to his senses.

I gave up on waiting for Cole years ago.

It can never be about more than sex. He can say no to sex. He can't say no to... all the rest.

He can fantasize about Cole. He can jerk off to thoughts of Cole touching him, sucking him, fucking him. But he can't let it be more. He can never let it be more.

His sobs calm to an occasional sniffle. Ren wipes his eyes, stands up and takes off his shirt, lets it drop to the floor; he doesn't care about anything right now. He takes one look in the mirror, shakes his head at his puffy, still-desperate eyes and walks to the shower, where he'll wash away the want, cry some more, and let every dirty thought, every desire and every last wish wash down the drain.

As he passes the door he hears a soft knock, so soft it sounds as though it might be someone knocking on a different door. Curious, he looks out the peephole and... there he is. *Cole.* Although his image is distorted by the tiny round lens, Ren can clearly see him standing with his back to Ren's door, his hand running roughly through his thick hair.

As if he can feel Ren's eyes on him, Cole turns and knocks again, louder this time. Ren holds his breath. He can't answer. He shouldn't answer. He won't.

"Ren. Open the door."

Ren exhales and steps back as if he's been burned. He will *not* open the door...

"Ren. *Please.*"

The urgency in Cole's voice is palpable; Ren recognizes it as his own. Suddenly he's not thinking anymore. Suddenly he's moving toward the door, hand unlocking the chain. Suddenly his fingers are on the handle—

"Shit!"

Ren realizes he's about to answer the door completely naked and runs back to his pile of clothes. Just as he slips on his jeans, Cole bangs on the door loudly; so Ren forgoes his shirt, runs back to the door and yanks it open.

"Stop! You'll wake up the other—"

Before Ren can finish admonishing him, Cole's mouth is on his. He backs Ren into the room, kicking the door shut behind them. In no time he has Ren pushed up against a wall, his hands digging into Ren's hips, holding him in place. Cole devours Ren with his mouth, kissing him so hard it hurts, nipping at his bottom lip, his chin, his throat. It's fast and desperate, and Ren can't catch up, can't do much of anything but hold on.

"Cole—"

"Please, Ren. Don't say no. I *need you*," Cole pleads.

Somehow, Ren finds it in him to reach a hand in between them. He pushes on Cole's chest, willing him to stop, but hoping he won't. Cole tenses and pulls back to look at Ren. He's letting Ren see all of it now: He's begging with his eyes, his hips, his hands.

Ren bites his lip and watches Cole's eyes as he stares at Ren's mouth. His body is humming with anticipation; it's as if his cock *knows* Cole will get him off in the most spectacular way. It was never like this with Paul, with anybody. But they can't. They shouldn't. They will regret this forever.

Bodies pressed together, their eyes lock, and Ren makes a decision.

"One night," he says, his hand still between them.

Cole grabs both of Ren's hands, places them over his head, against the wall, and holds them there. "I want so much... everything... Ren, I can't—"

"I know."

"One night. I have to... please can we just... I *have* to fuck you. *Now.*"

And that is *it*. Ren is gone. He wriggles his hands free from Cole's grasp and reaches around the bathroom doorframe to find his toiletry bag on the counter. Cole attacks his neck, and yet somehow Ren manages to find a condom in the bag.

"Here." Ren holds up the condom triumphantly.

"But you're not ready."

"I um... I am, actually. I was trying to get off before you got here, and I'm... I'm good to go." Ren blushes.

There is a moment, just a second or two, when they could back out. But then it's gone, and Cole's pulling his shirt over his head, and Ren's peeling off his jeans, both in a kind of frenzy. Ren yanks on Cole's zipper and pulls down his jeans and underwear in one pass. They are barely completely off before Cole is back on Ren's mouth, hands everywhere.

"You deserve—" Cole starts, but Ren cuts him off.

"Just do it. We'll go again. We'll go until morning. Please just do it."

Ren tears at the condom and rolls it onto Cole's erect cock. Cole groans and kisses Ren's bruised lips, hoisting him up a bit and supporting him with his weight. Ren wraps his legs around Cole's waist, saying, "Hurry, hurry, please, please," as if he might die if Cole doesn't fuck him *right now.*

"Is there enough lube?"

"Yes, yes. I'm fine. Just do it. *Please.*"

Cole spits in his own hand, rubs the wetness on Ren's hole and then Cole is pushing in, and Ren is pressing down and willing himself to relax, and it's not enough lube after all but it's good, it's so good, and then Cole is all the way in, and Ren is filled with an overwhelming sense of... joy.

Cole stills for a moment and then says, "This is happening."

"This is *so* happening."

And then Cole is fucking him, and it seems like a miracle, like everything Ren's ever wanted. He fucks him hard and fast, and it's perfect, and he's completely at Cole's mercy. Ren cries out, his head banging against the wall, but he doesn't care. Cole is relentless, pounding years of frustration into him, again and again.

"Don't stop, don't stop," Ren pants.

"Ren, *fuck*," Cole says between grunts. Ren's digs blunt nails into Cole's back and mouths at his ear. Cole holds him up; Ren takes his own leaking cock in hand and starts pumping, the sight of which tips Cole over the edge. His thrusts uneven, Cole looks pained, as if he's trying to hold back.

"Don't wait. I want to see," Ren says, and with that Cole is coming, his head burrowed in Ren's neck.

"Jesus," Cole mouths at Ren's chest, lost in the taste of Ren's sweat.

"Can you just... don't pull out. Just a little more," Ren says. Cole shakes off the haze and he's fucking him again. "Yeah, that's it. That's it."

When Ren's long-awaited orgasm finally hits, it is so intense he makes no sound. His neck snaps back, and he's surprised to find Cole's hand there, preventing him from banging his head against the wall again. He feels as if he's falling but he doesn't care; he knows Cole will hold him up. The release is like fire and so, so sweet as he comes down, his head falling against Cole's shoulder.

Cole's breathing evens out first. He shifts his weight, holding Ren in place.

"Holy shit, Ren."

"Mm hmm."

"I'm sorry, I know that was... fast. I wanted to touch you and taste you and build up to—"

"What, you're worried we didn't have enough foreplay?" Ren asks, coming back to himself. He kisses Cole's neck, his jaw, his swollen lips.

"Yes." Cole rests his forehead on Ren's shoulder.

"Cole, what do you think we've been doing for the past fourteen years?"

Chapter 4

It takes them two hours to make it to the bed.

After the first fuck they slide to the floor, Ren in Cole's lap, kissing slow and sweet, as though they're just starting. Ren holds Cole's face in his hands and worships his mouth. He leaves little kisses at the corners, slips his tongue inside, and then presses his lips firmly to Cole's mouth in a kiss so deep Cole thinks he might pass out.

They're full on making out now—next to the used condom they had dropped carelessly on the carpet; this is the most impulsive and dirty Ren has ever been with anyone. He can't even remember the last time he actually made out with someone, kissed someone until his lips hurt, until the air was sucked out of his lungs. It had always been kissing as a means to an end, not just to kiss. This, he thinks, *this* is kissing for the sake of it, for the love of it, for the pure joy of it.

When Cole can't take it anymore, he takes Ren's hands and places them on his own back, engulfing him in a hug, a silent reminder that above all, they are friends. Ren relaxes in Cole's tight embrace, his chin on Cole's shoulder. He still can't believe Cole held him up on the wall so long. He knew Cole was strong, but that was... insanely hot.

"Thanks," Cole says.

Ren pulls out of the hug, eyes wide. "Did I say that out loud?"

"Yup."

"Oh, God." Ren covers his face with his hands. Cole runs his fingers up and down Ren's sides, and Ren drops his hands. "Oh, whatever. It *was* hot."

"Insanely so, yes," Cole says with a smirk.

Ren takes in Cole's body. He'd seen him naked before—skinny-dipping, changing for practice, being ridiculous at parties. But this is

Cole all grown up: muscles defined, soft hair on his chest, two-inch scar on his shoulder that Ren knows nothing about.

As if reading his mind, Cole kisses Ren's right shoulder, all open mouth and hot breath, and thrusts his hips up a bit. It's just a nudge really, a tentative question. Ren rests his hands on Cole's shoulders and answers with his hips, moving his in small, lazy circles. Soon they're breathing heavily, rutting against each other, getting hard again despite the alcohol and the fantastic fuck.

Ren braces himself on Cole's shoulders and leans back against the wall, his hips burrowing down into Cole's lap and thrusting up. The angle is odd, but he doesn't want to move from Cole's lap, so he reaches one hand down, takes both of their cocks in it and lines them up perfectly. He is momentarily struck dumb by the sight—how often he had fantasized about this!—and then shakes off the thought, willing himself to stay present, to not miss one second of this night, this surrender.

"Did you... fuck... did you mean it when you said we could go all night?" Cole asks, synching up with Ren's movements.

"The damage is done. We should... shit! Just a little faster. Yes!"

Ren can't believe they're at it again so quickly, after the best wall sex he's had in his entire life. The need to come is so strong, it's almost as if they never got off, as if they're still building to something, still desperate.

"We should what?" Cole adjusts Ren's hips just a few inches and then holds them down.

"We should just... *fuck*!"

"Yeah. Keep moving. Just like that."

Ren's breath is coming fast now, but somehow he manages to get it out. "We should just get it out of our systems. Even if takes... oh... yes... *yes*... even if it takes... all night."

They're rocking in a decent rhythm, but they keep slipping; soon they're both whining in frustration.

"Ren... can you—?"

Ren presses firmly on Cole's shoulders and pushes him onto his back, covering him. He spreads Cole's legs a few inches and lines up their bodies, his hips a bit lower than Cole's. He thrusts up hard, dragging his cock up and back again. He's digging in and dragging up and digging in and dragging up, and the friction is so good it's almost painful.

"Faster, faster," Cole pleads, his arms wrapped around Ren's back, pressing down hard, holding them together. He meets Ren's thrusts every time, and it's perfect slippery magic now, all grunts and groans and the smell of sex and sweat and cologne and *Cole*. His name is a mantra in Ren's head as he ruts harder, faster, harder faster. *Cole. Cole. Cole. Cole.*

"Good. So good," Cole mumbles, eyes rolling back in his head.

Ren is on the edge now, pressing down, pressing in, harder, more, closer still. He pushes his forehead into Cole's shoulder and wills himself to keep the rhythm sure and steady so as not to break the delicious build.

Could I melt into his body, fuse with his skin, his muscles, his bones? Could I line my heart up with his and sink in, take over? Could I have this forever? Could I keep him?

No. But I can have this night.

Ren comes first this time, letting the internal mantra fall from his lips. "Cole, Cole, *Cole, Cole*." He wants to collapse but he keeps moving, deeper, harder, faster, pressing Cole into the carpet.

Cole tenses and arches his back up off of the floor, pushing Ren up with him. "Oh God, oh God," he screams, as he comes all over Ren's belly.

Ren falls onto him, but the mess is too messy. He rolls over onto his side next to Cole, hip to hip. They both pant, Cole with one arm thrown over his eyes.

"Holy shit, Ren."

"You keep saying that."

And then suddenly they're laughing, giddy with the release of their age-old tension.

Ren's whole body shakes, and Cole seems lost to it, as if he can't stop, as if they've just shared the funniest inside joke ever told. Ren laughs until he feels tears at the corners of his eyes.

When was the last time I was this happy? I can't remember. Maybe laughing with my brother. Maybe sitting on the little bench in the dressing room, watching Mom try on outfits for "date night." Maybe lying in the grass with Cole in that field behind the Science Hall, sharing earbuds and staring up at endless sky. Maybe never.

Cole grabs his shirt and wipes the come off of their chests, stomachs and thighs. He tosses the shirt across the room. They turn to face each other. Cole's eyes are shining, and Ren can't stop himself from touching his face. He wants to stay cool, casual, to keep the happy down so as not to betray his feelings, but it's nearly impossible—especially when Cole gives him a giant smile that reaches all the way up to his eyes.

Cole reaches for Ren's other hand and plays with his fingers. "You're not shy."

"This surprises you?"

"I always pictured you... I imagined having to draw you out," Cole explains.

"Yes, well, you weren't wrong. But that was then. We're grown-ups, Cole."

"I know." Cole threads their fingers together. "I know."

Ren watches their joined hands for a moment, then says, "I like sex."

Cole chuckles. "I got that."

"So spill. The fantasies. I'm demure Ren, and you're what, my mentor, seducing me? Getting me comfortable with my body? Helping me discover my sexual appetite?" Ren is full-on teasing now, enjoying the bashful look on Cole's otherwise composed face.

"Not exactly."

"What, then? Tell me. Because you know far too much about my first boyfriends to ever think I'd be shy in bed."

"I know. But I still... I guess when I... imagine you... I still think of you at sixteen, nervous about sex, afraid to watch porn because you were sure Father Ian was some sort of super-spy who could see your browser history—"

"Hey! He was *everywhere*."

Cole smiles and turns to look at the ceiling, moving clasped hands to rest on his damp, sweaty chest. "Remember the time Ash downloaded that video of the naked muscle guys sitting in a classroom, learning how to give proper blowjobs?"

"Oh, God. He wanted his girlfriend to watch it—"

"Something about 'educational purposes' and 'for the good of all concerned'—"

"Yes! That was some bloody nose she gave him. What was her name again?"

"Um... Sheila?"

"Susan!"

"Right. Susan. Poor Susan. Anyway, I still remember you standing back from the screen. You had your hands over your face, but I could see one eye peeking out from between your fingers."

Ren gives Cole a playful slap on the side. "It was weird, okay? I had this massive crush on you—"

"Aww—"

"—And watching... *that*... with *you*... was just beyond uncomfortable."

"But you looked. You still looked."

Cole lets go of Ren's hand and runs his fingers over Ren's belly. He traces the outside of Ren's belly button with his index finger. Circle. Circle. Circle. Circle.

"I couldn't help myself," Ren says, more in breath than words.

"Did you learn anything?"

"About what?"

"Blowjobs." Circle. Circle. Circle. Circle.

"You know you're embarrassingly obvious, right? And a bit juvenile," Ren teases. "You're practically middle-aged, Cole. If you want a blowjob, just ask."

Cole's fingers move down, tracing the line of fine hair from Ren's navel down to his well-groomed cock. His touch is feather-light, almost tickling, as he traces the line up and down. Up and down. Up and down.

"I'm thirty. Thirty is hardly middle-aged. And you'll be thirty in no time, Ren. Are you saying you think of yourself as middle-aged?"

Ren finds it difficult to concentrate now, with his entire being focused on Cole's one finger. Still, he manages a comeback. "Cole, no matter how many birthdays I have, I will never be middle-aged. You, on the other hand—"

Cole's finger moves down, down, down, hovering over Ren's cock. "Yes? What about me?"

"Um—"

Cole runs one finger along the underside of Ren's cock and back again. Ren gasps, mesmerized. Despite all of it, Ren is getting hard again. "I... ah... I don't think my cock knows how old I am."

"*What?*"

"I'm pretty sure my cock thinks I'm seventeen," Ren says.

Cole stops the sweet torture, his head collapsing onto Ren's stomach as he laughs and laughs and laughs. Ren laughs with him, winding his fingers through Cole's curls. He can't see Cole's face, but he can feel his smile on his skin. It's so easy now, this thing between them that used to be fun and sexy but so very, very difficult.

"I mean, it's almost like, at the very sight of you, my cock has some freakish flashback and acts like I don't have anything better to do but spend all night getting off with you." Ren's chest rises and falls with every giggle.

Still laughing, Cole says, "You really think your dick has a mind of its own?"

"Clearly, it does. Isn't that how we ended up here?"

Cole lifts his head and looks at Ren, who stretches up on his elbows to look him in the eyes. "No. It really isn't."

Ren looks at him for a moment, mouth open. Then he smiles. He touches Cole's cheek, reaches up to kiss his lips, the tip of his nose, his forehead. "I know. I was only teasing."

Cole relaxes, rests his head on Ren's stomach again. "I'm not used to you saying the word 'cock.'"

"I suppose not. It's not a word I would use with you unless—"

"Unless we were lovers," Cole finishes.

"Yes. That's right."

They're quiet for a few moments, listening to each other breathe over the low hum of the air conditioner on the other side of the room.

"Cole?"

"Hmm?"

"This is amazing... right?"

"Completely."

"Is it—" Ren trails off, searching Cole's eyes for the answer to the question he cannot ask.

Cole shifts off of Ren and onto his side, and now they're mirroring each other, caressing faces and holding hands. "Tell me," he says.

"Okay. Okay, I will. But first, can we agree that everything we do tonight, and everything we say, will never leave this room?"

"Absolutely."

"Then... then I want to say that I am ridiculously happy," Ren says. Cole's eyes light up. There's that smile again. "I think we've needed this for so long, and... just let me get this out, okay?" Cole nods and squeezes Ren's hand.

"You were brave, when you said you wanted me," Ren continues. "I... I should have said it back to you, but... we've both wanted this for so long and it was keeping us from truly being happy. Because this was inevitable... wasn't it?"

"For sure." Cole holds both of Ren's hands in his and rubs his thumbs over Ren's wrists as he's done so many times before, as he did last night, and everything seems so right Ren doesn't want to say what he know needs to be said.

He says it anyway.

"So it wouldn't have been fair, marrying Paul without first—"

Cole tenses for a moment and Ren trails off, nervous; but Cole recovers quickly.

"Getting it out of our systems?"

"Right. Yes. So you understand?" Ren asks.

"Of course. You're saying we had to do this, so we can truly give ourselves to Liam and Paul. I'm not sure they would agree with your theory, but they don't have to know."

Ren sits up suddenly. "They *can't* know, Cole."

Cole tenses up again. Ren wants to climb inside of him and live there forever, to ease his worry from the inside out, to stay. He wants more than he'll ever admit; and he won't admit it because Ren isn't just Ren Warner anymore. He's Ren Warner and Paul James. He won't admit it because Ren has a beautiful, magazine-perfect life and what he wants, what he *really* wants is too much to ask of his friend who loves someone else. He won't admit it because Ren is a fucking master at managing disappointment.

He *rocks* disappointment. But *this,* this all-consuming, electric joy, this he does not know how to do.

Cole turns away. "Look, Ren, we're on the same page here. Let's just... can we just agree that we have this crazy chemistry—"

"*That* is an understatement, Cole. It's like saying the atomic bomb was a little intense."

Cole laughs and turns back to Ren. He looks a little sad, but it could be guilt or exhaustion; his expression is too small for Ren to tell for sure. Cole runs his fingers through Ren's hair and smiles when Ren leans into his hand.

"Okay, so we agree that we can't tell them. And we agree that we have to stop, come morning. And we agree that we can say anything to each other tonight, and it won't be repeated. Yes?"

"Yes," Ren nods, kissing the palm of Cole's hand.

"Then, as much as I would love to tell you my secrets and bond over our shared... frustration... I only have a few hours left to do everything to you I've always wanted to do. So I need you to shut up now. Okay?"

Ren tries not to swoon. He nods. "Okay, but—"

"But what?"

"We haven't even left the hallway—"

"And?"

"You do know hotel rooms have beds, right?"

Cole gives Ren's cock a squeeze. Ren whines and Cole laughs, getting to his feet and holding out a hand for Ren. "Come on, you. Shower first, then bed."

Ren takes Cole's hand and follows him into the bathroom. They catch sight of their dual reflection in the mirror: all mussed hair, wide eyes and flushed skin.

"We look like the spokespeople for sex." Ren leans into Cole.

"Huh?"

"Well, I was going to say 'poster children' for sex, but somehow that just sounds wrong," Ren explains, giggling.

Cole squeezes Ren's bicep and goes to start the water. Ren can't take his eyes from his own reflection. He looks brighter somehow, in focus, as if he just woke up from a very long sleep. Ren quickly checks his toiletry bag for more condoms, left over from Paul's last visit to Santa Fe. He takes the condoms out and sets them on the counter. He turns to look at Cole, water cascading down his chest like some wet dream come to life.

How many times did I imagine this? How many times did I play out this scene in the communal showers, rushing to get off before anyone else came in? It's hard to believe he's here, waiting for me.

I should feel guilty, but I don't. Maybe I'll feel guilty tomorrow.

"Ren," Cole says, and his eyes are asking again.

"Coming."

⊞

During his entire junior year at Saint Benedict's, Cole's number one
(secret) mission was to be on the receiving end of a blowjob. He thought
about it—wet, pink lips wrapped around him, making him hot, making
him beg, making him come—far too much for his own good. It wasn't
that he felt ashamed; he was perfectly okay with the deluge of sexual
thoughts that ran through his mind daily (usually centered around a
nondescript, half-naked, dirty-blond surfer). He figured that, at any
given time, you could peek inside the minds of a roomful of "Bennies"
and see at least two dozen sexual images floating around in there; he was
no different. It was entirely age-appropriate.

The problem was this: *Because* his teenaged mind conjured up images
of blowjobs approximately every three minutes, and *because* after Ren
transferred to Saint Ben's sophomore year they did just about everything
together, and *because* Ren was frighteningly hot, Cole inevitably dropped
hunky surfer guy and started imagining getting a blowjob from Ren.
And that was *so* not okay.

But he imagined it anyway.

Ren.

Ren giving him a blowjob.

Ren giving him a blowjob anywhere and everywhere and anytime he
wanted it. In the library, Ren hiding under the table while Cole tried
to hold it together. On the couch in the common room after curfew; in
his bed, both of them trying (and failing) to keep quiet; in the woods
past the chapel during lunch, where they could be quick and dirty and
loud; in Ren's car; in Cole's car; in the men's room at Perkin's; at the
movies; in the shower.

Cole couldn't possibly count the number of times he got off to thoughts
of Ren blowing him. Even in recent years, he'd pulled that old fantasy out
a few (dozen) times. And it was good, as a schoolboy's fantasy always is.

But this...

This is better.

This is amazing.

This is the single best blowjob Cole McKnight has ever had in his
entire fucking life.

Just the sight of Ren on his knees, eyes closed, his swollen lips dragging down Cole's cock and up again like a pro, is enough to send Cole over the edge. It doesn't help much to look away, because his mind just floods with images from his old fantasies, and that—combined with the reality of Ren's masterful head—is too, too much.

Ren works him over with *purpose*. He is *not* messing around.

"Jesus, Ren. How—?"

He feels Ren smile around him now, and hum, and dear lord that's good. A slow lick up the vein on the underside of his cock, a few shallow sucks around the head, a twist of the wrist and then back to that dirty, rhythmic suck, suck, suck. Cole is in awe of Ren, the way he takes Cole in deep, his mouth enveloping Cole's cock, straining his lips. Cole is stupid now. Dizzy. Lost.

He wants it to last, to feel that swipe of Ren's tongue right... "There. Oh God. Again. Oh God." He wants to hold Ren's head tight and still and fuck Ren's mouth, scream his name, watch Ren jerk himself off as he takes all Cole can give.

But he knows Ren wants other things, and he's not sure he can deliver if they keep this up.

"Stop. Ren. Don't... oh fuck... stop!"

Cole whines when Ren pulls off. Ren strokes him with one hand. "Stop or don't stop?"

Cole waits for the oxygen to return to his brain. After a few moments, he tugs on Ren's hand and motions for him to stand up. Ren looks confused, but happy. He rests both hands on Cole's hips while Cole licks Ren's bottom lip, dips his tongue into his mouth and lets the kiss shake him out of the need for immediate gratification.

"Who *are* you?" Cole says finally.

"Stop it." Ren actually has the nerve to look embarrassed, shy even.

"You're like, the Jedi Master of blowjobs." Cole presses their foreheads together. He wraps his arms around Ren, taking his splashes. The water is running lukewarm now, unsurprising since they've been in here forever.

"Dork." Ren smiles. "I *do* like to achieve mastery in all of my endeavors."

"If you want to keep going, I need to stop."

"Still not making sense, Cole."

"I don't know if I can come again after this."

"Oh," Ren says, getting it at last.

Ren slips out of Cole's grasp and turns his back to him. He turns off the shower and steps out, reaching a hand out for Cole. "Come on. I want to fuck you on the bed."

"Yeah. Good."

Cole wants to apologize for sounding like a caveman, but instead he grasps Ren with one hand and palms the two remaining condoms with his other hand as they leave the bathroom. He admires Ren's strong, lean frame, his pert ass more perfect than Cole remembers.

They're on the bed in seconds, soaking wet, dripping water onto the cream-colored duvet, Ren's smooth chest pressing down onto his own. Ren sucks a raspberry-sized mark onto Cole's shoulder while Cole moans and slides his fingers down Ren's back to his ass.

Ren lifts his head up and says, "Wait, *do* you want me to fuck you?"

"Yes, God yes."

"I mean, I just assumed... but maybe you don't—"

"It's been years. Liam doesn't like to top," Cole says. Ren raises one eyebrow and Cole sighs. "Don't. Just... please, *please* fuck me."

Ren plants both hands on the bed on either side of Cole's head and swoops in for a kiss so deep, so forceful, it knocks Cole senseless.

Ren breaks the kiss to grab the lube, and Cole imagines Ren alone in this room just hours before, fingering himself, trying to get off to the memory of Cole's hands on him. He remembers the feel of Ren, hot and tight and waiting, squeezing around his cock and holding him inside as though he belongs there. And then Ren's finger is inside him, and another, and then it's "yes, yes, yes" and "more, more, more," and Cole whispers Ren's name with every exhale.

Three fingers, and then bliss, pure hot bliss, and then Ren leaves him empty. He feels Ren's lips on his belly, the inside of his thighs, sweet and reverent; he hears the sound of a foil wrapper ripping, of slicking-on latex, and then Ren is hitching one of Cole's legs up onto his shoulder and pushing his other thigh out, spreading him wide.

Ren hesitates, and Cole looks directly into his eyes. He sees it, now: pure adoration. Ren hasn't looked at him like this since that week they spent at Cole's grandparents' cabin in Wisconsin, the summer before college, when they spent every day at the lake, pushing buttons and boundaries. Ren had given up on something after that, or packed it away, or just *stopped*. But here it is, the look, shining down on him like a gift, the *best gift*.

Cole reaches up, palm flat over Ren's heart. He knows this could be the end of it. This could be the last time he has Ren as he's always wanted him, and they only just got started. "Hold on as long as you can," Ren says, reading his mind.

"Don't touch me, then. Just fuck me."

Ren plants a kiss on Cole's leg and pushes in carefully. Cole is grateful, but it's not what he wants. "I'm okay. Really. *Please*," Cole pleads. Ren nods and then bottoms out in one thrust, earning a guttural moan from Cole. "Fuck, *yes*."

Ren lifts Cole's hips, just barely, enough to get exactly the right angle. Ren is deliberate, rhythmic; he never misses a beat. He pushes Cole's thigh out even wider, holding him open. When Cole lifts his head up a bit *to see*—to *see Ren fucking him*, Ren as he imagined him so many times, Ren claiming him, loving him, filling him—he sees that Ren is watching, too. Head down, he seems mesmerized by the sight of his own cock pumping in and out of Cole. Cole groans, his head falling back on the bed.

His thoughts come quick and messy as he pants and whines.

Let me take a picture, let me hold onto this moment and keep it in my pocket, in the corner of my heart, in my dreams. Let me have it. Wasn't this always mine? Ours? Let me have it. Weren't we always this? Haven't we always been here, in this breath, in this pain, in this heat? Let me have it.

Cole loses himself with Ren inside him. He is anything and everything and nothing matters but *this, this, this*. He is so gone he doesn't notice the familiar tug until he is seconds from coming; and then all he sees is silver and black. Every cell in his body wakes up, as if he had been dead for years, as if he is awake for the first time. Pleasure rips through him like fire and fills him, white and hot, like liquid washing over his bones.

He is useless, so happily wrecked, and so willing to let Ren pound into him now as he searches for his own release.

"Oh... *shitshitshit*—"

Ren's babbling now, sweat at his brow, and Cole realizes that up until now, Ren hasn't spoken a word this whole time.

Cole struggles to keep his eyes open, to focus on Ren's face as he comes. He is certain there is no one more beautiful than this man, this man who used to be a boy, a boy who captured his attention and his heart.

Ren collapses on Cole, his body thrumming. He grips Cole's hips, all shallow breaths and little whimpers. Cole reaches up and holds Ren in a tight hug and he realizes they've been hugging all night, in between everything, during, after. He kisses Ren's hair, whispering, "Thank you, thank you, thank you."

When Ren rolls off to the side, Cole sees the tears in Ren's eyes and his own fill up at the sight. "We're not doing this, right? We're just... we're not stopping to do this," Cole pleads.

Ren rubs his face, wipes his eyes and says, "No. No, we're not."

They lie next to each other, staring at the ceiling, hands intertwined and resting between them on the bed. Ren rubs his thumb absentmindedly across Cole's knuckles. Cole rests his foot on Ren's ankle. "God, I want to go all night, but—"

"It's almost morning," Ren says.

"I'm spent."

"Hmm. Nice. I like that word. When it's earned."

Cole turns on his side, leans on his elbow. He looks down at Ren and beams. "Best. Night. Ever."

Ren smiles and pulls Cole in for a kiss. "Even better than what's-his-name?"

"Who?"

"Adam something or other. You know, *the guy.*" Ren smiles up at Cole. "In college. You dated him for a week or something. Remember? I came down to visit you, and you fucked him on the air mattress in the living room."

"Oh. *That* guy."

"We all heard you, and when Jeremy asked you about it you said it was mind-blowing, the best night ever."

Cole runs his thumb across Ren's chin, then up, and lets it slide into Ren's mouth and out again. "You never visited me again."

"No." Ren sits up, and then he's gone.

Cole glances over to the windows, frowning at the soft pink light peeking through the heavy drapes. He remembers that morning, after his one and only time with Adam, when Ren smiled too brightly and couldn't really look Cole in the eyes. He remembers waiting for the bus from Chinatown the following month, holding a tray with two coffees and a chamomile tea, so excited to see his best friend. And he remembers Jeremy stepping off the bus alone, shaking his head at the question in his eyes. He felt the tether go slack, then, and his shoulders sank with his heart. But still, he didn't fix it. He was too young, too clueless; he didn't know how.

Ren returns a moment later, cleans them up and then drops the damp washcloth on the floor. "Come on, under the covers."

"I don't want to sleep."

"I know. But I'm cold." Ren turns down the bed. Cole stands and somehow they both slide into the bed and into each other's arms without a question of sides or position. Ren snuggles in, rests his head on Cole's shoulder and immediately starts rubbing lazy circles around Cole's chest, playing with his hair. "I love this," he whispers.

Cole, one arm around Ren, kisses the top of his head. They're quiet for a long time, just listening to each other breathe, offering gentle touches, exploring, comforting.

"Feel better?" Cole asks, and he's asking about all of it, the last fourteen years of *not* feeling right, and Ren knows.

"Almost."

"Yeah. Almost."

After a few moments, Ren slips out from under Cole's arm and crawls out of bed. He crosses to the window and pulls the drapes open, letting in the first blush of morning.

"We're missing the sunrise," Ren says. He climbs back into bed and turns to face the window, pulling Cole over to hold him from behind. Cole throws an arm around Ren's waist, and Ren covers it with his own, silently imploring him to hold him even tighter.

The sunrise, bright orange and soft pink waking up over the mountains, is the stuff of epic poems and happy endings, and Cole *hates* it. He burrows his head into Ren's neck and whimpers. Ren just squeezes his hand tighter, tighter, until he lets out a shaky breath and disentangles himself from Cole completely.

"You should go," Ren says.

"Okay."

Ren watches as Cole dresses. They don't speak; they don't even look at each other. Cole wonders if Ren thinks it's the guilt that keeps him from looking at Ren; that would be another misunderstanding, another missed opportunity. He doesn't feel guilty, not at all. How could he? This is honoring an old, unspoken promise. It has nothing to do with the men they have promised to love now. Still, the way Cole slouches and moves slowly, head down, eyes on everything but Ren, he probably looks as though he's letting shame seep in.

If he thinks that, he's wrong. I'm just too sad, too close to fucking everything up. If he asks, I won't be able to say no.

Cole crosses to the bed, leans down and kisses Ren. For a moment he thinks he'll be pulled back in, under the covers, to roll around with Ren in this bed forever. Ren has his hand on the back of Cole's neck, he's up on his knees now, pressing naked skin to Cole's clothed body, and Cole has his hand on Ren's ass, and it's so hot and perfect and *them*.

Ren pulls his lips off of Cole and presses their foreheads together. "Go."

Cole kisses Ren one last time and steps away. He doesn't look back, not even when his hand turns the doorknob, not even as the door shuts behind him. He just walks. Down the hall, to the elevator, through the lobby, out the door, down the street. He walks and walks, and with every step he feels more and more... angry. He can still feel Ren on him, inside him, around him. The loss is too much, and he loathes this place they've let themselves get to. He is so angry with himself, and with Ren, for being brave about so many things, but never about this. Never about them.

He walks with balled up fists now, eyes dark and desperate.

Without thinking, he goes into the Starbucks. It's just opening up for the day. He walks up to the counter, orders two Americanos. And then he's walking again, coffees in hand, back down San Francisco Street, up the steps, through the lobby, down the hallway.

He stands in front of Ren's door. Room 415. Was it just a few hours ago that he faced this door, knowing that what he was about to do was crazy, that it was wrong, and that he had to do it anyway?

He knocks and Ren opens the door. He is red-faced, puffy-eyed, with a towel wrapped around his hips.

"It's still nighttime in Hawaii." Cole hands Ren his coffee.

Ren ignores it and throws his arms around Cole's neck. He kisses him again and again, little pecks on his cheeks, his lips, his forehead.

"What are we doing?" Ren asks.

Cole steps forward, pushing them back into the room. He says it before he thinks about it, before he realizes what it means or what he's asking of Ren and himself, before he changes his mind, because he really doesn't know *what* he's saying. "You're here for ten more days—"

"Twelve."

"So give me all of them."

Chapter 5

Three hours is not enough sleep, but when the phone rings to wake him at ten a.m., Ren wiggles out of Cole's tight hold and slips out of bed. He knew it was a bit scandalous to ask for a wake-up call *at seven in the morning*, but he didn't want to use the alarm on his phone. He knew there would be a text message or a missed call from Paul, and he just couldn't face it, not then.

He can't face it now, either.

Ren looks down at Cole, the duvet just barely covering his ass, and despite his lack of sleep and a nagging sense of apprehension working its way up his spine, he feels happy. Giddy, even.

They're on borrowed time. Stolen time, really. They're stealing moments from Paul and Liam and probably making a huge mistake, but he doesn't care. He'll worry about it when he gets back to New York, when this affair (*shit, is that what this is?*) is but a memory.

Ren is ten minutes into his long, hot shower when he realizes he's humming "Feelin' Groovy" by Simon and Garfunkel. It's such a Cole thing to do, so corny, so cliché, so *not Ren*. He sings a few bars; the sound of his own voice, scratchy from crying, from a lack of sleep and from giving one seriously intense blowjob, surprises him.

He used to sing with Cole, sunroof open on Cole's BMW, as they drove I-94 toward Minneapolis, toward "all-ages nights" and dancing and freedom. He used to sing alone in his room, softly, as he organized his closet or flipped through photos. He used to sing with friends at parties. He used to sing when he worked, polishing, sanding, soldering, making something beautiful.

When did I give it up? When was the last time?

Maybe he sang along to the national anthem when Paul, with a nudge and a million-dollar smile, forced him to join in while visiting then-Governor Landry's box at Yankee Stadium. He can't remember. There have been too many tiny, perfectly reasonable compromises and sacrifices, too many subtle shifts away from himself, to count. They all run together now, like a watercolor in the rain, and he can't put his finger on the exact moment when he stopped believing his own hype and acquiesced to a different life, a life that many envy; a life that he still can't imagine for himself, even though he's living it.

Ren finishes his shower, wraps a towel around his waist and walks back into the room to get ready. He goes through the motions, deep in thought, his movements slow and methodical.

Did I sing "Happy Birthday" to Meg at her last birthday party? When was that... wow, was that two years ago already? Or did I sing it into the phone last year? I've never even sung for Paul. Not one song. He'd probably be too embarrassed, anyway. It's been so long since...

I forgot. I've forgotten so much.

He's half dressed, slipping one arm into his button-down shirt, when he notices Cole staring at him from the bed, arms curled around the pillow under his head. Ren blushes, wondering if Cole heard him sing in the shower.

"I like watching you," Cole says.

Ren smiles. He sits next to him on the edge of the bed, shirt open. "Hey," Ren says softly. He runs two fingers through Cole's wild hair.

"Hey." Cole pulls one hand out from under his pillow and reaches for Ren, placing his hand flat on Ren's belly.

"I have to go see a woman about tile," Ren says.

Cole presses Ren's skin, feeling his abdominal muscles. He slides his hand up Ren's chest, presses two fingers into Ren's collarbone and reaches up to cup his chin. "Okay."

Ren leans down and presses his lips to Cole's. It's a soft ghost of a kiss—he's not starting something he can't finish—but Cole gasps nonetheless. Maybe this is how it will be every day until they part: heightened reactions to every little thing, panting and gasping and tugging and pleading and grabbing and holding on just a little too long. They've spent far too much time building up to this, or avoiding it, or both. Probably both.

Definitely both. Everything is urgent now; the clock is ticking, and Ren is damn sure of one thing: They will never be satisfied.

Suddenly it occurs to Ren that they're not stealing moments from anyone, not really. They're reclaiming the moments they left behind.

"Do you have to work today?"

Cole nods and stretches, his toes pointing toward the television. The sheet slips off, covering just the tops of his calves. Ren can't help but look at Cole's body: tan skin, strong thighs, his interested cock thick and perfect. So perfect. He wants to take Cole into his mouth, work him over until he's mad for it and then ride him until they both scream.

Ren licks his lips and looks back at Cole's face. He's smirking. "You know you want to," he teases.

"True. But if I miss this appointment, I won't get another for weeks, and I'm not coming back to Santa Fe just for tile," Ren says.

The words are out of his mouth before he realizes what he's saying, before he can figure out a better way to say he just wants to be finished with this job, not Cole. "Sorry. That didn't come out right. I just meant... I didn't mean I don't want to come back... to you. Not that we have that option—"

"It's fine. I'm fine. We probably wouldn't be here anyway. We'll finish up in a couple of weeks, I imagine. Unless Alegra changes her mind about something."

Ren takes hold of Cole's hand, intertwines their fingers and places their palms together, flat, as Cole did the night before last.

They've held hands before, many times. That first day they met behind the chapel, when Cole pulled him from one life into another. The night he moved into the dorm and Cole held his hand through two episodes of *Project Runway* to help calm Ren's nerves about starting at a new school. They held hands to offer each other comfort, reassurance, an anchor.

And sometimes they held hands because they couldn't bring themselves to do anything more than that, like that night at Dean's bachelor party when they held hands under the table, thumbs rubbing over knuckles, wrists, palms, keeping their attraction a secret from the group and from themselves.

That was five years ago; the last time they saw each other in person. They had never spoken of it.

Cole watches Ren's face as he reminisces. He must look pained, because Cole asks, "Are you okay? You look sad."

"I think maybe we're insane." Ren stares at their hands.

"But not wrong. Never wrong."

"That's debatable."

Cole pushes back on Ren's hand a bit. "It can't be helped, Ren. You know that."

"I do, yes."

Ren pushes back on Cole's hand one last time and then swoops in for a brief, hot kiss. He stands, buttons up his shirt, puts on his shoes and packs his phone and wallet in his bag, all while Cole's eyes follow him.

"See you later?" Cole asks, as if it's normal, as if this thing they're doing won't wreck everything, as if it won't kill them.

"Of course. When?"

"Dinner? I'll be done around eight, I think. Maybe earlier. Alegra's husband is flying in for the benefit, and she'll want to break to have dinner with him."

"Great. See you." Ren leans down to give Cole's thigh a quick squeeze.

He's halfway to the door when it hits him: He doesn't really know how to *do* the next twelve days. Will they spend every spare moment in his hotel room or Cole's? Will they behave as two old friends would, except more (so much more)? Will they have a chance to be together, to really *be together*, if just for a few days? Or is that asking too much?

Ren turns back and stands at the edge of the bed. He tries to get the words out, but so much has changed between them, cracked wide open and set on fire, that he can't remember the rules anymore—what can be said, what must remain unsaid.

He's silent, fiddling with the strap on his messenger bag, trying not to look nervous, when Cole says, "Tell me."

Ren exhales. "So can I take you on a date, or is this strictly a hotel thing?"

"We didn't cover that this morning, did we?"

"We didn't cover much."

"Is that something you wanted to do? Before?"

"Of course. But that's not really a secret, now, is it? I mean, I told you how I felt about you at the bonfire, Homecoming."

Cole's smile is rueful, but he doesn't explain it. Instead he crawls over to the edge of the bed and pulls Ren down to sit next to him. "What about now? That was just a crush, right? And you're not in love with me, now; you're in love with Paul. So, would you... is that something you want to do now?"

Ren wants to tell him it wasn't just a crush; it was everything. It was everything and it was too soon, and he was so fucking angry about it, because who gets to keep everything at sixteen? Why couldn't it have happened later, when he knew more about himself, when he'd seen enough and loved enough and discovered enough about himself to say, "Yes, I'll have this, I'll take this everything and keep it forever?"

Instead, Ren says, "Maybe we can... just for these days we have left—" Ren sighs, unable to say what he means because he's not really sure himself. "I don't want this to seem like an affair... even if that's exactly what this is."

"That's not what this is."

"Okay, so—" Ren stops himself from asking, *so what is this then?*

Cole lets the silence fall between them and then grabs Ren's hand again. He leans in, hot breath on Ren's neck, and kisses him in the spot right under his ear. Ren turns his head to look at Cole, who offers up one of his all-over grins and says, "I'd love to go on a date with you."

"It seems so wrong to call it a date."

"*You asked.*"

"I know, I know, but, hearing you accept, it sounds so—"

"Stop. Seriously, just stop. I don't want to spend all of our time together worrying about what's right or if we should go to the fucking movies or not, or hold hands in public or not, or anything else we want to do. I'm in this, and I'll accept the consequences when it's over. Until then, I want to just do whatever we want to do, whatever feels right."

Ren sucks in a breath, because this is Cole, wanting to be with him without limits, even if just for a few moments, and he can't walk away from that now.

"Okay. I'm in," Ren says.

Cole holds Ren's face in his hands and looks right into his eyes. "No rules."

"No rules," Ren agrees.

"No worries."

"No worries," Ren agrees.

"No regrets."

"No regrets." Ren gives Cole a quick kiss on the lips. "For now."

Cole takes another sip of his energy drink and tries to decide if he should just tell her the truth, or let her wonder forever. Everyone saw their intense make-out at The Pink last night—the band, Gretchen, everyone. And they all know Liam. Gretchen adores him, in fact. But Cole knows that if he asks them to, they'll keep their mouths shut. They probably wouldn't say anything to Liam even if he didn't ask for their silence.

But still. It's not over yet. So there's that. He can't pretend it was a one-time thing, something his friends can easily overlook. And he doesn't intend to cheapen what he has with Ren by sneaking around as if what they've done is wrong or shameful. Because it isn't. At least, it doesn't *feel* that way. Not yet. And his friends are bound to see them together at some point; they'll get to watch it unfold and come apart, so what's the point of lying now?

"I was worried as fuck, Cole," Alegra continues, mid-rant. He had tuned her out five minutes ago, trying to sort out a reply to her earlier question. "Answer your fucking texts, why don't you?"

"I'm sorry. Really, I am. I didn't think to check my phone."

"So did you or didn't you?" And there's the question again, so bold and finite.

Did I let myself be, for once? Did I give in? Did I do what I should have done years ago? Did I finally learn what it feels like to lose myself in someone completely? Did I have the most amazing night of my life with my dearest friend in the whole entire world?

"Yes. Yes, I did."

"Fuck."

"I know. But I'm not sorry."

"Are you a thing, now? Finally? Or what?"

"Yes. For twelve days."

Cole explains their agreement, lays it all out for her. He tries to make it sound sensible, but it's difficult, because he knows their situation is anything but.

Alegra listens carefully, and then says, "Cheating on Liam—"

"I *know*—"

"Hold up. Listen. Cheating on Liam is the *least* of it. Last night... you weren't just dancing with Ren. You were *clutching* him, Cole. And you weren't just kissing. That was pure worship. That was an *embrace*."

Cole lets out a heavy sigh and sinks down into the leather couch. They're alone in the studio—the others are out to lunch—so he lets himself fall to pieces under her watchful gaze.

"I'm so fucked," he says.

Alegra slips off her stool and sits next to him. She bumps her knee against his playfully, letting him know she's not judging him, that she's just his friend, just *here*. This is major, and there will be casualties. Everyone will be worried about Liam, but she's worried about Cole. She knows that his heart is about to break into countless tiny pieces, so many he'll never find all of them; so many he'll never be whole. And it won't be because he'll lose Liam. It's Ren who will break him, and there's nothing anyone can do or say about it, least of all her.

"What the hell are you going to do?"

He looks at her now, jaw set, his eyes wet with unshed tears. "Take everything he'll give me until the very last second."

She doesn't try to talk him out of it; there's no point. She just leans into him again and says, "Oh, Cole... how are we going to put you back together again?"

"It doesn't matter. He's worth it."

They both lean their heads back on the couch. They're quiet for a few minutes, contemplating ceiling tiles, listening to the low hum of the electronic equipment, and then Alegra kills the moment. "It was that fucking song, wasn't it?"

And they laugh—big, full-body, silly laughs, feeding off of each other, stupid with it, rolling around on the couch until they make themselves stop.

When they calm down, Cole looks back at the ceiling. "You're my favorite."

"I know, dear one. Fancy a burger? My salad is for shit."

⌗

"So Deidre says, 'But *Ren*, we've done this all wrong. Trinity Stupidbitch insists that, in Santa Fe, you start with the door FIRST and then build the house AROUND it.' God. Is this my life? Because if this is my life, I want a do-over," Ren says.

"Trinity Stupidbitch?" Antonio tries not to laugh.

"Whatever. She's stupid and she's a bitch. I can't be bothered to remember her actual name, so I made one up that suits her better."

"Yeah, but... *Trinity*?"

"Oh I didn't make that part up. That is her first name."

"I can't imagine Deidre Alexander hanging out with anyone who has conviction, much less someone who comes from a family so devout they named their kid after the Holy Trinity."

They're killing time in the FedEx line, waiting for an obnoxious woman to finish harassing the poor college-age kid behind the counter about missing boxes. She's screaming about small claims court, and something else about "the hand of God," when Ren's eyes fixate on the small gold cross hanging from Antonio's neck. Suddenly he's very embarrassed.

"I didn't mean to offend you," Ren says. Antonio looks at him quizzically and Ren explains. "About Trinity. I mean, you're... well, I don't know *what* you are, exactly. But you seem to be... are you Catholic? I mean, are you religious? I probably shouldn't even ask. I mean, we've never talked about this before."

"You can ask. I was raised Catholic, yes. But I only go to Mass when my mother asks me to now, holy days, family celebrations, that sort of thing," Antonio replies. "The cross is from my grandmother. She was Tewa, from the Nambé pueblo, but raised Catholic. I wear it mostly for sentimental reasons."

"Why don't you go to Mass anymore?"

"Well, some say all religions are imperfect in some way, that I should just overlook the things that piss me off and focus on what's really important, but I just can't do that."

"What pisses you off, exactly?"

"Hypocrisy. The Pope's stance on birth control, abortion, homosexuality. The massive sexual abuse cover-up. Should I go on?"

"No. Believe me, I get it. Catholic school survivor here."

"I do miss the ritual of it all, though. Sometimes I go to the Cathedral—"

"The one off the Plaza?"

"Saint Francis, yes. Sometimes I go there and light a candle for my grandmother and just sit in a pew and pray. It's simpler that way. It's just me and God. It's nice."

Ren is quiet for a minute. He'd had such disdain for Catholicism in school—the forced confessions, the mandatory religion classes, twice-weekly Mass, monks doing in secret what they condemned in public. His parents weren't practicing Catholics, but had sent him to Saint Benedict's in an effort to give him a stellar education and get him away from the league of assholes he grew up with in Two Harbors. He never had decided which was worse—"up north" hicks making his life a living hell or the dogmatic oppression at Saint Ben's.

"I don't miss any of it, especially confession. Did you ever go?"

"Every Friday."

"And did you... did you feel better, after confessing your sins?"

"It always feels better to talk to someone about your problems, sure. But I don't really believe in sin the way my family believes. I believe sin is acting against your own truth."

"Like knowing what's right and doing the opposite?"

"Sort of. It's more like, knowing what's right *for you*, and going against that. I'm oversimplifying, but you know, that's the basic gist of it."

A supervisor ushers the irate woman off to the side and the shell-shocked kid waves Antonio and Ren forward. Antonio's words hang heavy in the air as they step up, setting their two boxes of tile samples on the counter. Ren knows Antonio and Sarah saw him dance with Cole, saw him give himself over to the moment as if they were the last two people on earth. He wants to tell his friend he's in trouble, he's headed for a breakdown and he can't stop. He wants to tell him he had it all figured out until last night, until Cole uttered those four simple words: "*I've always wanted you.*"

He wants to tell him everything because he needs a friend, someone who won't judge him, someone who didn't know them before, when they were kids and made all the wrong choices...

"Ren? Overnight?"

"Hmm?"

"You want these boxes to go overnight, right?"

"Oh. Yes. Morning delivery, please."

Ren decides to keep his confession to himself for now. He smiles at Antonio and says instead, "It's a beautiful necklace, Antonio."

"Thanks."

Ren texts Cole on their way back downtown. There's this little Italian restaurant he's been meaning to try, just a short walk from the Alexander house. It has a New York feel, small, with clean lines, white tablecloths on square tables, simple flower arrangements and an excellent wine list.

Ren: Meet me at Il Piatto on Marcy Street at 8:30?

Ren tries not to look at his screen. Cole is working; he won't get back to him right away. He's busy.

His phone buzzes not thirty seconds later.

Cole: Yes. Perfect.

Ren imagines the two of them eating and talking and staying too long, and then walking back to the hotel, hand-in-hand, sneaking glances...

"You know what I think is the worst possible sin?" Antonio interrupts Ren's daydream.

"I'm afraid to answer," Ren teases. "Faux leather? Wearing a cowboy hat from Target?"

"Chickening out."

"On what?"

"The life you were meant to live."

Chapter 6

It's impossible to remember all of the wasted moments, much less add them up to make sense of how things went very and truly wrong, but Ren is giving it a good try anyway. Sitting on the floor in Deidre Alexander's enormous guest bathroom, he stares at the row of tiles lined up along the baseboard—indigo, midnight, ocean—and tries to piece it all together.

All through high school, Ren held out hope that Cole would get his shit together. Every time they were alone together he wondered, "Is today the day?" They had taken at least a dozen day trips to quaint little homophobic towns with antique shops and cherry festivals and pie, and had spent countless hours in each other's dorm rooms, cars and other intimate spaces. They had wandered off from at least seven Bennie mixers with the St. Margaret's girls so they could gossip or just talk about whatever crucial revelation one of them had had in the four and a half hours they hadn't seen each other. And of course, there was Jeremy's Stupid Camping Trip.

Through all of the moonlight and darkness and quiet, the firelight on young faces in the great hall, the haze of Asher's mystery drink, the accidental brushing of legs and stocking-covered feet on twin beds, the cloud formations and piles of autumn leaves and the sweet-smelling rain, the *proximity*, Ren had expected Cole to take advantage of one, *just one* of those "movie" moments and kiss him senseless. But he never did.

The way Ren saw it, these were Cole's wasted moments, not his. He had stated his intentions and played along and waited patiently for the big moment, the revelation, the declaration of love that never came. Wisconsin was the end of that, because in Wisconsin it was Ren who wasted the biggest moment of all.

Uncrossing his legs and bringing his knees up to his chest, Ren remembers water lapping against the sides of a dock in a lake far away, a pink, green and yellow glow reflecting in blue eyes on a night long ago.

It was the moment to end all moments. They were skinny-dipping in a lake, under the northern lights, a short walk from a parent-free cabin; it was a now-or-never moment if there ever was one. And Ren blew it. He took one look at Cole's expectant gaze, placed two hands flat on the dock and pulled himself up out of the water and away from any chance that they would finally get what they both wanted.

It wasn't the last time Ren wasted an opportunity to reach out and grab this thing between them and hold it steady, to let it land and settle between them and allow it to ripen and grow and shape them into the men they were always meant to be. But it *was* the last time he hoped they would get their own movie ending, because for the first time, *he* was the coward.

It was the realization that they were *both* cowards that inspired Ren to make a decision: He would learn how to be happy living a different life, without Cole.

From that moment forward, he held them both equally responsible for the wasted moments. And soon enough, the business of growing up eroded their everyday familiarity and these moments wound together and formed the DNA of their relationship; these moments *defined* them, in the same way their love *should have* defined them. And it all felt wrong, so very wrong.

Until they actually did the "wrong" thing and everything felt so very *right*.

Ren shakes off the memories and pulls his phone from his pocket. He's been avoiding Paul all day, afraid to let reality seep into the lovely awesome that has enveloped him ever since Cole showed up at his hotel room door. His finger skates through the texts, expecting to find a dozen or more anxious messages, but there are only four:

Paul: Did I miss you again? Still burning ALL of the candles at both ends here. We may have a deal with Tobias. Not sure yet. Love you.

Paul: Damn. I keep forgetting the time difference. You're probably still sleeping. Call me when you get this.

Paul: Forgot to ask about work. How is Mrs. Crazy? Are you done yet?

Paul: Just tried to call you. Dinner break. Thought I'd spend it with you.

What are we doing for Christmas? Can we be in NY on the 27th? I might
have a thing.

He knows he should call Paul, even if it's just to leave him a voicemail,
but he doesn't want to hear Paul's voice. He's afraid that even his short,
businesslike recorded message ("If this is an urgent matter, please contact
my assistant, April Clark at 917...") will be the pinprick that bursts the
highly inappropriate, delicious bubble he's been living in for the past
twenty-two hours.

It's not as though they haven't gone weeks without talking before, what
with Paul's commitments to President Landry and Ren's willingness to
let him disappear into his work without complaint. Paul can wait. As
long as Ren sends him a text, Paul won't miss him much; even if he does,
he'll be too busy to do anything about it.

Ren: Got your messages. Working hard to get this done to avoid a second
trip. Dinner meeting tonight, sorry. Good luck with everything.
Keep me posted via text, if you can. Yes, NY on the 27th is fine. xxoo

And there it is: the first outright lie.

Dinner meeting.

*Since when do I send little x's and o's? Trying to get my fiancé to text me
so I don't have to hear his voice. I'm a liar. A liar and a cheat. And a liar.*

Ren stands and makes his way through the house, touching walls,
brushing fingertips on polished wood, the backs of chairs, the dining
room table.

He's reminded of a conversation he had with his mom just before
Sean's wedding. They had stayed up until the wee hours, rethinking the
seating chart longer than was actually necessary, his mom nervous about
letting go of her eldest son and Ren nervous about seeing Cole in a tux.
Somehow they ended up talking until dawn, two empty wine bottles
and a half-full bowl of pita chips between them.

He didn't talk much about Cole that night, though he did discuss other
boys he dated and liked and kissed, the boys with whom he had shared
firsts. His mom didn't discuss her true feelings about Sean's milestone
either, instead choosing to match Ren's stories with her own dating
adventures. It was somewhere around four a.m. when she admitted to
once cheating on one of her boyfriends, a tall-ish firefighter she once
loved enough to practice saying her first name with his last.

At the time, Ren was shocked; her secret seemed incongruous with the warm, pleasant, unwavering loyalty his mother possessed. When he asked her if she had ever come clean, she looked right at Ren and said, "Honey, confessing to an affair that's over, well, that's just selfish. Sleeping with Steven didn't change my feelings toward Brian one bit. Telling him would have made *me* feel better, sure, but it would have broken Brian's heart unnecessarily."

She smiled at his wide eyes, then, adding, "It was my mistake, so I chose to live with the guilt. And believe me, that stuff eats you up inside. It's a harsh punishment. Thank goodness your father didn't care one bit about my past."

Looking at Deidre's still-unpainted kitchen, Ren wants to call his mom and tell her everything. He wants to lean into her soothing voice, rest his worries on her wisdom and let her unconditional love wrap around him and shield him from the guilt rising in his gut. He knew it would show up eventually, because as much as he is part of her, influenced by her example and sage advice, he is, above all, his father's son.

And Erik Warner never lies.

Ren closes the blue door behind him and makes his way from the Alexander house to Cole. *Cole.* Cole who is *on his way to meet him.* Cole who is his *date.* Cole who is not his fiancé. Cole who belongs to someone else.

How can two cheaters go on a date? Is that even possible? Is it called something else? Is it a rendezvous? A hookup? A big fat lie dressed up to look like something normal, something real?

Ren's thoughts overwhelm him, churn in his belly and twist up his spine until he feels a little bit sick. It's only a short walk to Il Piatto and he's early, so he decides to do the only thing that will make him feel better. He thumbs through his contacts, brings up the familiar face and presses "Call."

The phone rings twice and then, "Ren? What's up, buddy?"

"Hi, Dad."

"You okay?"

"Sure. Yes. I just haven't talked to you much lately, so I thought we could catch up."

It's almost ten o'clock in Minnesota, and Ren knows his dad is sitting in the family room in his giant brown leather recliner, trying to stay awake long enough to greet Mom after her three-to-eleven shift. The fact that his parents haven't altered their routine since he and Sean lived at home is more than just a comfort for Ren; it is the constant that keeps him from feeling lost, even when he is.

"Something's bugging you," Erik says.

"Not at all... I—"

"Ren, just tell me. What's going on? What do you need? Do you need something?"

Do you need something?

"Why would you say that? I'm fine," Ren says, hurriedly. There is a short pause and then he asks, "Why *did* you say that?"

"I don't know. You just seem... not yourself." Erik's tone is careful. "*Do you need something?*"

Do I need something? Fuck yes, I do. I need to feel like this is all okay, that I'm not a total and complete bastard. I need to confess. I need forgiveness. I need more than twelve days. I need—

"Ren, I can't help you, buddy, if you don't tell me what's up."

"I'm in Santa Fe," Ren starts.

"Yeah? You're still working on that job, then?"

"Yes... Dad—" and he can't say what he needs to say, so he diverts. "Did you know that you can see four mountain ranges from here?"

"No kidding? I'd like to see that."

"I finally get that whole 'purple mountains majesty' thing."

"Nice sunsets, I suppose."

"Yes. And sunrises." Ren pauses, takes a deep breath and lets out a heavy sigh. "I ran into Cole."

"Where? In Santa Fe?"

"Yes. We're staying in the same hotel."

"You just ran into each other? I thought he was living in England or something."

"He is."

"So I'm guessing there's a problem somewhere in this story, or you wouldn't be calling me. Is Cole okay?"

"Yes, yes. He's fine. He's good. It's, uh, complicated."

Ren hears his father sigh and move about in his chair. He imagines him there, in that room filled with family pictures and framed football jerseys, sitting up and forward in his chair as if Ren were right there in front of him, just as he did whenever Ren was in trouble.

"Just how complicated are we talking here, Ren?"

"Um... very?"

"Christ."

"Dad, I—"

"Now, Ren? After all these years, you two decide to do, whatever it is you're doing, *now*?"

"I know, it's crazy, *we're crazy*—"

"Does Paul know?"

"No, God no. Never," Ren insists.

"Never, huh? Exactly what are you and Cole doing here, kid? Because if it's what I think it is, you have to tell Paul. And if it's what *you* have convinced yourself it is, you still have to tell him. You can't be a liar, too, Ren."

His father's words are like a blow to the gut. Ren stops and grabs hold of the nearest wall for support. He doesn't say anything for a moment, just lets the silence and the weight of his deeds hang between them as, fourteen hundred miles apart, they both swallow, take a breath, and swallow again.

Just then, he spots Cole not a block away, walking up Marcy Street toward Il Piatto. Ren slips into the entryway of a shop and tries to mold himself against the blue door—always the same Santa Fe blue—as he watches Cole look up and around and finally notice the restaurant.

Cole looks gorgeous in his dark denim, a crisp, soft pink button-down and a brown, tailored leather jacket. Ren watches him take a moment to look at the menu posted on the glass outside and has to look away so he doesn't shout out to him, run to him, grab him in a crushing embrace and never let him go.

Ren looks up and notices the Marcy Street Card Shop sign. He peers in the window at the darkened store, at shelves of greeting cards and love notes and handmade paper, and says the thing he hasn't told a living soul.

"It *is* what you think it is. I'm hopelessly in love with Cole, and he came for me, and I couldn't say no," Ren says. "I couldn't say no."

"Jesus. I should have locked you two in the basement years ago. But somehow I think even if you were stranded together on a friggin' deserted island, you still wouldn't man up and do what needs to be done."

"I'm not going to argue with you, Dad. You're right, of course. I've spent the last few hours running over every time... well, it doesn't matter. What matters is we were both stupid—"

"And chickenshit—"

"Yes, that too. But we're not doing that anymore. Now we—"

"Now you're engaged, Ren. And Cole, is he screwing around on anyone?"

The words cut right through Ren's heart. But he deserves it. Every bit of it. So he fights the urge to hang up and answers: "Yes. A boyfriend."

"And he loves him?"

"Yes. I think so."

"And you still love Paul?"

"I do love Paul, but—"

"Never mind. I know it's not the same. Anyone who ever spent even five minutes with you two together knows you and Cole have that star-crossed chemistry thing going on. How is Paul supposed to compete with that?"

"He doesn't have to. As soon as I'm done with this job, I'm going back to New York, to Paul. Cole and I agreed."

"So you're just going to mess around on your future husband for a few days and then never tell him?"

Ren can hear the disappointment in his father's voice, and he wants to reach through the phone, get on his knees and beg for his forgiveness.

"Dad, I don't know what to do. I just... I can't stop. Not now. I just... I *need* this."

Erik heaves a big sigh and Ren imagines him rubbing his jaw, his face stern and his eyes filled with anger.

"Look, kid, you know I love you no matter what, but you have to do the right thing here. And I can't tell you what that is. I know you called me because you want me to tell you, but you're a grown man, Ren. You need to figure out what's right for you and have the courage to make it so. Even if it's the hardest thing," Erik says. "Except that part about telling Paul. Whatever happens, you owe it to him to tell him the truth. All of it. Not just this Santa Fe stuff. *All of it.*"

"Okay, Dad."

"Okay, then."

"I love you, Dad."

"So much, kid."

"Don't be worried, Dad."

"Fat chance."

"Thank you. Bye."

"Bye. Take care of *you*."

Cole sits at the table Ren reserved, a small square table for two in the corner near the window, feeling at once seventeen and ancient. He's nervous, and it's more than just first-date nervous, it's *first-date-ever* nervous. But after a long life of dashed hope and longing, he's also weary. Without Ren next to him, the flood of hell-to-pay creeps in and even though he can't—*won't*—do anything to stop it, it's there, right there, at the base of his skull. He wants to jump around *and* take a nap.

But isn't that how it always is with us? Aren't we always two things, or many things, or everything all in one moment? Will this ever make sense? Could we ever just be? After this... even after this?

Cole fiddles with his phone and calls up Liam's email for the third time that day. He'd canceled their Skype date, knowing full well he'd probably be tangled up in Ren's sheets by midnight and wouldn't want to stop in order to have Skype sex with his boyfriend. It felt wrong, the thought of leaving one man for another in the same night, but not in the way he expected it to feel wrong. He canceled his plans with Liam because it felt oddly as though, if he went through with this very simple thing he often did with his boyfriend, he would be betraying *Ren*.

> Cole,
>
> Why do I get the feeling you're out there, lost in the desert, and may never come home? Tell me I'm wrong. Tell me I'm just missing you and freaking out for nothing.
>
> Call me when you can.
>
> Liam

It wasn't the first time Cole had canceled something with Liam. He made work his priority, often staying late at the studio or playing an extra set at the tucked-away pubs he frequented. He reasoned that he was just one of those people who needed a lot of time alone, who was dedicated to his work, who liked to keep some things to himself. But deep down, he knew it was more than that. He'd never really given himself over to anyone, not really.

He loved Liam, partly because Liam was the first guy who accepted his inherent distance, the first guy who just let him go off and do his thing without grumbling about it, or questioning his fidelity or interest. It was easy. They had fun. The sex, while not satisfying, was regular, and they rarely argued. Their relationship was comfortable, but he never felt that all-consuming, hot, firework kind of love with Liam, not even in the beginning. If he were brutally honest with himself, he would have to admit that he got more goosebumps after receiving a text from Ren than he did while receiving a blowjob from Liam.

Sex with Liam was like getting off with a friend.

Sex with Ren was like setting his soul on fire.

Sitting in this tiny Italian restaurant, waiting for this boy he's always loved, Cole knows now that his relationship has worked so far in spite of him. Liam always compromised and waited patiently without protest. He took what he could get from Cole and never asked for more. That which is good between them is all Liam, and he's starting to feel mighty guilty about it.

His entire time in Santa Fe, Cole had been pulling away from Liam, beyond the norm. He used everything as an excuse—Alegra's whims, his muse, the demands of the record company—but he knows now what kept him from truly engaging with Liam these past few weeks. He was preparing for this, for Ren. Now that they are wrapped up in the tether that binds them together, he knows that he has been waiting for him here, in this enchanted, dusty city, all along.

Liam deserves more, so much more, and Cole doesn't want him to worry unnecessarily. So he shoots off a quick, short email. Liam will receive it when he wakes up.

Liam,

I haven't been myself lately. I've had a long day and I'm turning in early.

I'll call you tomorrow and tell you everything.
Love,
C

Cole regrets sending it almost immediately. He didn't address Liam's concerns and he outright lied about going to bed early. And "everything?" He doesn't even know what that means. Is he going to tell him the whole story, or just portion it off, leaving out the stuff that would kill what they have?

Is Liam my backup plan? Was he always? Can I spend the rest of my life with a backup? Doesn't Liam also deserve this mind-blowing, life-defining love?

He wants to call Liam and confess, promise to work on their problems when he returns or set him free, but he knows he can't do either of these things. Liam is sleeping, but that's the least of it. How could he tell him any of this without sounding like a prime asshole, without breaking his heart?

Just then he hears a familiar voice in the main dining room near the entrance. "Warner. But I'm meeting a friend—"

Ren's body is stiff. Cole knows he's stressed about something. He watches Ren weave his way through the tables, smiling down at other diners as he slides through the tight spaces.

Cole's heart races; his palms sweat. He's known this man for more than a decade, known him since before he needed to shave, before he fell in love with furniture design and sushi and Patsy Cline, before he discovered Armistead Maupin and Bombay Sapphire gin and Yaz, before he could vote or make lobster bisque or navigate the subway without a map. He's had sex with this man, but still, *still*, he feels the same heady anticipation he's felt ever since he realized he was in love with his best friend.

Ren makes his way to their table and Cole can see the precise moment when his shoulders relax and he lets go of the worries he carried in with him. Cole stands, ready to hold out his chair for him, but Ren stops him cold with a raised eyebrow. He hangs his bag off his chair and sits down, eyes locking with Cole's. Their grins take the place of words and they stay like that, staring, smiling, the air between them charged and thick with promise. Out of the corner of his eye, Cole sees their server start toward them, size up the scene and then step back and lean against the bar, waiting.

Cole reaches over and takes Ren's hand in his own, his eyes fixed on Ren's lips, the faint red mark just below his left ear, the blush on his cheeks. Ren squeezes and thumbs the back of Cole's hand, back and forth, back and forth, back and forth, and it sends a jolt of *amazing* and *holy shit you're gorgeous* straight to Cole's heart. They stay like that for a few minutes, long enough for the nearest diners to notice.

Then, just when Cole wonders if they should just ditch the restaurant and make a run for the hotel, Ren leans in to whisper, "I already love this night."

Cole gasps. He *gasps*. Like a teenaged girl.

Ren squeezes Cole's hand one more time and then leans back in his chair, his smile almost a smirk, but not quite. Cole laughs and nods at the server. She bounces over, all blonde hair and brightness.

"May I take your drink order, or would you like to hear the specials now?"

"We'll take a bottle of Prosecco," Cole replies.

"May I ask your name?" Ren asks.

She brightens and replies, "Gloria."

"We'd also like a bottle of Pellegrino, Gloria."

"Perfect. I'll be back in two shakes."

"Who says that?" Ren asks, after she scurries away.

"Gloria, apparently."

Ren licks his lips. It's an absentminded gesture, one that reassures Cole. Ren is nervous, too. They're quiet again, not sure how to start. They both look down at their menus—just meaningless letters floating on paper the color of wheat—searching for something to say.

Gloria returns before long, opens the Prosecco, splashes the first taste into Cole's glass and offers it to him. He's practiced in his inspection and appreciation of the Italian wine, drawing on his country-club-prep-school-garden-party upbringing with ease.

Cole doesn't like to call attention to this aspect of his past, and does his best to avoid any and all functions where he would be expected to behave in a way "befitting the McKnights of Edina." He left that behind when he said no to his father's Harvard dreams and followed his own.

This is the sort of thing a first date wouldn't know. He'd have to work up to it, peel away layers slowly until he revealed his true self. But Ren already knows the real Cole McKnight. He knows that proper etiquette is second nature to him, but that he really doesn't give a damn about tasting the wine *before* they actually drink it; they ordered it, so they'll drink it.

As Gloria recites the specials in minute detail, Cole pretends to listen attentively; he's just going to order the steak, anyway. He steals a glance at Ren, who isn't listening at all. He's staring at Cole, a knowing smile at his lips, making it very difficult for Cole to keep up his good manners. Gloria somehow manages to get their orders out of them.

As soon as she leaves, Ren leans in again. "I knew you would order the steak. You're so poised tonight, so dapper. You know it's just me, right? You can tuck the breeding in your back pocket, if you like."

"I know," Cole replies, feeling uncomfortable.

"Manners are important, of course, but you're holding yourself like you're on display at one of your mother's fundraisers," Ren chides.

"Sorry, I—"

"What?"

"It's just, I'm sort of at a loss here. You already know everything about me."

"And?"

"And it's messing with my first date game."

Ren laughs and says, "Since when do you have game?"

"Hey, now—"

"You want to tell me all about your childhood, your hopes and dreams?"

"Stop teasing."

"Come on, give me your best first date story. I want to hear you tell it."

"No way. You'll laugh."

"Probably. Do it anyway." Ren fixes him with a darkened stare. "Give it to me."

And then it hits Cole—oh yeah, this is them. This is Cole and Ren volleying again, pushing the limits, getting off on getting each other riled up. Except this time is different. This time, there's no pulling back. This time, all of their play will lead to something. Something awesome. It's just them, minus the hellish sexual frustration. He sets his first date jitters aside and relaxes into it.

"Shit. *Okay.* I went to an all-boys Catholic boarding school in Minnesota," Cole begins.

"All boys? Do tell."

"We were prep school kids, never out of uniform—"

"Are you sure you're not confusing your life with porn?"

Cole glares at Ren, but there's no heat behind it. He's fine with the teasing, more than fine with it. He's happy to let Ren tease him for years, decades even, all the way to the old age home.

He teases back. "*This* is how you would genuinely respond to my story on our first date?"

"If I didn't know you? Probably. Maybe. Go on," Ren urges.

"One summer, just after school got out, a bunch of us decided we'd go camping up in the north woods," Cole continues, eyes gleaming. "We planned the trip to the letter. Everyone had a list of stuff to bring. It was so well organized we might as well have been military school brats. Except for one teeny tiny little problem..."

Cole watches as Ren's eyes get big and his cheeks flare.

"Oh, no—" Ren says.

"Oh, yes. So this friend of mine, my best friend—my *gorgeous* best friend—"

"Thank you."

"Well, you were."

"I know. Please don't go on."

"My friend was assigned to bring the big eight-person tent his dad had agreed to let us borrow. Except what we didn't realize until we pulled into the campsite—after dark, no less—"

"Stop, just stop—"

"—My friend forgot to make sure the tent poles were in the bag. We ended up sleeping in the car, rain pouring down on us—"

"Seriously, Cole? *This* is the story you tell all of your dates?"

"No. Not really."

"And it was *not* raining."

"Was too. Sheets! Sheets of rain—"

Ren starts to laugh. "Oh God, and we were all packed in Jeremy's SUV like sardines—"

"Like *drunk,* sweaty sardines."

Ren loses it. He laughs so hard he throws his head back and clutches the table. And Cole loves this—Ren, unwound over a shared memory, loose and happy and silly. All too soon, though, he remembers his surroundings and calms himself down, wiping tiny tears out of the corners of his eyes.

"It's funny; I thought of that trip earlier today," Ren says, taking a drink of wine.

Gloria returns to the table with two Caesar salads and a pepper mill. She lingers too long, clearly wanting in on the joke, but Cole shoos her away with a kind, "Thank you, Gloria."

"So what else?" Ren asks.

"What else what?"

"What else do you talk about on a first date?"

"I don't know. I don't really plan these things."

"Sure you do. You've got this whole relaxed, musician-slash-record producer, expat thing going on, but you're still a planner, Cole McKnight."

"Okay. I like to do the 'proudest moment, deepest regret' bit," Cole starts.

"Very 'job interview,' Cole. Hot."

"I ask first, of course."

"Of course."

Cole puts on his earnest face and interview voice and asks, "So, what is your proudest moment, Ren?"

Ren tries not to giggle. "Proudest moment, proudest moment... the day Mom and Dad and Sean signed a note—in *blood*—that they would never, ever shop at Wal-Mart again."

"Good one. And your deepest regret?"

And oh, maybe this wasn't the best idea Cole's ever had, because Ren is frowning now. He looks worried and sad and somehow smaller than he did just one minute ago.

"Ren, you don't really have to—"

"Wisconsin."

"Sorry?"

"My deepest regret is Wisconsin."

"Oh."

"Yeah. *Oh*," Ren says, lifting his eyes up from his lap as though they weigh ten pounds.

With that one word, *Wisconsin*, Cole is transported back, not just to the day and the dock and the boy, but the feeling. He had pushed past their boundaries and outright asked Ren for his virginity in exchange for his own, and it was one of the stupidest things he'd ever done. Because when he said, *"We could, you know, be each other's first,"* what he really meant to say was, *"Could I be yours, and would you be mine, first and last, in everything, for as long as we both shall live?"*

"For a moment there I thought you were going to say yes," Cole says out loud.

"I was. I would have. But—"

"Ren, wait. We said no regrets and we need to stick to that, or this is just going to suck for both of us," Cole interrupts.

"Of course. You're right."

"I know I asked. I wasn't thinking." Cole reaches across the table to thumb Ren's wrist.

"No, it's fine. Really." Ren takes his hand back and smiles to let Cole know it really is okay. He takes a few bites of his salad. After a moment he pushes the plate away and says, "I do want to talk about some of it, though. I want it to be okay for me to ask you a few things, to tell you a few things. Because we have this brief time together when we can just tell the truth and, I don't know, *clarify* things, and I want that. I want clarity, Cole."

"About the past?"

"Yes."

"Not about the future?"

"No. I think we're pretty clear on the future."

Cole looks down at his plate and marvels at the way they manage to jump from joy to sadness in a heartbeat. Maybe clearing the air about a few things would help even things out, unravel the tension and give them the freedom to enjoy each other until they can't anymore.

"Don't you want to know things? Haven't you always wondered what I was thinking in... certain situations? I'll give you an example," Ren says, taking another drink of wine. And then he leans in again and whispers, "That night I caught you jerking off in the communal showers not five minutes after we got back from the midnight showing of *Rocky Horror*—"

Cole's breath catches in this throat and his cock twitches under his napkin. *Shit.*

"You said you were getting off on Rocky in his gold shorts, but were you... were you getting off... on me?"

Ren bites his lip, and because of this Cole knows that he's not trying to turn him on; he really does want to know. Except that Cole *is* turned on. Incredibly so.

"Yes," Cole answers.

"I knew it!" Ren sits back in his seat. He's triumphant, shoulders squared and mouth set in a satisfied smile. He reaches behind him to rummage through his bag, digging out a small tube of lip balm.

"It's so dry here," Ren says, as though the fact that he just unlocked one of Cole's secrets is nothing, as though his own dick isn't bothered by it one bit.

He opens his mouth and rubs the waxy substance into his lips. Cole's eyes follow Ren's index finger as it rubs first his bottom lip, and then the top. Cole realizes he has to even things out or he's going to be stuck here for hours, eating fucking tiramisu and drinking tawny port until he wants to cry.

"I *was* thinking of you, Ren," Cole starts. He's using his lower register, which gets a raised eyebrow from Ren but nothing else, so he presses on.

"I remember exactly which part of you I was thinking about: your thighs. That night you had kind of scooted your ass down in the seat next to me, letting your thighs hang over the seat a bit and part, just slightly. I was so used to your legs, one crossed over the other, and that was bad enough, but that night you scrunched down and relaxed and—"

"It was preemptive ducking, Cole. I didn't want bread or water in my hair." There's a slight hitch in his speech, and Cole knows he's getting to him.

"Your jeans, they fit your thighs like a glove, and I kept imagining running my finger along the inside seam, unbuttoning your fly—"

"Uh, Cole, this isn't really the best time to—"

Ren is fidgeting now, playing with his fork and looking around nervously, one ear trained to Cole and the other to the nearest conversations.

"—Pulling down your jeans just a bit, just enough to—"

"I get it—"

"—But not enough to uncover your thighs. And then I would kneel down, and feel the denim straining over your thighs as I dipped my face between your legs—"

"Gloria!"

Ren is breathing heavily now, glaring at Cole with a smile in his eyes. He was too loud, calling their server over, but neither of them seem too worried about it. Without a word from Ren, Cole has his wallet out before Gloria arrives at the table.

"Everything okay?" she asks.

"Perfect. Can we get our entrées to go, please?" Ren's voice is strained.

Gloria looks confused, but agrees and rushes off to the kitchen, Cole's credit card in hand.

"Do we have to wait for the damn food?" Cole asks. "We can order room service."

They look at each other, and then back at Gloria's retreating form, and then at each other again. In a flash they're both up and out of their chairs, making a beeline for the bar.

"Do you run the cards? I need to sign. Can I sign?" Cole asks the bartender.

They're out of Il Piatto in three minutes flat, walking briskly up Marcy Street, toward the Eldorado Hotel.

"I hate that I can't just hail a cab in this town," Ren says.

Cole has his hand on the small of Ren's back and he's not trying to rush him, he really isn't, because they're only a few blocks away, but he does give him a little push. Just a tiny one. And then his hand is on Ren's ass.

Oh God, Ren's perfect, perfect, perfect ass.

He needs it. He needs to see it, and touch it, and taste it and fill it.

Ren groans. Cole reaches around and palms Ren's cock through his jeans as they walk.

"Cole! Fuck!" Ren bats Cole's hand away. "Are you kidding me right now? I am not coming in these jeans in front of all of these tourists!"

"Sorry, sorry. I don't... I've never done that before. I don't know what—"

"Just keep walking."

Cole knows Ren is just frustrated with the four blocks between them and their hotel, at their lack of wings, at their inability to teleport directly to Ren's bed. Or his. Maybe his.

They're both hard and finding it difficult to walk quickly, so Cole takes Ren's hand and gives in to the stroll. But not a minute later he's sliding his hand up Ren's arm, down his back, under his shirt, and into the back of his jeans, trying to get at that perfect, perfect, *perfect* ass.

"Jesus, Cole! Go. Go to the other side of the street," Ren demands.

"What? No."

"You're like a fucking animal, Cole, and I'm good with it. *Believe me*, I am, but you can't keep your gorgeous hands off my ass or my cock, so we need to be separated. Like unruly children."

"Or horny teenagers."

"Whatever. Go."

Ren folds his arms and waits until Cole crosses to the other side of San Francisco Street. Cole turns to face him, holding his hands out wide and says loud enough for Ren and several bystanders to hear, "Really, Ren? Really? This is silly."

"Just walk!"

They mirror each other as they walk, sneaking glances, trying to keep up with each other. Ren's hands are in his pockets, and Cole wonders if Ren can feel the throbbing of his own cock through the fabric. He wants to *be* Ren's hand, his pockets, the boxer briefs he knows Ren is wearing. Cole stops for a moment to steady himself and sees he's steps from the Starbucks, where just this morning he made the decision to give in to this beautiful thing.

Across the street, Ren stops and waits. When Cole finally gathers his wits, he falls into step with him. Cole picks up the pace, and Ren follows. They both stop at parallel curbs, waiting for two lazy cars to slide by, and that's when they both turn to look at each other. Their eyes lock, and then they are walking fast, the Eldorado in sight, taking their eyes off of each other only long enough to make sure they don't run straight into a pole. Cole is eye-fucking Ren from *across a street* and Ren is giving it right back to him. The energy between them is tight. Crackling. Bright.

They're almost running when they reach the steps of the hotel, taking two at a time and bursting through the heavy lobby doors as if the doors were fakes, as if they were paper. They don't touch; people know them here. Cole slows, eyes still on Ren, as they make their way to the main elevators.

As they pass the front desk a clerk calls out, "Mr. Warner, I have a message for you—" but Ren keeps walking, eyes focused straight ahead.

Tapping his foot, he pushes the "UP" button three times too many. Cole wants to say something, anything, but he's afraid it will be like a match to gasoline, so he keeps quiet.

In the elevator, he wants to push Ren up against the wall, shove his knee between Ren's thighs and let Ren grind down on him until he can't *help* but come in his jeans. But he settles for standing one inch apart, intertwining fingers, as they both watch the numbers light up like a slow-motion replay. First floor. Second. Third. *Fourth*. It's only when the elevator dings and the doors fly open that Cole realizes they've both been holding their breath.

Ren is shaking, so he hands Cole his key card and with one swipe they're in, back in the same hallway where they fucked the night before. Cole grabs Ren's ass before the door closes, and Ren whines, "Please let me get to the bed."

They're stripping now, a trail of clothes and shoes and underwear behind them. Ren pushes Cole down onto the bed and crawls on top of him, straddling his thighs.

Cole bucks up, looking for anything, but Ren leans down and stills him with a brush of his fingers through his hair. He touches Cole's cheek, gentle and soft, and then sits back up. There is silence then, like earlier at the restaurant, like the last minutes in Ren's apartment before Cole left for Europe, like the first time they woke up together in Cole's dorm room, still in their uniforms, hazy and at a loss as to why any of their rules or boundaries mattered.

"This is going to kill us, you know," Ren says, pushing his thumb into Cole's mouth.

Cole nips at Ren's thumb. He whispers, "Shh. Shh."

Ren pushes two fingers in now, letting Cole suck and bite and suck and bite until they're both moaning.

"Let me ride you," Ren says.

Cole pulls Ren's fingers from his mouth. "God, yes."

Ren lifts up a bit and reaches two wet fingers around behind him. Cole wants to see. He has to see. He reaches over to the nightstand, grabs the lube and sets it on his own belly. "I want to watch. *Please*."

Ren palms the lube, climbs off of Cole and says, "Switch. I need to lean against something."

Moments later Cole is at the edge of the bed, facing Ren, one hand holding him up, one hand on his dick. Ren is up against the headboard, thighs spread wide on display, two lubed-up fingers pumping in and out of his ass. He groans and adds a third finger, never taking his eyes off of Cole.

Cole asks, "Is this where you were... last night... before—?"

"Yes," Ren squeaks between pants.

Cole inches closer and stares at Ren's fingers, his hand, the flexing of his thigh muscles as he readies himself for Cole's cock. "You were thinking of me?"

"Yes. Yes. But I couldn't—"

Ren cries out and Cole watches his body contract for a moment, and then he's back at it, working his fingers in deeper, stretching, pushing.

"Couldn't what, baby?"

Ren looks startled at the endearment, but doesn't object. "I couldn't get off. I tried. I tried so hard I actually cried."

Would I call him baby? Or honey? Or sweetheart? Would I call him darling, or beautiful, or love? If we had a thousand days, if we had forever, would I give him secret, sweet names that twist his insides when I whisper them in his ear? Would I have a look, just for him, a look that told him it was time to go, time to leave this party and get lost in each other until the world's protests grow loud enough for us to hear?

Cole finds the last condom. He slips it on and then reaches over and grabs Ren's wrist, pulling his fingers out with a gentle tug. Ren wipes the leftover lube on Cole's dick and pushes Cole back on the bed. He straddles him again, placing Cole's hands on his thighs.

"Why couldn't you get off?"

Ren places his own hands on top of Cole's and leans back a bit, pressing down. He lets Cole's cock brush his entrance. "Because it wasn't you."

Cole leans up as far as he can go, and Ren meets him halfway. Ren's lips are warm and firm and taste like Prosecco. He hangs on to Ren's waist for support as he fucks his tongue into Ren's mouth and then it's hands in hair and little moans and cock against cock and he never ever wants it to end. *Never.*

When Ren can't wait anymore, he pushes Cole back on the bed again, positions himself over Cole's cock and sinks down, down, down. He holds still, eyes closed, and they wait.

"Remember the graduation party?" Cole asks, trying to keep still.

"Which one?"

"At Jeremy's house." Cole's thumbs dig into Ren's inner thighs.

"Yeah. That was fun." Ren rests his hands on top of Cole's and presses in, willing him to grip tighter, tighter, tighter.

"You got a bit drunk and... God...shit, Ren... you danced, and danced." Cole's voice is soft and desperate.

Cole feels Ren relax around him, but still he waits.

I'll wait forever for Ren.

Wait. What?

"Yeah. What about it?" Ren asks. He tilts a bit, sinking down even further, and lets out a low whine.

"Were you doing it for me? Was the dancing for me?"

Ren opens his eyes and looks down, a sweet smile on his face. "Yes."

"Do it again."

"Do what again?"

"Dance. Now. On my cock."

Ren sucks in a breath, flashes Cole a wicked smile and starts moving his hips in slow, tight circles. His muscle control is nothing short of amazing. He picks up the pace but keeps a steady rhythm as he grinds down and lifts up a bit, returning to his circles each time he bottoms out.

"Fuck, that's good. Yeah. That's it."

"Is this what you wanted? I saw you and Jeremy watching me. Your eyes were glued to my hips, and my ass. Were you imagining me riding you like this? Even then?"

"Yes! Fuck."

Ren plays with his own nipples, pinching and twisting, and it drives Cole absolutely mad. He thrusts up, meeting Ren as he slams down, and they're good together in all the ways he knew they would be, and in ways he never imagined.

Ren's riding him hard now, humming a tune too softly to make out. Ren is in his own world and Cole knows he's close, so close, so he thrusts harder and gets to work on Ren's cock. Hips swiveling, ass pressing down and lifting up, thighs trembling, Ren is so beautiful Cole can barely breathe.

Ren tenses, and Cole lets go, and they come, following each other like two singers in a round, Cole's *fuck, fuck, fuck* followed by Ren's high-pitched *oh, oh, oh, oh, yeah, more, oh, oh, yes, yes.*

Ren collapses on Cole. Cole, loose-limbed and moments from sleep, wraps his arms around Ren's back and holds him there, dick still inside.

"Don't pull out," Ren whispers into Cole's chest. "Let's just lie here, for days, until they find us shriveled up from lack of food—"

"Hey, you started it," Cole teases, nipping at Ren's earlobe.

"No, seriously. Just stay. Stay in me forever."

⊞ Chapter 7 ⊞

Ren is admiring a table base with deep curves at its center. It looks like an exaggerated, angular hourglass. He runs his hands along the sides: It's metal, probably steel, and it feels familiar, like touching the '68 Aston Martin Vantage his Dad bought the summer before his senior year. He looks for markings, any clue that will help him find the designer of this gorgeous piece. He has to have it.

As he caresses the base, he imagines it in the homes of various clients, in his apartment, as the chef's table at the new restaurant opening he'll start on after the holidays. He wants to ask the artist who made it to teach him everything he knows. Or she. It could be a she, but somehow Ren knows a man designed this, made this with his tools, his hands, the muscles in his back, the beauty in his heart.

He feels a hand snake up the inside of his thigh—*When did I get naked?*—and squeeze. He senses someone behind him, someone important, someone who could change everything.

His pulse quickens and when he whispers, "Love, I know it's you—" his voice surprises him. It booms and echoes back to him, as if he's standing inside a bell.

The hand squeezes again, and then it's all feather-light touches, brushing up his belly, over his nipples, down his chest and back again. In the distance he hears someone call his name, but he can't stop looking at the metal base, as if it is somehow connected to the hand, to the caress, to the love.

He hears a phone ring. It's a foreign sound, not his cell. He ignores it, covers the hand with his own, and now he's sure he feels someone breathing behind him. The ringing stops, starts up again moments later.

Suddenly Ren is awake, in his hotel room, no table base to be found. He was dreaming of furniture again, and something else, *someone* else, a hand—

"Make it stop—" Cole mumbles into the space between Ren's shoulder blades. Ren shifts in Cole's arms and pushes him back flat against the mattress as he reaches across his chest to the nightstand.

He picks up the phone, but before he can spit out a greeting a voice says, "You're in trouble."

Instantly alert, Ren rolls halfway onto Cole for a better reach, his mind racing with thoughts he never imagined he would have.

Who saw us? How much do they know? Who else knows? Will they tell Paul? How could they possibly know anything? Wait—

"Who is this?" Ren asks.

"It's your fucking client."

Oh. Damn.

"Deidre. Hi."

Relieved, Ren relaxes and wiggles so his body is flush with Cole's. Eyes still closed, Cole wraps his arms around Ren and pulls tight, cracking his back. Ren's on alert now but still melts a little, his body slack.

"Wow," he exclaims.

"Wow? *Wow?* You didn't answer your cell last night, so I left a fucking message for you with that useless idiot at the desk. *Gawd*, his FACE! Bastard prick. He wouldn't tell me which room you're in. Can you believe those assholes? I'm *paying* for the fucking room, fucking tell me the goddamn room number."

Ren offers up a silent thank you to the Eldorado Hotel's policy manual and then snaps to attention. "Wait, did you say '*his face*?' Are you in the hotel?"

"Yes I'm in the fucking hotel, Ren. What's your room number?"

"I'm in 415," Ren replies, regretting it immediately. And before he can ask Deidre if they could just meet in the lobby, he hears a click and then a loud, annoying dial tone.

"Shit. Shit. Shit. Shit. Shit!"

Ren tries to wiggle off of Cole, slapping at his hips to get him to move. "Get up, get up, get up!"

Cole reaches out to still Ren's hands, grabs his wrists in a tight hold, and then opens his eyes. He speaks in even tones: "Stop. Breathe. Explain."

"My client, Deidre, she's on her way to the room. Why did I give her my room number? It's you and your face and your body and *your face.* You distract me! She'll be here in seconds, Cole! We have to get up." Ren tries to ignore Cole's solid grip, the rise and fall of his chest, his drowsy, soft expression.

"Just put on a robe, answer the door and don't let her in. Tell her you need five minutes," Cole reasons.

Ren laughs and wrenches his hands free. "You have no idea, Cole. No idea."

Ren hops off the bed and struggles into his discarded jeans. He jumps up and down as he tries to wedge himself into them; they went on so easily the night before. Well, *easier.*

Cole stares at him and laughs, cheeks pink and lips swollen. "This is awesome."

"Shut up."

"Would you like some help? Or did you want to just keep jumping?"

"Ugh! All that salt and booze and... fuck!"

"—'Cause I like the jumping—"

"Why? Why don't I think before I speak?" Ren stops himself from falling back onto the bed. "And why did I let you talk me into nachos— *nachos!*—and champagne? Who drinks champagne with nachos, Cole? Hmm? Who?"

"We do."

"I *don't*, Cole. Or I didn't. Shit," Ren says, still trying to wiggle into his jeans.

"Our choices were limited. We didn't stop fucking until after midnight, and by then—"

"What is happening to me? Nachos. Cheating on my perfectly respectable boyfriend. No sleep. Lying to my perfectly respectable boyfriend. Nachos. *Nachos*, Cole—"

"Perfectly respectable, huh? That's hot."

"We're not doing that," Ren says, still trying to twist into his jeans.

"Right. That was rude." Cole reaches out to fondle Ren's ass. "So perfect. And by the way, he's your fiancé."

"That's what I said. Isn't it?"

"No."

"Well I meant that. *Fiancé*. WHY AREN'T YOU MOVING?"

"Don't panic. You don't have to let her in, you know."

Ren glares at Cole, but Cole just smiles up at him, his hand reaching out again. "Kiss?"

Jeans finally on, Ren slips on a shirt and starts pulling on Cole's hand. "Get up! You have to hide."

"I have to *what*?"

Ren lets go of Cole's hand and lifts the duvet up to look under the bed. "Shit! The frame is too low, there's no way you'll fit under the bed—"

"Like I would get under there anyway—"

"Why not?"

Cole sits up and watches Ren flit about the room, picking up condom wrappers and clutching Cole's clothes to his chest. "Is this a fight? Are we fighting? Because if we are fighting, I should probably tell you that I'm really turned on right now—"

"Cole!"

Cole rubs the sleep out of the corner of his eyes, barely moving as Ren scrambles. "I've seen this before. This is like a bad episode of... something—"

"Are you a sloth? GET UP!"

"And when I get up, where do you want me to go?"

There is a loud knock and Ren's hands fly to his mouth, smothering his own scream. Cole laughs, and then Ren's hands are off his own mouth and covering Cole's.

"Coming!" he shouts.

Cole licks Ren's palm, looks up at him with *those eyes* and it's all Ren can do not to cry out, push him back into the bed and do his best to forget all about Deidre Alexander and whatever hell she brought with her.

"Not. A. Word," Ren whispers, slowly removing his hand from Cole's mouth.

He pulls Cole to his feet, picks up Cole's jeans, underwear, jacket, shirt and shoes, drags Cole to the bathroom and pushes him inside.

"Ren! I can hear you! Open the fucking door!" Deidre shouts from the hallway.

"Shower!" Ren says, as forcefully as he can manage with his whisper-soft voice.

Cole shakes his head, and then Ren is in the bathroom with him. He tries to yank the linen shower curtain back one-handed, his clothed body pressed up against Cole's *amazing naked amazing naked naked naked* self.

Cole's hands encircle Ren's waist as he struggles with the curtain. "Let's just stay in here until she gives up," Cole whispers, his lips ghosting Ren's cheek.

Ren gives Cole a gentle push, and Cole steps into the shower. Ren tosses Cole's clothes at him.

"Really, Ren?"

"Shh!"

Ren closes the bathroom door halfway, smooths his hopelessly wrinkled clothes and opens the door for Deidre.

"Hey, Deidre. Sorry. I wasn't really awake when you called—"

"You're always up early," she says, pushing past him into the room.

Deidre Alexander is tiny, blonde, just over five feet tall and, thanks to her liquid diet and endless Pilates sessions, way too skinny. Underneath her impeccable five hundred-dollar dye job and three thousand-dollar ensemble, she is a too-smart-for-her-own-good brunette from Paramus, New Jersey.

Her eyes sweep the room, look him up and down, and before he can interrupt her train of thought she flops down on the unmade bed, the bed where he's had the best sex of his life. He's worried she'll sit in something she really shouldn't, or just smell something she really shouldn't, like sex. Hot, awesome, record-breaking sex.

"Apparently that fucking front door is a life-or-death decision, so I'm here. Get dressed and let's go."

"You flew all the way here because you wanted to pick out a door? I just overnighted you a box of tile for your final sign-off."

"So I'll have Janet overnight them back here. I like it better when we're looking for tile on 16th Street, together."

"You mean checking out one store and then drinking four Bloody Marys at Coffee Shop until I call your car service to take you home?"

"Yeah, that. I just like it better when you're in New York. I missed you. Fuck. Why do you make me say these things?"

"I'm choosing rugs today, Deidre. Antonio and I are driving up to Chimayó. No doors today."

"So I'll come with you."

"So you'll come with me. Great. Why not?"

"Get dressed, already. I'll just flip through the channels."

Ren winces as he watches her search for the TV remote in his rumpled bedding. What if she finds the wet spot? What if there's more than one wet spot?

Then he remembers: There is *definitely* more than one wet spot.

"Deidre, stop. I'm not that friend, okay? I'm not going to get dressed in front of you and let you look at my ass and dish with you about all of your former men and listen to you tell me how you can't orgasm on Vicodin. Just give me an hour and I'll meet you in the lobby—"

"Forty-five minutes."

"Fine. Forty-five minutes."

When Deidre stands to leave Ren lets out a sigh of relief he hopes goes unnoticed; but he panics when she says, "I have to pee," and pushes open the bathroom door.

"No! Deidre!"

"What the fuck, Ren?"

Ren braces himself for the questions, the tongue-lashing, the shattering of this private, beautiful thing. He hopes Cole has clothes on, at least.

"You scared the shit out of me! It's not that messy, Jesus!"

Ren peeks around Deidre into the bathroom. Thank goodness, Cole is hiding behind the shower curtain.

"Just, can you use your room, Deidre? I'm sort of private—"

"I'm not staying here. I'm up at Ten Thousand Waves, where I can get a proper facial and some fucking peace. I need to pee. I'll do it with the fucking door open, I don't care. So if you want to see my Brazilian, just keep standing there." Deidre marches into the bathroom.

Mortified, Ren looks down at the carpet as he slowly closes the door behind her, sending silent, urgent messages to Cole: *Quiet as a mouse. I'm so sorry. Quiet as a mouse. Please don't be mad. Quiet as a mouse.*

When did his life become a bad rom-com, complete with (gorgeous) secret lovers hiding in bathrooms? And nachos?

He wants to listen at the door, but that's just beyond creepy, so he tries to spray the sex out of the room with a few spritzes of the latest Tom Ford cologne.

Ren holds himself very still, bracing himself for Deidre's scream. After three minutes, which seem like three hours, his mind starts racing.

What if she finds out? She can probably tell I've had someone in the room. But would she even care? She's not exactly a walking example of moral fortitude. Maybe she'll let it be our secret... and hold it over me for the rest of my life, forcing me to remodel one Southwestern monstrosity after another. Maybe even in Texas.

Ren shudders and sits down on the bed, legs crossed, his foot bouncing nervously. He'd bite his nails if he could find a decent manicurist in Santa Fe to fix the damage. The toilet flushes. No screaming yet. The faucet turns on. Still no screaming. The faucet turns off. Still nothing.

Finally Deidre pushes the door open and says, "You've got forty-one minutes. Don't be late. I'm already bored."

And with that she opens the door to his room and leaves without a backward glance. Ren can't *believe* they got away with it.

"I can't *believe* we got away with that!" he exclaims, racing into the bathroom.

Cole pulls back the shower curtain. He's in his boxers now, his clothes and shoes in a pile in the bathtub, arms folded.

"She peed, Ren. She peed in the bathroom. With me. In the bathroom."

"Oh my God, Cole! I'm so sorry! I didn't know what to do!"

Cole is clearly pissed. It reminds Ren of that time Dean pantsed Cole while they were walking over to the track to run laps. They were all stressed about the upcoming meet, acting crazy, when Dean suddenly came up behind Cole and pulled down his hunter green sweatpants. If looks could kill, Dean wouldn't have made it to graduation.

Ren has never been able to take Cole's pissy look seriously; it just looks so wrong on his face. Sure, he'd seen him genuinely angry—during that infamous dinner when Cole and his father had argued about his father's refusal to stop donating to politicians with homophobic policies, even after Cole practically begged him to do so.

And there was that time the East Coast members of the class of 2003 met at a club in New York, each visiting from their respective colleges.

Cole discovered Caleb, Ren's first boyfriend, "kissing" another guy, and pushed him out of the bathroom, past their table, out of the bar and onto the street.

It took Cole forever to come back inside, and when he finally slid in next to Ash, he looked as if he'd seen a ghost. Everyone tried to get Cole to tell them what he and Caleb had talked about, but they never could pry more than, "I'm so sorry, Ren," out of him. He looked *really* angry, then.

But this isn't angry Cole. This is super-annoyed, put-out Cole. And it is hilarious.

Within seconds, Ren is doubled over laughing—at Cole's expression, at the absurdity of the morning, at the reality of their situation. It's another one of Cole's "aerial" moments, but this time the image of the two of them, standing in this bathroom, in this swank Southwestern hotel, in this tiny, dusty, ancient little freak show of a city, is somehow hysterically funny.

"Not. Funny."

"Come on, Cole," Ren says, still laughing. "You never peed in the same room with one of your girlfriends? They're always following me into the men's room at clubs because the line to the women's is too long—"

"That's not the same, and you know it."

Ren crosses to the tub and runs his arms over Cole's taut shoulders. "Are you scarred for life now, Cole? Is that it?" he teases.

"I just... I don't like all of these... shenanigans."

Ren giggles and kisses Cole on the mouth, all while trying to get Cole to unfold his arms. "Shenanigans? You're adorable when you're annoyed. Your inner grandpa comes out."

Cole finally releases his arms and wraps them around Ren's back. Ren revels in the embrace as he rests his head against Cole's bare chest. He listens to his heart, still beating fast from nerves and total irritation.

Cole slips one hand up to the back of Ren's neck and holds his head there, almost cradling Ren against his chest. It takes him back to the dance that triggered this heavenly mess, to the song that carried them right to the edge, drew their hearts out from separate places of deep slumber and reignited a flame that had been slowly burning for nearly half their lives. Ren sways a bit, or maybe Cole is rocking him gently, he's not really sure.

He can hear the echo of Alegra's haunting voice and remembers how she sang them right out of the ache and into something even more dangerous. Ren knows he is on a runaway train, and there's no stopping it. He knows Cole wants him. He knows Cole loves him, too. But Cole also loves another, in a way he never loved Ren and most likely never will.

Ren is almost thirty years old, and the single most important lesson he's learned is, life is not black and white. There is so much gray area—*He wants me, my body, my laughter, my touch, he may even love me more or differently than I realize, but I'm not his, I was never his, because if I was ever his, he would have told me so*—and he has to learn how to live in that gray space, where he can't have it all and everything is complicated. He has to be okay with it, to find happiness in it, even if his heart yearns to hear the words, "It's you, it was always you, and no matter what you do, or say, or decide, no matter how much you change or don't change, it will always be you."

But I can't think about that now. In this moment, and for a few precious days, I still have Cole, complicated or not, and that's all that matters.

"I like you flustered," Ren says finally, kissing one nipple, then the other. "I like you human."

"Can't get more human than us right now. I just... don't want to be that guy who has to hide in the shower, you know? I don't want us to be *that*."

"But we are... that." Ren burrows further into Cole.

"But that's not all we are. It's not like we're two lonely strangers who met in a hotel bar and decided to hook up for a few days. There's miles of us before this, Ren."

"I know."

Cole kisses Ren's forehead and pulls him closer, closer, closer. He whispers in his ear: "Last night you said... you said—"

"Stay inside me forever," Ren whispers back.

"Yes."

"People want things, Cole. It doesn't mean those things are actually possible," Ren says, his sigh heavy with the end that is still days away.

"Are we talking literally or figuratively here, Ren? Because I'm quite aware of the fact that, as much as the idea appeals to me, I can't actually keep my dick in your ass for all of eternity," Cole teases.

"Both."

Cole is quiet for a few moments, then gives Ren a gentle squeeze. "Okay, Ren. Okay. Shower?"

"Yes, but just that. I really do have to make it out to Chimayó today and spend tens of thousands of Clint Alexander's dollars on rugs for a house he'll most likely never visit."

"Fun."

"If you say so."

They shower together, taking turns washing each other's backs, hair, thighs, shoulders. They kiss each time they shift positions, never saying a word, just washing and kissing and moving as if this is a well-practiced dance, as if they've done this everyday thing together for years. Ren wants, and Cole wants, and if there were no rugs to buy or songs to record they'd give in again, and again, and again. Instead they wash, and kiss, and caress, and move around each other, behind each other, lean against each other, until they are both clean and warm and buzzing with thoughts of *later, tonight, tomorrow and tomorrow.*

After they dry each other off and Ren starts pulling on a fresh pair of vintage straight jeans, Cole slides into his "date night" clothes. "I have to change and make a phone call. I'll see you tonight?"

"Yes," Ren says, with a kiss to Cole's jaw.

Cole turns to leave and then turns back. "Last night, you were talking in your sleep. What were you dreaming about?"

A hand. A voice. A love.

"Furniture."

Cole laughs and kisses him again, this time a bit dirty, and strong, as though he's trying to push him over. After a few minutes he pulls away and says, "I'll call you."

Jacket draped over one arm, Cole makes his way to the door. Ren watches him go and feels his heart *tilt.* He laughs, remembering his mother's warning whenever he twisted his face into a pout: "Be careful. Your face might stay that way forever." Will his heart stay this way forever, tilted toward someone he cannot have?

Twenty minutes later, he's dressed and coiffed and ready to face Deidre and the day. He's at the elevator with two minutes to spare, not that he's genuinely concerned about being late. His phone rings, and he smiles at the sight of the caller's name.

"Tell me it's not true," Antonio says, before Ren can say hello.

"It's not true?"

"I'm not her goddamn *servant*, Ren—"

"I know, I know. It's just for a few hours—"

"If she pulls anything I will stop the car and *kill* her, Ren, with my bare hands—"

"Just—can't you ignore her? I'll keep her occupied, I will. Besides, she'll get sick of rugs and want to come back to Santa Fe to drink and talk trash for hours, so really, it's me that gets the short straw. Not you."

"Ren—"

"Are you out front?"

"Yes, goddamn it." Antonio hangs up without saying goodbye.

Ren finds Deidre perched on a bench in front of a large fireplace in the lobby, arguing with someone on the phone; Clint, most likely. He doesn't want to hear one word of what is likely a rant about Antonio, who probably refused to let her come with them today. So he wanders around the lobby, picking up brochures and putting them back down again.

He finds one about Chimayó, the little town where the Espinosa family weaves their highly sought-after rugs. He reads about the chapel there, about the dirt that is supposed to have healing properties, and about the thousands of devout Catholics who make a pilgrimage to Chimayó every Easter, some walking hundreds of miles with wooden crosses on their backs. He doesn't get it—the closest he ever came to a pilgrimage was a visit to Coco Chanel's Paris apartment—but he slips the brochure into his messenger bag anyway. Maybe this trip will help him clear his mind; maybe, even though he doesn't believe, Chimayó will heal his heart before it breaks.

Ren catches Deidre's eye and points to a large clock on the wall, willing her to get off the phone. When she nods and marches out the front door, cell phone plastered to her ear, he walks over to the front desk and surprises himself when he says, "Hi. I'm Ren Warner, in 415. Could I possibly get an extra key card?"

"Certainly Mr. Warner. Do you have a guest arriving?" the cheerful girl asks.

"Guest? No. I just... well—"

"It's no problem at all, Mr. Warner," she says, saving him.

She hands him a key card, which he slips into his wallet. But instead of closing the wallet, he stares for a moment at the edge of key card peeking out of a pocket, thinking about what it means. If this thing with Cole, this *affair*, were something else, if it were true and unfettered, this key card would be a real key, and it would signify a change, a commitment.

If, instead of eleven days, they had a few years, or a lifetime, this would be the point in their relationship when Ren would hand Cole a little box with a key to his apartment tucked inside. And he'd say something like, "It's not the key to my heart, because I gave that to you ages ago. It's a key to my everything." And Cole would smile too big, and press the key into his palm and say, "I'll carry it with me forever." And it wouldn't matter that they were both ridiculously cheesy in their sentiment and optimistic in their promises; it would be a milestone, with the intention of someday having more milestones, bigger milestones, the biggest.

But they'll never have those normal, sweet, breathtaking moments—the first "I love you" without the implied "as a friend, of course;" their first place together; their first "someday" conversation. ("Someday, would you like to have children? Someday, would you like to buy a little summer place in Montauk? Someday, would you like to vow to love me in sickness and in health?") There would be no exchange of rings, or promises, or last names. No, this is just a key card so Cole can let himself into Ren's room, so he can wait for him and come and go as he pleases. It's a convenience. That's all.

Closing his wallet, Ren tries not to think any further about how it could be so much more, or how he's already *had* so many of those "someday" moments with Paul, or how those other "somedays" are like a popular song played on an out-of-tune piano.

Realizing he's been staring at his wallet longer than one would deem normal, he smiles at the girl behind the desk, looks at her name tag and says, "Thank you, Amy."

He's still thinking about key cards, and Paul, and what it all means, when he walks out into the blaring New Mexico sun and gasps at the sight before him: Antonio and Deidre standing next to the Range Rover, talking to Cole. *Cole.* Gorgeous, clean-shaven, sexy-hot Cole who should be in his room, or on his way to Galisteo, or anywhere but here.

Ren straightens his shoulders, slips on his sunglasses and walks over to the trio. Cole notices him; his smile is part smirk, part apology, part "help me," but only Ren would know that. To the rest of the world, Cole is the picture of composure.

"I ran into Antonio on my way—" Cole starts.

"He's coming with us," Deidre says.

"Deidre, meet Cole, my friend—"

"I know who he is. He told me. Best friend. High school. Got it. He's going to keep me awake by telling hilarious, embarrassing stories about you." Deidre slips into the front seat. She shuts the door before Ren can argue with her.

"You're not coming," Ren says emphatically.

"I think I am."

"But you have to work—"

"Gretchen texted me. Alegra is spending the day with her husband, and since she's not available, Mitch decided to go see his friend in Corrales, so I have nothing else to do anyway," Cole explains.

He looks absolutely determined, and Ren should be happy to spend more time with Cole, and he *is*, but not like this. Not with her. And besides, he kind of needed the break from Cole. Every minute with him eats away at his resolve, and now there is no hope for a reprieve.

"But you said you had to make a phone call—" Ren starts, and then regrets it. Antonio probably figured they were up to something and now he has them figured out for sure.

"He, uh, wasn't home," Cole explains.

"We could use the backup," Antonio says.

"This is *not* a good idea," Ren pleads.

"Just let me run inside for a minute. I need to... just hold on, okay?" Cole says, darting off without waiting for an answer.

Antonio waits until Cole is inside before he says, "Ren, I didn't want to say anything yesterday, but—"

"Stop. I can't. I just can't, okay? Can we just, *not*?"

"Whatever you say."

"Thank you." Ren smiles up at him. "You're a good friend."

"Fort Knox, remember?" Antonio tips his hat. "You know I'm going to kill her, right? I know places. They'll never find her body."

"Ugh. Maybe it is a good idea for Cole to come along. He can charm anyone into submission," Ren says.

"Apparently," Antonio teases with a wink.

"Shut up."

After Ren and Antonio get in the car, there is an awkward, too-long silence before Deidre says, "So how come my fucking kitchen still hasn't been painted?"

Ren groans. He is trying to come up with an answer that will placate her when she inhales and starts clicking her tongue. She's looking at the hotel entrance; Ren turns to see Cole walking toward the car.

"Yes, that man is definitely worth the risk," she says.

"Deidre, *do not* try to fuck him," Ren warns.

"Wasn't planning on it. I don't shit where I eat."

Before Ren can ask her what she means by that, Cole opens the door and slides into the backseat, next to Ren.

"Ready when you are."

Ren thinks Cole, with this expectant expression on his face, looks like a five-year-old who has just been told he's going to Disneyland.

Antonio starts the car and pulls out. Deidre reaches to fiddle with the radio and he says, "Don't touch that. My car, my music."

She huffs and turns in her seat, and just as Cole inches his hand over to cover Ren's, she turns to face them. "So, Cole, now that I've peed in your presence, don't you think we should get to know each other a little bit better?"

"Oh fuck." Ren hides his face in his hands. Cole is speechless, his face as white as Ren as ever seen it. Ren wants to vomit, to run screaming from the car. Suddenly the trip to Chimayó seems less like a pilgrimage and more like a death march to hell.

Antonio changes lanes. "Remember, I know where we can hide the body."

Chapter 8

After Deidre teases Ren and begs for details, after Antonio tells her to shut up and turns off the radio, after Ren bites back at her and squeezes Cole's hand so tightly it hurts, they all settle into a prickly silence.

As the landscape rolls by, bleached dirt on rolling hills and round, green, short trees that look more like bushes poking up here and there, Cole silently counts the number of people who know he's having sex with Ren. Alegra. Gretchen, probably. And if Gretchen knows, maybe the entire band. And Mitchell. And if the entire band knows, then maybe friends and acquaintances back in London. Maybe Liam.

He tried to call him this morning, but Liam didn't answer his cell or show up on Skype. So Cole changed and left his room in search of coffee and a copy of *The New York Times*, something to take his mind off of Liam. And Ren. And what he might say to Liam *about* Ren.

He doesn't know; he really doesn't. They made a deal, and it was evident, even after last night, and the first night, even after Ren whispered, *Stay inside me forever* into Cole's skin and straight through to his heart, that Ren had every intention of seeing their deal through. Ren was settled. Content. This thing between them, would it... *could* it change that?

I'm completely at his mercy. I'll happily take everything he's willing to give me, every scrap. June was right. I am his. But he's not mine. So do I let go of Liam, knowing I'll never have Ren?

It's a ridiculous question, for which Cole doesn't have an answer, so he keeps counting. Alegra and Gretchen make two. Deidre. And now Antonio, though Ren might have already told him. That's four. And the bellhop from last night. That's five.

Cole looks over at Ren, who is staring out the window looking at his
own set of brown hills and shrubby green trees, and chuckles at a memory
from last night. Ren had lifted his head off of Cole's chest with a start
and said, "We're out of condoms!" Somehow they had both forgotten
to buy any, and suddenly the situation became desperate.

"I don't want to get dressed," Cole said.

"I don't want to move," Ren replied.

And then Cole said, "Hold on to me, okay? Don't let go."

He rolled them slowly, careful to stay inside of Ren, careful not to crush
him, until he was on top and could reach the phone on the nightstand.

After the front desk clerk forwarded him to a bellhop, Cole said, "I'm
in room 415 and I'll give you two hundred dollars cash to run out and
get me a pack of condoms—"

"Large," Ren interrupted.

"—*Large* condoms. Now. Like, right now."

"Yes, sir. Right away, sir," the bellhop replied, as if Cole had asked for
a pizza or something.

Cole hung up the phone, looked down at Ren's flushed face and said,
"I can't believe I just did that."

And then they both got the giggles and started laughing until they
were shaking from it, Cole with his head buried in the crook of Ren's
neck, each trying not to move too much for fear of hurting the other.
Soon it was too much, and they both winced.

"I have to pull out. I'll come back, I will. Just let me—"

Ren nodded, and Cole watched his face carefully as he slowly pulled
out of him. Cole pushed a few strands of Ren's hair back from his face
and kissed his forehead. Ren wrapped his arms around Cole's neck and
pulled him in for a kiss that was all gratitude and heat.

Now, sitting in the back of Antonio's car, Cole wonders if five people
are too many or not enough.

"I said I won't say anything," Deidre pleads.

"You're not getting the story, Deidre. Tell Paul, tell your friends, tell
the goddamn gossip queen from hell—"

"Who? Marjorie Willhem?"

"Barbara Davies," Ren replies.

"Oh, no. I *loathe* her," Deidre says.

"Who *are* these people?" Cole asks.

"Harpies. Or friends. Whatever," Ren says.

"I hate New York," Antonio says.

"Of course you do. You're just like him, with the horses and the space. All that space," Deidre says.

Cole is thoroughly confused. The three of them seem to have their own language, and he's reminded how little he actually knows about Ren's life now.

"Will you tell me all about it later? After?" Deidre's voice is so small she almost sounds contrite. Cole wonders if she feels badly about calling them out, but he can't really imagine her feeling badly about anything.

"Probably not," Ren says, arms folded.

They settle into yet another awkward silence as Antonio turns off the main highway onto a winding, two-lane road. Cole notices more green in the landscape as the hills come close and bank them in. The history of the place surrounds them; they pass adobe buildings that appear to be as old as time. They're just twenty minutes outside of Santa Fe, but it seems as if they've entered another dimension entirely. Gone are the beautiful iron gates and dripping bougainvillea adorning well-kept historical homes. Here, they see cars up on cinder blocks and bars over windows and crumbling, ancient walls. Many people struggle here, that much is clear.

"See that house?" Antonio asks, pointing to a small, single-story adobe house that looks just like all of the others. "I met my wife because of a boy who lived there."

They're all content to let Antonio diffuse the tension, so he does. "His name was Jimmy Padilla, and he was gay, but that's really not okay up here, you know?"

Ren and Cole look at each other because, yes, they do know.

"Sarah knew him. He came to Alex Marin House when he was twenty, a bit too old for the place, but he had nowhere else to go. He'd been up to Vegas, I think, or maybe it was Reno, trying to be himself and make a go of things in a place where people wouldn't judge him. He never found that place. Instead he got sick. I guess he must have had HIV since he was a kid, which really pisses me off, thinking about what he got into up there, but by the time he made it to Alex Marin House, he had full-blown AIDS."

Cole takes Ren's hand and leans into him a bit, listening.

"See, Jimmy never had the money for the drugs or treatment he needed to fend off the virus, so he really didn't have a chance. Maybe he didn't want to live anymore, who knows. Anyway, it was Thanksgiving morning, and my grandmother was in the hospital, recovering from surgery. I came in early to sit with her for a while, and when I left, I ran right into this beautiful girl in the lobby. Sarah. She was crying her eyes out. She said, 'Excuse me,' and I don't know what happened to me, but I knew. I knew right then that she was all I would ever need."

Cole slides even closer to Ren, wraps his arm around him and pulls him closer still.

"And I don't know why she thought I was okay to talk to, but all of a sudden she's telling me Jimmy's story, and I'm holding her hand in the waiting room. She tells me she tried get his family to come, that he didn't have much time left, but they kept saying no. I guess they knew he had AIDS, or had been told, but couldn't accept it because, to them, that meant he was gay. So they acted like he, I don't know, had a bad flu or something. Like he'd be just fine."

Deidre leans back against the headrest and turns her head toward Antonio. They're all focused on him now, eager to hear the end of his story.

"Sarah kept saying, 'They won't come. Why won't they come?' It broke my heart, it really did. She told me she couldn't leave him alone. She said, 'Nobody deserves to die alone.' And then she thanked me, you know, for letting a total stranger cry on my shoulder and went back to sit with Jimmy. But I couldn't get her out of my head, or him, so I went up to the nurse's station and asked this girl I knew, Maria, if I could get his address. She shouldn't have done it, but she kind of owed me one, so the next thing I know I'm skipping Thanksgiving and driving out here to Jimmy's parent's place."

"What did they say? Did they come? What happened?" Ren asks.

"They were sitting down to Thanksgiving dinner, like nothing was wrong, like they didn't have a son dying not half an hour away. I begged them to come. I didn't even know Jimmy and there I was, begging these people I didn't know to come and visit someone I had never met. But they refused."

Antonio is quiet for a moment, and then continues with his story. "I dropped by my mom's and packed up some plates, and then drove back to the hospital. When I walked onto Jimmy's floor, Sarah was holding a phone, I guess maybe getting up the courage to talk to Jimmy's family again. She looked up at me, kind of surprised to see me, and I said, 'They still won't come. I tried, but they won't come.' And then she smiled at me, which I didn't expect. I guess she was happy someone else cared enough about Jimmy to try. And then I sat with them, in his room, and we tried to eat some Thanksgiving dinner and pretend that he had all the time in the world, that he'd get better."

"What happened to Jimmy?" Deidre asked. "When did he die?"

"That night, after I left. Sarah held his hand until the end, wouldn't leave his side," Antonio replied. "And you know what, I couldn't have asked for a better way to meet the love of my life."

"But it's so sad," Ren says.

"It is, but I met her at the same moment I realized life is precious and short, so I never hesitated. I never pretended not to be interested in her or played games. I just went after her like she was the best thing that ever happened to me, because she was. And Jimmy caused that."

They're quiet again, except this time the silence is reverent, for Jimmy. Cole decides that maybe he loves Sarah; that maybe, even though they only just met, they could be best friends. He vows to make it over to Alex Marin House the first chance he gets. Maybe Ren would come with him. Maybe they could go tonight.

"This is it." Antonio pulls into a parking lot. "There's a little chapel down the hill. It's kind of a tourist thing. Cole and I will be down there."

Antonio gets out of the car. Ren looks up at Cole with a question in his eyes.

"It's fine. I don't really want to look at rugs, anyway," Cole says.

"I'll try to be quick."

Cole watches Ren and Deidre disappear into a large, whitewashed adobe building and then follows Antonio down a gentle hill, into a little valley. The trees grow tall here, and there's a tiny village, which he assumes is Chimayó. He sees a chapel, with a courtyard in the front and tourists milling around.

"This is a holy place," Antonio says. "People come here for healing. Go through the chapel and into the back room and you'll find offerings, candles and prayer requests and little pictures of people who need miracles. Inside the room you'll find a hole in the ground. That's holy dirt, or so they say. You can take some. They have little containers, or you can buy a locket or something up at the store over there."

"I'm... I haven't been to Mass in years," Cole says, entranced by the simple beauty of the building.

"Doesn't matter. You can still go in. Unless you're good. Maybe you don't need a miracle," Antonio says. "It never worked for me, anyway. It's just something to do while the two of them argue about color palettes and whatever the hell else they talk about. I'm going to go buy a candle for my grandmother at the store. Do you want to come?"

Cole eyes the chapel and decides to go with Antonio instead. The store is full of kitsch and postcards and little self-published books about the area. He looks at silver jewelry in glass cases, at woven baskets and little clay dolls. Antonio buys two tall votive candles and then finds Cole.

"*Milagros*," Antonio explains, looking at the basket of tiny tin and pewter charms next to Cole's hand. The old woman behind the counter smiles at Antonio knowingly. Cole is so out of his element here and yet so entranced by it all: the ritual of everything, the sacred quiet, the vibrant colors. It's a sharp contrast to the severity of Saint Benedict's— monks in black habits, immaculate hallways, rows and rows of polished pews.

"Miracles?" Cole asks, remembering his high school Spanish.

"Yes. They're offerings. You see how some of them are shaped like body parts?"

"Yes."

"You choose one that represents that part of you, or of someone else, that needs healing. Then you place it in the candle and leave it at the altar, inside," Antonio explains, gesturing toward the chapel.

Cole runs his fingers through the bowl of tiny charms and, without thinking, picks out four hearts. He doesn't believe in this, he doesn't. But what does he know about miracles, really? Except that yes, he probably could use a miracle today... or eleven days from now. Or anytime, really. Like, right now, even. *Yes, now would be good.*

"I'll take these, and three candles, please," he says, handing a few dollars to the old woman.

They walk to the chapel and slip into the dark room with the other tourists. Antonio dips his fingers in a bowl of holy water at the entrance and crosses himself. The chapel is tiny, quiet; it seems as though it's been here in this valley forever. Antonio stops but does not sit; Cole waits for him. He notices a poem on the wall and reads it, silently.

"If you are a stranger, if you are weary from the struggles in life, whether you have a handicap, whether you have a broken heart, follow the long mountain road, find a home in Chimayó."

Unlike the classic art in the churches of his youth, folk art adorns the back wall of the chapel. A large cross, rough-hewn, hangs turned on its side. After a few moments they walk up to the altar and turn left, through an even tinier door, and into a room no bigger than Cole's en suite bathroom back home in Minnesota.

There are votive candles everywhere, *milagros* of every kind, letters and photos, little stuffed animals offered up in hope or remembrance. He follows Antonio's lead, lining up his three candles next to each other. He places one heart in one candle and lights it for Liam, the second heart in the second candle for Paul. Then Cole places the two remaining hearts in the third candle and lights it for two of them, for this love he feels for Ren, for their hearts. It is a wish, a deep and profound wish for a miracle he can't ask for out loud.

He notices the hole in the dirt floor. People crouch down to dig, placing dirt in plastic baggies, in paper cups and small boxes. Antonio hands him a cup and again, Cole finds himself moving without thinking. Using a small shovel, he digs up a little dirt and places it in the cup. He's overwhelmed by all of the desperation and hope in the air, and the room starts to close in on him.

He doesn't deserve this—this room, this dirt, this place, this moment. He's nothing but a coward; even in finally giving over to his feelings for Ren, he's a coward. He comes to this moment unclean, burdened by too many betrayals of self, and heart, and friendship and truth.

"I have to get out of here," Cole says suddenly, ducking out of the exit door. He walks out behind the chapel, finds a bench and sits. He looks out at green, so much green it's startling. There is life here—trees, and grass, and more trees dotting the creek bed, now dry in the summer heat.

Cole sticks his fingers into the dirt in his cup. It's just dirt, but in his hands it somehow it feels like so much more. The feel of it grounds him, and just like that, he knows what he must do. Maybe it's Antonio's story about Jimmy Padilla and the fragility of life, echoing in his heart; maybe it's the landscape, the valley dipping from high desert into this tiny oasis; maybe it's the Santuario, the dirt healing not his wounds, but his regrets.

Whatever it is, Cole has never felt more sure of anything in his life: He will break things off with Liam and with every other man who tries to be his everything. He will spend his life saying "no," waiting for Ren to say "yes."

When Antonio finds him, Cole says, "You lit two candles."

"One for my grandmother and one for Jimmy."

They sit together for an hour or so, staring out at the green and brown, watching tourists order flavored tortillas from a nearby stand. They exchange easy conversation and benign facts, nothing that would betray the decision Cole has just made, until they hear the fast-paced walk of two New Yorkers approaching behind them.

"We have rugs! Can we go?" Ren says, eyeing them warily.

"I'm ready. You ready, Cole?" Antonio asks.

"Yes. Absolutely."

Antonio turns on the radio for the drive back, and Cole listens to Deidre and Ren talk about tile and glassware and a party they both plan to attend in October. The largest rug is too big to fit all the way in the trunk, so part of it rests on top of the seat behind them, between him and Ren. Cole wants to curl into Ren, kiss his neck and earlobes and tell him what he plans to do, but the rug is in the way.

"Ren tells me you work with Alegra," Deidre says, shaking him out of his thoughts.

"I do in fact work with Alegra, yes."

"You write songs?"

"Sometimes. I used to," Cole says.

"He writes beautiful songs," Ren insists.

"Sing something for me," Deidre commands, because she is just that gauche.

"Antonio's car, Antonio's music," Cole quips.

"Hey, I'll turn it off if you want me to," Antonio says. "Or not."

"It's been a long time since I wrote anything," Cole stalls.

"Ren, I've never heard you sing. Do you remember any of his songs?" Deidre asks.

Cole wonders how Ren could possibly remember any of the songs he wrote in high school and college. He remembers Ren poring over his journal, reading the lyrics in blue ink bleeding through and onto the back of the page. That was years ago, a decade ago. How could he remember? Surely he doesn't—

But Ren is singing, that song he wrote his first year at Berklee, before he let other boys in, before they grew up, before he gave up. It's amazing and perfect and Cole wonders if he's ever actually *heard* Ren sing this song before. He remembers singing it himself in the showcase, remembers Ren's rapt expression as he strummed and sang his heart out, hoping Ren would understand that he could sing what he could not say.

Ren's voice is otherworldly, haunting, pure. With the rug in the way, Cole can't look at him, so Ren slides his hand across the seat and places it on Cole's thigh. They haven't said a word to each other about this morning, or this day, or about why Cole is holding a paper cup half-full of dirt. But somehow this is all that needs to be said, this song. And somehow this is all that needs to be done, this hand on his thigh.

Ren sings, and the words, *his own words*, are like a revelation to him. He barely remembers writing them, but he definitely remembers the feelings that inspired him to write the song.

When they pass Jimmy's house, they all turn to look; and, each in their own time, Antonio first, turn back to look at the road ahead of them. Cole takes Ren's hand again.

Will I always take it? Will I always reach for his hand, wrap it up in my own, hold it tightly, again and again? Will I always have the chance to hold it and never let go?

He lets Ren's voice wash over him, lets a tear fall, and then another, silently, so silently, as if he's sitting in the Santuario, praying.

Chapter 9

Between Chimayo and the drive to her work-in-progress house, Deidre used the words "fuck," "fucking," or "fucker" a total of twenty-seven times.

Cole counted.

While watching the three men unload obscenely expensive, beautifully crafted rugs, she pulled out the words "bastard," and the oh-so-eloquent "*cocksucking* bastard," several times (in reference to her husband).

Tensions are high now, all four of them still reeling from the emotions of the day. Antonio heaves exasperated sighs and glares at Deidre while she continues to talk trash and hurl obscenities at every single little thing, living or dead.

Cole does his best to ignore it, choosing instead to watch Ren move, make decisions, change his mind, give in to impatience, contemplate, hum and softly sing what sounds like an old Florence & The Machine song under his breath. Ren mediates, keeping Antonio and Deidre at least five feet apart. Every so often he smiles apologetically at Cole and mouths, "Sorry," or, "It's fine if you want to just go." Each time he does this, Cole just shrugs his shoulders as if none of it matters and shakes his head. He's not going *anywhere*.

They're hours into the rug relocation/optimal placement dance when Antonio quietly invites Ren and Cole to join him for Friday night dinner at Alex Marin House.

Deidre must have supersonic hearing, because almost immediately she sidles up behind him and says, "Are you fucking serious, Ren? I thought we were going out. Haven't we spent enough time with this judgmental asshole? You know he hates me. His wife will hate me even more, because that's what they do, jealous, prissy motherfuckers—"

Apparently, the word "motherfucker" is the last straw.

"That's it!" Antonio shouts, lunging for Deidre. She ducks behind Ren; Cole does his best to hold Antonio back. It's a bit like trying to wrangle a charging bull, but Cole is strong, and Antonio doesn't really have it in him to hurt anyone, anyway. He just wants to scare the living crap out of her.

Ren turns to face Deidre and grabs hold of her upper arms. "Now you listen to me, crazy girl. I'm going to tell you something that could probably cost me this contract, and many future contracts, but I have to do it, because otherwise I might slap you. And despite my commitment to pacifism, if I slap you, it will hurt. It will hurt like a *bitch*. And I don't want to hurt you, Deidre. I don't. I just want you to zip it. Zip it for all good people. Just bottle up all of your pain and keep it to yourself for one night like a good little socialite. Drown your neuroses in booze and pills, I don't care. Just shut. The fuck. Up."

Ren's speech leaves Deidre stunned and quiet, Antonio amazed, and Cole so turned on he has to literally *step back*, away from Ren, so as not to maul him right there on Deidre's clay-colored rug.

"Antonio, Cole and I would love to join you and Sarah for dinner with the kids, Right, Cole?"

"What? Oh, yes. Of course. We'd be delighted," Cole replies, staring at Ren's ass. He can't help it—Ren has been bending over and crouching down and scooting across the floor *for hours.*

"And Deidre, if you can tame your rage for a few hours, you are welcome to join us. Otherwise, I'll see you tomorrow."

"Only if he promises to be nice to me," Deidre says, in a soft voice.

"Ren, are you serious with this?" Antonio is genuinely angry now, and Cole wonders what Ren is thinking, inviting her along.

"I'm not going where I'm not wanted," Deidre says.

"Good. You're not wanted," Antonio barks.

"Antonio, stop. It's fine. She'll behave." Ren starts for the door. "And besides, if you just put out a swear jar, Sarah will probably have half her annual budget covered by the time we get to dessert."

Antonio stomps off, brushing past Ren on his way to the car. Ren motions for Deidre and Cole to follow, and then shuts off the lights and locks the door behind them. He walks in step with Cole and says in a hushed tone, "They're like bratty, neglected children."

"Will I get you alone tonight? Or are you on mom duty?" Cole asks.

Ren laughs and says, "Tonight, you get me any way you want me."

Cole feels as if he's seventeen, all hormones and nervous anticipation. How does Ren *do this*? They were wrapped up in each other not fifteen hours ago, and still Cole is almost desperate with want.

Cole stops Ren before he can slide into Antonio's backseat, and whispers in his ear: "I've been hard for you for hours. I won't make it through dinner."

Ren kisses Cole firmly on the mouth, causing Cole to lose his balance. Ren reaches behind and steadies him just in time, his hand on Cole's lower back.

"You have a rental car, right? So we'll take your car and leave early," Ren offers.

From the front seat Deidre says, "I can hear you, you know."

Thirty minutes later, it's official: Ren is driving Cole insane. Brushing up against him during Sarah's tour of the warm and inviting Alex Marin House, resting his hand on Cole's ass while they study the photo mural residents made for their rec room, eye-fucking him unabashedly while Cole tunes his guitar. If they hadn't accepted Antonio's dinner invitation and promised to sing some songs with the kids who lived there, Cole would have tied Ren to a bed hours ago.

Cole is singing a stripped-down version of the summer's biggest Top 40 hit when Ren excuses himself from the group of enthralled teenagers and makes his way to the kitchen. Just before he disappears, he turns to give Cole one last look, a slow burn that lasts six full seconds, causing him to screw up the song. Ren giggles and ducks into the room to join the other adults.

Cole answers a few questions about Alegra, about London, about the music business. He's grateful Ren is out of earshot when Teddy, a tall boy no more than sixteen with platinum blond hair, asks, "What's your boyfriend like?"

"He's cute. Sweet. Generous," Cole replies, trying to end the Q&A as quickly as possible before he forgets and adds: *"But he's not the one, not by a mile. Let me tell you about the man who IS the one. He's strikingly beautiful. He's brilliant and gifted, with an obscene amount of talent. He's layered and brave and his touch is addictive, like scorching desire and coming home all at the same time. No, my boyfriend is not the man of my dreams. The man of my dreams is right over there."*

He's saved from himself and the prying questions of excited teenagers by Sarah's call from the kitchen. "Kitchen duty, you're up. Who's cooking?"

Teddy stands and holds his hand out to a shorter boy, also blond—Wyatt, maybe? They shuffle into the kitchen just as Sarah, Antonio, Deidre and Ren walk out and sit down at the large dining room table.

Cole excuses himself from the other kids, but leaves his guitar for them to "mess around" with. He pulls up a chair, and Ren scoots his own chair closer to him, takes his hand under the table and rests both of their hands in Cole's lap. It reminds him of Dean's bachelor party, except this time, there's no desperation, no pretense.

"So this concert—" Deidre starts, looking at Sarah.

"Oh, you should join us! Antonio's sister was planning on coming, but her daughter has the flu, so she can't make it," Sarah says, ignoring Antonio's warning glare.

Cole was right about Sarah: He just loves her. Fresh-faced and makeup free, she is patient, and kind, and dedicated; and if he weren't so eager to get Ren alone and naked, he'd want to sit and talk with her for hours, and then make plans to do the same thing again, very soon. He can see why Antonio is still so deeply in love with her—she glows with a light that only people who live in their purpose possess. She is not yearning for anything; she's right where she's supposed to be.

"I'm sure you couldn't possibly find me a ticket," Deidre says, in an affected tone.

"No, like I just said, I have an extra ticket in our row—"

"I'm sure it would be impossible to find a seat for me. Unless you have a VIP ticket. You probably have at least *one* VIP ticket left, but I'm sure it's very expensive." Deidre says.

"I don't understand... you can have the ticket—"

"How much did you say your VIP tickets are again? Twenty-five thousand?" Deidre pulls out her checkbook and starts writing, her handwriting the swift, long strokes of someone accustomed to spending boatloads of cash on a regular basis.

Sarah gasps and Antonio's mouth falls open. Ren reaches across the table to take Sarah's hand. "She's trying to make a donation, Sarah, but she doesn't want anyone to know she has a soft heart underneath her trash mouth and thick skin."

When Sarah jumps up and hugs her, Deidre's arms reluctantly reach around and hug Sarah back, and Cole is stunned to see a small, genuine smile on Deidre's face. Maybe she's doing it for Jimmy. Or her guilty conscience. Or because she wants to help these kids. Whatever the reason, Cole dislikes her a little bit less—though, unlike sweet Sarah, he cannot imagine ever being real friends with her.

Dinner is strange and wonderful. Not because the kids are boisterous and inquisitive and show off like peacocks—*Were we like this, once upon a time, in our maroon and gold uniforms?*—but because the grownups are treating them like a real couple. They don't bat an eye when Ren leans in close and whispers in Cole's ear, "Look at Teddy and Wyatt. Aren't they darling? So in love." They smile knowingly when Cole offers to trade plates with Ren so Ren can have more chicken and Cole can have more pasta. And when Cole starts to squirm in his seat, the proximity to Ren too much to handle without kissing him, they rightly assume that the two lovers will soon make their excuses, express their thanks and slip out before dessert.

Which is exactly what they do.

Twenty-three minutes later, Cole has Ren panting, zipper down, legs apart, in the front seat of Cole's rental. They haven't even made it out of the Eldorado's parking garage.

Cole's hand trails down Ren's stomach as he mouths at Ren's neck, flushed red with want. He slips two fingers under the waistband of Ren's briefs, rubs the pads of his fingers against Ren's soft, hot skin. Back and forth, back and forth, back and forth. Waiting.

It's everything he dreamed about all those years ago, jerking off in his dorm room, imagining Ren in various states of undress as they gave in to the awkward, delicious, first-time moments of sexual awakening.

"Do something, *God*, " Ren says.

"Will you let me get you off?"

Cole adjusts his hand so that his two fingers dip lower, his thumb rubbing along the outside of Ren's briefs. He thumbs Ren's cock, breathing into his neck, moving slowly, so slowly, waiting for an answer.

"We're steps... from the hotel—"

"Please. I can't wait. I need to see you come."

Ren grabs Cole's hand and pushes it down, under the soft cotton. Cole takes hold of Ren's cock with sure fingers, his own breath quickening at the feel of it.

"So hard for me," Cole whispers.

"*Yes.*"

Cole strokes whimpers out of Ren as he kisses confessions right into his mouth. "I wanted this. I wanted to reach over, unbutton your jeans, dip my hand into your underwear and touch you, feel you, have you all sweaty and relaxed and—"

"When?" Ren kisses him back.

"After the movies. After coffee. After shopping. After any of it. After all of it."

Ren reaches down and places his own hand on top of Cole's, moving with him, guiding him to go faster, just a bit tighter, twist, now faster again, *that's it*, more, tighter, faster, more.

"I would have let you, would have shown you—"

"How you like it? How to make you come apart—"

"I would have done anything... *please, shit...*. don't stop—"

"Would you have let me get you off every day, like this, just like this, my hand in your pants—"

"Yes, *yes*. Every day—"

"You'd trust me with your body, with everything new and confusing and hot—"

"Yes, everything..."

"—And you wouldn't even be scared—"

"Because it would be you."

Their hands move in unison now, driving Ren perfectly, *perfectly*, and Cole can see Ren's orgasm build in him, see Ren chase it, expect it, need it.

"Come on—"

"*Cole*—"

"I thought about this *so much... that's it, come on*—"

Ren arches his back and comes over Cole's fingers, his own fingers squeezing down on Cole's hand *hard*, as though he needs him, as though his hand is a lifeline. Cole rests his head on Ren's shoulder and looks down at Ren's lap, at the trail of soft hair down his stomach, at his firm, muscled thighs spread out to the edges of the seat.

Suddenly he's crying again, his tears silent, warm and salty as they slide down his cheeks in single file, wetting Ren's shoulder. He hears the song, *his song*, his song *for Ren,* and remembers all of it. Every hopeful thought. Every wish. Every disappointed sigh. Somehow, all the mind-blowing sex they've had in the past two days pales in comparison to this simple thing. Because this is how he always pictured it, the first thing, the thing they'd do a hundred times before they did anything else, the thing that would start their *forever*.

He'd thought about giving this to Ren every time they pulled into student parking, every time they drove to the stupid mall, every time he pulled up to his parent's house with Ren in the passenger seat, ready to jump out of the car and start their weekend of platonic fun. And now they've come full circle, here in the shadows of this parking garage, surrounded by concrete and dust-covered cars.

Ren moves their hands, zips up his pants and turns in his seat to face Cole, gently knocking Cole's head off of his shoulder. He takes Cole's face in his hands and kisses Cole's forehead, his eyelids, his cheeks, his lips. It feels a lot like love.

"Let's go upstairs. Okay?" Ren says.

"Okay."

Ren is silent as he leads Cole by the hand, through the lobby and up to his room. Cole wonders if he knows. He doesn't want to freak Ren out before he's had a chance to make sure Ren understands that he's serious. He wants Ren to know without a doubt that Cole chooses him, over everyone else, and always will. He won't stand a chance with Ren otherwise.

Cole is still feeling bittersweet, moving slow under the weight of memory, while Ren strips off all of his clothes, sits down on the bed and pulls Cole toward him. He wastes no time taking off Cole's jeans and underwear, his face level with Cole's cock. He tugs on Cole's shirt and says, "Off."

His shirt is half off when Ren takes him in hand, and it's everything Cole can do to stay upright. He looks down at Ren, adoring him, and feels the temporary melancholy leave him. Ren is pressing hot, wet, open-mouthed kisses to his belly, working him over with *intent*.

"It's okay," Ren says. "I know what you need."

Cole is all about one goal now, as he pushes Ren back on the bed. He's on his knees, sliding his hands up Ren's pale, strong legs, kissing Ren's calves as they hang off the edge of the bed. Ren lifts up on his elbows, looks down at Cole and raises an eyebrow.

Cole presses into Ren's thighs with his thumbs. "Spread your legs."

Cole holds Ren open with both hands, licking, tasting, fucking into him with his tongue. He moans around him, *in him*, and Ren babbles and curses, arching up off the bed and flopping down again, over and over again until he's begging, "Please, *oh God,* Cole... Cole... you're not going to do this for *hours*, are you? Just... please... I can't... so good... shit—"

And then Cole is pressing lubed fingers inside Ren, and Ren is hissing, pleading, thanking him. He was right: This is exactly what he needs.

Let me watch you fall apart. Let me take you there, out of time, to that place where you have nothing and everything and all you see is me, all you smell is me, all you know is me, and I am yours. Let me find you there, giving in to me, over and over and over again, until all that we have left is each other and this, this, this.

When Ren is stretched, open, waiting, *waiting*, Cole stands up, leans over and says, "Wrap your legs around me."

He reaches under Ren, lifts him just a few inches up off the bed and moves them across until they are both fully on the bed, Cole on top of Ren.

He doesn't want to use a condom, not now, not ever, but this thing between them isn't settled. It may never *be* settled, so he forces himself to slip away for a moment. The condom in place, Ren moves to turn onto his stomach, but Cole stops him.

"You like this position, huh?" Ren says, eyes dancing.

"I like looking at your face."

Ren smiles and folds his knees up.

Cole is fucking him slow and deep when Ren says, "You wanted that for a long time... *shit*... in the car... your hand—"

"Since forever," Cole says.

"You wanted me—"

"In so many ways, Ren." Cole tries to keep the same rhythm as he leans down to kiss Ren, tongue on teeth. He thrusts deeper, a little bit faster, his head facedown on Ren's shoulder.

"What else?" Ren asks, his mouth pressed up against Cole's ear. "Tell me everything."

"I would sneak out after curfew, open your door and find you there, your back against the headboard, your pajama shirt open—"

"Yes—"

"—Pants pulled down to your knees, touching yourself."

"Yes, yes... yes, more—"

"—And you'd—"

Cole stops, sucks a mark into Ren's shoulder, feels the pressure pool at the base of his spine, like hot liquid, and climb up his back; bright, wide fire-licks of want. If he could just stay still for a moment, if he could hold this feeling back and stave off the inevitable, it could be the best ever.

"What? Please tell me. What would I do?" Ren pants, his hips making small, tight circles.

Cole kisses along Ren's jaw, and whispers, "You'd let me watch."

"Holy *hell*. Come *on*. Just fuck me, *please*."

"I am fucking you."

"No, just do it. Do what you need. It's okay, please, I want it," Ren begs. "If you were seventeen, eighteen... if you could have had me then—"

And then Cole is all in, pushing Ren's thighs wider still and his knees further back, fucking him with such force they are both reduced to grunts. It's so base, so dirty, he has a fleeting thought that his teenage self would never allow him to do this, to let go and *be this* with Ren, or with anyone... but he would want to.

Ren comes after just a few pulls on his cock and then holds his knees up as Cole continues to pound into him with urgent, desperate thrusts.

"Do it. Yeah. That's it," Ren commands, his voice disarmingly deep.

Cole cries out when he comes—maybe he says Ren's name; maybe he swears a blue streak, or thanks God; maybe he even confesses his love. He's not sure; whatever he said doesn't seem to upset Ren, who is wrapping him up in his arms, his legs, his soothing voice, helping him come down.

After a few minutes, or maybe twenty, Cole lifts his head and looks at Ren with concern in his eyes.

"Don't ask me if I'm okay," Ren says, rubbing Cole's back. "I'm always okay with you."

In the morning they shower, dress and walk the few blocks to Pasqual's for breakfast, both with big days ahead of them. The restaurant teems with life, every table full and seemingly engaged in fascinating conversation. Overhead are strings of multi-colored Tibetan prayer flags; all around them, modern New Mexican art.

Cole gulps down his glass of freshly-squeezed orange juice in one go and orders a second, which earns him a big smile from Ren.

"You're feeling better, then?"

Cole blushes and nods, runs his thumb over Ren's cheekbone.

"You don't cry, not often," Ren observes, sipping coffee.

"Not often, no."

They discuss their plans for the day over plates piled high with eggs and green chile and chorizo and sweet cornbread. Ren *will* order a door today, while Cole heads over to the Santa Fe Opera for sound check. Again, Cole is struck with the realization that they are acting very much like a regular couple and, instead of pointing it out to Ren, he keeps it, like a tiny treasure sewn into his pocket.

Maybe Ren feels it too. Maybe he doesn't want to upend this beautiful thing between them, so he's keeping it to himself. Maybe he's keeping other thoughts and feelings and truths to himself as well. Maybe he's waiting for Cole to get his shit together once and for all. Or maybe none of that is true. Maybe he's just doing what he said he would do: giving himself over to Cole for eleven, now ten precious days, before he returns to the life he's made for himself.

Maybe.

"So I got you a key card, to my room," Ren says, interrupting Cole's thoughts. "I just thought, well, since we're both working during this... moment... thing... whatever—you shouldn't have to wait for me in your room. You could wait for me in my room. If you want."

Ren slides the key card over to Cole, and Cole laughs, remembering what he did yesterday morning, just before they left for Chimayó. Ren looks put out, but Cole holds him off with a raised hand and reaches into his wallet.

"Here," he says, sliding an identical key card over to Ren. "I got one for you, too. Now you can come up to my room whenever you like."

"Okay, then."

"Okay."

Chapter 10

"Tailgating? At the Opera? Are you serious?" Ren asks Antonio, his mind flooded with memories of boring Vikings games, his brother and their dad inhaling bratwurst and hamburgers as if they were in some sort of eating contest. The last thing he wants to do is wrinkle his two thousand-dollar suit sitting in a rickety lawn chair, drinking beer from a can.

"It's not what you think," Antonio answers, pulling into a parking spot marked "Reserved."

"It sounds awful," Deidre says. "Why did I agree to this?"

"You paid twenty-five grand for the privilege of doing this," Antonio reminds her.

"Right. I'm a fucking idiot, apparently."

As he steps out of the car, Ren takes in the panoramic view from the Opera's perch—the Sangre de Cristo Mountains before him, the Jemez to his left, and a rolling landscape of piñon-dotted desert. From here he can see the top of the impressive, modern amphitheater. Its infrastructure of white poles looks like a design by NASA.

Antonio starts off toward the main parking lot, away from the amphitheater's main entrance. "This way," he says.

But before Ren takes a step, Deidre grabs hold of Ren's arm and tells Antonio, "We'll catch up to you."

Antonio waves her off, happy to be rid of her. When he's out of earshot, Deidre turns to face Ren. "Look, I just want to say that I'm sorry, okay? I didn't mean to be such a bitch yesterday, I just—"

"It's fine. I know who you are. I get it," Ren says.

"You make me sound so... Jesus, Ren. I'm not a *total* bitch."

"Not totally, no," he says with just a hint of a smile.

"And you were right, about my rage thing. It's a bit out of control, I know. And that's my own shit, not yours. But still, I really think you need an intervention. Someone has to tell you what's what."

Ren leans back against Antonio's car and sighs. "Just get it over with, then."

"You're in love with that man—" Deidre starts.

"Straight to the point, I see."

"—And you're dangerously close to blowing it with Paul, no matter what bullshit story you're telling yourself. And you *would* be blowing it. I may only be a few years older than you, but I know what I'm talking about. What you're feeling... it's all sex and lust and unrequited hotness—"

"—Unrequited hotness?"

"Whatever. It's sex after pining. Lots and lots of pining. I mean, *that song* you sang in the car. Lord. I can't believe you didn't drop your pants and bend over the moment you heard him play it." Deidre fans herself. "But it's not the thing you base a marriage on, Ren."

"Do tell me what *your* marriage is based on, Deidre. Is it love? I think not." Ren is all hard edges and clipped tones, his body tense with anger.

"You can't let yourself get caught up in this. You can't let yourself make big, life-altering decisions while you're caught up in this—"

"Like you've ever made an emotional decision in your life—"

"I have. I did. There was... someone. Once," Deidre says, looking out into the crowd.

"Oh, dear, he's not here is he? Is he that janitor over there? Or the box office guy? Is he the *valet,* Deidre? This isn't your pathetic attempt to recreate a scene from *The Notebook*, is it?"

He's joking; she knows he's joking. And he's trying to hurt her, just a little bit, because she's getting to him. "Your life is miserable. You hate almost everything about it, except the money. Why would I *ever* follow your advice about love or marriage?"

"I'm not some cautionary tale," Deidre bites. She pauses. "Okay, I am. But that doesn't change the fact that you are contemplating trading in a man who adores you and wants to marry you, a man who could very likely be the next governor of New York, for a man with whom you've had the best sex of your life. BUT—and that's a big juicy but, Ren— you're trading in your future husband for a man who still loves you 'like a friend.' A man who is living with another man, in another country, on another continent."

Ren can't help but wince. *Future husband.* It's all wrong, and he knows it, but what can he do? If he says anything—if he tells the truth, if he admits that when he hears the words "future husband" he really only thinks of one man, one gorgeous, soulful, ever-present man—he'll likely break several hearts. Paul's, for sure. His own. And maybe Cole's heart, too, when for the second time in their lives, he admits he can't love Ren the way he wants to be loved. Because he'll have lost his friend. They'll all be losers. Lost. Broken.

"Remember that scene in *When Harry Met Sally*?" Deidre asks.

"There are lots of scenes."

"The one where they're arguing about the ending of *Casablanca.* Sally argues that Ilsa was right to leave Rick and get on the plane with her husband, and Harry thinks she should have stayed, because Rick was the love of her life—"

"—And the best sex she'd ever had. Yeah, I remember—"

"Right. Well I agree with Sally. I mean, what the hell was she supposed to do in Casablanca, anyway? Hang out at the fucking bar? Wait for Rick to come home? That place was a shithole."

"So you're saying I should forget about Cole?"

"No. How can you? I'm just saying you should get on the plane, Ren. Get on the plane."

"Is that what you did?"

"Maybe," she answers, avoiding his eyes.

"There are so many things wrong with everything, *everything* you just said, Deidre. First, Cole and I have always been more than friends. We're just—"

Ren hesitates, trying to come up with a short, articulate explanation for fourteen years of longing and missed opportunity.

He chuckles, remembering Antonio's words. "We're just chickenshit, Deidre. And we have been for like, ever. And what you're seeing between us now is the opposite of that, or almost the opposite of that. And I know Cole has a boyfriend and lives three thousand miles across a very big ocean. I know that Paul loves me and that to everyone else, we make sense. But I also know that, while Cole may not be in love with me the way I am so hopelessly in love with him, his love for me extends beyond friendship."

It's the first time he's said it out loud, and it shakes him to the core because, really, he *doesn't* know the full extent of Cole's feelings. Sure, he'd seen him break down yesterday, *twice*, and that look Cole gave him after he sang Cole's song in the car was pure love, no denying it. But was it *love,* love, the kind that's worth wrecking your life over?

Despite all of the letting go, and giving in, and sharing of regrets and fantasies and *tenderness*, they're still playing that game, breathing in all that is left unsaid and letting it enter their lungs, their bloodstreams, their hearts. They're still unsure of themselves, and each other, and that—well, that could go on forever. It seems as if it already has.

"And secondly, are you for real? Ilsa *absolutely* should have stayed with Rick. Everyone knows that. She left because Rick forced her to go, not because she thought she'd be better off with what's-his-name," Ren says. "And if they made an obnoxious sequel to *Casablanca*, it would have been all about Ilsa looking for Rick after the war and trying to get him back. Because they were meant to be."

She looks at him as if he's speaking a foreign language. "If you tell Paul, you'll lose him."

"Probably."

"And Cole? Has he said even one word about what will happen after you go back to New York?"

"No."

"Has he promised to leave his boyfriend for you?"

"No."

"Has he confessed his undying love for you and asked you to be his forever and ever?" Her tone is mocking, as if he's some lovesick, clueless teenager who can't be bothered with reality.

"No, okay! No to all of it."

"Well—"

"Just shut up. Shut. Up. I liked this town much better when you were far away, ensconced in your penthouse, making out with a vat of gin."

"Ouch."

"That was low. Sorry."

"It's okay. I've said worse."

"Yes, you have."

They're quiet for a moment, staring out at the view of the Sangre de Cristo Mountains, the desert sun softening into lavender hues. It's foreign to them, unsettling, all of this big sky and ancient earth. They both feel New York buzzing under their skin, beckoning them home. This place is crazy-making, the way it strips you down and leaves you bare, and they just want to get back to the noise of the city, let it lull them into a sense of calm, false or not.

"I hate this town," she says. "I can't believe I agreed to live here even part-time."

"You'll get used to it."

Ren extends his arm, and Deidre slips hers through it. They wind their way through the throngs of Santa Feans dressed in black-tie and sitting next to their Mercedes and Ferraris at card tables covered in the finest linen, leaning up against luxury SUVs (dinner served from the hatchbacks) or standing next to decadent spreads laid out on the hoods of Range Rovers and BMWs. There are candelabras and elaborate floral arrangements, champagne and sangria and the finest tequila, tapas and filet mignon and the most decadent chocolates. It's absurd and wonderful and odd, and Ren is a little bit giddy at the sight of it all.

They find Antonio and Sarah sitting at a table for twenty that is covered in a soft pink tablecloth. Delectable appetizers and desserts are arrayed on artfully mismatched fine china. Dozens of tiny votive candles glow; the wine flows freely.

Antonio gestures to the chairs next to him and, despite his blatant hatred of her, stands until Deidre is seated. The party is made up of Alex Marin House board members and major benefactors, all relaxed and smiling, taking in the night as if this happens every day. Just a few feet away, the residents of the house sit at a smaller table, laughing and trying to act as though they belong here.

Ren snaps a few pictures on his phone, and then leans over Antonio and says to Sarah, "My dad will *not* believe this. It's not exactly his idea of tailgating."

"It's really an Opera thing. And yes, they really do love the Opera as much as your Dad probably loves football," Sarah explains, holding out her glass for Antonio to refill it.

"Thank you again, for inviting me."

Sarah beams at him. "I want you here. Antonio thinks the world of you, and it's an honor to have you with us."

Ren relaxes in his chair and lets the conversation wash over him. He catches Mitchell, the producer and owner of the Galisteo studio, looking at him and smiles at him. Mitchell smiles back and winks. At this point, he realizes, it would be a miracle if Paul didn't find out about this affair. Too many people know. Too much has happened. Too much has changed.

Through the toasts and stories, Ren slips into a nice warm buzz. It's not long before everyone starts to move toward the amphitheater. Volunteers stay to clean up as Sarah, Antonio, Ren and Deidre make their way to their seats. They are in section F, three rows from the stage, and from here Ren can actually see into the wings.

The venue is gorgeous, like nothing he's ever seen before, with the audience facing west toward a perfect view of the sunset. Ren is overwhelmed with the *rightness* of the night. He feels lucky and proud to be here with everyone—even Deidre.

Mitchell takes the stage, says a few lovely words about his passion for Alex Marin House, and then introduces Sarah. The applause is deafening—clearly she is well loved and well respected. Ren hears the boys calling out to her from across the aisle. As she speaks about the work she does, about the kids she loves, about the futures they now have thanks to everyone in the room, Ren cannot help but tear up. If he hadn't had his supportive parents, if he had been born into a frightened, ignorant family, any one of their stories could have been his own.

Because Sarah is awesome in so many ways, her speech is over before anyone can get too blubbery. She squeals when she thanks Alegra, and Mitchell, and Alegra's band, and then she's off the stage and back in her seat in a flash.

"Was that okay?" she asks, reaching out for Antonio's hand.

"It was perfect, sweetheart."

The house lights down, Ren notices lamps everywhere in yellow tones: the motif for the night. The band takes the stage, and Ren strains to see Cole in the darkness but can't make him out.

Alegra takes the stage to more applause, looking *fabulous* in a high-wasted black cocktail dress. She greets the crowd. "I'm just tickled to be here, and thrilled to have the chance to support Alex Marin House, a place that lights the way for so many kids who are lost in darkness."

The piano kicks in with the opening bars of the biggest hit from her last album, a fast tune that makes everyone smile and want to get up and dance. She is in top form, and Ren lets himself get caught up in the night, lets himself feel okay with his choices, lets himself stare unabashedly at Cole. *Cole.* Cole, who looks like a fucking rock star up there in his black suit, pants tight, hair wild. He's playing guitar and singing backup vocals, and if Ren weren't so madly in love with him already, he would fall for him instantly.

On the next song, one Ren doesn't recognize, Cole comes forward for a guitar solo, Alegra beaming at him as she steps back a few feet. Ren leans forward, his ass nearly off his seat. Cole is killing it, and the song is gorgeous. She's just reached the end of the song when his phone vibrates in his pocket.

Cole: Are you enjoying yourself?

Ren: You're texting me from the stage.

Cole: Obviously.

Ren: But aren't you supposed to do something with that guitar right about now?

Cole: Probably not. We're trying something different with the next song.

Ren: Still. This is pretty tacky, Cole.

Cole: True, but necessary.

Ren: Necessary? How so?

Cole: I have to tell you something.

Ren: So tell me.

Cole: Alegra and I worked out the set list for tonight.

Ren: Okay. Am I missing something?

Cole: Just listen to the song. I asked her to sing it.

Cole: For you. She's singing it for you.

He looks up from his phone and sees Cole looking in the direction of their row of seats, smiling that earnest, movie-star smile he loves so much. Ren's pulse quickens, and even though it's probably the worst idea ever, he leans over to Antonio and says, "She's singing it for me. He dedicated the next song to me."

Deidre's eyebrows shoot up and Sarah squeals, while Antonio turns to look at Cole.

The piano comes in, and as soon as Alegra starts singing Ren's breath catches in his throat. It's her new song, "Forever Man," the one they keep trying to get right. He grips his phone tightly, as if it were Cole's hand, as if he could reach through the phone and grab him. He looks at Cole, fights back tears and listens to every word.

"You're not a sometime thing, no. You're not my summer fling. You're not a line drawn in the sand," Alegra sings, pure and strong. Ren can tell she's looking for him in the audience, and it seems so surreal, to have Alegra singing to him, willing him to listen on behalf of Cole, this boy, this *man* he's loved so long.

Holy shit. Is Cole in love with me? Does he want to be with me? Is this for real?

"You're not my maybe, baby. You're not my compromise. Darling, you're my everything, forever man," she sings, her eyes landing on Ren. She pours everything into the song, and Ren's eyes dart from her to Cole and back again, not sure where to focus.

"Well, *shit*," Deidre says. "I guess you're not getting on the plane."

He looks over at Cole, who hasn't stopped staring at him, and lets the tears fall. Suddenly Ren is that boy again, drawing their names in his notebook, fantasizing about Cole McKnight: savior, confidant, friend. He's that boy with a lonely heart, holding out for happiness, biding his time until he can escape to a place where people will accept him, befriend him, celebrate him. He's that boy who moons over his best friend, waiting for him to notice him *that way*, to claim him, to ask him, to want him, to fight for him, to declare his love and lay down his heart for him.

He's long since given up being serenaded by Cole. Even when Cole sang his own songs, even when it *sounded* as though he *might* have written the song for him, Ren never knew for sure. Because Cole never said anything, and Cole never sang to him, or about him, just *with* him.

And now this. It's not Cole singing—it's freaking *Alegra*—but this time Cole was clear. *I asked her to sing it. She's singing it for you.*

Ren wants to run to him, wring the truth out of him, kiss his palms and rest his head on his chest for years and years. He wants to hold him, to sway with him as they did that night that seems like *ages* ago. He wants to *know*, to hear it from Cole's lips, to see the truth in his eyes.

Alegra sings and it goes right through him, like a gust of wind. "*If there is only this, if there is only you, then I'll be happy 'til my dying day. There is nothing temporary about that thing you do or the way my heart asks to stay and stay.*"

He turns and finds Antonio and Sarah looking at him, smiling; Deidre pinches his arm. It's too much, the magnitude of the moment. It's the big reveal, Ilsa confessing her love for Rick at their clandestine meeting, Harry confessing his love for Sally on New Year's Eve. But instead of feeling joyous or even relieved, he suddenly feels trapped. It feels as if all of the air has left his body and he can't catch his breath. Everyone and everything is crowding him—the faces, the music, the promises, the stares.

Ren can't believe he's actually feeling claustrophobic in an amphitheater, but *he is*. Rows upon rows of strangers unknowingly watching his life officially fall apart—or get made—it's too much. Everyone is smiling and happy and he just wants to run, run, run.

He's up out of his seat before he can think twice about it, his pace quickening as he makes his way to the end of the aisle. Within minutes he's back in the parking lot, doubled over, chest heaving as though he's having an asthma attack.

"Ren?"

Ren turns to see Cole standing not five feet away, a bit out of breath.

"Did you mean it?" Ren asks.

"Yes."

"You're in love with me?"

"Yes."

Ren doubles over again, trying to catch his breath. Cole crosses to him, rubbing his back, saying nothing. After a moment, Ren straightens up and asks, "How long?"

"I want us to be together—"

"No. How long have you been in love with me?"

The answer to this one question is all Ren needs to know. Because this man, this friend, this lover of his has always given in to whims and drama and intensity, and Ren has to be sure that he is not *that*. He has to be sure that this is not *new*.

Cole steps into Ren's space, tilts his chin up and kisses him. The kiss is firm, an answer, a promise.

"I can't remember a time when I *wasn't* in love with you."

"What? Just... *what?*"

"You heard me." Cole's voice is gentle, but firm; unwavering.

"That can't be... how can that be?"

Ren holds his stomach, sure that he'll vomit on his Ferragamo loafers. He expected a different answer, a story of how Cole fell in love with him over time or all at once, but later, not from the beginning. They couldn't have been in love with each other at the same time, this whole time. Could they have? Because that would be insane, and tragic and *insane*. He expected an answer pulled from the past, but not from the very start of it all.

It would have made more sense if Cole had said, *I fell in love with you that Christmas, when we picked out your tree together and stayed up all night staring at it and talking.* That year Cole showed up at the Warners' unexpectedly. It was their last holiday break as college students. Their friendship had started to fade in the wake of new experiences, new interests, new friends, new everything. Ren hadn't talked to Cole since October, so he had no idea if Cole planned to come home for Christmas.

It was tradition for the boys to pick out a tree with their dad, so Ren's parents had waited until he arrived from New York to get a tree. Cole showed up just as they were pulling out giant plastic tubs from the basement marked "Christmas Ornaments" and "Lights: Color." Cole wore a bright smile on his face, his navy pea coat covered in a light dusting of wet snow. Ren was flustered but ecstatic, and suddenly they were all climbing into Ren's Navigator en route to the same firehouse tree lot from which they had purchased trees since Ren was in grade school.

Ren never asked Cole why he showed up that night, but everyone assumed he'd stay through dinner, through hanging lights and stringing popcorn and cranberries, through trimming their giant, fat tree with every ornament they owned.

After Sean hung the star, after his parents went to bed and Sean left to meet a friend, Ren and Cole turned out all of the downstairs lights and talked for hours, Ren's feet in Cole's lap. It was easy and sort of magical; that could have been the night Cole fell in love with Ren. That confession would not have taken him by surprise, not at all.

Or if Cole had said, *It was that night I called you from London and we talked for nearly four hours.* Cole was a little drunk and a little sad that night, having just put his parents on a plane after a tense visit. Ren sat on the rooftop of his Brooklyn apartment and watched the Staten Island Ferry go back and forth across the East River as he listened to Cole rant, and qualify, and fight back tears. He clung to his phone like a lifeline as they tested and teased each other, and sighed heavy sighs when the unspoken, lingering want became too much. Ren would have accepted that Cole fell in love with him that night—hell, after *that* marathon call he half expected him to show up on his stoop the next day.

Or it could have been any number of moments Ren never witnessed, moments when Cole looked at old photographs and suddenly everything clicked and he just *knew;* moments when he was caught up in conversation with someone Ren had never met, talking about old friends, and his best friend, his Ren, and he would finally get it; moments when he compared a boyfriend's face to Ren's face and realized, in an instant, that he had fallen madly in love with his most treasured friend.

But no. It goes back to the beginning, to a time when Ren thought he was alone in his desires, his vision for the future, *their* future. He can't wrap his head around it. It's amazing and thrilling and too much.

So he asks again.

"You're *in love with me?*"

"I am."

"Since—"

"Since forever."

"No, no. *No.* You didn't want me... you said—"

Ren sways a bit. He might fall, just collapse right there in the Santa Fe Opera parking lot where not two hours ago he was sipping champagne and laughing at all of the wonderful running through his veins.

Cole grabs his elbow to steady him, and Ren tugs his arm away and sits on the ground. The asphalt is smooth and dirty, but he can't bring himself to care about the damage to his pants. Cole flops down beside him, close but not too close, and reaches for his hand. Ren hesitates but takes it, bringing their joined hands into his lap. Still slightly nauseated, he takes a few deep breaths.

"The other night, at The Pink, when you told me that you've always wanted me, I thought you meant sex. Just... sex."

"If this, *this*," Cole says as he squeezes Ren's hand, "were just about sex, we would have fooled around ages ago. It's always been more than sex."

"Of course it's more than just sex. That's not what I meant. It's more because we're friends. We used to be best friends, and sometimes we still are. I know it's *more* than just sex, I know we love each other like family, but—"

"You *are* my family, Ren. You're the only family I'll ever want," Cole says, and Ren is stunned silent again. He stares at Cole, looking for something, some clue as to what the hell is going on with him. Ren is still not sure this is real, and if it is, well, he can't even *think* about that right now.

"You... the things you *say*, Cole—"

"I mean every word—"

"We haven't seen each other in five years, Cole. How can you—?"

"Four. It's been four years."

"Whatever. It's still years. *Years*. And now this... just.... out of the blue—"

"That's what I'm trying to explain. It's *not* out of the blue."

Ren looks away. "I feel like I've had the wind knocked out of me."

"I'm sure. And I know none of this is simple, and I have a lot of explaining to do, but just so we're clear," Cole says, shifting to face Ren. "When I said I've always wanted you, I meant *all* of you: your body, your ideas, your memories, your whole heart. I want your dreams, your spare drawer, your mornings, your worries. Your triumphs, your laughter, your bad nights and your quiet days. I want your *future*, Ren.... just so we're clear."

"Holy hell, Cole. Did you practice saying that?"

Cole shrugs and smiles. "Well, I am a songwriter. I may have practiced, but it doesn't make any of it less true."

Ren searches Cole's earnest face. He looks nervous, as if maybe Ren will reject him. The long-awaited turnabout is not as delicious as Ren had imagined years ago; he's not entirely sure that he *won't* walk away from Cole. The stakes are higher. Everything is different. They're all grown up, now.

"I would never give you a spare drawer," Ren teases, trying to smooth Cole's furrowed brow with words. "I need *all* of the storage."

Ren leans over and places a soft, tentative kiss on Cole's lips. As he pulls away, the questions and concerns remain behind Cole's eyes.

"Cole—"

"It *was* more than just sex for you, right? This thing between us, it's always been more than this crazy chemistry. Right?"

Ren wants to agree, to come back with something like, *Yes, it's always been everything,* but he can't say it. He can't confirm or deny his feelings, or give Cole a chance to exhale and think his admission was worth it. Because if he does, if he admits to loving him and needing him, if he admits that no other man has ever even come close to claiming his whole heart; if he admits that he's been pining for Cole for so long it's a fucking *lifestyle,* that he's good at it, that he's used to it, that he might not know who he is without the ever-present shadow of unrequited love at his heels, he'll have to start over.

If he confesses this one, sacred, life-altering truth, he'll have to let go of every self-deception, knock down every wall, reveal every choice made in the name of vanity, or conformity, or "personal growth," and embrace the man he was meant to be. Because loving Cole has never just been about loving Cole; loving Cole has always been about *becoming,* about meeting his own destiny and saying yes to a life he hasn't planned out to the letter.

Somehow, he's always known this to be true, but it's only in this moment that he realizes it. So he can't say everything that needs to be said, or admit to all of his feelings. He needs to think. To breathe. To take this night apart and put it back together until his life makes sense again.

"Cole, this is a lot."

"I know, I know. I'm sorry I sprung this on you, but I had to do it."

Cole takes his other hand and runs his thumb along the inside of Ren's wrist. As always, it works like a charm, calming him enough that he can think straight. His nausea subsides and he listens to Alegra's voice, floating over them and into the desert night. It's another one of her new songs, and though he can't make out the words, somehow it sounds like the words that have haunted him, and altered him in just a few short days.

Do you need something?

I've always wanted you.

I can't remember a time when I wasn't in love with you.

He knows Cole wants an answer, and he also knows that Cole will wait for it. Because Cole is a gentleman, and kind, and because Cole is his dear, dear friend. So he kisses Cole on the neck and then tilts his head up to look at the stars shimmering in the sky, the sky that, uninterrupted by skylines and progress, seems to go on forever and ever.

"Can you believe the stars, Cole? It's even more than we can see back home," Ren says finally.

Cole looks up. Ren can feel him smiling. Maybe it's a rueful smile, or maybe Cole is all lit up inside, relieved after his confession; Ren can't tell from this angle. But at least he's smiling, whatever the reason for it.

"Mitch says they have meteor showers this time of year, the Perseids, he called them. If we're lucky, we'll spot some this trip. The best time to watch them is just before dawn."

"I've never seen a meteor shower. Have you?"

"No. But I know I will someday."

"How do you know?"

"Because Mitch said the Perseids have been coming every August for two thousand years. They are a constant, and they'll be visible here and other places next year, too. I'll see them eventually."

Ren stares at the sky for a few moments; then he stands, pulling Cole up with him. He dusts off his pants and brushes a few pebbles from the backs of Cole's thighs. Cole looks resigned now, as though he knows he's not getting what he wants tonight. Ren could let him off the hook—he could. But he needs to think. He has so many questions—for himself, for Cole—and he can't really handle hearing the answers right now.

"May I have tonight?" he asks.

"Yes. Anything."

Ren cups Cole's face in his hands and kisses him again. It's wet and beautiful, and Ren feels it down to his toes. Cole wraps his arms around him and pulls him close. When their lips part, he holds Ren protectively, as if he's fragile, as if he's something precious.

"Meet me for coffee tomorrow?" Ren asks.

"Of course. Text me when you're ready and we'll walk together."

"Okay."

As Ren makes his way back to his seat and Cole back to the stage, Alegra sings a cover of the standard "When I Fall in Love." Ren feels as though he's walking in a strange, wonderful, terrifying dream, a dream in which he gets whatever he wants, but a minute too late.

When he finds his seat, Antonio and Sarah are in their own little Nat King Cole bubble, nuzzling and squeezing each other like two kittens, just schmaltzy enough to give Ren fodder with which to tease Antonio for days. Deidre stares at the adoring couple, arms crossed, pouting. He ignores her, sits down and searches the stage for Cole, but it's just Alegra and the piano right now.

Will he come out again at all? Maybe he's losing it, too. Maybe he feels the weight of it, his whole world crashing down around him and every single fucking dream coming true all at the very same time. Maybe he's dying inside, because I couldn't tell him. Maybe he thinks I'm chickening out again, that this is just another repeat of the same story—a story that always ends in disappointment.

Ren remembers Cole singing this very song at that piano bar, Marie's Crisis, in the West Village. Cole and his Canadian boyfriend Trevor came to Manhattan for a getaway, and Ren and his then-boyfriend Miles met them for dinner. Someone suggested the piano bar, and before long they were shutting down the place, Ren and Cole taking turns singing until the piano player had enough.

A few songs before they closed up for the night, Cole handed the piano player a twenty and begged him to break the rules and play one song *not* from a musical. Ren feared the worst—Madonna or some throwback boy band tune—and so was surprised when he heard the first notes of the song. Cole sang it to the wall, to the room, to the rim of his glass, never once making eye contact with anyone—not Trevor, and certainly not Ren.

As lovers do when someone croons a romantic song, Miles squeezed Ren's hand, but all Ren could offer him was a terse smile. Would he ever find someone for whom it would be worth laying down this persistent crush, this gorgeous unnamable thing?

Alegra's voice blends with Ren's memory, the past and present in perfect harmony. After she finishes the song, Alegra excuses herself for a moment, and the band continues to riff on the classic tune. The audience assumes it's part of the show, but Ren suspects her absence has something to do with Cole, because moments later he walks back onstage, slips his guitar strap over his head and stands front and center with the other guitar players.

The band is quiet now, waiting. Before the audience has a chance to get restless, Alegra's backup singers start in on her biggest hit. Everyone is out of their seats, clapping to the beat, and as Alegra walks back onstage singing the first lines of the song, the audience goes mad. The band kicks in. Ren's eyes are glued to Cole, ever the professional. Looking at him, you'd never know he just confessed a secret he's kept half of his life.

Ren gets caught up in the song along with everyone else, lets the music take him out of his head and back into his body, into the amazing that is Alegra. The past few days have merged to become one, giant "pinch-me" moment. She is part of that moment, Alegra, this icon that is now Cole's friend, this artist whom Ren has often referred to as "genius" and "stunning" and "epic," but who is also this woman who knows all about Ren and Cole and cares about what happens to them. He could never have dreamed this night for himself.

When she finishes the song, the crowd screams and applauds. Ren wonders how far the sound will travel across the high desert.

Alegra says, "Thanks for coming out tonight, guys. Thanks for supporting Alex Marin House. We're going to end the night with "How We Loved.""

"Oh, shit," Ren says, a bit too loudly.

"What?" Deidre asks.

"This song." Ren sinks back into his seat. He looks for Cole, but he's stepped into the shadows and Ren can't see his face. Did he choose this song, too, or is it just her standard encore song?

"*I know,* this song pisses me off so much," Deidre says.

She doesn't know. How could she? She wasn't there at The Pink to witness them give in to age-old desire, to see them fall into each other, desperate with want. She didn't see them clinging to each other, sinking; she didn't see them lost in each other's eyes, twisting hands in each other's shirts, gripping. She didn't see them kiss for the very first time, then again, and again, and again, all full of heat and loss and anticipation.

Suddenly, Sarah reaches over Deidre's lap and takes Ren's hand in her own. He looks over at her, expecting a placating pity of a smile, but all he sees is love. She's not sad for him; she's overcome with happiness. It's all over her face, as though she knows this song wasn't the beginning of the end for him, but the beginning of everything that matters.

"You were there," he says, remembering, and she nods. He's so grateful for her blanket acceptance.

She pulls him closer to her, so close he's almost in Deidre's lap, and says, "It's supposed to turn your life upside down. That's the *point*."

"What the fuck is she talking about?" Deidre asks, thoroughly annoyed.

"Love. She's talking about love."

Deidre is not amused. She wiggles a bit and uses both hands to push both Sarah and Ren back into their seats. Alegra is singing her heart out. Ren listens intently, joins in when she asks the room to sing along, and lets go of the sadness this song once held for him.

The song used to be about pain, the anthem of missed opportunities and what might have been. But now it's the song he danced to with the man he loves. The song used to be about longing for the love of your life, knowing you can't change the outcome. Now, it's the song that changed everything.

Cole slumps down in the chair, his head low and resting on the edge. He needs a few minutes to compose himself before he faces the band, Gretchen, the Alex Marin House kids and board members, and anyone else with VIP privileges. Maybe Alegra will let him off the hook, let him wallow backstage in her dressing room until he can safely slink off to his hotel, alone.

He can feel the headache work its way up the base of his skull when Alegra walks into the room and shuts the door behind her.

"I'm sorry—"

She holds one hand up to stop him. "Don't. I'm not angry. I know you'll never run off the stage during a concert again. Right?"

"Right."

"Good."

Alegra faces the mirror and begins taking it all down—her hair, her jewelry, her face. He likes her dress. Classy and girly, it's a throwback to her early style, so he tells her so.

"I forgot to tell you—you looked beautiful tonight. You were amazing."

"Thank you. Hubby's here though, love, so you can lay off the flattery. He's been telling me I'm beautiful since the moment he stepped off the plane."

"Where is Stephen, anyway?"

"Chatting up some cowboys, probably. The way he romanticizes American mythology—"

"Cowboys are real, Alegra."

"Whatever," she says, winking at him in the mirror. When she's finished she stands up and says, "So are you staying in here to watch me strip down to my knickers, or are you going to face the lot outside that door?"

"May I stay here? I won't look. I'll just close my eyes."

"Turn 'round, *and* close your eyes. I'm a modest, married woman," Alegra teases.

Cole snorts. He shifts in his seat and closes his eyes, happy to be sheltered by her. He takes comfort in her quiet, steadfast support, lets it soothe his pride and allay his fears.

From across the room Alegra asks, "Gretchen is telling everyone you broke up with Liam. Is that true?"

"It is."

"And how was that, then?"

"Awful."

"I bet."

"Necessary."

"For you and for him," Alegra agrees.

"I tried to tell him yesterday, but I couldn't get through. He turned off his phone, went up to his mother's house for the weekend. He was avoiding me. He knew it was coming."

"And what did you say to make it better for him?"

"I told him I wanted to love him the way he needed me to love him, but I was wrong to try, because it was impossible."

"Did it work?"

"Of course not. There's no way to make this better, or right. I fucked up. I never should have let him love me."

"Well, it's not like you have much say in that sort of thing now, is it? But you did fuck up. Every minute you let this nonsense with Ren go on, you were fucking up. Do you not think you're worthy? Is that it? Are you punishing yourself for something?"

Cole rubs his temple, his headache worsening by the minute. "I don't know. I... there were so many different reasons for not telling Ren how I felt, I couldn't even tell you all of them."

"You can open your eyes."

He doesn't want to open them. He wants to stay here, in this chair, in this dressing room, until someone fixes everything and he can just run into Ren's arms and stay there forever. He didn't expect his confession to cause Ren to nearly pass out from anxiety. He had hoped that Ren would return his feelings, that they would both promise to take a chance, but now he's not even sure if they'll fulfill their promise of twelve days together. And if that's all over now, he'll leave his eyes closed, thank you.

When he finally does open his eyes, Alegra is fully dressed, slipping on her boots. "That was the second time Ren ran off during one of my songs. I mean, what the fuck, Cole? He's going to end up with a conditioned response—what's that experiment? You know, the one with the dog?"

"Pavlov's something or other?" Cole asks.

"Did it work, then? Did you get him back?"

"Back? We were never together—"

"Oh my lovely, I mean this in the nicest possible way: Please take your head out of your arse. You two are blind as bats, and willfully so," Alegra says, hugging him from behind. "You may not have been very good at it—distance and boyfriends and bullshit and all that—but you were most definitely together. Ask around, your prep school friends. I'm sure you'll soon discover you were in a relationship with Ren all this time, and you were the only two people who didn't realize it."

Cole stares at her, dumbfounded. He was used to imagining what it would be like to be *in* a relationship with Ren. He hoped and fantasized so much he could win an Olympic medal in pining. But he never considered the fact that he actually *was* in a relationship with Ren.

"If Ren and I have been together all this time, then someone should punch me in the face, because I've behaved terribly," Cole says.

"Don't start the self-hate crap. You'll just waste even more time sorting this out," Alegra warns.

"No, I suck. I really and truly suck."

"Come on. Let's get you back. You can order ice cream and vodka and fall asleep with your clothes on."

"That sounds disgusting. And perfect."

"I know, dear. It's never just one thing at a time, is it?"

Cole does end up schmoozing with Alex Marin House benefactors, the elite of Santa Fe society in their layers of organic fabric and twenty thousand-dollar crystal pendants. He does manage to avoid Gretchen's glare and the band's inquisitive stares, however, as he makes his way through the crowd to Sarah.

"He left," she says, anticipating his question.

"I figured."

"Thank you again for joining us last night. The kids can't stop talking about the two of you."

"It was our pleasure." Cole likes speaking for both of them, as if their lives are already intertwined.

"That was a bold move... the song."

"I tend to indulge in grand gestures."

"Hmm. Ren seems like the type of person who appreciates all things grand," she says, with a twinkle in her eye.

"Usually, yes." Cole smiles warmly at her, and then remembers an earlier conversation with Alegra. "We'll be back at The Pink on Monday night. Will you and Antonio join us?"

"Are you kidding? Hell yes, we will!"

"Great. I'll see you there, then. Do you have a way home?"

"Yes. Antonio is coming back for me. That is, if he hasn't strangled Deidre and is busy disposing of her body in Diablo Canyon."

"Is there really a Diablo Canyon, or is that just a thing?"

"It's real, and not far from here." She reads a text on her phone. "He'll be here soon, actually, so I'm covered."

"Okay. See you."

She kisses him on the cheek and gives his shoulder a reassuring squeeze before she joins Mitchell at the little post-event bar set up backstage. He wonders how much she knows. She was sitting right next to Ren the entire night. Did she let him freak out and tell her everything? Did she give him advice?

Cole is on autopilot from the moment he pulls out of the parking lot. It's a fifteen-minute drive to the Eldorado, but when he pulls up to the valet it seems as if it's only been a few minutes. His head is throbbing now, and his vision is starting to blur.

Cole knows he has maybe half an hour before he's dealing with a full-on migraine, so once in his room he goes straight to the bathroom in search of his prescription. He splashes cold water on his face, slips off his shoes and stops cold when he steps into the main room.

"Hi."

Ren is perched on his bed, eyes red from crying, legs crossed, both hands holding onto his knee. He looks exhausted: His skin is blotchy, his shoulders sag under the weight of revelation, and his hair is most definitely in need of a do-over.

He's the most beautiful sight Cole has ever seen.

"I used my key card, your key card, the one you gave me," Ren explains. "I hope that's okay."

"Of course. Yes. Absolutely." Cole doesn't make a move; he's afraid he'll spook him, and Ren will run again, like a scared animal. "I thought you wanted to talk tomorrow, over coffee."

Ren throws his hands in the air, gestures toward his disheveled state and laughs. "Cole, *Cole*... we're such fuck-ups. This is *crazy*."

Cole is on his knees in front of him in an instant. Ren uncrosses his legs and makes room for Cole to scooch up as close to him as possible. Cole places one hand on each of Ren's knees and begins rubbing them with his thumbs, in tiny circles.

"I wanted to tell you. I *tried* to tell you," Cole says, his pleas careful and quiet.

Ren takes a deep breath. "So tell me now."

"I didn't know at first. I couldn't recognize it. I thought we were just friends. The feeling I had whenever you were around, and that other feeling, when you *weren't* around, it was new, and confusing, and we were young. By the time I realized I was in love with you—*so, so* in love with you—I was worried you wouldn't feel the same. And then I was worried that if by some miracle you did still care for me, it could eventually end and our friendship would be ruined. And then at some point confessing how I really felt became this insurmountable thing—"

Ren nods. "It was easier to leave it wide open—"

"Yes, and I kept thinking, 'If he wants me, he'll tell me.' So I poked, and teased, hoping one day you'd just take the hint."

"But I never did."

"Granted, some of my hints were vague, and some were completely juvenile." Cole breaks out in a grin.

"Completely."

"I was a coward, Ren. And I'm... I'm so very sorry."

Ren touches Cole's cheek. "You were an idiot."

"I was an idiot."

"I was an idiot, too. I still am, I think."

"Why do you say that?" Cole asks, his heart in his throat.

"Because this idiot is hopelessly, madly, undeniably in love with you, and has been for a very, very long time... and, aside from admitting to a schoolboy's crush once upon a time, never did a damn thing about it."

Cole lets out a breath he didn't know he was holding. His head drops in relief, falling on Ren's thigh, and he's kissing Ren's hand—fast kisses, a dozen or more, in gratitude.

"Oh Ren, *Ren*. Say it again. Say it a thousand times."

Ren lifts Cole's head just as he did not two hours before, holds his face in his hands. But this time is different. This time he looks down on Cole with shining eyes and says, "You are so in love with me."

Cole whispers, "Yes, yes, yes."

"And I am so in love with you."

"Oh, God. *Yes.*"

Their kiss is long and deep. Cole can feel it in every cell in his body: this opening up, this rightness. When it's too much, he pulls away, plasters his face into Ren's neck until he catches his breath and then dives back in again, taking hold, slipping every secret wish into Ren's mouth as his tongue lays claim over its contours. He feels as if Ren is sucking the truth right out of him, pulling him down, down, down until they are both panting and dazed with the enormity of it all.

Let me live in this moment forever, and if this is all we have, let me die here; let me lie with this man until I take my final breath. But please, please, let there be more. Let me keep this. Please. Please.

"Please what, my love?"

"I... I didn't know I... I was praying, asking—I didn't know I said that out loud."

"You were praying?"

"I was pleading—"

"For me?"

"For more."

Ren kisses him softly, gently, his hand at the nape of Cole's neck. Cole winces; suddenly, the migraine hits him full on. He burrows his head in Ren's lap and cries out in pain.

"Migraine," he says, anticipating Ren's question. "I already took something for it."

"What do you do for it? Should I turn off the lights?"

"Bed. I need to sleep. I'll feel better in the morning."

Ren undresses Cole, pulls back the covers and helps him into bed. He pulls the curtains closed, and after undressing himself, turns off the lights and slides in next to Cole.

"May I touch your head? Would that help?"

"Just hold my hand. And stay close."

"Okay."

They lie there in the dark, listening to each other breathing, until Ren stifles a giggle.

"What's funny?"

"You tell me you love me, and I almost have a panic attack. I tell you I love you, and you get a migraine," Ren explains, giving over to laughter.

"Maybe we're allergic to confessions," Cole offers. "I know you hated it."

"Hush. Your brain hurts, remember?"

They are quiet for a moment, and just before he nods off, Cole says, "For the record, it was at Dean's Anti-Prom party, junior year. I was watching you—I was always watching you, God, could that have been a clue? You were standing with Jeremy's girlfriend, the redhead, adjusting something on her dress. She must have said something funny because you laughed. You laughed so hard you threw your head back, put your whole body into it, really, and it hit me all at once. I literally heard a voice in my head say, 'Cole McKnight, you are in love with Ren Warner.' I heard it plain as day. And that was it. You just... laughed, and I was gone. I was yours."

⚙ **Chapter 11** ⚙

When he wakes up, Cole is holding him, one arm across his waist, the other underneath him, just barely touching his back. He settles into Cole's loose embrace, listens to him breathe, watches his eyelids flutter as if trying to open. The room is cool and dark, save for slivers of the blazing New Mexico sun fighting to get in through the heavy curtains.

He wants to curl into Cole and drift off, get lost in the lazy Sunday morning they never got to have and wake up an hour or two later to Cole's soft kisses. He wants to order room service and eat it on the bed, naked, wrapped up in the sheets and Cole's smile. More than that, he wants to see Cole's face the moment he wakes and realizes Ren is with him, that he wants him, that he *loves* him. So he waits, eyes focused on the relaxed features of Cole's gorgeous sleeping face.

It's only the fourth day of the twelve he promised Cole, and already it seems as if they've been together for a lifetime. In a way, they have. He's certainly loved Cole for most of his life. He's thought about him every day.

Sometimes it's just a passing thought—walking by the ice rink at Bryant Park and wondering if Cole found a new skating partner in London, smiling into his coffee when he hears one of their old favorite songs blasting out of the Mudtruck. And always, it comes when he searches Paul's lovely brown eyes for hints of blue.

Sometimes his thoughts of Cole last longer. Sometimes he stands at the Mudtruck, or in the elevator, or in the produce section, and listens to the entire song, his mind full of honey lips, smiling; of summer-tanned arms hanging out of car windows, tapping a rhythm on the door; of the flirty tenor of Cole's voice, beckoning him no matter how many days and miles and walls he puts between them.

Then there are the days he thinks about Cole *all day long*, which usually culminate in a Meg Ryan marathon and a box of cupcakes from Magnolia Bakery. Those days are few and far between—he's had six, maybe seven all told—but they sneak up on him without warning. He'll be fine, really quite fine (thank you very much), happy, even. And then he'll suddenly have an entire day to himself with no commitments, chores or responsibilities, and by midmorning he'll be in full-on Cole mode, sorting through an old box of theater programs, silly notes and mementos.

On those days, he considers calling Cole, or texting, anything to connect and get them riled up, get them back into their thing, to get Cole thinking about *him*, but he never follows through. On these *all day long* days he'll turn off his phone, or, if necessary, march down the hall to 31B and ask Mr. Walker to hang on to it until morning. He does this because on those days, calling Cole is dangerous. On those days, he could lose everything.

The last day like that was years ago—two, maybe. As usual, nothing specific brought it on, but by the end of the day he was a complete wreck, thumbing over Cole's name in the contact list on his phone.

He tests the memory of that last day now, runs it through and around his mind. He expects it to taste like baker's chocolate and go down hard, but he finds none of that. It doesn't feel pathetic anymore, all the pining and fantasizing; their confessions have already begun to ease the pain of old habits and disappointments. What does it matter, anyway? They're here now, aren't they?

Cole wakes suddenly, eyes big and searching. As if on cue, he says, "You're still here."

"Is there anywhere else?"

Cole's smile reaches all the way to his eyes, and his arms tighten around Ren, pulling him in, close, still closer, and it's good, it's very good. He can feel Cole's excitement buzz beneath his skin, can practically hear his mind burst with little revelations—*Love! Possibilities! Sex without limits!*

He presses his face into Cole's chest and giggles at the thought, his mouth right over Cole's heart.

"What?" Cole's voice is light and teasing, but his grip is sure and firm.

"I can hear you thinking."

"You're a mind-reader now?"

"I can hear some version of what you're *probably* thinking. There are a lot of exclamation points."

Cole chuckles and kisses the top of Ren's head. Ren feels the affection all the way down to his toes. He allows himself to love this moment, to revel in it, to let it be *all* wonderful and deserved, not the slightest bit bittersweet.

"What did you dream?" Ren asks.

"Who needs dreams?"

Cole's words flip a switch. Ren lifts his head and crushes Cole's lips with his own. He licks at Cole's bottom lip, and then Cole's hands are on the back of his head, pulling him down, taking him in. They suck in each other's gasps and moans, swallow contented sighs and let them slide down their throats and seep into their bones. There is only sweetness and want now, the kind of want that makes a person feel strong, beautiful, worthy, the kind of want that is *returned*.

It feels like a first kiss.

"Hi," Cole says. One of his hands is at the back of Ren's neck, and the other presses into the small of his back. Cheeks flushed, those deep blue eyes dancing, mouth curved into a soft smile, Cole is the very definition of beauty.

"How... how do you do that? Take my breath away after all this time?" Ren asks.

"I don't know, but I'm profoundly grateful for whatever it is."

Ren burrows in and pushes close. They are quiet, content to just *wallow*. To be in Cole's arms *and* to know his heart is bliss to Ren, and he's quite sure he never really understood the meaning of that word until now.

Ren pushes up and rolls himself on top of Cole, who steadies him with both arms wrapped securely around his back. When he scoots up a bit to meet Cole's eyes, he can feel Cole getting hard, his muscles taut, his body strong and willing. Ren looks down at him, eyes sleepy and warm and so, so happy.

Cole beams. "Tell me again," he says.

"You are so in love with me. And I am so in love with you."

Cole trails two fingers down Ren's cheek, grabs his chin and pulls him in for a kiss. Deep and unrelenting, then hard little nips at his bottom lip and under his chin; this is Cole staking his claim. And with every push back, Ren goes willingly, sinking deeper into him. He lets Cole take all of his weight and hold him tight. They're both hard now, but in no hurry. They'll get to that. They'll get to everything.

Ren pulls back to catch his breath and says, "I adore you."

Cole's whole faces lights up. "Thank *God*."

"I don't want to move."

"So don't."

"Would you hold me all day?" Ren feels light-headed, giddy with the knowledge that he can ask for what he wants without fear of rejection, that he can have this.

"Oh, please, *yes*."

Cole rolls them, slips his hands out from underneath Ren and places them on either side of his head. Ren settles down into the rumpled linens. "I like this... looking up at you."

Their kiss is a tease, a promise of things to come, as Cole dips and pulls back, swoops down to nibble at Ren's shoulder. When he comes back up they've already started rocking. He can feel Cole's cock against his stomach, and reaches down to adjust them both for what's next. It's a slow build, a perfect, sweet torture, as if they've practiced this moment in dreams both day and night.

Ren bucks up, twists his hips and spreads his legs a bit. Just then Cole stops moving. He runs two fingers through Ren's hair, brushes the tip of his ear and moves down, the two fingers gently pinching Ren's earlobe. He looks down at Ren, his face at once awed and worried. "I want you to know... about Liam, I—"

"Let's not. Not right now, okay? Just keep going."

Cole hesitates for the briefest of moments and then starts up again, this time with purpose. He's holding Ren down with his weight, with the motion of his hips. It's fast and delicious and everything Ren wants.

How does he know me so well, like we're old lovers, when we've only just begun? How does he give me what I want before the thought even occurs to me?

Ren lifts one knee, shifting the angle just *so*. They're both panting now, bodies still in rhythm but faster, still faster, the drag made easier by sweat. There's so much to say, so much to ask of each other, but instead they do this. Instead, there is friction, and heat and the slide of bodies so perfectly matched.

There are no words now; just huffed breath and *uh uh uh*. Ren's hands press into Cole's back. He loves the sounds, the squishes, the skin. He loves the knock of the mattress hitting the wall, Cole's grunts as he pushes them closer to the edge. He loves all of it.

It's over in minutes, Ren tipping first and Cole following seconds after, backs arching, hands gripping, muscles straining until they both give in and give over to it.

When Cole can move, he pushes himself up and scoots down the bed until he can comfortably rest his head on Ren's belly. Ren plays with his sweat-soaked curls and says, "How's your head? All better?"

Cole laughs into Ren's skin. "I woke up with a dull ache. But, uh, after that... yeah, it's gone now."

"That's good. I was worried about you, love."

"*Love,*" Cole echoes, twisting the word in his mouth as if testing the feel of it on his tongue.

"Is that okay?"

Cole nods, buries his face in Ren's skin and rests his palm flat over Ren's belly button. His fingers play with the soft hair trailing down, and Ren can hear Cole take him in, smell him, all the sex and sweat and yesterday's soap.

"I don't remember you getting migraines," Ren says. "Just headaches from time to time."

"It started a few years ago. A gift from my mother."

"How does she deal with them?"

"Naughty little pills. They don't really work, not for a full-on migraine, but she takes them anyway. Liam says—"

Cole tenses. Ren isn't ready for Liam and Paul to enter this dreamy, all-I-ever-wanted Sunday morning bubble they've created, but he asks anyway. "What does Liam say?"

"He says I need to learn to meditate."

"You? Meditate?" Ren's laugh turns into a full-on guffaw, forcing Cole to sit up.

"What?"

"I just can't imagine it." Ren pushes up on his elbows.

"I can meditate. I *can*."

Ren twists his smile into a smirk. "Total silence. Sitting still for longer than ten minutes—"

"I could work up to it... *what*?"

"Nothing. Let's get you a book, or a video, or a guru or something." Ren pushes his toes into Cole's thighs.

"A guru?"

"I bet we could find one around here."

"I'm sure you're right. Probably a dozen."

"A whole set. A guru set," Ren teases. He loves this, the back and forth and the lazy ease of it all. It's intimate in a way they've never been before, but also entirely familiar. "Do you have to work today?"

"Tomorrow. But there's this thing tonight, at the Encantado. I should make an appearance," Cole says. "Come with me?"

"Yes."

"No hesitation, huh?"

"No."

"I like that."

"Me too."

Cole syncs his body up to Ren, hip to hip. He picks up Ren's hand and plays with it as he talks, threading their fingers together and then pulling them apart.

"It's an industry party, music execs mostly. Nothing official. Most of the guests are Mitch's old friends," Cole explains.

"Can we invite Deidre?"

"Sure, but—they've been up in Taos all weekend, some sort of spiritual retreat, so I have no idea what the mood will be."

"In other words, get Deidre to be less 'Deidre'?"

"Is that even possible?"

"Depends. If she has sufficient motivation, maybe."

"We don't have to be there until late, which means we have about..." Cole looks over at the bedside digital clock, "... nine hours to kill."

"Or use wisely." Ren swings their clasped hands back and forth between them.

"Or use wisely."

Ren squeezes Cole's hand and holds their clasped hands to his chest. "Are you going to sex me all day long, Cole McKnight?"

"I'd sure like to. But first—I do think we should talk about this."

"You mean you want to talk about them."

"This is huge, Ren. It's everything," Cole starts. "But it's also a big mess, and we have to do this right—"

"Could we wait until later, just a few hours?" Ren lets go of Cole's hand and props himself up on one elbow, his right hand tracing circles on Cole's arms. "I only just got you."

Cole stills Ren's hand, raises Ren's fingers to his lips and kisses the tips. "You've always had me."

"That's not what—"

"Shh. Of course. We'll talk later."

"Thank you."

Ren knows he's avoiding the inevitable, but it's too much to think about—leaving Paul, possibly leaving New York, possibly *not* leaving New York; becoming more of everything that matters. He can't think about all of that *and* process this remarkable, precious gift that is Cole McKnight, loving him.

From somewhere across the room he hears the telltale chirp of an incoming text message, probably from Paul. It could mean anything: Paul misses him; Paul needs Ren to help him rally; Paul has news about the deal. He hasn't been reading *The New York Times*, or listening to NPR or reading the blogs, so he has no idea if they've made any progress in Washington. The bill is so vital, so much a part of his relationship with Paul, it seems strange to be so disconnected from it now.

Ren slides out of bed to retrieve his phone and is both relieved and slightly disappointed to find the text isn't from Paul. Why did he ever think their situation was okay, with Paul gone more often than not and Ren working all hours? He scrolls through the message, and Cole motions for him to come back to bed. Ren takes his phone with him and hands it to Cole.

"Deidre. Apparently she's going for contrite today," Ren says.

Cole reads her message. "Ten Thousand Waves?"

"It's a Japanese spa just up the mountain. She stays up there whenever she's in town. I've never been."

"She must feel really guilty."

"We don't have to go. We could just stay in bed all day—"

Cole wiggles his eyebrows. "Or we could indulge in a little hot tub sex—"

"Hmm... wait. No. You can't be the first person to get that idea, which means other people have done it."

"Let's not think too hard about it or we'll never get in the water." Cole hands Ren his phone. "If you're into it, text her back and tell her we'll go. We're due for a celebration, right?"

Ren looks up from his phone, takes in Cole's gorgeous, carefree smile, and for the very first time lets his heartbeat pick up speed without concern; he lets the goosebumps rise on his skin, lets the butterflies fly free in his belly. He's allowed. It's supposed to feel this way, this crazy, inevitable, life-altering love. No more hiding, or pretending his feelings aren't real, or worthy, or true. This is that feeling: Cole under his skin and in his veins. He'll show him all of it now.

He leans in for a kiss, his lips just a breath away from Cole's, and says, "You wreck me, in the best possible way."

Cole kisses him quickly on the lips. "Soooo... yes, then?"

"Yes."

Passing through the dark, carved wooden doors, Ren is pleasantly surprised by the sophisticated, natural beauty of Ten Thousand Waves. He marvels at the wooden pagodas, the winding paths lined with wildflowers, the bright orange and golden koi swimming in clean, clear ponds, the gentle sound of bubbling water.

"Wow," Cole says, looking at the photos of tubs near the reception desk.

"What is wrong with me? This place is amazing. I should have stayed here instead of the Eldorado," Ren says.

"But then we would have missed each other." Cole tugs on Ren's hand.

"Maybe," Ren replies with a soft smile. Before Cole can respond, a fresh-faced girl with pink hair, wearing a Ten Thousand Waves T-shirt, greets them.

"Welcome to the Waves. Please sign in. Are you here for tubs or treatments?" she asks.

"Both. Our friend booked it for us. Deidre Alexander?"

Her face scrunches up before she can stop herself, and then she quickly looks down. Ren rests his arms on the counter and whispers, "We're not terrible. I promise."

The girl looks up from the appointment calendar, her cheeks pink. "I'm sorry. I just... I've never met anyone like her before."

Cole laughs and slides the sign-in book over to Ren. "Me either. Maybe we need to start a club: People Who Met Deidre Alexander and Lived to Tell About It."

The girl relaxes. "I'm Lou, by the way. I take it this is your first time at the Waves?"

"Yes, because we're idiots," Ren says.

Lou giggles and launches into the rundown of their day, then asks for their driver's licenses. She hands each of them a cream-colored cotton kimono, rolled up neatly with its belt wrapped around it. A small locker key with a numbered tile is pinned to each belt.

"Your first tub starts in twenty minutes, so you have plenty of time. Just walk out that door, make a left, and you'll find the men's room. Come back and let me know you're ready and I'll give you the key to Shoji."

"Thank you. Will you come look for us if we get lost?" Cole asks, putting on the charm.

"Oh, I... you won't get lost—"

Ren smiles at Lou and says, "Ignore him. You've been so helpful. Thanks!"

Cole winks at Lou and takes Ren's hand, guiding him through the next set of doors.

"You're always so flirty when you're happy," Ren teases.

"I only use my powers for good. She's totally going to look the other way when we return the key with crazy happy sex smiles on our faces."

Ren's breath hitches. "Cole, these tubs are *outdoor*—"

"So we'll be quiet. Or at least try to be."

"And 'crazy happy sex smiles?' Is that a thing?"

"Not yet. I just made it up. It's when you feel super relaxed and goofy at the same time. Like you didn't just have amazing sex, you had amazing sex with someone you love. Imagine the Buddha's face after he got high and then got laid."

Ren looks around at the Japanese-inspired architecture and design. There are Buddha statues everywhere: tiny Buddha hidden among succulent plants, personal shrine-sized Buddha being used as doorstops, a large Buddha holding court in the resting area.

"First to find that expression on one of the Buddha statues pays for drinks tonight," Ren says.

"I would have bought anyway."

"Or tried to." Ren turns to face Cole, leans up against the wall next to the Men's Changing Room sign and puts on his best coy smile. "And have you seen this crazy happy sex smile on me?"

Cole nods and comes in close. "Once."

"When?"

"The first night. In the hallway... after."

"Right. So it's the same smile *you* had, then?"

"The very one."

They make quick work of showering and changing into their kimonos and rubber sandals. Ren loves the smell of the yuzu shampoo, the sound of rippling water, the feeling of soft organic cotton against his skin.

After Lou explains how everything works, hands Cole the key to Shoji and gives him directions, Cole asks, "Lou–is it short for Louise?"

"Lou Ann."

"Lou Ann. Pretty name. Thank you so much, Lou."

Again, he takes Ren by the hand and leads him away.

"You're just awful. You're encouraging her to crush on a gay man just so you can get in my pants without repercussions," Ren says.

"You're not wearing pants," Cole says, guiding him on the charming, stone-covered path. "Besides, every girl needs a gay crush. We're often cute, always fun, and we're not thinking about their boobs while we pretend to listen to their life stories. We're awesome."

It's all so light and relaxed between them; so much so that Ren is shocked when, mere moments after entering the Shoji suite, Cole is on him, full-force: Cole's hands cupping Ren's ass, tugging at the belt of his robe, sliding up his chest as though he's art, as though he's a fucking wonder. It's as if he left charming Cole on the other side of the wooden door because this is first-time Cole, desperate Cole; this is too-hot-to-resist-even-though-it-will-surely-ruin-my-life Cole.

They're naked before Ren can really register what's happening or take in their surroundings. Cole has him in a tight hold, one hand at the back of his neck as he kisses him as if he's his *only good thing*. When he pulls back, he takes Ren's cock in hand and lines it up with his own, and Ren can't believe he still has the strength to stand.

Cole says, "I'm going to get us off, and then I want to fuck you deep and slow, for as long as we can take it."

Ren is so on board with hot, desperate, first-time Cole, he doesn't think twice about sliding three of his fingers into his mouth. He sucks. He slides his tongue between Cole's fingers and pulls them out of his mouth, wet.

Cole wraps his hand around them, pulling Ren in for a hard kiss. Then it's mouth on mouth, and Ren mutters, "Shit, *shit*," against Cole's lips.

The first orgasm is quick and dirty, Cole's hand moving fast and sure. When Ren comes, his knees buckle. Cole, still hard, helps him to the wooden bench and then, legs on either side of Ren's knees, brings himself off right in front of him. Cole, still standing, bends over as he comes and lets Ren take his weight.

He's had this type of sex before, this heady, too-fast, just-right sex that is all about getting off and nothing about connecting to the other person. With others he'd take a beat, straighten himself out and, after the appropriate niceties, leave to enjoy the benefits of stress relief and knots untied in the privacy of his own apartment. Now, despite the fact that this is all instinct and sweat, he feels closer to Cole than ever before.

Up until this moment, sex with Cole has been an expression of all they'd left unsaid. Burrowing his head into Cole's belly, Ren is thrilled to know that sex with his love can be this too, when they need it to be. Even their hot fuck against his hotel room wall was full of emotion and unspoken desires, so to get this base release and know that Cole is so very good at it is a relief.

Moments later, Cole, kneeling on a folded-up towel on the cedar plank deck, pulls Ren down into his lap and, after mouthing the back of his neck for a few minutes, gently pushes him forward until Ren's head is resting on another towel, his ass in the air and on display.

Cole grabs and squeezes, presses his thumbs in and pulls Ren's cheeks apart. He can feel Cole staring, and giggles when Cole mutters, "Thank you, *thank you*."

"You're welcome."

Cole laughs. "I wasn't talking to you."

Cole leans back and fumbles around for something, and then suddenly Ren has a lubed up finger in his ass as Cole whispers unintelligible nothings into his back. Dirty? Sweet? He doesn't know and it doesn't matter.

It's not long before Ren is pushing back on Cole's fingers, trying to get back into his lap. Cole pulls out, taps him on the waist and says, "Turn, baby. We're going to do this face to face."

Ren stands up and turns just in time to see Cole tearing open a condom wrapper with his teeth. He lowers himself onto Cole's lap, reaches down to pull and tease and stroke him ready. More lube and Ren is raising up, and sinking down, waiting out the pain until he can ride Cole in earnest.

"Lie back." Cole gently pushes on Ren's chest, urging him down.

"What? I thought—"

"Just lie back slowly, until you're on the floor, with me still inside of you."

"Okay... I've never done it this way before."

"Good. I was hoping you would say that," Cole says, suddenly bashful. "I haven't either. I wanted us to have a first, together. This is something I imagined doing... with you."

"And you never tried it with anyone else?"

"I couldn't. I... Ren... *Ren*—"

Ren steadies him with a kiss. He understands. It hurts too much to think about all of the lovers they've had, all of the sex they've genuinely enjoyed, all of the firsts they'll never share. But it never occurred to him that Cole would save something for him, knowing full well it might well be a fantasy he would never see fulfilled.

Ren leans back, grateful for his flexibility as his thighs stretch and his back arches. It's not that different from missionary, but with his ass high in Cole's lap and his shoulders on the floor, it's different enough that he can feel the possibilities.

As if reading his mind, Cole says, "This position is supposed to make it easier to last. And I want this to last as long as possible."

For what has to be at least an hour but seems like *days* they get close, and pull back, and get close and pull back, Cole still inside Ren, Ren hanging on by a thread. When Cole tires, Ren pushes up with his hips, riding Cole from the floor, the angle strange and perfect and new. When Ren tires, Cole holds onto his hips and fucks him slow and deep.

Ren mutters, "I can't, I just can't," too many times to count, and cries out just as often.

He loses himself at least twice, head turned to the side, body limp like a rag doll, until Cole squeezes his thighs and says, "Baby, come back, come back to me."

Cole struggles, too, holding himself back from thrusting in hard and fast and ending it all too quickly. His moans sound as if they're coming from a man past the point of no return, but he stays with it, holds them to it, sees it through. And Ren is so grateful sex with his love can also be this: a slow, sweet burn that takes him right out of his head and into bright, sweat-soaked pleasure that aches in all the best ways.

When Cole finally reaches down and pulls him back into his lap, Ren is so far gone he'll do anything to come. "Can we please?" he asks.

Cole just grunts and leans back, pulling Ren on top of him. He winces, probably from staying on his knees for so long, and struggles to get his legs out from under him. Ren lifts up, allowing Cole to move freely.

Cole stretches his legs, and then pulls Ren back down. "Come on, come on," he begs.

When he reaches behind for Cole's cock he notices the condom is loose and slipping off. "Cole, tell me you brought another condom."

"What? Yeah. In my robe. *Jesus.*"

Ren is off Cole in a second, rummaging through the kimonos. He finds two condoms and over his shoulder says, "Optimistic!"

"Now that I have reason to be, fuck yeah, I'm optimistic."

He's back on Cole's cock in under a minute, but Cole is already too far gone. He's a begging, almost incoherent mess, cursing and whining Ren's name. So Ren rides him hard, pushing him over the edge quickly and then jerking himself off in rapid strokes, Cole spent and useless, splayed out under him.

Sore in all the right places, Ren slides off Cole and rolls into his side. Cole wraps one arm around him loosely and kisses the top of his head. In the quiet, they orient themselves to the space, to the air around them, to the sound of water and faraway laughter. Ren hears the muffled sounds of other guests in the adjacent tub and realizes what they've done.

"Lou is going to kill us," he says.

"I might already be dead."

Ren laughs, and then Cole laughs, and then Ren smiles big because *this is them*. "We laugh," he says. This earns him a halfhearted "huh?" from Cole. "We laugh. That's our thing. Our sex thing. We laugh in bed, almost every time," Ren explains.

"We have a sex thing. I love that."

They hear a beep, and then Lou's voice over the intercom, located near the door. "Shoji, this is your ten-minute warning."

"Thank you!" Cole says loudly.

"I don't think she can hear you."

"God, let's hope not."

Ren says, "I can't believe we didn't use the tub at all," and they're laughing again, back to easy, back to friends; friends *in love*.

Somehow, they manage to rouse themselves, clean up, slip on their robes and make it back to the front desk in ten minutes. Ren averts his eyes, pretending to look at cucumber-scented candles while Cole turns in the key and learns where they are to go next. Just as Cole predicted, Ren can't keep the giant, goofy smile off of his face—so he holds the candle up to his nose to hide his mouth.

"In twenty minutes, you have a ninety-minute couple's massage with Paula and Rain, followed by Nightingale facials in separate rooms. Your last tub is One Wave, and you'll have to come back to the front desk to get the key."

"Thank you, Lou. You're wonderful." Cole flashes her the smile.

"Umm... you have time, if you need to, you know, shower," Lou says, her voice barely above a whisper.

"Again, thank you," he says, tugging at Ren's hand. Cole's been leading him around by the hand all day, but Ren is not complaining. The feel of Cole's hand wrapped around his own is familiar, and today, today he is happy to follow this man anywhere.

Cole is still guiding Ren by the hand when—twenty minutes later, after separate showers in neighboring stalls—Paula and Rain lead them to the small pagoda where they will likely pass out from sex-induced exhaustion. How the hell are they supposed to stay awake in the most serene place on earth... during a massage... after *that*?

The room is jade and cedar, eucalyptus and sandalwood, soft music and the Buddha, always the Buddha. They are left alone to disrobe and get on the padded massage tables. Cole, ever the gentleman, covers Ren with the thin, soft sheet before he slides in under his own.

The tables are about three feet apart, close enough. Cole reaches his arm out toward Ren, and they touch fingers, just a brush, a reminder of how it all started.

Paula, with dreads down to her ass, and Rain, with her sleeves of superhero tattoos, are both vegan-skinny yet surprisingly strong. They start on the shoulders first.

"You are super relaxed," Paula says to Cole.

"I have Mr. Jell-O over here," Rain echoes, working her way up to Ren's neck.

Thankfully, neither of the women follows the conversation to its natural conclusion. Instead, they ask safe questions: "What are your trouble spots?" "Are you just visiting?" and, "Where are you from?"

They both have the same answer to the last question: "Minnesota."

Ren is too relaxed to wonder why he didn't say *New York*, or why Cole didn't say, *I live in London*.

The ladies share their opinion of the state, make small talk, but mostly they're quiet, clearly intent on massaging Cole and Ren into a coma.

They've turned onto their stomachs and are both receiving a most awesome thigh rub when Ren opens his eyes to find Cole staring at him. This time, it's Ren who reaches out his hand, and Cole who takes it willingly. It's a brief moment, but long enough for Paula to mutter, "Aww," which sparks Rain's next question.

"So how long have you two been together?"

They both answer at the same time.

Ren says, "Seventeen hours."

Cole says, "Three days."

It's the first time they've acknowledged their relationship publicly. Ren feels Rain's hands still, momentarily, and then pick back up again as she moves down to his feet. He can practically see her next question in the air, like a thought bubble above her head, the words "What's the story?" in Comic Sans font.

Ren says, "Fourteen years, three days and seventeen hours, give or take a few months."

"There's a story there," Paula says, beating Rain to the punch.

Rain bounces on her heels. "I bet it's epic."

Cole smiles at Ren and says, "It is."

Ren falls asleep during his facial, leaving the warm cocoon of the treatment room in a daze. He wants to get Cole, go back to the hotel and sleep for days. He finds him in the resting area, sound asleep. The teak chaise is built for two, so Ren climbs in next to him and dozes off to the sound of people chatting, wind chimes in varied tones and water bubbling in a nearby fountain.

He wakes to the sound of Lou's soft voice, trying to wake them. Ren looks at her through half-lidded eyes.

"Do you want to just skip your last tub?" she asks.

"No. I'd like to actually get in a tub while we're here," Ren says without thinking. "I mean... yes, we'll take our slot."

Lou blushes and hands him the key to One Wave. "It's just around the corner, much closer to the waiting area than Shoji," she says, her cheeks a bright shade of pink. "And you only have forty-five minutes this time."

"I understand. Thank you, Lou."

She smiles warmly at him. Ren kisses Cole awake.

"How long was I out?"

"Don't know. Our tub is ready."

They walk silently, side by side, to One Wave: a sunken wooden tub, also teak, with a deck and benches. It's not as elaborate as Shoji, but the view of the mountains is spectacular.

Once in the water, Ren pulls Cole to him, wraps his arms around his waist and holds him loosely, back to chest.

Ren is waking up. From the moment he ran into Cole, he's been peeling off layers of sleep, wiping the film from an old picture that tells the story of his life. Here, in this healing place, in this "Land of Enchantment," Ren feels as though, up until this very moment, his life has been a very long dream, a dream in which he kept forgetting to show up.

"I'm beginning to understand why people come to Santa Fe and never leave," Ren says. "It feels like I could be anyone here. This place doesn't even feel real."

When Cole chuckles, Ren looks down at Cole, eyebrows raised. "What?"

"You don't like it here," Cole says.

"I never said that."

"You were counting the days until you could leave."

"I was counting the days because that's all we had," Ren corrects. He fights the worry creeping in, pushes aside the small reminder that they are more than this moment, that they both have ties, and promises and hearts to break. He wants *this*, without everything else. He wants this day, this moment, this life, to be all there is, and all there ever was.

"Not anymore." Cole pulls Ren's arms to fit tightly around him.

"No. Not anymore."

They stay that way for some time, silent, until Cole turns in Ren's arms and kisses him. It's a tender kiss, a kiss that says, *I have everything I want, and everything I want is you.* Ren feels himself getting hard again, and reaches down between Cole's legs. He needs more than water to work him open, but he lost track of the lube in Shoji.

"Hang on." Cole raises up and leaning over Ren to reach for his kimono. Ren sucks on one nipple while he strokes Cole's cock, and this time when Cole comes back in for a kiss it's sloppy and wet.

"Are we really doing this again?" Ren asks.

"Fourth time's the charm." Cole lifts to give Ren easy access to his ass. He holds Ren's head to his chest while Ren fingers him open.

"Turn around," Ren says, his voice just barely loud enough to be heard over the sound of the jets.

Cole holds his gaze for a moment and turns to face the cedar wall, kneeling on the tub's interior bench. He bends over, resting his belly on the edge of the tub. When Cole's hot skin touches the hard deck he flinches and says, "Cold, *fuck.*" The sun is low and the desert air cool.

Ren covers him, skin to skin, chest to back, and rubs his hands down Cole's arms, back and forth, for friction. Cole relaxes, presses himself flat, and after a moment, Ren whispers in his ear, "Better, love?"

"*Yes,*" Cole exhales.

"Lift your right leg, like this," Ren says, slipping his hand under the water and down the back of Cole's thigh, pushing gently when he reaches the tender spot behind his knee. Cole lifts his leg without resistance, rests his foot on the bench and looks over his shoulder at Ren.

"How long do we have?" Cole asks.

"I have no idea. I've completely lost track of time," Ren replies, pressing soft, wet kisses to Cole's back.

"She'll give us a warning," Cole reminds him, pushing back on him a bit. "Just do it."

Ren slips a condom on and eases into Cole, but he has no intention of going slow. Within minutes Cole is back to cursing, and Ren is fucking him hard and fast. The fact that he knows just what to do to make Cole whimper and beg, to get him off quickly and well, almost stops him cold.

I know him like a lover knows. I know what he likes. I know the sounds he makes, the way his eyes roll back and then close tightly when he comes. I know how he takes it, how he needs it, how he loves it. I know his body, and now I'm sure of his heart.

They're halfway out of the tub, building up to it, trying to be quiet, when they hear the intercom beep, followed by Lou's voice. "One Wave, this is your ten-minute warning.... but, umm... if you need an extra five, that's cool."

Ren picks up the pace, chasing it with everything he has. Cole pushes back on him, and lifts up a bit to fist his own cock.

"*Ren*... fuck! See... *ahh, oh God*... see what a little charm... gets you?"

He can feel a giggle snaking up his chest along with his orgasm, and he can't do both, *he can't.*

"Stop, just... let me... *shit,* Cole. *Cole.*"

He buries himself in Cole in one, long thrust. "Yeah, that's it, baby," Cole says, and Ren comes hard, still fucking into Cole, still giving him what he knows he needs.

His head resting on Cole's back, Ren keeps up as best he can and whispers, "I am so in love with you."

With that, Cole comes on the deck, his back arching, lifting Ren up even further out of the water.

"Damn, you're strong," Ren says, the words pressed into Cole's skin.

Cole chuckles and says, "I love you, too."

⊞ **Chapter 12** ⊞

The Encantado is luxe and gorgeous, and the outdoor patio Mitchell's friends reserved is pure heaven. They're all crowded around the massive round fire pit, some on the oversized creamy, crescent-shaped "couch," some milling about, feet too close to the fire. Most are from L.A. or New York; all are "searchers" looking for meaning in wild sunsets, in the art and traditions of Native people, in this sacred desert. They're hoping to see a meteor shower, a sure sign that they're on the right track, that their lives are on purpose, that they matter.

Ren sits next to Mitchell, one ear on his conversation with Alegra and one eye on Cole. He watches as Cole shakes hands with a short, young, dark-haired man in brand-new cowboy boots he'll probably forget he owns after this trip.

"Who's that?" he asks Mitchell, leaning into his space.

"Shep Vasovic. He's the kid behind Scout."

"He doesn't look like a kid."

"He does to me."

"Scout. That's a record label, right?"

"No. That's *the* record label."

"So he wants Cole to produce?"

"Nope." Mitchell takes a drink of his beer, and looks at Ren as though he's noticing him for the first time. "Maybe you can convince him."

"Convince him of what?"

"To take the deal. Shep's been trying to get Cole to sign on for the past year, but he refuses."

Ren looks over at Cole. He's talking with his hands in big sweeping gestures. Shep grins, pats Cole on the back, and they go their separate ways. Ren's eyes track Cole as he tends to Deidre, caught up in a pointless flirtation at the edge of the party. Cole leans in to ask her something, his hand on her arm, and she laughs, really laughs, and there's that feeling again.

Cole, so charismatic, so genuine, so magnetic, mesmerizes Ren. He looks especially good tonight—tight, black tailored pants and an indigo V-neck cashmere sweater, summer weight. He's pushed up his sleeves to his elbows, showing off his delicious forearms. Ren watches him order drinks at the bar, slip a large tip into the giant tumbler on the rail. He watches him smile, take notice, compliment, listen. Ren lets himself stare, lets his body feel loved and important, lets the day be what it is: the beginning of *the rest*.

He's so wrapped up in the gorgeous *everything*, so completely sated with life, that when Cole returns, drinks in hand, he doesn't think twice about leaning over and kissing him on the neck, just below his ear. Cole returns the kiss, this time on the mouth, and Ren scoots back against the seat and closer to Cole, his right leg almost in Cole's lap.

"Hi," Cole says.

"Hi."

"You're half asleep. Let me take you back."

"No, I'm fine. Just relaxed. Very, *very* relaxed."

In the fire pit the flames race up toward the stars, taking him back to the bonfire that Homecoming night when he told Cole, "I like you, like... a lot. Like, more than friends."

Cole, the firelight reflecting on his face, had looked so shocked that Ren had to fight the urge to play it off as a joke. Instead, he pressed on: "I think about us, being together. Do you... think about me?"

It took everything, making that confession at sixteen. And even though he knew there was a good chance Cole wouldn't return his feelings, Cole's gentle, dumbfounded rejection stung. Cole shuffled his feet, looked down at the ground and said, "Isn't best friends enough? Because to me it's... the best thing ever and—I'm so sorry, Ren."

Cole's touch brings him back to this day, these flames, this love. He gives Cole a lazy smile and is rewarded with a squeeze on the thigh.

Letting his eyes wander, Ren notices a man—tall, mid-forties, definitely gay—watching them from a group of newcomers who are standing off to the side. When he realizes Ren has caught him, he takes it as an invitation and walks over to them, squeezing between Ren and Mitchell.

"You probably don't remember me, but we met last year, at the HRC Gala," the man says, reaching out his hand. "Jakob Winters."

Ren sits up a bit, shakes his hand and instinctively slides his leg away from Cole. "I'm sorry, I don't recall meeting you. But don't take it personally. I met a lot of people that night. This is my friend, Cole McKnight."

"Nice to meet you, Jakob," Cole says.

His eyes still on Ren, Jakob shakes Cole's hand and says, "Likewise. I'm sorry if this is inappropriate, but I have a copy of *New York Magazine* in my house with an article about Paul James, and I could swear you're in it. There's a picture of you and Paul in the kitchen you renovated, the one with the punched tin backsplash?"

Ren freezes. He can feel Cole tense up beside him. He takes a sip from his drink, then another, and finally says, "Yes, that was me. You have a good memory."

"Oh, I just covet that kitchen, is all," Jakob says, looking uncomfortable.

"I love that kitchen," Ren says.

"It is a great kitchen," Cole adds.

"You've never—did you read the article?" Ren asks Cole.

Cole turns to look at Ren and says, "I might own a copy."

"Look, I just wanted to say I'm in awe of the work you and Paul are doing for the community, and I'm grateful. I really am," Jakob says.

"Thank you. Paul's the crusader, but I do my part."

The tension is thick and awful, but Jakob doesn't seem to be motivated to move. Ren is just about to stand up and make excuses for leaving the party early when Jakob says, "You're lucky, you know? To have someone like Paul. I think you should know that other people... we look up to Paul, and you... other people want what you have."

His words run like ice-cold water down Ren's spine. Suddenly overcome with anxiety, he focuses on keeping his gaze steady, his hand still on the glass, his voice even. "I do know that... I don't need a reminder."

Jakob looks pointedly at Cole. "I think you do."

Ren is speechless, squirming, ready to leap off the couch and run all the way back to the hotel when Cole puts his hand on Ren's knee and squeezes. He turns to Jakob and says, "Haven't you ever loved someone so deeply it defied reason?"

Jakob is stunned; that is clearly *not* what he expected to come out of Cole's mouth.

"Jakob, it's amazing that you care so much about Paul and Ren, but trust me when I say, as cliché as it sounds, this is not what it looks like."

Jakob stammers, "I have eyes. I'm not stupid—"

"I'm not insinuating that you are. I'm just stating a fact. This. Is not. What it looks like. This is something rare, and perfect and *inevitable*. This is something we've wanted for nearly half of our lives. You think you're looking at a train wreck. But what you're really seeing is an answered prayer."

Ren is torn between the urge to smack Cole to get him to stop talking and a desire to climb right into his lap. Jakob looks down at his hands, mutters something Ren can't make out and stands to leave.

"I'm sorry I'm not who you thought I was," Ren chokes out.

"So am I."

Ren doesn't watch him leave. Instead he gets up and walks over to the darkest edge of the patio, away from prying eyes. He can feel Cole's approach. He knows what he'll say before he says it. Cole takes Ren's hand, turns it over and presses into Ren's wrist with his thumb, back and forth, back and forth, back and forth.

"Baby, it's time."

Ren sucks in a breath, lets it out slowly and says, "I know."

It's after two a.m. when Cole slips out of bed, pulls on a pair of jeans, grabs a blanket from off a nearby chair and quietly exits his room. He can't sleep; the complete joy of the day is marred by words left unsaid, like the sound of a beeping alarm punctuating a lovely dream. They had agreed it was time to talk about what they had done, and who they would end up hurting, and how they should move forward; but now it looks as though that talk will have to wait until morning.

By the time they'd made it back to the hotel, Ren was asleep. He used all of his remaining energy to walk to Cole's room and dump his clothes on the floor before falling on the bed. Cole slid into bed next him, kissed his shoulder, his hair, his hip. The heady smell of herbal massage oil still lingering on Ren's skin brought him back to the day, the day to end all days, the first day of their forever. They'd waited long enough to have the "hard talk," but he couldn't bring himself to disturb Ren's sleep. So he lay there, eyes trained on the rise and fall of Ren's chest, waiting.

Now, standing in the elevator, he wishes he could skip to the next part, just pass right over all of the mess and hurt that is sure to come. He can't believe that his life was made in just four days, but he knows for sure now that he and Ren are meant to be. *What you're seeing is an answered prayer.* When he said that to Winters, when he told him that he and Ren were inevitable, he could feel every last lingering doubt leave him. He hoped it was for good.

He's not sure why he feels so entitled; it's never been his way. But he *does* feel entitled... entitled to Ren's love, his body, his future, his everything. He'll make amends to Liam somehow, and Paul, well, he'll find a way to apologize to him someday.

He and Ren have been so very stupid for so very long, and unfortunately included others in their cowardice; but damn if he is going to let him go now.

Stepping onto the roof—all clay colors and big sky—Cole realizes he forgot his jacket in the room. The cool air hits his skin like a slap. He's always surprised to feel the chill of the desert at night, the way it comes on unexpectedly and obliterates the warmth of the day, as if the sun in all of its certainty never shone at all.

He wraps the blanket around his shoulders and tries to imagine a future with Ren, a future with Ren as *his*. He's never let himself really think about it seriously, not since they were kids. Would he move to New York, or would Ren follow him to London? Would they start fresh, someplace new? Would they get married and raise children together? Would they stay the course with their careers, follow new dreams, or dig up the old wishes and put them back together again?

New dreams and old wishes. Earlier that night at the party, when Shep asked for the millionth time if he'd sign on to Scout, Cole shocked them both by agreeing to meet with him before Shep went back to L.A., after his trip out to Bandelier. Though he fought it for years, he's thrilled by the thought of finally doing what he always wanted to do, the thought of dusting off old songs and writing something new, something for Ren.

The old songs are for Ren, too. They are all for Ren, which is why he kept his notebooks and sheet music locked away in a box marked "Taxes." This is also why, rather than share them with friends, instead of recording them and releasing them into the world, he played his songs at pubs frequented by people who would never ask him for more information than he was prepared to give.

He sang and played and was met with warm smiles and misty eyes on faces he didn't know and would not likely see again, faces of people who somehow knew his dormant heart as they knew their own.

He sang and played, and in these unfamiliar faces he recognized his own regret, shared knowing looks with strangers who doodled remembrances of unrequited love on cocktail napkins, their hands, an empty envelope.

He sang and played and felt the room fill with sweet nostalgia, bodies gently swaying, worn boots tapping, hands interlacing, as those listening remembered their own sweet moments, their own top-down Friday nights, their own days of possibility.

And once in a great while he looked out among the sea of faces and saw him. *Ren.* There would be a young man about the right age, with similar hair or some other shared trait: long legs, broad shoulders, blond hair falling down over his pointed stare. He'd look at this stranger and see Ren. He'd sing for him—not *to him*, because that would be creepy and weird—he'd sing for the stranger, the stranger who was Ren, with a voice charged with purpose: to make sure *this* Ren knew how much he loved *his* Ren... how much he loved the man who was *almost* his.

On these nights, so rare and emotionally charged, the audience would be on their feet demanding more, always more, and he would stare at the floor and let their applause and praise wash over him until he felt seventeen again, until the memory of playing for a boy he always loved and could have had settled into his bones, until he could look up out into the crowd and see *him*, clapping and smiling and looking at Cole as though he were the best thing ever.

Later, after he sipped on drinks given by his one-night-only fans, he'd turn off his phone and hide it in his guitar case for the long walk home, because nothing good could come from giving in to desperation in the middle of the night.

Maybe I'll say yes. Is it really possible to get everything you always wanted? It seems like too much, to get Ren and the music. Could I be this lucky?

He feels something vibrate in his pocket, and realizes he left his phone in his jeans when he chucked them earlier.

Ren: Where are you?

Cole: Rooftop.

Ren: Don't jump. ;)

Cole: Funny. Talk me down.

Ren: Sleeping.

Cole: Good thing I'm not really suicidal.

Ren: Very good thing.

Cole: Come on. Give me all the reasons.

Ren: You have a great ass.

Cole: That's supposed to keep me from hypothetically jumping to my death?

Ren: You have a great ass and I want to touch it.

Cole: Better. What else?

Ren: You have a great ass and I want to touch it forever?

Cole: Okay. You convinced me. I'll stick around.

Ren: Good. I love you.

Cole: Are you awake enough to find your way?

Ren: Coming. Wait for me.

Cole looks out over the edge onto the ancient city below. As they usually are at this time of night, the streets are dead, just the occasional bar patron walking home. Even from here, in the center of the city with lights from adobe buildings fighting for dominance, the sky is full of stars.

He settles into a chaise lounge, narrower than the one he had shared with Ren earlier that day at Ten Thousand Waves, and stares up at the moon. In Santa Fe it's so easy to forget about everyone else looking at the same moon, everyone who will surely find fault with his actions, everyone who will be shocked to discover he's not one hundred percent gentleman after all.

He goes through the list of people who will understand, who won't even ask him for an explanation. His fellow Bennies: Dean, for sure, and

Jeremy. And Ryan, his friend from college who heard one too many of Cole's drunken confessions *not* to understand. It's an awfully short list, and soon Cole is wondering why he insists on making mental lists to feel better when they so rarely help.

The door to the rooftop squeaks and he turns to see Ren padding toward him wearing a pair of Cole's sweatpants and one of his Berklee T-shirts.

"Shove over," he says, climbing in next to him. He scoots in close, throws an arm and a leg over Cole and ends up with his body half on the chaise and half on Cole. "Should I ask why we're up here, or is it best if I don't?"

"I come up here when I can't sleep," Cole says. "I was just thinking about who will support us when they hear about us. I only came up with three people, besides Alegra."

He slips his hand under Ren's T-shirt and traces circles on his back.

"Does it matter? I mean, I know you're worried about what other people will think—"

"I'm not worried."

Ren lifts his head so that Cole can see him roll his eyes, and plops back down onto Cole's shoulder, tucking his head in under Cole's chin.

"You're not used to people not liking you," Ren says.

"You think people will stop liking me?"

"They might. I'm fully expecting judgment and recrimination from all camps."

"You would," Cole teases.

"I'm a realist. You're not."

"Come on. It's not that black and white. You're here with me, really *with me*, and I think that it took at least a little bit of idealism to admit you love me."

Ren lifts his head again, stares directly into Cole's eyes and says, "No. I had no choice. It wasn't some sort of... perfect hope that made me finally admit it. There was no coming back from what we started. You see? Realist."

"Maybe I am idealistic, I don't know." Cole takes a deep breath, unlocks his eyes from Ren's and looks up at the moon. "I left Liam."

Ren sits up immediately, pulling away from Cole. "You what?"

"We broke up. *I* broke us up."

"Please don't tell me you broke up with your boyfriend over the phone."

"I couldn't very well get on a plane, and I had to tell him, so I could—"

"When? We've been together almost nonstop—"

"Saturday, before the concert."

Ren pushes off of Cole and swing legs over the side of the chaise. He looks down at his hands and whispers, "So you could tell me you love me."

"Yes."

"Shit, Cole. Shit. Shit. Shit." Ren stands up and starts to pace around the swimming pool, the floodlights casting shadows on his face. "What did you say to him? Is he okay? Did he argue with you?"

"Not really, he just—"

"What is he going to do now? Did he cry? Oh my God, I'm going to be sick. *What were you thinking*, Cole? Shit!"

"Do you want me to tell you?" Cole lets the blanket fall as he sits up and forward in the chaise.

"You should have told me *before* you told him!"

"Why?"

"So I could tell you not to tell him!"

"I would have done it anyway. It was the right thing to do."

"No, telling him in person would have been the right thing to do. This is just... Cole. *Cole*. He deserves better than that, *more*. I can't believe.... *Shit*."

Ren looks at Cole and shakes his head, backing up toward the edge of the roof all the while. "Did you... did you tell him about me?"

Cole hops off the chaise and crosses to Ren in two seconds. He takes him in his arms, squeezes, makes little shushing noises and tries to calm him down, but when Ren pulls back, his eyes are wild, as though he can't stop the worry. "Did you? Did you tell him?"

"No. He guessed."

"He guessed you were having an affair with your old dorm buddy who you just happened to run into while staying at the same hotel?"

"He guessed that I was in love with someone else. He doesn't know it's you. He wasn't happy about it, and it wasn't pretty. I let him scream at me and copped to all of it. The first mistake I made was trying to be with someone other than you, and he knew. He *knew*."

Stepping back from Ren, Cole steadies himself. He rests his hands on the wall at the edge of the roof, the rough stucco pressing uneven patterns into his skin. He hasn't seen this side of Ren since the night he threw Caleb out of the bar. Not wanting to disrupt the gathering any further, Ren had put on an air of relative calm all night, until the door to the apartment he shared with a roommate shut behind them and Cole was met with Hurricane Ren. He couldn't tell Ren what he saw in the bathroom that night—Caleb pounding into a barely-legal, watered-down version of his gorgeous, amazing, perfect boyfriend—so he put up with the hurricane that was Ren pacing and yelling at him, begging to know why, until they were both too tired to stay awake.

Ren runs his fingers through his hair, pulls on the hem of Cole's T-shirt and does his best to fight back what looks like a flood of tears. He looks at Cole with the same pleading expression he wore that night all those years ago, asking for answers, willing Cole to make everything okay.

"Ren, they have to know. We never should have involved them in the first place—"

"What's that supposed to mean? You're saying I shouldn't have dated Paul, or anyone, or said yes to Paul's proposal, because I can't shake my love for you? Is that it? I was supposed to just wait for you and never love anyone? Never have a family, or anything real, just because we were idiots and couldn't get our shit together?"

Ren is pacing again now, his hair wild. He wipes away a few stray tears before they have a chance to stain his face. "I have a *life*, Cole, a whole life... I can't just break that over the phone. I can't... Paul is in D.C., and he needs to know I'll be there when he comes home. He can't fight this fight alone. He can't deal with a breakup when he's so close to winning, Cole. He can't. I *can't*. I'm sorry."

The truth hits him harder than the thought it would. Cole knew Ren may not want to tell Paul right away, that he might ask for time to sort things out, but this is so much more than that. This is Ren in mourning for his other life, afraid to leave it, afraid to embark on a new life with a man he may not fully trust, a love he's only just received.

It's then that he realizes the difference between them: Cole never pretended he could make a substitute life without Ren, while Ren tried like hell to make something worthy and beautiful of his life without Cole.

"Baby, listen. Come here. Please," Cole says, holding out his arms.

Ren comes willingly, drawn to him like a magnet, and lets Cole wrap him up and hold him tight.

"I understand it's not simple, and maybe I was wrong to tell Liam over the phone, but it's done now, and I don't regret it. Could we just... make a plan for you to tell Paul? I need to know what comes next. I need to know when I'll see you again, when we can be together."

Ren is quiet for a few minutes, resting. He wraps his arms around Cole's waist and pulls his arms up around his back, much as he did during their first dance at The Pink.

"I'll tell him when I get back to New York," Ren says, in a voice so soft Cole can barely hear him.

"And when will I see you again?" Cole asks, his heart in his throat again.

"Will you come to New York? Can you get away?"

"When?"

"After I tell him. Will you come as soon as I call you?" Ren lifts his head. Cole still sees worry behind Ren's eyes, but he's calmer now, and there is no trace of anger.

"We have maybe two more weeks of work before Alegra's album is finished. I'll come as soon as we're done. Even if you haven't told him yet, I'll just fly to New York and wait. I'll wait until you call me and then I'll come for you. Okay?"

"Okay. Yes."

He gives Cole a soft kiss and Cole decides that all of their future arguments should be fought while intermittently hugging and kissing. He laughs at the image of Ren squirming to escape Cole's grasp, turning his head away from kisses with a huff. It's the first picture of a proposed future with Ren that he's allowed himself to see, one not likely ever to happen, but he's grateful for the thought. They have so much to negotiate, so much to discover about each other—how they'll fight, how they'll solve problems, how they'll divide up responsibilities, how they'll stand for each other against the world.

I'm ready for all of it, even if it means living with Hurricane Ren, or any other less-than-wonderful side of my love, my man, my heart. I'll take all of him, thank you.

When Cole gazes up at the moon this time, he sees what he's been waiting for. "Look up," he says, hand under Ren's chin.

There they are. The Perseids: meteors shooting across the sky every few seconds, like dozens of wishes coming true. He watches as Ren's eyes turn from worry to wonder. His grip on Cole loosens and he relaxes into it, leans against Cole without fear of falling, a smile forming at the corner of his lips.

Ren kisses him again. "What if I hadn't said it back?"

"Hmm?"

"You broke up with Liam before you knew for sure if I loved you."

"I had to take the risk. I wasn't going to miss my chance with you again, no way. I needed to cut off all other possibilities, and it wouldn't have been fair to Liam if I told you I loved you before letting him go."

They both look up at the sky. Cole counts under his breath. "One, two... three... four... there's five—"

"Six... and seven."

"Eight—"

"It looks like a Disney movie," Ren quips. "You know, the logo right before the movie starts?"

"It does. Nine... there's ten—"

They settle back into the chaise longue and count meteors while huddled under the blanket. With each one that falls, Cole tries to push down the uneasy feeling that they might not be together right away, that Ren might want to wait until Paul wins his fight. For now, he'll take every second he can get with Ren and hope that Ren too will be willing to risk everything for Cole. Until then, he'll wait.

"Beautiful," Ren says, after they've lost count, the first pink of sunrise coming up on the horizon. He kisses Cole's cheek in thanks, as if he had ordered the Perseids just for Ren. "I can't believe we get to see this."

Cole returns the kiss, this time on the lips, and says, "I knew they'd come."

They've taken over three tables on the outdoor patio at The Pink: the band, Mitchell, Gretchen and Alegra; and Cole and Ren with their guests, Deidre, Antonio and Sarah. Ren is deep in discussion with Alegra, while Cole listens to Sarah share Alex Marin House success stories, her face lit up with pride. He hasn't seen Ren all day—both of them busy with their respective projects—which is why he's been holding Ren's hand under the table since the moment they sat down.

He wants to lock it down, the next steps for everything, the where and the how. He wants a written plan detailing the logistics of merging two lives; he wants to make it official. But where he was living on the periphery of his life in London, enjoying Liam's friendship and loving presence but never counting on forever, Ren is fully enmeshed in his life with Paul. He knows that the thought of untangling two lives held up as an example for all of New York to see is overwhelming for Ren, and complicated, so he doesn't push. Instead, he just holds his hand and tries to stay rooted in the moment.

The sun is setting, the band's cue to move inside to the back room and set up, but Cole still won't let go of Ren's hand. He nods politely at Sarah's enthusiastic tales and asks questions, but all he wants to do is lean into Ren and nuzzle his neck, ask him to dance, find a corner and kiss him slow and sweetly until the ice melts in their glasses and their friends have all gone home.

"Thank you for telling me! It changed my life, too, you know," Alegra says, loud enough for Cole to hear.

"I remember. You said that in your Grammy speech," Ren says.

"Oh God, you were one of those kids watching at home, weren't you?"

"Guilty," Ren says, and Cole doesn't have to see Ren's face to know he's blushing.

"Was it your song, then? Did you sing 'How We Loved' for days, thinking of our poor Cole?" she asks. Cole tunes Sarah out in favor of hearing Ren's answer.

"You would think, right? But it wasn't. I love the song, of course—"

"Of course. Jesus fuck, Ren, everyone loves that song. I don't need you to love it, too," Alegra teases.

"But I do, now for different reasons," Ren says, touching her arm as though they're old friends. "I'm sorry, I still can't get over the fact that I'm having a conversation with *Alegra*."

"I'm sitting right here, you know. Just a person." She's smiling, and Cole can tell that she's impressed with Ren.

"Sorry. Yes. It takes some getting used to," Ren says, blushing again.

"It's fine. Cole looked a wreck the first few months I knew him, always standing at attention like some military school brat."

"It wasn't a military school. It was a Catholic school," Cole says, over Ren's shoulder.

Alegra rolls her eyes. "Whatever."

She flashes him a big smile and then gives him a look. He knows that look. It's the same look she gets when she's about to surprise him, or prank him, or embarrass him in front of thousands of people.

After Alegra takes the stage again, everyone moves back inside. Ren claims a table for six and Cole tilts his head at Deidre and motions for her to join him at the bar.

June is minding the store tonight in full bouffant, her eyes made up like peacock feathers. She winks at him and says, "Champagne?"

"No. Margaritas. Two, no salt."

"I thought you were celebrating," she says, a twinkle in her eyes.

"Celebrating what?" Deidre asks.

"That he got what he wanted, that he's his, and vice versa, all that good stuff," June says.

"What's she talking about?" Deidre asks, clearly annoyed with June's big hair and cryptic, all-knowing self.

"Deidre, this is June. And she's about to tell me she told me so," Cole says, laughing.

"Well, I did. So how about a little champagne on me, then?"

"Pour one for Ren, too," Cole says.

"But of course."

He's about to walk the champagne over to Mitchell's table when he notices Ren excuse himself and answer his phone.

Deidre turns to see what he's looking at and says, "It's Paul. I can tell by the way he's holding the phone."

Cole watches, his irritation growing with every passing minute. He gulps down half of his champagne and sets the glass down on the bar. He's suddenly quite desperate to know what Ren is saying. Paul is amazing—great-looking, accomplished, devoted, not afraid to love Ren, to tell him how he feels, to promise him forever. Cole's only just getting around to all of that; he's acutely aware of his disadvantage.

"Comparison is the thief of joy," June says suddenly, topping him off. "Roosevelt said that, so don't go thinking I'm a genius or anything."

"Franklin D.?" Cole asks, his eyes still fixed on Ren. He looks for clues in his posture, his stance, the way he grips the phone.

"Teddy."

"So you're saying I'm stealing my own joy?" Cole turns to look at her at last.

"Well, you're a human being. That's what we do."

"Who the fuck *are* you?" Deidre asks.

"I'm June, as this lovely man already told you. And you, my dear, sad woman, are too wrapped up in the consequences of your own fucked up choices to listen to anything about anyone but yourself."

The guests applaud as Alegra finishes the song. Cole makes a break for it, avoiding the storm brewing at the bar. He takes Ren's champagne, walks over to him and places it in his hand. Ren, still on the phone, looks surprised to see him and a little guilty. Cole ignores it and smiles. He knows what he has to do. He finds his guitar in with the gear, and looks over to Alegra. Like June, she winks at him, and that's all the encouragement he needs.

Alegra waves him over to the stage. "Hush up, now. No more chatter. We've got something unbelievably special happening right now," she says to the crowd. "Our Cole has been holding out on us for years, but it seems he found his balls and now we get the rare gift of hearing a Cole McKnight original."

From the stage he can see Ren's mouth agape. He's off the phone in seconds. Cole pulls a stool over and adjusts the microphone. "She sure is short," he jokes, and the audience laughs off their secondhand nerves.

"I don't usually sing in front of people I know, unless I'm backing up this lady," he begins, nodding toward Alegra. As he speaks, he tunes his guitar. "But I wrote this song for a dear friend when I first moved to London. He's the love of my life and he's never heard me sing it. And since he's here tonight, I thought I'd give it a try. Are you all good with that?" he asks the audience.

Really, he's asking Ren. He can hear Antonio's "Damn right!" and June's high-pitched hoot in the chorus of yeses. Ren stays rooted in his spot.

The moment Cole starts playing the simple melody, the easy strumming takes him over and he's not afraid. Everything is open and on the table now, and he can share this song with people who know his story, his laugh; he can sing this song for Ren without concern that he'll mess it up.

Ren walks toward him slowly, tentatively, his hands in his pockets. He's looking at Cole as if he's seeing him for the first time, as if he's a mystery, and Cole realizes that Ren hasn't heard Cole sing in years, not since Dean's bachelor party.

Out of the corner of his eye, he sees Antonio wrap his arms around Sarah from behind as they sway together. June, who has hopped up onto the bar, swings her legs next to Deidre who, for the moment, seems to be less annoyed than usual.

Ren continues toward the stage. Cole sings right to him. Alegra, who has been standing back with the band, joins him on the chorus, careful not to overpower his voice. A few people find their way to the dance floor, but most stay in their seats, listening, watching Ren and Cole as they move toward each other, one in body, one in voice.

He needs this; he needs Ren to know that they weren't just words. *I can't remember a time when I wasn't in love with you.* He needs him to understand that no matter how difficult the transition is, no matter how long he has to wait for Ren to let go of everything he's built, his plans and his compromises and everything wrong and right about Paul and their love, he'll wait. He'll wait forever.

The song has a simple chorus; he can see people mouthing the words as the song picks up and fills the room. Just a few feet from the stage, Ren smiles in wonder, places one hand over his heart and sings along.

⚏ Chapter 13 ⚏

Home Depot is packed for a Tuesday morning. When they arrived, Ren pushing an unwilling Deidre toward the entrance, he spotted one of the men from his paint crew walking out with what looked like four gallons of Lavender Morning (*ugh*). Despite Ren's frustration, he didn't chase the man down to demand an explanation for the crew's daily no-show. No. He was past that, now. He would paint the damn kitchen himself, because that's what Warners do.

That it took nine weeks, true love and a dozen orgasms for him to realize this is beside the point.

The point is, today I remember. Today I remember who I am.

Because the store is packed, they're still waiting for their paint order; which is why Ren has enough time to wander into Aisle 15 and try not to think about the other, much more significant ways in which he has *not* been behaving like a Warner. He'll think about building materials instead.

He knows he should go find Deidre before she wrecks something, or someone, but the beautiful steel bars lined up in neat little rows call to him like long-lost friends. He runs his index finger down the flat surface of a forty-eight-inch crown bolt, so simple, so nothing, really, and imagines all that it could be. *Just give me a few hours, a jig and a pair of suede work gloves (blue, preferably, or lime), and that bolt will meet its destiny.*

It's been so long since he actually *made* something.

As his eyes scan rows upon rows of opportunity in the form of flat metal sheets—galvanized steel, zinc-plated, aluminum black lincane, diamond tread—he can hear his own ecstatic voice shining through a transatlantic phone call, dying to tell his dearest friend about finding the workshop space on Third Avenue, to make it all the more real.

"Cole! It's just seven blocks from my apartment in Park Slope. And it has this old freight elevator and two crazy performance artists down the hall and seven outlets in my area alone and—Cole! It's perfect. It's just perfect!"

It was his pair of postmodern, brushed-steel deck chairs that landed him the job at Blue in SoHo; and though he created many pieces for the showroom in his first few years working there, high-profile interior design jobs soon took precedence over time in the workshop.

Then, shortly after he moved in with Paul, he gave up his beloved space. He'd spent many late nights cutting, sanding, shaping and dreaming in that space, and yet, when the time came, he let it go without so much as a tear or heavy sigh. By then, he'd moved on to this other life; he was practiced at giving up on dreams, after all.

Whenever his old New York friends asked when he'd get back to the work he loved, he'd say, "I haven't found the right space in Manhattan." But he wasn't really looking. High-end furniture design is a risky, competitive game. Why would a sought-after interior designer in a saturated market give up everything to make furniture he might not be able to sell?

Despite Ren's best efforts, the urge to create something of his own often bubbled to the surface. He'd ignore it until he felt as though he might jump right out of his skin, his hands aching for the familiar, repetitive movements, and say, "I need to make something beautiful." To which Paul would always reply, "But you make everything beautiful," missing the point entirely.

Walking over to the fine-gauge wire, Ren has that nagging feeling again, as if he forgot something—something he was supposed to do, someone he was supposed to call. He reaches out to touch copper, brushed steel: a reunion.

Paul. Sweet Paul. Earnest, heartfelt, *clueless* Paul.

He was genuinely excited to hear Paul's voice last night when he called and, thanks to that third drink, he let himself forget for a moment that he was about to break the poor man's heart.

"Paul?"

"Hello, stranger. I was afraid Deidre locked you in the basement."

"Adobe homes don't have basements."

"God, I miss you. Can you talk? Please tell me you can talk."

"I'm at a bar, but yes. Of course. How are you holding up? What's happening? Are you getting any sleep?"

"Not much. Either I'm in a meeting or in session, or too wound up to sleep. If we don't come to an agreement by Sunday, it's not going to happen."

"Shit."

"I know."

"What can I do?"

"Just let me hear you."

"Okay."

"Tell me everything. I want to hear about beveled windows and crazy Deidre and how you can't wait to get out of hellish New Mexico. Tell me all about it."

"I met Alegra."

"What? Are you kidding? *The* Alegra?"

"She's recording an album out in Galisteo with an old friend of mine."

"Really? That's amazing. Who?"

"What, who?"

"Who's the old friend?"

"Cole McKnight."

"Cole, Cole?"

"Uh-huh."

"Small world. How fun for you. Tell him hello for me. So what else? Tell me more."

He cradled the phone and told Paul about choosing between three doors, about the unpainted kitchen and the silver serving tray he'd found at the Nambé outlet store on San Francisco Street and willed himself *not* to start his next sentence with, "Speaking of Cole..."

He let the sound of Paul's agreeable, loving voice drown out the ambient sounds around him, the sounds of truly special people he'd just met who knew him in ways Paul never would. It wasn't Paul's fault. How could he understand that Ren had kept the truth hidden all these years, even from himself?

Then, he did the worst thing. He hung up on Paul, let the mere sight of Cole preparing to sing take precedence. And, as his phone vibrated in his pocket, Ren continued to ignore Paul's calls.

Later, after he nuzzled his face into the back of Cole's neck at his hotel room door; after they kissed for an hour and then an hour more; after he climbed into Cole's lap, naked, and teased him mercilessly until he finally let the tip of Cole's cock slide in, just a bit, just enough; after Cole cleaned them up, and held Ren's hand, and kissed the tips of his fingers; after he traced pictures onto Cole's back and whispered *love, love, love* into his ear, Ren sat on the edge of the bed and texted Paul an apology and a crappy excuse about poor cell reception in the bar. *Another lie.*

Ren somehow managed to put the lying out of his mind until just before he fell asleep in Cole's arms. But then, as he listened to Cole's soft, contented breathing, it was all he could do to push the sound of Paul's voice out of his head. *How fun for you. Tell him hello for me.*

Shaking the memory off, now, Ren backs down the aisle, eyes fixed on the materials he wants to twist and mold into something else, something new—and bumps right into Deidre.

"You left me in the ninth circle of hell. Do you hate me? Is that it?"

He laughs. "It's only paint, Deidre."

"People were staring." She grips his hand.

"No doubt because you look like a Gucci ad and swear like a sailor," Ren teases. "Is the paint ready?"

"Maybe? I went to look at the fucking flowers and got lost. Do you need something from this aisle?"

Ren looks at her blankly.

Do you need something?

Doesn't she know?

No, how could she know that he used to live for these materials, for thick sheets of aluminum, for wire cutters and table saws and mallets of every size? He wants to tell her everything, show her renderings, drag her through the homes of old friends who still proudly display his "almost" and "not quite" pieces like treasures, like art.

Do you need something?

Do you need to make something beautiful with your own two hands?

Do you need a different Wednesday, or winter, or next year?

Do you need something you left behind, something you forgot you loved?

Ren turns to her, takes both of her French-manicured hands in his own and says, "Let me make you a table. Or two. Let me make you two tables!"

"You want to make me—?"

"For the courtyard, to go with the wrought iron set we just bought."

"Ren, of course, but—"

"I can do it! You know the stainless steel fainting couch in my office? The one with the lilac cushions? I made that," he says, eyes bright. "It was years ago, and I don't have the tools here, but I'm sure Antonio can help me find someone who would have—"

"Ren! Stop. What the fuck? First you want to paint the kitchen *yourself*, and now you want to *make* my furniture. Who *are* you?"

She looks worried, like a little girl watching her first scary movie, afraid to find out what will happen next. He lets go of her hands, offers a small smile and then tucks her perfectly-styled blonde hair behind both of her ears. "Just me," he soothes. "Still me."

"Fuck. You're leaving New York, aren't you?"

"Did you ever wear your hair like this? Away from your face?"

"Yes. When I was *nine.*"

"I like it. You have a sweet face."

"You say that like you've only just met me." Deidre tugs on the hair behind her ears. "And you didn't answer my fucking question."

Ren sighs, kisses her forehead and says, "You're running out of houses for me to decorate, anyway. You'll just have to resign yourself to being my friend."

She wraps her arms around his waist and gives him a quick hug, her head resting on his chest just a few seconds longer than normal. For Deidre, it might as well be a declaration of love. When she pulls back, her smile is radiant. She looks him up and down and says, "Is the sex really that good?"

"For what?"

"For you to break up with your perfect fiancé, create the scandal of the season and move to another country in shame?"

He laughs, ignoring the truth in her question. "No, I mean, *yes,* holy wow the sex is *amazing,* but we haven't decided. I'm not sure what I want to do. I can't even figure out how to tell Paul, or when to tell him."

"Or if you want to tell him," she adds, which earns her his steely glare. "What? I thought we were best friends now."

"You're not ready for that, honey."

"Whatever. You know I'm right."

Ren turns on his heel and marches toward the paint section, where Lucky, the six-foot-four college student who put up with Deidre's mouth and misgivings, has loaded two gallons of Wheatgrass, a roll of painter's tape, one roller and three brushes of varying lengths into their cart.

"Thanks, Lucky. You're a sweetheart," Ren says.

"No problem. You need some help with that paint job? I get off at three." Ren looks up from the cart to see Lucky winking at him, trying to flirt. He takes in Lucky's shoulder-length, strawberry blond hair, his slightly bloodshot blue eyes, and smiles.

"I'm too old for you."

"You're not, but I know when someone is trying to let me down easy."

Deidre catches up to Ren at the paint counter and pokes him in the side. "So, can you really bend steel?"

"Sure."

"Dude! Superpowers? Are you sure you don't wanna hook up?" Lucky says, leaning over the counter.

"He's taken. So taken. *Double* taken," Deidre teases.

"Stop," Ren warns.

"Kinky, huh? It's like that?" Lucky asks.

"No, it's *nothing* like that."

Deidre leans over the counter, right next to Lucky, invading his personal space. She touches his nametag, letting her fingers linger over his name. "Is this your real name, *Luck-y*?"

"Okay, okay. Enough paint fumes for you," Ren says, dragging her away. "Thank you, Lucky!"

After the cashier rings up the sale, after Ren covers Deidre's mouth to stop her from cursing at the woman behind them in line, after they load up Deidre's rental and head up Cerrillos Road, back toward the Plaza, Ren finally lets himself think about the promises he's made—to Paul, to Cole, to himself. He settles into it, this new side of him he can no longer run from: the liar in him, the cheater, the selfish asshole who is lucky enough to get two perfect men in one short lifetime.

They're halfway back to Deidre's "godawful house" when he realizes she's right. It isn't that he doesn't want to tell Paul about Cole right now; he doesn't want to tell Paul about Cole at all.

It's evening, close to eight o'clock, when Antonio pulls up to the Alexander house and offers to help Ren with the second coat. They're finished by a quarter after ten, walls glistening, backs aching, brushes clean. Cole won't be out of the studio and back in Santa Fe until at least eleven, so Ren accepts Antonio's invitation and they head over to the Cowgirl Hall of Fame for two-dollar beer (for Antonio), margaritas (for Ren) and ostrich burgers (for both of them).

The crowd on the Cowgirl patio is young, yet distinctly "Santa Fe"– girls in peasant skirts and ratty band T-shirts, and boys in skinny jeans wearing more jewelry than the girls: turquoise chokers, hemp bracelets, crystal necklaces, Celtic symbol earrings. These are the transient Santa Feans who, in a few weeks, or months, or maybe years, will move to Boulder, or Austin, or Nashville, always chasing the next experience.

They sit in overlapping groups, laughing and talking over the sound of a local, pseudo-grunge band playing inside.

"Don't let me drink too much tonight. I have to head out to Taos early in the morning," Antonio says, as they grab a table next to the stone wall bumping right up to the sidewalk just barely at knee level.

"Normally I would say, 'I'm not your mama,' but I don't want to get drunk tonight, either, so—"

"I bet you don't."

"Must you? I thought we agreed you were done."

"I'll stop, I'll stop!" Antonio holds up his hands in mock surrender. "I'm just feeding off your happy vibe. You're more fun to tease when you've had something other than a stick up your ass."

Ren kicks Antonio's foot. "You're lucky you're not wearing sandals."

"Sandals? I don't wear sandals."

"Ever?"

"I didn't even wear sandals on my Super Romantic Hawaiian Vacation," Antonio says, in his best game show host voice. He looks out over the crowd and waves a server to their table.

"Don't sound so excited about it," Ren says, settling in. He places his phone on the table, in case Cole calls or texts, along with a pen and a small, leatherbound notepad he picked up at the Marcy Street Card Shop earlier that afternoon. Reasoning that he needed to get practical and stop fearing the inevitable, Ren had planned to make a list of all of the tasks he'd have to complete in order to start fresh with Cole. He'd even jotted "FRESH START" at the top of the first page of his notepad. But when he still had nothing after staring at the mostly blank page for twenty minutes, he gave up and watched the paint dry in Deidre's kitchen instead.

"I'm not much for forced romance," Antonio says.

"Please tell me you didn't wear cowboy boots on the beach," Ren says.

"I went barefoot."

The server arrives, a young woman with her hair in a loose bun through which she has stuffed two pencils. As she takes their orders, her expression blank and body rigid, Ren asks her name. "Jillian," she replies, "but I prefer Jill, and before you ask, no, I did not come tumbling after."

Ren says, "Of course not. Anyone can see you're a modern girl. You know how to turn on the damn faucet." This earns him a belly laugh and a pat on the shoulder from Jill before she marches back to the main bar.

"Nice," Antonio says.

Ren shrugs. "It pays to have them on your side."

"I'm glad you came out tonight."

"Me too. I've been meaning to—I want to apologize. I should have accepted your invitations on earlier visits. Your wife—Sarah's lovely. And the kids at Alex Marin House, and just... I'm sorry. I should have said yes more often."

"Don't stress about it. We're cool."

"I tend to judge things too harshly, and too soon. I don't *hate* New Mexico. It's—I'm not sure yet, but I might even like it."

"Another couple of days and you won't want to leave," Antonio says. Ren shudders, his face a mask of mock horror.

"It's unnerving, this place," Ren says, fingers twisting the thin blue ribbon bookmark in his notepad. "I've been knocked off my center, you know? It's both exciting and nauseating."

"Are we talking about New Mexico or Cole? Because there's no stopping the Cole Train, magical desert or not."

"Antonio. The *Cole Train*?"

"What? That's what he is—a train that was coming whether you liked it or not. Chugging down the road, following the tracks straight to your station."

"Chugging? To my station?" Ren says, trying not to laugh.

"Listen, man, it's a solid metaphor."

"So Cole is a train that travels all over the world—"

"I didn't say all over the world, I said—"

"And I'm a decaying building just waiting for him to arrive? Is that it?" Ren is using his "just kidding" voice, but really, the analogy does hit too close to home. He was always waiting for Cole. Even when he thought he had stopped—after that night under the northern lights, after he slept with the super-cute "boy-who-isn't-Cole" just to get it out of the way, after Cole left for London, after they couldn't get their shit together for the four-hundredth time.

No matter how many times he forced himself to move on and carve out a life that worked—a life that looked like something people like him should want, a life that was a fair substitute for feeling wildly happy, for being stupidly in love with someone who felt the same—he couldn't shake the sixteen-year-old boy mooning over the friend who, with the simple touch of his hand, had awakened his soul and cut him off from every other chance at real happiness.

He was always waiting for Cole, no matter how wide his smile or how sure his proclamations, no matter how many lies he told himself to prove otherwise.

"And I didn't say 'decaying,' either," Antonio says, interrupting Ren's thoughts. "Sounds like you've got some boxes to donate."

"Sorry?"

"You know, boxes of old crap taking up space and messing with your life. Whenever I'm holding onto stuff from the past, Sarah says, 'Time to donate that box, Antonio'. It's helpful to think of it as useless junk."

"So I'm a *hoarding* train station—"

"Okay, stop with the train station stuff—"

"You started it."

Antonio sighs and looks out onto the sidewalk and across to the Zia Diner, to the map store Sarah loves, to the Jean Cocteau cinema, its age-old marquee dark for the night. Ren follows his eyes and whispers, "I'm sorry. I sound like a crazy person, I know."

"I don't want to tell you your life," Antonio says at last.

"You keep saying that, but you *are* telling me my life. Can we just agree that as much as you don't want to butt in, you can't help yourself? And as much as I don't want to be told what to do, I really do need your help figuring all of this out?"

Antonio's smile is so warm Ren can't help but smile back. "You're a good friend, Ren. I think a lot of you, crazy talk and harsh judgments aside."

"Thank you." Ren plays with his pen. "After this is all over, you may be my only friend."

"Come on. Everyone makes mistakes. Besides, I can't be the only person on this planet who knows. You two radiate soul-love like a freaking neon sign."

"Soul-love?"

"You're the one who feels it—why do you need me to tell you what it is?"

Ren looks down at his hands, a small smile on his face. He knows. He knows all about how it feels to love someone across time, to hear his heartbeat over his own.

But he doesn't know what having a soul-love *means*, or how long you can have it before something goes terribly, horribly wrong. He doesn't know if it's fragile, or forever; he doesn't know if it's a guarantee of happiness or heartache.

He starts to say as much, but he's cut off by the arrival of their drinks. "Ostrich burgers will be right up," Jill says, before she dashes off to another table.

"Ostrich burgers?"

Ren looks to his right and sees Cole leaning against the stone wall, arms crossed, staring up at them. He looks tired, but good-tired, the way you look when you've been hard at work doing something you dearly love.

"Hey! You're off early," Ren says, leaning down for a kiss. "How'd you know where to find us?"

"Sarah," Cole mumbles into Ren's mouth, his lips full and warm. The kiss is a bit dirty for a public sidewalk, so Cole ends it with a chaste peck and backs away toward the entrance. Ren leans right to watch Cole bounce up the stairs like a kid, denim stretching across his toned thighs as he takes them two at a time.

"It seems Sarah and Cole are getting to be good friends," Ren says, turning back to Antonio. He raises his glass, and his eyebrows, which earns him a clink from Antonio's glass.

"Cheers to that," Antonio says. He slides a nearby chair to their table, and waves Jill over to take Cole's order.

"Thanks." Cole shakes Antonio's hand. "Get a lot done today?"

"We have a green kitchen, yes," Antonio says.

"Wheatgrass," Ren corrects.

"Whatever. It's green."

Cole plops down in the empty chair and looks right into Ren's eyes.

"Hi," Ren says, grinning.

"Hi," Cole replies, smiling back.

"I was just thinking about you," Ren says.

"I thought about you all day."

"I was hoping you'd be done early."

Cole reaches over and thumbs a spot under Ren's ear. "You have a little paint on your—let me—"

He licks his thumb and rubs the spot again for a moment, eyes locked with Ren's. "There. Better."

"I missed you," Ren says, taking Cole's hand in his own.

"I like it when you miss me," Cole replies, intertwining their fingers.

There's a cough, and someone is talking, but Ren is suddenly, completely lost in Cole's eyes, every worry completely gone from his mind. Lost, that is, until Antonio kicks him under the table.

"Ouch! *What?*"

"Are they always like this?" Jill asks.

"They haven't gotten to always yet," Antonio says. "New lovers; you know the drill."

"Right. So, do you want anything?" Jill asks, nodding at Cole.

"The sign says two-dollar beer," Cole says, finally giving her his attention. "I'll have a beer, and the ostrich burger. Why not, right?"

"You don't want the two-dollar beer. Trust me. I'll bring you a local brew, off the tap." Jill marches away before Cole finishes saying, "Thank you so much."

"So what are we talking about?" Cole asks.

Before Antonio can launch into a new lecture about trains, or soul-love, or whatever desert voodoo he wants to impart, Ren opens the notepad, folds over the page marked "FRESH START" and says, "Zozobra. Antonio was just telling me about this tradition, of burning a giant man in drag—"

"I said he *looks* like a man in drag."

"Whatever. Apparently, we are supposed to write down our regrets and worries and somehow stuff the paper inside this giant Zozobra man and then burn him to the ground," Ren says, pen at the ready. "So, is it just our regrets and fears of this past year, or—?"

"Hold up. Why are we doing this?" Cole asks.

"So, you know about Fiesta—the burning of Zozobra is the final night of Fiesta, when Santa Feans burn 'Old Man Gloom' to the ground and start the new year fresh, free from the burdens of regret, fear, worry, negativity—basically, we burn up everything bad and wipe the slate clean."

"That sounds amazing. How do you get the paper into the Zozobra guy?"

"There are boxes all over town. There's one near the Eldorado, if you want to participate," Antonio explains.

"Yeah, I do. Is this the thing Sarah wants us to come to?"

"We'd like you two to come, yes, but I wasn't sure if you could get the time off. We go down to Fort Marcy field in the afternoon and have a picnic. It's a local thing. You'll like it. After he burns, we have a party at our house."

Ren's heart flutters. *You two.* They are "you two," and "us" and "them;" like before, like when they were joined at the hip, blazer-to-blazer, but different. More. *Everything.*

"I'll make it work," Cole says, looking at Ren with a question in his eyes.

A fresh start? A chance to bury old regrets and new worries and wipe the slate clean?

Ren smiles and squeezes Cole's hand. "Yes. We'll absolutely be there."

On Wednesday, Ren sends the new door back. It fits, and Deidre likes it, but it's just not right. He thumbs through the pictures on his phone—koi, orange and gold, swimming in a pond up at Ten Thousand Waves; the red rug he left behind in Chimayó; the rows and rows of doors and the row of three he'd asked the guys to line up for inspection. Has it only been one week since that first night at The Pink?

Paul calls once more, but doesn't leave a message. Ren knows he should call him, but he can't; their five-minute conversation rattled him so completely, he can't go there again.

Not yet.

Not yet.

With the house almost complete, Cole at work and Deidre up at the Waves for a spa day, Ren has time to figure things out. He could fill up his entire notepad with ideas, and plans and to-do lists. But, just as before, he's terrified by the endless options and the finality of putting pen to paper, so the pages remain blank. Instead, he accepts Sarah's offer to join the Alex Marin House crew at the Hysterical Parade on the Plaza. They agree to meet beforehand to wander downtown.

Sarah slips into alleys and down ancient, narrow streets, showing Ren *her* Santa Fe. They shop, and laugh and find the best leather, and silver and art. He gently pushes her past the matchstick skirts and toward something fashion-forward but quiet and elegant, like her.

When she twirls out of her dressing room, shiny and bright in a white eyelet dress, Ren revels. She's not worried about image, or labels or public perception. She just wants to feel pretty.

By the time they wind their way to a tiny candy shop, Todos Santos, Ren is in love with Sarah, too. She introduces him to her friend Marcus, the proprietor, and starts collecting little candies in a small basket.

Ren bends down to look inside the glass cases, admiring the wrapped candies in brilliant colors, the chocolate skeletons covered in edible gold leaf, the bite-sized marzipans shaped like chile peppers.

"This is art," he says, mentally choosing pieces for everyone he knows.

"See? You find the best places when you just keep turning the corner." Sarah asks Marcus to pack up six chocolate squares covered in crushed pistachio and tie the box with a bow. "A Fiesta present, for Antonio," she explains.

"Is that tradition? To give a present for Fiesta?"

"Not really. But I always do, because for Santa Feans it's like New Year's Eve and Yom Kippur and Winter Solstice all wrapped up in one—no disrespect to those who understand Judaism and Paganism better than I do."

"I wouldn't know," Ren says, sifting through a basket of Our Lady of Guadalupe charms.

"So I give him something, just a little trinket or candy, or whatever, to let him know I'm letting go of my regrets, and starting over in *all areas*, including our marriage. It's surprisingly effective," she says, bumping Ren's shoulder.

"How so?"

"Let's just say that after Zozobra it's all very... *fresh*." She giggles and Ren joins in, trying *not* to think about Antonio getting it on with this lovely flower.

"What are these?" he asks Marcus, pointing at gold and silver candies shaped like human hearts.

"*Milagros*—'miracles.' They come in many forms, representing the miracle you're hoping to receive," he replies. "They're my specialty."

Ren says, "They're beautiful," his voice almost a whisper. He thinks about his heart, and Cole's, and the men they are leaving in honor of their own miracle.

"I'll take that one, the one in silver. And could you wrap it?"

"For Cole?" Sarah asks.

"Yes. For Fiesta."

They both watch as Marcus places the silver heart in a small black box, wrapping it in bright red paper.

Sarah's hand finds Ren's own, resting on the glass. "It's perfect. He'll love it."

"Anything else?" Marcus asks.

"So much, yes. Will you ship to Minnesota?"

Later, at the parade, Ren holds Sarah's bags and lets her stand on the bench behind him for an unobstructed view. The Alex Marin House kids, dressed in their most outrageous attire, take pictures, and clap and scream; they are at home in the wildness, in the *different*. The event reminds him of Pride—carefree people dressed in random costumes, making joyful, riotous noise.

It reminds him of times when he and his friends fled Saint Benedict's after hours and escaped to Minneapolis to dance at First Avenue. He and Cole, Dean, Jeremy and Asher would all cram into Cole's BMW, laughing and singing, buzzing with excitement at the chance to shuck their uniforms and be themselves, if only for one night. At the club, they would dance for hours—in celebration, in defiance, in *honor* of all the fabulous, strange and unique beauty in life.

It all seemed so possible, then.

He's let so much slip by, blending in and staking a different claim among powerful people with long-term vision who rock the boat in careful, predictable ways.

The parade is familiar in the most perfect way. Ren laughs, and forgets about blank pages and unspoken confessions, and instead texts Cole about every little piece of awesome. He takes pictures for his father, and for Antonio and one of a hippie football player/go-go dancer he'll send to his brother Sean. He feels good. And right. And more like himself as each float passes by.

The city is growing on him. *Imagine that.*

Slowly, as June predicted, he's remembering.

He's remembering who he really is.

Chapter 14

With all of Santa Fe in Fiesta mode, Alegra decides they'll push hard on Wednesday and Thursday so everyone can attend Zozobra; which means the first opportunity Cole has to meet with Shep is late Wednesday night. He hasn't seen Ren since this morning: his eyes a soft gray in the morning light, his smile warm and lazy. It seems as if it's been days, not hours, since he kissed the back of Ren's neck, gave his duvet-covered ass a squeeze and made his way out to Galisteo.

Ren has texted and sent him pictures throughout the day: Ren arm-in-arm with the Alex Marin House lovebirds, Teddy and Wyatt; Sarah in a white dress, winking at the camera; a vintage VW bus painted in crazy colors, leading the Hysterical Parade; Native American dancers in traditional costumes; a pile of hot-pink feather boas, abandoned on the sidewalk; Sarah kissing Ren's cheek.

Cole's texted back when he could, but the day was long and the work important, so he mostly just scrolled through Ren's latest messages during lunch and dinner breaks, texting responses for each and every one.

It reminded him of college, both of them at schools they loved in cities that promised acceptance and adventure. They'd text each other several times a day, share photos of new friends and ridiculous strangers, of beautiful architecture and awesome bargains—pictures of *life*, a life that didn't seem real unless they shared it with each other.

His phone vibrates again as he pulls in behind a Range Rover on Canyon Road, just a block from El Farol. He's not surprised Shep wanted to meet here. Mitch had told him once that the restaurant and nightclub was a favorite hangout for local musicians—"*Successful* local musicians," he'd amended—but Cole had yet to check it out.

After turning off the ignition, Cole takes out his phone to read Ren's latest text and give him his ETA.

Ren: How did it go? Will I see you tonight?

Cole: Just getting to the meeting now. Wait up for me?

Ren: Of course. Did you eat?

Cole: Yes. I'll just have one drink and head back. Maybe an hour?

Ren: Take your time. Just text me when you leave, okay? Come to my room.

Cole: :)

Ren: Really? I ask you to come to my room and I get a smiley face?

Cole: Do they have dirty emoticons?

Ren: I'm sure I wouldn't know.

Cole: I'm sure you WOULD know.

Ren: Just exactly who do you think I am, Cole McKnight?

Cole: I can't say. My answer is too cheesy.

Ren: That bad?

Cole: So bad you might deny me sex.

Ren: Nothing is that bad. Tell me.

Cole: You're the love of my life.

Ren: Aww.

Cole: ?

Ren: Is that your way of asking me if you can still sex me up tonight?

Cole: Yes.

Ren: Punctuation. Hot.

Cole: Call me Casanova.

Ren: 8===>).(

Cole: Wow. Does that mean what I think means?

Ren: Come knock on my door and find out.

Cole laughs out loud. Here in the confines of the car, he can tell that his laugh is different, that it's a good laugh, the kind you only have with a lover or an old friend. That he is laughing at an exchange with a man who is both his best friend and his lover is not lost on him. This is how it's supposed to be: deep affection; ease; a pure moment. He pockets his phone and makes his way to El Farol with an extra spring in his step.

He's on the verge. Everything is happening now, and it all comes down to Ren. *Ren. Love. His love. His.* He can't believe his good fortune; he thought for sure he'd used up all of his chances. It's enough to make him believe in God again as he used to; as a child believes, staring up at the night sky in wonder. He's giddy with it, with the sweet, unexpected delivery of all his dreams in one searing kiss.

Once inside, he spots Shep right away, his head bobbing along to the warm, complicated tones of the jazz fusion band just a few feet away. He's claimed what appears to be the best table in the house, upon which sits a bottle of Patrón and two large shot glasses. Even in this ancient city of no more than eighty-thousand people, Shep Vasovic knows how to VIP.

He wonders why Shep is going to so much trouble. Cole is mostly a music producer now, his performing aspirations long tucked away into a box of old letters and dreams. He sings backup, and plays guitar and piano and makes good songs better. His own melodies, the truths that run through him and scream to get out, they're for strangers, for fleeting connections and singular moments of understanding, not masses of people.

At least that's what he used to tell himself. *Before*. Now, he's thinking he might actually say yes. What does he have left to hide? He's no longer running, or wishing for another life. If he can have Ren, surely he can have this, too, right? *Maybe*.

Shep spots Cole and waves him over, points to the empty chair and fills both shot glasses to the brim. The music is too loud for conversation, so the two clink glasses, down their shots and settle in for the rest of the set. The tequila goes down smooth, *too* smooth, and Cole makes a mental note to cover his glass when Shep tries to refill it. He has plans for tonight, plans that do not include dragging his drunken ass back to the Eldorado only to pass out next to a very flirty, very willing Ren.

Letting the music wash over him, he imagines what it would be like to move people with his own music, beyond the joints he wanders into every so often, guitar and heart in hand; to share something so deeply personal with the entire world. It's been so long since he's been in front, taking the lead. Now that his heart is right side up, he can admit that he misses it. Not all the time, not every day, but sometimes—often enough that he knows it's still in him.

Shep doesn't waste any time on pleasantries. After the cellist promises they'll be back in twenty, he leans forward and says, "Just tell me when you can deliver twelve tracks, and I'll call legal."

It's too abrupt, too final, and Cole shrinks back. He hadn't expected this. It's a big step, *huge*. The opportunity is so golden it seems as if it could be too much, too fast. He needs time to think it through.

"I haven't said yes yet."

"So say it, and let's do this," Shep counters. His smile is earnest. From his friends in the industry, Cole knows that Shep will treat him right and that he has the best of intentions. Cole couldn't find a better home for his debut album, really.

Debut album. It's been so long since he entertained the thought of recording his own music, much less aspired to make something great.

Before Cole can respond, Shep chimes in again. "I told you I saw you perform at that dive in London, but what I didn't tell you is, I asked Curtis Fogg to track you down in the pubs, recording performances whenever he spotted you."

"Really? I didn't realize—"

"He's a sneaky little fuck, so I'm not surprised you didn't catch on. I'm not sorry about it, either, even though it does officially qualify me as a stalker."

Shep pours amber liquid into the glass in front of him. When Cole shakes his head and covers his own glass, Shep sets the bottle down. "You kept saying no, and I had to find out why. So I asked around, and when no one seemed to know, I sent Curt to see if he could find the answer in your music."

"And did you find it?"

"I think I did," Shep replies, his expression softening.

Cole looks at him, lets the silent stare between them go on a moment too long and says, "I don't want to leave Alegra. Her album is my priority, and I'm supposed to tour with her next summer."

"Fine. Good. Anyone on deck to open?"

"Not yet."

"Why don't you open for her, then? Keep it in the family."

"It's not up to me."

Shep sets his glass down hard, as if he's decided something. "Right. Listen, Cole, I can get you all the way to Oz, but I can't make you knock on the door."

"I know."

Cole is quiet again. He decides he can handle half a shot more, so he pours it and downs it, trying not to think about how—through practice, avoidance and denial—he'd taught himself how to hesitate. It was an easy habit to slip into, what with the conditioning his parents provided once they realized he would never belong at the Edina Country Club. There's so much mistrust of freethinkers and musicians and *queers* in his "illustrious" family, it's a wonder he was able to stop doubting himself long enough to make any decision at all.

But that was before—before the miracle, before *I'm so in love with you and you're so in love with me*. Now, now that he knows what it feels like to get everything he ever wanted, he's ready to reach out and grab the brass ring.

"I'll talk to Mitch, see if he'll help me with the demo," Cole says finally.

"That's who you want, then? Because I can get any producer you want."

"I want Mitch. I'll record it here."

"Do you have enough for an album, or do you need time to—?"

"I have dozens of songs," Cole interrupts.

"So we do a soft launch before Alegra's release and then push hard right before the tour."

"I need to talk this over with a few people. Alegra, and Mitch, and... someone very close to me."

"I'll send over the papers. I need the demo by the end of September, just your best stuff."

September. He promised Ren he'd show up in New York as soon as they wrapped. Would Ren come back to Santa Fe so soon? Would he understand if Cole had to leave so soon after they were officially reunited?

"I'll let you know by Monday," Cole says.

"I'll have my assistant email a contract to your manager in London, and overnight a hard copy to you. You're at the Eldorado, right?"

"Yes. Room 206."

"One more, to celebrate." Shep refills their glasses. Cole nods, decides to leave his car on Canyon Road and walk back to the hotel. He's only slightly buzzed, but not clear-headed enough to drive.

Shep raises his glass. "Here's to finally saying yes to the best thing that ever happened to you."

"Finally," Cole agrees, a smile at the corner of his mouth.

Cole texts Ren that he's on his way, but walking; and after shaking Shep's hand, he heads downhill toward the Plaza. It's busy for a Wednesday night, with more tourists than usual and everyone in a celebratory mood. He picks up the end of the Old Santa Fe Trail and crosses to San Francisco Street when he reaches the Cathedral. He can see the Eldorado about ten blocks ahead and suddenly realizes he's walking the same path he took from The Pink that night that changed everything.

Has it really been a week? It feels as though it's only been a day since my life was officially made. No, that was days later, when I finally told him of my promised heart, and he took my hands in his and confessed he felt the same. Still, it's a week since we gave in, since I came for him; since we forgot about who we'd become and remembered who we once were, what we wanted and would always want, no matter what. No matter what.

He sees the two of them everywhere on this street. He sees Ren's face, bathed in lamplight that first night as they walked by darkened shops en route to Deidre's house. He sees himself, stepping off the curb to run down the middle of the one-way street to get to Ren—*faster, faster, hurry, faster, this is it, this is your chance, faster, don't fuck up, hurry, faster, faster.* And again, the following morning, walking on autopilot, two coffees in hand, resolved to take whatever Ren was willing to give. He sees the two of them walking on opposite sides of the street, aching, drawn to each other like moths to a flame.

He sees them everywhere: San Francisco Street. A path in Brooklyn, covered in cherry blossoms. A weathered dock in Red Cedar Lake. Asher's basement. A chapel. A dream.

His phone vibrates, shaking him out of his reverie. As he unlocks the screen he thinks, *Hell yeah, I can write new songs—just you wait.*

Ren: Come to my room, but don't knock. Use your key card.

Cole's heartbeat quickens and he picks up the pace. He's past the front desk clerk in minutes, in the elevator in seconds and at Ren's hotel room door before he has time to wonder what Ren has planned. Whatever it is, it will be hot, and amazing, and so, so right.

He swipes Ren's extra key card and smiles when he thinks about this time last week, when he was stuck on the other side of the door, begging Ren to let him in. Now, just seven days later, Ren is waiting up for him, for *him.*

"Ren?" he asks, slipping off his shoes in the hallway. He hears a soft moan from the main room, and the unmistakable sound of...

"Holy fuck."

Ren is on the bed, his back up against the headboard, wearing maroon and gold-striped cotton pajamas. He's left his shirt unbuttoned and open, revealing his toned chest, and he's pushed the bottoms down around his knees. He's flushed, legs splayed as far as the fabric will allow, one hand working his hard, perfect cock.

"Is this how you pictured it? I wore silk to bed back then, but... *mmm*... but I found this today and... *yeah*... Bennie colors—"

Ren notices that he's rendered Cole speechless, so he slows up on his pace a bit, smiles wickedly at Cole and says, "You said you wanted to watch."

Cole swallows, his eyes fixated on Ren's hands as if he's sixteen and watching a man jerk off for the very first time. Ren arches his back, lets his head fall back on the headboard and gives in to it, one hand on his cock in long, sure strokes, the other teasing one nipple and then the other. He's close, holding himself back.

After a few moments, Ren sits up a bit. "What would you have done? What next? *Shit*, Tell me. Tell me what you would have done if you found me like this, if I let you—"

"Take off your pants. All the way." Cole's voice is so desperate and gravelly he doesn't recognize it as his own.

There's that wicked smile again, and Ren is pushing his pajama pants down to his ankles, one hand on each leg. He pulls them off, tosses them to the floor, and then looks up at Cole expectantly, as if to say, *Tell me what's next.*

"I... may I sit?"

"So polite. Yes. Sit," Ren replies, hand back on his cock. Cole unbuttons the top of his pants and pulls the zipper down before sitting on the very edge of the bed.

"No touching. Not yet," Ren warns.

"Ren—"

"Come closer. I want you as close to me as possible."

"Without touching," Cole says, crawling up toward Ren.

Ren's breath hitches. He watches Cole's slow approach. "Without. Touching."

Cole knows the game now. It's push-pull; no one is in charge. First Ren leads, then he leads. They'll both hold back, and they'll both give in, taking turns, feeling their way. He can *so* do this. He's waited his whole life to do this—not just for Ren (though, yes, always for Ren, *always*), but also for himself.

He's wanted this all along, looked for it in others: an effortless sex life and a partner who is confident, dirty, a bit silly and so, so willing. He's wanted every intimate moment they've shared together so far, as if he's been checking off his fantasies one by one, as if he could see the future: deep, hot, desperate, profound. And silly, like friends, like *best friends*. He never doubted that he and Ren would be compatible in every way, but he's so thrilled to find that he was absolutely right.

Cole settles in on his knees directly in front of Ren, his pants now riding low on his hips, revealing a pair of Ren's dove-gray boxer briefs.

Ren stares at Cole's cloth-covered bulge, at the glimpse of trimmed brown pubic hair peeking out over the waistband. His breath is so uneven now it sounds as if he's panting, but somehow he manages to croak out "*Mine*" as he reaches for Cole's cock.

"Yours? Oh, right. I, ah, borrowed these this morning. I hope you don't mind," Cole teases. "Or were you referring to something else?"

Although it seems impossible, Ren's eyes darken even further. "I want them back," he says, holding out his hand, palm up.

"Right now?" Cole teases.

"Right now."

Ren resumes stroking, spreading his legs wider now that he can. He watches as Cole sticks his thumbs in the briefs, ready to pull them down, and whines when he stops.

"Come *on*," Ren pleads.

"Ren."

"Yes?"

"I want something."

"*Anything*, yes... what is it?"

"I want to watch you get off, and then I want to fuck you—"

"Yes, just, please—"

"No, listen. I'm not finished. I want to see your face when you come, and then I want to kiss you, cover you and let your come stain my shirt.

Then I want to turn you on your side, open you up, press up against your naked body and fuck you with my clothes still on."

"Oh *fuck*." Ren arches his back. "Were you always this dirty? Or is it... new?"

Cole can tell Ren wants to ask something different. *Is it me? Do I make you dirty? Or have you said these words to someone, everyone, anyone else?*

Cole leans forward a little, drawing it out, careful not to touch, eyes darting between Ren's neck, taut with pleasure, and the tight fist of Ren's hand. "You remember, don't you?" Cole asks. "That night, the winter before I left for London, the night you sent me a picture of the hot couple in front of the tree in Rockefeller Center..." Cole looks for signs of recognition on Ren's face. There's love, and desire, and promises of ever after, but he's still so unsure of so many things.

Does he remember what I remember? Were there moments that meant more to me than they did him? When the boys were sweet, and felt almost right, did he yearn for me in the same way, then? Or was my voice just an echo? Did he get lost in the skilled hands of other lovers, like I did, when not-right lips were less wrong, and the ache subsided long enough to forget?

"You walked me home," Ren says, interrupting his thoughts.

"I... what?"

"You called me, right after I sent the picture, and I asked you to walk me home."

Cole laughs—Ren remembers it better than he does. *He'd* forgotten that part, the part where Ren said, *"I'm cat-sitting for a friend on 78th Street. Walk me home?"*

They stayed on the line for twenty blocks, Ren intermittently describing window displays, a bad fashion choice, a restaurant he'd like to try. Every few minutes Cole would say, *"Where are we now?"* and Ren would rattle off the street number. Cole had felt so close to Ren then, despite the tension, the boyfriends, their looming futures.

Cole says, "And it seemed like four minutes—"

"—But it was more than twenty-five—"

"—And when you arrived at the building, you said you didn't want to stop talking—"

"—And I sat on the stoop and we talked for a while longer—"

"—And that's when you told me about your fantasy, the one where you're naked and someone fully clothed fucks you from behind," Cole finishes.

Ren stops, looks right into Cole's eyes and says, "Not someone. *You.*"

Cole's eyes mist over, which causes him to snort at the ridiculousness of it all: He's getting emotional about one of Ren's dirty sexual fantasies simply because he's always wanted the starring role.

Ren sees it all on Cole's face and laughs. They're bound by the same story, the same thoughts, the same want. "So I give you one of your fantasies," Ren says, thumbing over the tip of his cock for emphasis, "and you give me one of mine?"

"Fair is fair."

Ren glances at his pajama top, most of it bunched up under his ass now. "Do you want this off, too?"

"Leave it," Cole says, his eyes on Ren's cock.

"Okay," Ren whispers. He seems to sink into Cole's stare; it's everything Cole ever wanted, to worship this man.

Ren picks up the pace and settles into it, as if enveloped in the memory of dorm room fantasies and the promise of what's to come. He's full-on panting now, in between gasps and *hmm* and *ahhh* and *Cole, oh Cole*, and it's all Cole can do to keep his hands to himself. It's the *Cole, oh Cole* over and over again that really rattles him. If he could have heard those words slip out of Ren's pink lips just once back in prep school, he never would have let him go.

"You like watching me... *oh, shit...* come apart," Ren says.

"Were you thinking of me? In the dorm, when you put your hand down your pants, when you fingered yourself in the shower?"

"Always. Every time," Ren replies, and Cole can tell he's close—so close it will only take a few words, or his hot breath in Ren's ear, to tip him right over the edge.

"And since?"

"Yes."

"You still think of me when you get off?" Cole asks, his hands in tight fists as he fights the urge to touch, grab, stroke, kiss, feel.

"You know I do. That night. *Fuck.* Our night, last week," Ren pants, his hand moving furiously now. "I told you. It was you. You're my default. I have to make myself... *oh, oh shit... Cole, oh Cole*—"

"You have to make yourself what?"

"I have to... close. I have to—"

Ren lifts his ass up off the bed, and that's when Cole sees it: his hole, glistening, dark pink, open. *Ready.*

"Ren, did you... did you *prep* for me?"

"I thought, since it's our anniversary—"

"Ren—"

"You seemed to like it. You seemed... *I can't...* you were so hot for it, the thought of it, that you could just slide right into me—"

Cole can't take one more second of this. "Come. Come now so I can fuck you. *Come.*"

As if on command, Ren tenses up, mouth slack, and comes all over his stomach. His thighs shake, his brow is damp with sweat. Cole doesn't wait for him to come down. He quickly climbs up the bed, turns Ren on his side and lies down behind him, arm wrapped over Ren's chest. They stay still like that, listening to each other breathe, until Cole trails his hand up Ren's chest, his neck, his chin, and slips his thumb into Ren's pliant mouth.

He turns Ren's head toward him, fingers gripping his chin, and kisses him for the first time in fifteen hours. It's possessive, and a little sloppy, but Ren doesn't seem to mind. "You taste like tequila," Ren murmurs into Cole's mouth.

The angle is awkward, and when Ren moves to turn around, Cole stops him, pulls back from the kiss and whispers into his ear, "Let me fuck you, baby. Just like this."

Ren just nods; he's too spent to answer. He lets Cole maneuver him, lets him lift up his right leg and move it, positioning him just so. Cole traces two fingers over Ren's hole and then, without warning, he's inside, testing, teasing, making sure. He pulls his pants down a bit, takes his cock out, so hard, so ready. He rubs its tip along Ren's ass, his lower back, between his thighs. Ren is moaning now, desperate even in his sated state. Cole grabs Ren's right cheek, then reaches his hand down and pulls it apart just enough to let his cock slide in between.

This time there is no talking.

Cole molds himself to Ren's backside and fucks him fast. He lets the denim rub up against Ren's calves, makes sure Ren can feel the metal zipper on the back of his thighs. Ren, usually so full of praise and profanity, is reduced to whimpers as he reaches behind to grab Cole's ass, urging him to fuck harder, or deeper, or stay still for a moment when it's all too good, too perfect, too agonizingly hot to move.

He pushes back to get Cole even deeper, grabbing his hand and pulling it back over his chest. He intertwines their fingers and grips tightly, squeezing every time Cole grunts into his ear, his hair, his shoulder. It's dirty, so dirty, the sounds of sex and the sight of Ren's pale, naked skin against Cole's nearly clothed body.

Ren yanks their joined hands down to his cock, now hard again, and Cole just hangs on as Ren jerks himself with purpose. They're a mess—a sweaty, sticky, panting, grunting, beautiful mess. Cole feels the heat build and buries his cock in Ren's ass, and when he feels Ren start to come, Cole lets go and pounds into him until he comes, too, screaming into the back of Ren's neck.

In a million years, he never would have imagined Ren so free, so willing, so deliciously naughty. He would have taken him however he came, of course—restrained, nervous, vanilla, shy. But Ren is none of those things. He's Cole's very best match, the most perfect man in the whole wide world.

They stay in the same position for minutes, more, who knows how long, until Ren turns to face Cole, wincing a bit as he shuffles in and presses as close to Cole as possible. Cole wraps both arms around him, rests his hands gently on Ren's ass, and says, "You okay?"

Ren snuggles in deeper and nods into Cole's chest, and then he's shaking, and Cole thinks he's crying, in pain, or overcome with something—sadness? Worry? Overwhelm? But then Ren lifts his head and Cole can hear it before he finally sees Ren's face: Ren is laughing, so hard his whole body is about to fold in half.

Cole smiles, laughs a bit with him, but it's Ren's moment; he'll explain when he comes down. After a while Ren is calmer, still giggling a bit, but able to look Cole in the eyes when he cups Cole's chin and says, "Just so we're clear, you're the best I've ever had."

Cole beams. "Thank you. I'm sure I don't have to tell you it's mutual."

Ren laughs. "I mean—*Cole*. We are having seriously amazing sex. I have never—and I do mean *never*—felt the urge to scream, 'Thank you,

Jesus!' For obvious reasons. But I do now. I need someone or something to thank, because this is more than just good sex; this is life-altering sex. This is what people mean when they say 'earth-shattering' sex."

Cole is so proud he feels as if he could levitate right off the bed, his grin as wide as it's ever been.

"I used to tell myself that if I ever had sex with you, it would be a disappointment because I'd built it up for so long," Ren continues. "Like that time I met Zac Efron at this event at The Center."

"Was it before the hair, or—?"

"After."

"Ew. Okay. *Not* pretty."

"Right. Anticlimactic, to say the least. So many fantasies demolished in one handshake."

"Tragic."

"Quite." Ren shifts up onto one elbow. "Sometimes I had to convince myself that there was no way we could be as hot as I imagined it, that it would be embarrassingly awkward, mediocre. Or just bad. But, fuck, Cole. It's... I mean, you have to admit, it's almost unbelievably good between us. Like, no one should have it this good. Should they? It's almost unfair how good the sex is."

Cole grins, kisses the corner of Ren's mouth and says, "No it isn't. It's what it feels like when you love someone completely, without question."

Ren looks worried. "And... you've never felt this before?"

"What? No. Of course not."

"You talk as though you speak from experience," Ren explains, relaxing a bit.

"No. I just knew, that's all. I knew it would feel this way with you." Cole runs his fingers along Ren's arm. "I knew sex with you would be amazing, but I didn't know you'd be so fucking dirty, Ren. *God.*"

Ren smirks. "You bring it out in me."

"I do? You weren't... you haven't—?"

"What? Love, let's not pretend we haven't both had plenty of great sex—"

"Of course not, I just wondered what you're into, what you've done before and might want to do again," Cole explains.

"We can get to that, right? I mean, just... just know it may have been wild, but it's never felt like this."

Ren's kiss is sweet, and slow, and full of reassurance and *shhh, let's not do this, I love you, it was always you, yes you, no more, shhh.*

Cole wraps one hand around the back of Ren's neck and kisses him fiercely, tongue fucking into Ren's mouth and sliding on his teeth. He kisses his need, his love, his *gratitude* into him.

They're quiet again, thinking, happy. After a while, Cole cleans them up, takes off his clothes, pulls the duvet back up to the top of the bed and climbs in next to Ren.

"I can't believe you prepped yourself for me again," Cole says, eyes shining.

"Well, the first time was purely coincidental."

"And convenient."

"That, too. I thought it was appropriate, since today is our anniversary." Ren is drawing circles, or hearts, or maybe snowflakes on Cole's chest. He plays with Cole's nipples, the patch of dark hair just below his belly button, his hands.

"It's not our anniversary, by the way," Cole says into Ren's hair.

"It is so. I'm pretty sure it was a week ago today that you had me up against a wall."

"Yeah, well. I don't want to celebrate that."

"Why not?"

"Because I hadn't told you I love you yet," Cole explains, his voice soft and steady.

Ren lifts his head says, "Saturday, then?"

"Saturday."

"What should we do to celebrate?"

"Maybe go back to Il Piatto and try to make it through an actual dinner?"

"Yes. I'll make the reservations tomorrow." Ren snuggles closer. "Oh, wait! How was Shep? Did you say yes? Are you Scout's hot new recording artist? Tell me!"

"I gave him a strong maybe. I need to discuss it with a few people, and with you. I'll tell you everything in the morning—it means I'll be busy, *really* busy, and we're just getting started—"

"Cole, you can't—"

"Shh. We'll talk about it in the morning."

Ren hesitates but quiets, planting a soft kiss on Cole's chest. He mumbles, "Okay, rock star," and falls asleep within seconds.

Cole drifts—to Saturday, to anniversaries yet to come, to someday. He briefly wonders if it's right to plan anniversaries when there is still so much unfinished, when there are still so many ties to break and amends to be made. It all seems so tenuous, fragile; he wants solid ground under his feet and a firm commitment from his love as to when, and where and how. But he's too content, too stupidly happy to dwell on this for long. As his eyes flutter shut, his last thought is the same as it's been nearly every night since he was seventeen: *someday*.

⊞ **Chapter 15** ⊞

On Thursday Cole logs sixteen hours in the studio while Ren, Antonio and Deidre drive up the Old Turquoise Trail to Madrid to pick up three small paintings he commissioned on his last visit. Ren texts him photos of old mine shaft entrances straight out of a John Wayne film; Deidre perched on a motorcycle, clutching an impressive tattooed bicep; a wooden marquee next to a honky-tonk bar, on which a flyer promotes "Drag Bingo! Saturday Night!;" Antonio sitting on a too-small stool at a retro soda fountain; rows of mailboxes, painted fuchsia and dipped in glitter; a close-up of Ren's face, pointed toward the sun.

He talks to Mitch and Alegra after the dinner break. They are both overjoyed that he's finally decided to take Shep up on his offer, and suddenly there is a plan, and next steps, a path to something he's dreamed about since college.

By the time he makes it back to Ren's room it's after midnight. Ren is asleep, the room dark save for the soft light from the desk lamp. Cole empties his pockets and notices Ren's notepad, open facedown on the desk. He knows he shouldn't look, but picks up the book before he can stop himself. Ren's been staring at the thing off and on for a couple of days—he just wants to take a quick peek.

The page is blank, except for the words "FRESH START" written across the top. Confused, Cole flips through the remaining blank pages and notices a few pages have been torn out. His eyes immediately zero in on the trashcan under the desk and now he's officially snooping. He's not even sure why he feels the need to do it—he could just ask Ren—but something is pulling him forward.

He finds two crumpled balls and unfolds each one carefully so as not to wake Ren. Right away he can tell that these are discarded drafts of his Zozobra paper. Cole had dropped his final version in the box earlier that morning. Just three sentences encapsulated all of his regrets and his greatest fear:

Every chance I never took.

Every promise or declaration I made to anyone but Ren.

That all of this is but a dream.

He felt better after placing the twice-folded paper in the box, as if he were already letting the regrets and fears go. But he'd shown his paper to Ren before he left that morning. He'd let him read it and accepted his kiss of reassurance. Surely Ren would have shown him his paper as well?

His heart stops when he realizes Ren has written only one sentence on each page:

Loving Paul.

Hurting Paul.

Paul. These papers were both rough drafts of a paper that had gone into the same box into which Cole had dropped his own regrets. What was on the paper that finally made it into the box? And why, after days of trying, had Ren found it so difficult to make one list that would get him closer to a fresh start?

For the first time in days, Cole falls asleep with a troubled mind and a heavy heart.

They're not expected at Fort Marcy Field until three p.m., so the next morning, after a shower and coffee and a late breakfast of eggs and red chile at Tia Sofia's, they drive to Whole Foods to pick up picnic items to share with the group, then to Target for a blanket and a cooler. With an hour or so to kill, they decide to do the tourist thing for a bit, and drive back to the Plaza.

The last thing they expect to find at the Georgia O'Keefe Museum is a pack of kids running in circles in the lobby, but they are not deterred. Ren wants to see O'Keefe's desert, her ravens, her sky. Cole pays their admittance fee as a tall, thin woman, probably the mother, says to her harried husband, "It's just art. There's nothing here for kids."

Ren rolls his eyes and digs his fingers into Cole's arm.

"Don't bite your tongue so hard it falls off," Cole teases.

They wander the minimalist rooms, sometimes lingering together to look at a particularly stunning flower, hands and shoulders brushing; sometimes apart, reading plaques and taking their time. Ren has been sweet and flirty all day, but also distant and nervous. It's unsettling; it seems as though they aren't just killing time, but waiting for something, something terrible.

Cole knows it's probably apprehension about telling Paul. Ren's nerves are likely getting the best of him.

"Look, New York!" Ren says, his expression wistful and still a bit closed off. "I thought she only painted flowers and desert things."

"I guess not."

Cole lets his arm brush against Ren's back, leans further into his space, breathes him in. They are alone in this wing, the obnoxious family long gone. Cole contemplates kissing the back of Ren's neck, wrapping his arms around his waist and pressing his forehead to his back, pushing in and in, closer, still closer until his forehead rests in that sweet, sweet spot between Ren's shoulder blades.

Instead he slips his hand into Ren's. "Do you miss it?"

"Every day."

"And could you imagine yourself living anywhere else?" Cole asks, trying to keep the worry out of his voice.

"I don't know. I never tried, not seriously."

Ren pulls him into the last room, effectively closing the subject. They talk of art, and rumors about O'Keefe's sexuality and their favorite galleries. As they drive back to the Eldorado they trade stories about artists they've known, pieces they've loved. As they walk toward Fort Marcy Field, cooler and blanket in tow, they talk of the places they'd still like to visit while in Santa Fe—Taos, a return visit to Ten Thousand Waves, dinner at the restaurant at the Inn of the Anasazi. It's not strained, not at all, but there's a nagging feeling sitting squarely on the back of Cole's neck—a worry, a fear.

As they pay their entrance fee and walk onto the field, Cole stares up at giant "Old Man Gloom" all in white, his black eyes and red lips, and remembers the last words on his paper: *That all of this is but a dream.*

He'll watch it burn up tonight and the worry and fear will be gone, along with his regrets. They'll get their fresh start, surrounded by their new friends and twenty thousand Santa Feans. And in a few weeks, once everything has settled down, they'll come back to each other free, and ready; they'll begin.

"Look, Cole, he's wearing a bow tie," Ren says, poking him in the side.

"Are you finding this at all bizarre?"

"I think it's fabulous."

Despite the early hour, a large crowd mills about, looking for a place to squat, finding their groups.

"Antonio said meet them on second base," Ren says.

Cole glances around and notices a baseball diamond close to the main stage. A quick scan of the crowd and he spots them: Antonio, Sarah and the Alex Marin House kids, some in chairs, some sprawled on blankets. When they arrive, Antonio gives both of them a big hug, nearly lifting Cole off the ground.

"I'm *so* excited you came. You are going to have the best day. The *best day*," Antonio says, rubbing his hands together. "Can I get you anything? A beer? Sarah made sangria—"

"Don't mind him," Sarah says with a smile, kissing Cole on his cheek. "This is his favorite day of the year."

"Oh, I don't mind. I'm excited, too," Cole says, setting down the cooler.

"He's an enthusiast," Ren says with a wink. "It's a way of life."

Cole helps Ren spread out their blanket and organize their snacks. He catches up with the kids, all of them disappointed he didn't bring his guitar. He watches the crowd swell and is relieved when Alegra and crew show up in time to commandeer a space right next to them. She's dressed down, a giant floppy hat on her head to block the sun and hide from fans. He notices Deidre arrive with Mitch and asks, "What's up with that?"

Ren shrugs and says, "No idea."

After they're all settled, eyes glued to the darling Mini Mariachis—children dressed in full costume, performing their little hearts out—Cole leans in toward Antonio and says, "Help me keep an eye on her, okay? This is a big crowd, and I don't want anyone to get to her."

"No problem."

After a while, Sarah pulls a lightweight easel from her giant bag of tricks, unfolds it, and places an easel pad, half-used, on the ledge. The kids gather close, familiar with the tradition, and Sarah assigns teams. Soon they're all crowded around the easel playing a rowdy game of Pictionary (without the board). Ren sits in Cole's lap, learning forward when it's his turn to guess, shouting answers and slapping his thighs when he gets it right.

Cole wraps his arms securely around Ren's waist, pulls him back, and whispers into his ear. "I adore you. And this. I love everything about this day." Ren twists a bit to give him a kiss and then snuggles back in to watch Alegra draw for her team. She seems to be drawing the same thing over and over again—a train, with two straight lines next to it.

Over the ridiculous guesses from her team, Deidre finally shouts, "Goddamnit, Alegra, can't you draw something different?"

Alegra glares at her, and finally starts to draw something that looks like a map, but Cole's not sure; this is clearly not her game. Sarah calls time, and Alegra throws her hands in the air. "Orient Express!"

"What the hell are the two lines?" Deidre asks.

"Chopsticks."

They're all laughing now, even Deidre, Ren doubled over in his lap.

"Oh fuck off," Alegra says, reaching for her cup of sangria. "Talk to me when you have a dozen Grammys."

There is a collective, "Ohhh!" and then Deidre is clinking glasses with Alegra, and Sarah is teasing both of them, and all is well.

They pass around salads in Chinese takeout containers, a bowl of fried chicken, garlic cheese rolls, freshly baked chocolate cake. It's a hodgepodge, but Cole loves every second of it: the band; Alegra; his new friends; and Ren, always Ren. It's as if they've built a little community in just a few short days and he never wants it to end.

By the time the sun sets, they're all mildly drunk and anxious for the main event to start. Their blankets an island in a sea of people, they stand to see over the crowd, laughing at the fire dancers and shirtless drummers. It's all very pagan, despite the priests standing off to one side, blessing the event. Cole can feel the crowd pulsating in his own body; the anticipation is palpable.

Suddenly, Zozobra starts to moan, and growl and flail his arms. The lights on the field go out and the crowd chants, "Burn him! Burn him! Burn him!" He notices Antonio wedge in close to Alegra, standing over her protectively, as they all join in the chanting. Ren is laughing and shouting along with everyone else, his neck and wrists adorned with glow sticks, a gift from the kids. And once again, it seems as if they are suspended in time, neither here nor there. He wraps his arm around Ren's waist and tugs him close.

As the flames lick up the bottom of Zozobra's dress (it couldn't be called anything but), the crowd goes wild, screaming louder than he's heard at any arena. As the fire builds and crawls up the cloth body, stuffed with the worst of it: with everything that holds people back and haunts them and keeps them up at night; with everything wrong, and stupid, and worrisome and *bad*, Cole feels a calm wash over him.

As Zozobra wails and the fire consumes him, the crowd caught up in the crazy, dark joy of watching their troubles burn, the worry leaves him. The weight of regret disappears and he is suddenly both lighter and more grounded at the same time. He looks at Ren, the fire casting a glow on his jubilant face. *Does he feel it too?*

After the fireworks, after they pack up their empty containers, and coolers, and chairs and blankets, after they all walk the four blocks to Antonio and Sarah's lovely restored adobe, their crew expands to include other friends of their hosts, filtering in from the festivities. Cole helps Sarah set out several kinds of homemade salsa and guacamole as everyone else lends a hand with chairs, with playlists, with drinks and a table of sweet treats.

The party is jumping, yet easy, as good people laugh and get a bit too drunk. There is dancing, Antonio's playlist a love letter to Sarah. It's her music—soul and funk and some Motown, and nearly everyone takes a turn dancing, even Alegra. Cole flows in and out of Ren's orbit, standing close to him for long stretches, letting him mingle and laugh and shine in others. Most of the guests don't know their story, their past, their tangled web and plans unmade. They just see them as Ren and Cole, two men in love, and treat them as such. It's *heaven*.

But later, he notices Ren off to the side, staring into his drink. He remembers the crumpled papers, Ren's worst, the thing he wanted to see go up in flames. What had he written on the paper he dropped in the box? Maybe the magic of the night is lost on him. Maybe he's too burdened with the reality of breaking Paul's heart to let Zozobra do his job.

With the first few bars of a classic Otis Redding song, Cole pulls Ren onto the dance floor and into his arms. Here, surrounded by Sarah and Antonio's friends, Cole realizes they are a part of something bigger than themselves, something outside of the two of them and their age-old dance. He holds Ren a little tighter, lets Otis move them and tries not to think about all that's left to unravel and break, the blank pages, all the words unsaid.

Cole's love is a slow burn, hot, crackling under his skin like the small fire in the kiva not ten feet away. Are they all on fire tonight, all of these couples in and out of something great, dancing slowly and slower still, letting the music glue them together when words fail? Will all their regrets go up in smoke now, angry like Zozobra, wailing and fighting to hang on? Will they truly be able to wipe the slate clean and start over, or was it just a paper wish, a secret confession that cannot be absolved?

They dance like this for two songs, and a third, a haunting, sexy version of "A Case of You," covered by Prince. Ren laughs and says, "I think this is the only way Sarah can stand Joni Mitchell."

"Antonio likes Joni?"

"So much. It's disturbing." Ren cocks his head to one side. "Something wrong?"

"No. I'm good. I was going to ask you the same, actually."

Ren looks scared for a moment, starts to say something and then grabs Cole in a tight hug. "Just hold me close. Just dance with me and hold me as close as you can."

Most of their friends are dancing now, Antonio with Sarah, Teddy with Wyatt, even Deidre with Mitch. Ren presses his fist against the back of Cole's shirt, lets Cole lead their movements, follows his hips. It's not sexual, not yet. It's an exhale, a promise; the forging of two hearts.

Ren pulls back, slips his hand into Cole's and says, "Let's go back."

Cole nods, and they make the rounds, thanking their hosts and saying their goodbyes to the rest. They leave the blanket and the cooler, buried deep in the stack of Zozobra supplies, and make their way back to the Eldorado. They're quiet, the events of the night still on their minds as they approach the Plaza. Picking up San Francisco Street again, Cole has the beginning of a new song: a song about this street, this city, this gift to his heart, this chance.

They're still holding hands as they enter the lobby, happily buzzed, Ren mumbling something about which room they should stay in tonight, when a voice stops them cold.

"Ren! I've been waiting—you look—God, I missed you. You look amazing. Where have you been? I've been texting you for hours."

"Paul."

As Ren's hand slips from his grasp—fast, as if it's on fire—Cole can actually feel joy leave his body. It shoots out from the marrow of his bones and through his skin, every inch of it, disappearing into air, leaving him with the terrifyingly familiar ache that he'd thought gone forever.

Paul.

Paul isn't some abstract concept, a man he knew for an evening, a man he envied. He isn't Ren's biggest regret, someone to whom Cole will apologize sincerely and profusely and eventually forget as he and Ren walk off into their preordained life. Paul is a man with a platinum band on his ring finger and Ren's promise in his heart. He's real and standing right in front of them, *jubilant*.

Suddenly Cole feels as if he's watching his love slip away from him in slow motion, as if he's drowning, as if he's a spectator in his own life. Every gesture is exaggerated and every moment takes too long: Paul's face breaking out in a radiant smile; his arms opening wide and wrapping around Ren. It's the end of the movie, the last scene, as Paul squeezes Ren hard and lifts him up off the ground like two lovers reunited. Because *they are*. Ren and Paul are lovers.

Without Cole it's just the two of them, undeniably a couple, certainly friends. Between them are midnight confessions and shared plans and sweet, silly moments stacked up like bricks, fortifying. He stares as they hug and Paul chatters and Ren whispers back, and Cole realizes that the wall between him and his happy ending is much stronger than he had anticipated. *They are; they are lovers.*

Paul is here. *Paul*. Smiling, handsome, travel-rumpled Paul, who seems too focused on hugging his fiancé to notice that Ren was practically glued to Cole when they walked in the door. It's the proverbial slap that wakes him up to reality, to old doubts and new fears.

"We did it! Wilder caved and then Peterson had no choice but to agree and now it's done. It's done!"

Ren pulls back from the hug, grips Paul's biceps and says, "As in, *done*, done? As in they won't go back on their word?" Paul nods, and Ren sways a bit. "We're—that's it? It finally happened?"

Paul's face is lit up like Christmas. Ren's return smile hits Cole like a bucket of cold water. That smile, shining at him over coffee; on the dance floor; under a blue, sun-bleached sheet drying on Molly's backyard clothesline, his face turned away from too-fat dragons and cotton candy wisps floating across the sky.

It hurts too much to see *that* smile directed at someone else.

Paul takes Ren into his arms and lifts him off the floor again. He's easily six-foot three, his auburn hair, graying slightly at the temples, a compliment to Ren's blond. Ren squeezes him back, laughing. They look like an ad for Cape Cod vacation rentals; every caption on every picture of them might as well read, "My Fabulous Gay Life."

The sight of his love in the arms of another is too, too much, and Cole has to fight the urge to punch Paul in the face. In all the years he pined for Ren, he'd never wanted do harm to one of his boyfriends, not even when he was spitting mad at that cheater Caleb. Humiliate them with his vast knowledge of the many layers of Ren Warner, absolutely. But tackle them to the ground and beat the living shit out of them? Never. The desire to rip Ren from Paul's grasp and do just that is more than a little disconcerting.

"I had to see you. I had to come straight to you," Paul says, his body buzzing.

"But how could you leave? You must have so much to do—"

"Clark is bringing the vote to the floor as soon as we're back in session, but that's not until after Labor Day. Andy told me to take the weekend."

Weekend? He's here for the weekend?

Ren goes white, but he doesn't say, "No, no. You can't possibly stay. I'm in love with Cole, and we promised each other all of the days. All of them."

What he does say is, "You remember Cole."

"Of course! Ren mentioned you two ran into each other." Paul extends his hand. The sight of Paul's earnest face is enough to make Cole want to vomit all over the Navajo rug beneath them, but he shakes his hand anyway.

"Small world, and all that," Cole says, failing at everything. Paul's grip is strong, his skin warm.

"Come celebrate with us!" Paul exclaims. He is all trust and happiness; Cole can feel the bile creep up his esophagus.

"Yes! That's exactly what we should do," Ren replies. "Together. All three of us. They're still serving at the Agave."

Cole thinks Ren may have temporarily lost his mind.

"I don't—"

"*Marriage*, Cole. It means we're as good as everyone else, in every state."

Ren looks at him with pleading eyes, as if to say, "Don't leave me." But the urgency and precariousness of their situation is lost on him now. All he can see is Ren in a tux; Ren leaning into him as music plays and their nearest and dearest dance; Ren whispering into his ear, *This is how it always was,* as he slips his hand into Cole's pocket and pulls out the key to their room, his heart, their future.

"Please join us, Cole. I'd love to catch up with you, and share a toast to our new civil rights."

Cole gapes. *A toast to our new civil rights? Is he for real?*

"Of course. I'd love to. Thank you."

He knows that if this were a normal situation, if he weren't in love with Ren, if he weren't fucking Paul's fiancé, he'd politely decline and let the lovers escape to their room for the private celebration Paul no doubt had in mind. But this situation is anything *but* normal. This situation is pure hell and it doesn't come with a rulebook.

The Agave is buzzing with post-Fiesta revelry. Ren leads them through the maze of tourists and the occasional group of suits caught up in the citywide celebration, toward the back of the lounge. He zeroes in on a group of middle-aged women standing up to leave and claims their table. There is small talk as the women gather their things, talk of mariachis, and rebirth, and crowds and fireworks. Paul is rapt, asking questions about Zozobra while Cole merely nods and smiles in what he hopes are all of the right places.

"—And I really felt it, you know? The release? What did you burn?"

It takes him a moment to realize that the short, slightly plump woman is talking to him. She's glassy-eyed and bouncy and a bit too loud.

"Sorry, what?"

"What did you burn? You did write down your fears and regrets, didn't you?"

"Yes, I—"

"Wasn't it amazing? Watching it go up in smoke? Just poof! All of that ugly stuff gone for good—"

Before Cole can spit out an answer the woman is pulled away by her friends, en route to another bar. Paul settles in on the butter-soft oversized settee. He pats the cushion, urging Ren to sit down next to him. Cole sits in a chair opposite them, glaring at Paul as he tugs on Ren's waist to pull him closer.

A busser swoops in and clears their table, the server right on his heels. Paul orders without consulting them. "Veuve Clicquot and three glasses, please. We're celebrating!"

Cole tries to pay attention as Paul weaves his tale of how he pulled off the civil rights miracle of the decade, but finds it difficult to multitask— how is he supposed to keep up with this important conversation when he's busy counting the number of times Paul touches Ren?

One, the back of Ren's hand. Two, his forearm. Three, a shoulder squeeze.

"And you're sure Wilder won't back out this time?" Ren presses.

"I may have convinced him we had enough votes to kill his farm bill and make it look like his overzealous strategy was to blame," Paul says.

Four, the back of his hand again. *Is that their thing? Is that how he calms Ren down? Does it work faster than my thumb on his wrist?*

"But doesn't Landry support the farm bill?" Ren asks.

"He does."

Paul smiles at Ren, shrugs his shoulders. Ren frowns. "And Peterson? Why did he fall in line? You said he had no choice."

Five, hand squeeze.

"He wants that farm bill just as much as Wilder, but he doesn't want to alienate his voters," Paul explains. "I may have had a hundred or so kindergartners with same-sex parents draw pictures of their families and hand-deliver them to him to his office... just as Summer Davies showed up to interview him for a *Today Show* segment about his experience growing up in the foster care system.”

“Ha! I wish I could have seen that,” Ren exclaims.

“You will.”

Six, kiss on the cheek.

“So you think a bunch of kids with sweet pictures will change his mind about ‘dirty queers?’” Cole asks, remembering Congressman Peterson’s easy dismissal of gay rights in years past.

“No, he still hates us,” Paul explains. “I just handed him a very public reason for changing his mind, one that will appeal to most of his almost-moderate constituents, and made sure Ms. Davies was there to witness it. He gets his farm bill, secures some votes and gets media points for his ‘heartfelt transformation.’ Everybody wins.”

Ren smirks at Paul; he knows and appreciates his ways. Cole tries not to roll his eyes. They’ve only been sitting at the table for ten minutes—how is he supposed to get through the rest of the night without revealing their secret to Paul or knocking that satisfied smile right off his face?

“You *are* brilliant,” Ren says fondly, as if he’s reminding himself that it’s true. Cole shifts in his seat.

“It was you. Your belief in me, and in us, it carried me through and inspired me,” Paul says, his hand on Ren’s cheek.

Eight.

Cole tries not to vomit on the table. Paul’s smooth is too smooth, as if it comes from a can. *Maybe I could just accidentally kick him under the table—repeatedly.*

Ren looks down at his hands, folds the corners of his cocktail napkin down, one at a time. If Cole ever wanted a direct line to Ren’s brain, it’s now. He is at his mercy and he has no idea what Ren could be thinking.

Just then, Ren looks up at Paul. Behind his eyes there is sadness, but Paul’s smile remains. Ren tries to smile back, says, “I can’t believe you’re here.”

“Good surprise?”

“Of course.”

Paul relaxes his shoulders. “Good.”

Ren turns his attention to his champagne glass, spinning it to catch the flickering candlelight. Cole knows Ren likes the patterns the glass makes on the napkin and, because he knows this, he smiles.

From across the table, Paul offers Cole a toothy grin. "So Cole—"

"Hmm?"

"Wedding bells for you any time soon?"

Ren's gasp is a little thing, almost silent, but Cole can hear the plea of *oh God, not now; this is too hard* underneath it. As Ren drinks down a glass of water, Cole takes a long sip of his champagne, thinks about how to answer. He wants to follow Ren's lead, to make this easier on everyone, especially his love, but he can't give up all of the control. It's maddening. And it's making him feel hot and cold all at once.

Ren gulps too fast and coughs, sounding as if he's struggling for air.

"Okay?" Paul asks Ren, rubbing his back.

Nine.

"Fine. Just wrong way and all that."

Paul turns his attention back to Cole. "So? Any marriage plans for you and your—I'm sorry, I don't recall your boyfriend's name."

Paul takes Ren's hand and places it in his own lap, under the table.

Ten.

Shifting his gaze to Ren, Cole says, "I haven't proposed yet."

Ren's eyes go wide, but Paul doesn't notice.

"But you want to," Paul says.

"I do." Cole's eyes are still fixed on Ren. Between them is a trail of promises unspoken, like a thousand tiny boxes waiting to be opened. He holds Ren's gaze, willing him to open one. Just one.

"And now you'll be able to get married anywhere you want in your own country," Paul says proudly. "Just don't do it this January. We've got dibs."

At this Ren breaks the spell and turns to face Paul. "Wait—no. We said May, or possibly June—"

"Why wait? It's perfect. We'll marry in one of the holdout states, make a statement," Paul says.

"We can't... I can't get married in January."

"Why not? You already have everything planned out in that book of yours."

"I just can't."

Paul seems surprised to hear Ren's sharp tone. He leans closer, as if he wants to hug him, soothe him, love him up. But before he can, Ren slides away and gets up from the table. "I need the restroom. I'll be... I'll be back."

Ren checks his pockets, offers both men a small smile and then, as he walks by, a barely-there brush against Cole's back. It's nothing, but enough to bring a blush to Cole's cheeks. A blush is all it would take for Paul to pay attention, to assess Cole. And he can't have that, not until he knows how Ren wants to handle this.

Paul may be watching Ren, or watching Cole watch Ren, so he won't look. He won't look at him as he walks away, as he has watched his every move since that first Tuesday, more than a week ago; since the last chance, the one that fate gave them because they couldn't get there on their own; since before then, and every day; since the beginning; since the day he held his hand out to help a beautiful sad boy, when he was deaf to his own heart but looking, always looking; since what seems like forever. He won't look. He *won't*.

Except he does look for just a moment, mere seconds, but long enough to see Ren wind his way through the tables as he did that night at Il Piatto. And then he's still looking, eyes on Ren's back, his shoulders, his graceful stride.

When he turns back to Paul he is composed, all McKnight poise and demeanor, his forced smile masking the raging volcano in his gut. Paul is focused on his phone, texting a reply to someone.

Paul turns his phone over on the table. "Sorry. Bad habit."

Cole shrugs. "Work is work. Yours is more important than most."

"It's not, not really." Paul leans back, rests his arm on the back of the settee. "We all need teachers, and scientists, and skilled labor, and music, and design—I could go on, of course. The list of admirable and necessary professions is long. I'm just a guy with a dream who won't give up."

Is he for real?

The worst thing about Paul is, he's almost impossible not to like. Everyone likes him. Loves him. Even Ren. *Ren.*

Paul is passionate as he speaks about the inherent value of each and every person on the planet, wide-eyed and talking with his hands. With his strong jaw, broad shoulders and dazzling, perfect smile, he could convince anyone to reconsider their vote. Cole listens, and nods and smiles; his mother's best boy.

"Liam! *That's* his name." Paul interrupts his own monologue. "Your boyfriend. Ren mentioned him."

"We broke up."

"Oh, I'm sorry to hear that. But I thought Ren said—"

"We broke up."

Cole may be okay with using everything he learned at his mother's knee to hide the tension and turmoil inside of him, to keep him from claiming Ren in some ridiculous display, but he'll be damned if he's going to lie.

"You said you planned to propose. Someone new then?" Paul asks.

Cole looks directly into Paul's eyes and says, "Someone perfect."

"Whirlwind romance?"

Cole chuckles. "Depends who you ask."

"Hmm, you're holding on to that story pretty tightly," Paul teases. "Maybe we'll get it out of you with the next round."

Paul pulls the bottle from its icy bath and tops off all three glasses.

Cole sneaks a glance toward the direction of the restrooms. No sign of Ren.

"So, Cole, what do you know for sure?"

Really? The Oprah line? Cole tries not to laugh. "I know the Vikings can't defend against a long pass because their wideouts aren't fast enough."

"Vikings, huh? I'm not a football fan, though Ren's dad has taught me enough that I enjoy it somewhat. You know Erik and Linda, right?"

"Very well, yes."

Paul's phone vibrates on the table. He flips it over, looks at the screen and says, "Shit. I have to respond to this email. Do you mind?"

"Go right ahead."

With Paul engrossed in composing his email, Cole pulls out his own phone, intent on texting Ren to make sure he's okay. When he unlocks his phone he sees that Ren has already texted him from the bathroom.

Ren: I'm sorry. I'm in shock. Don't be mad.

Ren: Please look at your phone.

Ren: I'm not in the bathroom. I snuck off to the bar. I'm drinking tequila.
      The bartender is teaching me things.

Cole cranes his neck, looks around the room, but the bar is out of his sight line. He immediately types a reply.

Cole: This is crazy.

Ren: I know. I know. I panicked.

Cole: He's quoting Oprah. You need to come back.

Ren: ?

Cole: What do I know for sure? I know for sure that this is hell.

Ren: That's just his standard opener. He thinks he made it up.

Cole: Seriously? Doesn't she have that trademarked?

Ren: Cole! Focus!

Cole: Yes. Shock. Got it. Are you ever coming back?

Ren: Will you help me tell him?

Cole: Of course.

Ren: Right now?

Cole: Yes.

Ren: Oh God. He'll hate me.

Cole: He won't.

Ren: You don't know him.

Cole: I know he loves you.

Cole: And I love you.

Cole: And I could never hate you.

Ren: Deep breath.

Cole: Baby. Come on.

Ren: Follow my lead. I may not be able to do this.

Cole: You can. You will.

Ren: I'm walking back now.

Cole: I don't want him to think we were texting while you were gone, so I'll keep texting until you come back. I love you.

Cole: I love you. I love you. I love you.

Cole: Remember that night after the Spring Break Eve Party when we snuck out of the dorm with Dean's stash and walked out to that massive willow tree out by the boathouse?

Cole: You said you wanted the kind of love that could break your heart. You said you wanted to be at someone's mercy. And I didn't say anything. I held my breath because you were daring me to love you. To be that person. Or I thought you were.

Cole can feel him return, his love, but he keeps texting; he does not look up.

"I see you both are enjoying each other's company," Ren teases.

Paul holds up two fingers, his attention focused on his phone. Ren sits down next to him, sips his champagne.

"Almost done," Cole says.

Cole: The way you looked at me. You were daring me. I wasn't sure then. I
       was never sure enough to try. So I let the sun come up and that was that.

Cole: I am that person.

Cole: Don't forget that, baby.

Cole sends the last text, slips his phone into his pocket. He looks at Ren. "Sorry about that."

Ren smiles nervously, glances over at Paul. He waits; he does not fill the space between them with small talk, or pretend. Cole steels himself for what's coming. He studies Paul, his entire being wrapped up in somewhere else, some plan, and wonders if he'll go down lightly. Will he let Ren go without a fight? Will he unravel before them, his shiny brass armor falling to the hard Mexican ceramic tile floor? Or will he recognize the truth, that there will be no compromise, no negotiation?

There will be no deal.

When Paul finally looks up from his phone he doesn't pocket it or turn it off. Instead he slides it across the table and over to Ren, a giant grin on his perpetually photogenic face.

Ren covers Paul's phone with his hand and says, "Paul, I need to tell you something—"

"Read that," Paul interrupts, gesturing toward his phone.

Ren squares his shoulders. "Something's happened, and it was... it was bound to happen eventually, I think. *I know*. I couldn't—"

"Ren, whatever it is, I'm sure we can handle it. Please, just read the email on my phone."

Cole stares at Ren, at the way he grips the phone, his palm still covering the screen; at his somber face, his watery eyes; at his fear.

"Paul—"

"Darling, please."

Ren sneaks a quick glance at Cole and then, shoulders slumped, lifts his hand off Paul's phone and begins to read. In seconds, Ren's eyes bug out.

"What the fuck, Paul? Tell me this is just a draft," Ren says, his finger scrolling through whatever it is Paul wants him to read. "Tell me... *Paul*. Are you—tell me this is just a fucking draft."

Paul sits back a bit, smile faltering. "You're not happy?"

"You didn't even *talk* to me about this," Ren fires back, eyes still on Paul's phone.

"I thought—"

"You set a *date*?"

"It was hard enough to find a date that would work with Landry's schedule—"

Ren slams the phone down on the table and shifts in his seat to face Paul. "I don't give a fuck about the President. Just tell me, yes or no—is this press release a draft, or have they already sent it out?"

Paul frowns, then looks over at Cole and says, "Would you give us a few minutes?"

"He's not going anywhere," Ren says. "Answer. The fucking. Question. Paul."

"It went out a couple of hours ago."

Ren stares at Paul, silent, jaw set. It's only a few seconds but it seems like minutes, minutes that seem like hours, Cole's heart threatening to beat right out of his chest, until Ren finally says, "You couldn't find another way to get a prime spot on the morning news? A hundred little valentines weren't enough?"

Paul reaches for Ren's hand, but Ren pulls back, folding his arms across his chest.

"I wanted your approval, but I couldn't find you—"

"And it couldn't wait one day? Just one fucking day?"

"I thought you'd be happy. I thought—you wanted to set a date, we've been putting it off for so long."

Ren looks at Cole then, eyes filling with tears he seems determined not to shed. Then he looks up at the ceiling, pressing his fingers to the corners of his eyes.

He turns to Paul and says, "You should have talked to me first, even if you had to wait."

Paul leans in, takes Ren's left hand and kisses the ring on his finger. *Eleven.*

Cole stares, notices how the firelight hit the ring just right; how it's special; how it fits Ren's finger snugly, as it should.

God, I'm an idiot.

I haven't even noticed the ring. That hand has gripped my hip, pressed love into my spine, caressed my face and spread me open. I saw nothing but his elegant fingers, strong, the life lines on his palm telling me hopeful stories. It was there all the time and I saw nothing.

Cole turns away, focuses on the din in the room, the too-loud stories about forgiveness and rebirth, the laughter. He counts the *vigas* above him, Ponderosa pine beams stained dark. Purely ornamental, they bear no weight. He tries not to think. He won't think at all.

"We need to—let's go up to your room. We can talk this out. I'm sorry, I didn't want to—please let's—we haven't been alone together in so long. Cole won't mind," Paul says.

"You won't mind if I steal my guy away, right?" Paul asks.

Cole is on a rogue rollercoaster. He is careening down a deep gorge on a runaway train. He is falling, falling, miles beneath him and only sky above, sure to crash.

There will be no deal.

"Actually, Paul, I do—"

"No!" Both men look at Ren, surprised by his panicked tone. "Let's... not. We're here to celebrate," Ren says, his voice too sing-song to be trusted. He raises his hand in the air to get the server's attention.

No, what? Let's not, what? Tell the truth? Go upstairs? What?

"Ren," Cole presses, "you said you had something you wanted to tell Paul."

Ren ignores him, smiles at the server approaching their table. Tall and rail-thin, with blond dreadlocks pulled back from his face, he looks every bit the young Santa Fe, the picture of wide-eyed contentment.

"What's your name?" he asks the server, his body turned away from the table.

"Daniel, but my friends call me Dano," he says. He can't be a day over twenty-two.

"Daniel, I need you to set us up with six tequila shots, two for each of us," Ren says with a wink.

"Right away," Daniel says, before shuffling off to the bar.

"Ren—"

"*Paul?*" Ren replies, one eyebrow quirked up in challenge. He shifts back toward the table, pours the last of the champagne into his glass and drinks it down.

"Never mind." Paul settles back in his seat. He glances at Cole, a slight blush on his cheeks. "I swear, he knows the name of every person who has ever waited on us."

Ren leans back against the settee, arms folded, glaring at Paul. Cole forces a smile. They're off the rails. He should say something, say the thing Ren needs to say, anything to get them back on track, but the tension is thick, a knotted rope tied 'round his throat.

Paul fidgets with his glass, and then tries again. "Cole here was telling me that he broke up with Liam. But he said he's not single, so I'm—"

"Really, Paul? Really?" Ren interrupts.

"What? He said he wanted to propose. Am I wrong? Are you single, Cole?"

Cole shifts his gaze to Ren. "Not remotely, no."

"See? He doesn't mind talking about it," Paul says.

Ren rolls his eyes, stares him down. The silence is brief, but painfully awkward, both Paul and Cole trying to find their footing. *Why doesn't he just tell him? Why bother fighting over a wedding that will never take place?*

From under the table, Cole can feel Ren's leg bouncing up and down, a nervous tic. He watches as Ren's face heats up, his lips purse in a thin line.

"Darling—" Paul begins.

"All these years I've just been another item on your to-do list. Moving me around like a fucking intern. A fucking *intern*, Paul."

"That's not true—"

"It most certainly *is* true."

"Couldn't we go upstairs? We haven't been together in weeks," Paul pleads.

"Whose fault is that?"

Paul smiles nervously at Cole and says, "I'm sure Cole doesn't want to hear us fight."

Ren glances at both of them, then up at the ceiling again, his voice a loud whisper: "This is a fucking nightmare."

Let me climb across the table, to you, for you. Let me soothe your worry with reminders—a look, a nod, a thumbprint on your wrist. Let me get to you. Keep you. Let me try.

"Ren—" Cole starts, but before he can get another word out, Daniel returns carrying a tray laden with six generous shots of tequila, a dish of lime and lemon wedges and three tiny personal saltshakers.

"Blanco," he informs them, as he places everything on the table.

"Blanco? Is that a brand?" Paul asks, jumping on a chance to diffuse the tension.

"No. Blanco means it was bottled immediately after the distillation process," Daniel explains.

"It preserves the agave flavor," Ren adds, licking his the back of his right hand.

"You know your tequila," Daniel says.

"I'm learning." Ren sprinkles salt on his hand, licks it, and downs his first shot without sparing the rest of them a glance.

Daniel clears all evidence of their first round. "Flag me down if you need me."

Ren pulls a wedge of lemon from his mouth, wipes his lips with the back of his hand. Back straight and brow furrowed, he looks like a hurricane waiting to happen. "You two better catch up."

Cole and Paul follow suit without question, their faces grim as two soldiers about to be sent off to war. Ren wastes no time; he licks his hand again, readies the salt.

"Let's toast. Tonight is the beginning of the story, isn't it? The story we tell our grandchildren, about how this battle finally ended," Ren says, sprinkling more salt.

Cole follows on automatic pilot, stunned. Ren is angry, and buzzed, and on his way to blitzed. There's no telling what he'll say, or do.

Ren raises his glass high, a cue. He waits until the other arms are up and then looks at Cole, eyes beginning to mist. It's only two seconds more, but in that moment, in the waiting, is a longing Cole had thought was gone forever. There is want and the cage around it. There is hope, waning. There is despair.

And then, when the old familiar pain is almost too much to endure, Ren simply says, "To love."

Cole holds his gaze. "To love."

Ren brings his glass to his lips, offers Cole a sad smile. Paul mutters something about "the sweetest toast" as Cole chokes down his second shot, leaving the citrus in the bowl. *Let it burn. It's nothing compared to this.*

He lets his eyes wander around the room, everything turned up and everyone a bit off thanks to Old Man Gloom and third, fourth, fifth rounds of liquor. He lets the sound of Ren and Paul fade into the background as Ren bites and Paul works his charm—too smooth, too shiny. Cole lets his heart swell, bolstered by belief and sheer will, by ten thousand memories and days unspent.

The tequila races through his veins, settles into his face, the tips of his fingers. Silently he wills Ren to look at his phone, to come back to the task at hand, to remember. He's a witness to the drama of a relationship that should have been over by now. They should be up in Cole's room, his arms wrapped around Ren. They should be falling into sleep, his hand rubbing calming circles onto Ren's lower back, whispering, "Baby, I love you" over and over again into his hair.

It's a hideous feeling, waiting for the end.

Cole is drawn back to the table when Daniel appears again, saying, "What's up? Do you need something?"

Ren stares at him for a moment and then inexplicably starts to laugh. He flops back on the settee, his body loose and sideways.

"What'd I say?" Daniel asks.

"I have no idea," Paul says. He sighs, opens something on his phone and begins scrolling through it.

"Could you bring us some water?" Cole asks.

Ren sits up, still giggling. "And tequila!"

"None for me, thanks," Cole says.

Ren points at Cole, then Paul, and then himself. "Two, two, two. Set us up, Dano."

"His name is Daniel," Paul says, still looking at his phone.

"But we're friends. Aren't we friends, Dano?"

"No worries, man. You can call me Dano. I'll be right back with your drinks."

As soon as Daniel is out of earshot, Paul sets his phone down and turns to Ren. "You seem determined to do this here, in front of your friend, so I'll say this now before you drink so much you black out, " he says. "It's not like you to hold on to your anger like this, and it worries me. This crusade—isn't it ours? Aren't we together on this? I'm surprised you've taken this so badly, and I want to make it right, if I can."

"You can't—fuck, I'm all fuzzy. Just because I believe in your work doesn't make what you did okay," Ren says.

"You're right. I apologize for jumping the gun, for acting without your approval. I want you to be happy. It's all I've ever wanted. Please forgive me?"

Ren licks his lips, considers Paul. His face softens. "I wanted—I *do* believe in you. You know that, right?"

"Yes."

"And I'm so very proud of you," Ren says, his words slurring.

"I'm proud of you, too—"

"No, I—don't be. You shouldn't—"

"But I am proud of you, darling," Paul says. "This victory is as much yours as it is mine."

Ren's face falls. "Oh. I, uh... never mind."

Watching Paul miss the point is almost as painful as watching him touch Ren. Cole wants to fill Paul in, give this to Ren, help Paul get it just to see Ren smile at something true and beautiful, just to see Ren feel loved in all the ways that matter.

Ren is shredding the napkin now, no pristine folds, no pretty patterns. "I am angry. But I—we set it up this way, and I was okay with that, because—sometimes—I shouldn't have. Oh, fuck, this is hard."

"What's hard?" Paul asks.

Cole braces himself, lays his palms flat on his thighs to keep himself from jumping out of his chair and climbing into Ren's lap to block out the world, keep him safe.

Ren huffs out a little self-conscious laugh. "I'm—I'm a little drunk."

"It's okay. Could you—you know I meant well, don't you?"

"You always mean well, Paul. It's your best quality."

"You'll see. It will be beautiful—a winter wedding. And then we can finally get on with it."

Ren looks at Paul. His face is so sad, Cole can hardly stand it. "We have a lot of plans, don't we?"

"Yes. Yes," Paul says, leaning in.

Ren looks down at the napkin again, now strewn about in tatters. His voice is soft and liquor-lazy when he says, "*Do you* need something, Paul?"

"Sorry? I don't—"

"Something... else?"

"I have you, why would I need—?"

"Because I do."

Cole sucks in a breath, wishes for arms long enough to reach under the table so he can steady Ren's knees, hold his hand.

"I need something, Paul, and... and I didn't want to tell you like this, or ever, really, but—"

"Whatever you need, we'll get it. Okay? I know I've been gone a lot and maybe haven't noticed—"

"No, it's not about—oh God, I'm a little *too* drunk for this," Ren says, his face pale and flushed.

"Let's get you up to your room, okay? You need to sleep it off and then we'll start fresh in the morning. It'll be a new day. Because it is a new day, Ren. It's a beautiful new day in our country and we're going to be married and we did that, you're part of that, the way you loved me and supported me—isn't that something to shout from the rooftops? Isn't that something worth telling the world, even if it means answering a few interview questions?"

Damn. "A hundred little valentines," Cole mutters.

"Hmm? I didn't hear you," Paul says.

Cole looks at Ren, growing paler by the second, and says, "It was nothing. Doesn't matter."

When Daniel arrives with the drinks, Paul drops a wad of cash on the tray. "Thank you. This should cover everything, but we won't be needing the last round," he says, and turns to Ren. "Come on, let's get up to your room. We have a lot of catching up to do."

Ren stands up abruptly, a look of panic in his eyes. "Wait," he says, his hand on Daniel's arm. He picks up one of the shot glasses and swallows the tequila without ceremony. Very quickly, he moves on to the next. He's on to his third before either of them speaks up.

"Whoa, Ren—"

"That's enough," Paul says, stilling Ren's hand with his own.

Ren shakes off Paul's hand and downs the shot. "You both just move me where you want me, don't you? When and where—everything is you, you. Everything."

"Come on, let's get you upstairs," Paul says, nodding at Daniel in an effort to get him to leave.

One arm around his waist, Paul guides Ren to the door, Cole trailing close behind. Ren struggles a bit and then gives up, makes an effort to walk straight. "I'm fine with it. I'm so good at that," Ren mumbles.

When they reach the lobby Paul says, "Are you on the same floor—?"

"No, I'm on the second floor. He's on the fourth," Cole says. "Let me help you get him to his room."

"No, thanks. I've got him."

Paul starts to make his way to the elevators, and then turns to look over his shoulder. "I don't know his room number—"

Cole wants to keep Ren with him so badly he has to practically spit the words out. "Room 415."

Paul nods, whispers something in Ren's ear. He walks Ren past reception, past the giant fireplace, past the toffee-colored armchairs arranged in a square. There are too many touches to count, now. He's all over Ren, protecting him, keeping him safe.

Cole is under water. He is sinking, sinking fast. He watches as Ren's knees give and fights the urge to rush to him, to hold him up, to swim to the surface. *Let me.* He watches as the elevator comes down, the numbers lighting up at each floor, each second stretching out as though he still has a chance, as though he could make this right; as though he isn't at the bottom of the sea, tangled in kelp, praying to be rescued himself. *Let me.* He watches as the doors open and then close again, this time with his love inside. *Let me.* He can't hear Ren; he can't see his face; he is drowning.

By the time he makes it back to his room, Cole is beside himself with worry. His mind swims with too many questions, fueled by ancient insecurities he's slipped back into like a second skin, as if Santa Fe never happened... as if his worst fears did not burn up in flames tonight, but came true instead.

Chapter 16

It's still early when Ren wakes, the sun creeping into the room despite the heavy curtains, forcing him to face the day and all he has yet to handle. His head is caught in a vise-grip, his stomach empty but still tied up in knots. He'd complain, but he deserves every last agonizing moment of it.

Getting embarrassingly drunk was a dick move—he should have just told Paul right then and there, but he was already slightly tipsy by the time he and Cole left Antonio and Sarah's party and, in order to deal, to take care of two hearts and remember his own, he needed all his wits about him.

Opening his eyes all the way, he whispers, "You're full of shit." It's still too loud for this epic hangover, this massive mess.

In truth, getting drunk was the only way he could avoid sex without outright telling Paul why he never wanted any other man but Cole for the rest of his days.

Glancing around the room, he's not surprised to find the other side of the bed empty, nor is he surprised to find two little ibuprofen pills next to a glass of water on the bedside table. There's also a note:

Went for a run. Breakfast at ten and a phone interview (both of us!) at noon. It would be perfect if you would cancel your afternoon so we can roll around a bit until our dinner reservations at eight. April found a lovely Italian restaurant downtown, Il Piatto. Love you!

It's all very familiar—the hand at his back, the gentle persuasion, the surest fix for every problem. He'd long since abdicated to Paul; he let him lead, and fuss over him, and steer them in the right direction. He'd let him take over and paint their future in "appropriate" colors, fill in the gaps, patch up the holes. He let him do this because it wasn't something he'd yearned for, or planned for; it wasn't something he'd dreamed up one rainy day after a perfect boy took his hand and showed him a shortcut to the promise of total acceptance. For *that* future, he would have had much to say. He would have stayed up until the wee hours of the morning weaving possibilities with interlaced fingers, playing with ideas and soft hands, laughing, and planning, and plotting, and hoping and sharing in the creation of something inevitable, and rare and true.

But with Paul he just nodded and smiled. He rearranged his calendar, and toned down his wardrobe, and generally felt fine with all of it, his handsome compromise.

He *let him*.

Still, Paul also pulled a dick move. Sending out a press release about their wedding, setting a date without discussing it with him—it was classic Paul James. They were both dicks—the more so because they let it all play out in front of Cole.

He reads the note again and groans. He now has reservations at Il Piatto with two men—Paul at eight, Cole at eight-thirty.

Fucking hell. What is my life?

He spots his phone charging on the desk next to his wallet, which is open and lying flat. His clothes are folded neatly on the corner chair, the little in-room coffee pot full, a clean cup and saucer next to it. He's a bit woozy when he stands up and stretches the kinks out of his back. *How the hell am I going to make it through this day?*

He pulls out the desk chair and sits, reaches for his phone and turns it on. He sees a few texts from Deidre, one from Antonio and several from Cole, all unread. The latest from Cole shows up on his screen at the very top.

Cole: Call me when you wake up. I need to know you're okay. And please read all of my texts.

He ignores the other messages and reads through his entire text exchange with Cole, including the last few he hasn't seen.

I love you. I love you. I love you.

I am that person.

Don't forget that, baby.

This. This is how he will get through the day. Somehow he will find the courage to tell Paul everything and send him back to New York to dismantle the life they built together. He'll call Deidre and Antonio and explain that he needs to take the day and, when it's all over, he'll meet Cole at the restaurant. He'll be ready, then—to start over, to become the person he was meant to be and be with the man he has loved so long.

His forefinger hovers over Cole's name in his phone—how many times had he called him? So many, too many, and not enough. The marathon phone sessions when Cole was this miracle, this boy who was proof of all that is good in the world, this giant. The shorthand. The drawn-out calls they'd had trying to fit in every detail of their big, beautiful, grown-up lives. Then, the distance in Cole's voice. The too-long, awkward pauses. The goodbyes.

He thinks back to the first time he called Cole, so nervous to make good on his promise to "call if you need to talk;" how he looked at Cole's name in his phone as if it was his secret gift and then, mustering every bit of courage he had, touched Cole's name with his finger—the same finger poised to call Cole now—and called the boy who made him smile.

Cole answers on the second ring.

"Ren?"

"I'm okay. Terribly hungover, but okay," Ren says, his voice hoarse from screaming at Zozobra the night before.

"Do you need some ibuprofen? Can I bring some to your room?"

"I took some. Thank you. Cole, I'm so sorry—"

"Don't. It's a mess. You were upset. I get it."

"It's going to be okay. Right? Can you tell me that?"

"Of course. Maybe not at first, but—you're strong, baby. You can say what needs to be said. You'll be okay."

"I wish you could be here with me."

"I'll come right now."

"No, I... I need to do this alone." Ren moves to the door, listens carefully. "He'll be back soon. I'm going to tell him this morning and then I'll come to your room. Will you wait for me?"

"Are you sure you don't want me to help you tell him?"

"No, no. That was a bad idea. I need to give him the respect of privacy."

"He can be very... never mind."

"What?"

Cole sighs. "He can be very convincing, Ren."

He hears the concern in Cole's voice, shaky and soft. So Ren says, "He can try to change my mind all he wants, but that has nothing to do with my heart."

Cole is quiet for a moment; Ren hears just the sound of his breathing. And then, "I'll be waiting."

"Go back to sleep. Keep your phone near you, okay?"

"Yes. Of course. I won't be able to sleep, so call me anytime."

"Cole?"

"Yes."

"I love you, too."

Ren hurries through his shower, not wanting Paul to return before he's finished and get the brilliant idea to join him. As he goes through his routine, he practices what he'll say, how he'll start. "I'm in love with Cole," he says, as he washes his hair. "I can't marry you because I love someone else," he says, as he works conditioner into his hair from roots to ends. "I've been lying to myself, and to you, and I'm so very sorry," he says, as he scrubs his body too harshly, skin red from the friction and heat. "Please forgive me," he whispers, as he stands under the shower spray, rinsing clean.

He runs a towel over his hair and then ties it around his waist. He brushes his teeth. Just as he's coming out of the bathroom he hears it: a knock.

Him. It began with a knock. No. It began with a hand, holding mine. No, no. It began with a smile, a tiny kindness, a wish.

Assuming he must have changed his mind and come to help him tell Paul, Ren steels himself to see Cole when he looks through the peephole. Instead it's Paul in his running clothes, hair wet with sweat, waiting. He opens the door.

Paul looks him up and down and smiles appreciatively. "I hope you knew it was me when you opened the door."

"Yes, I checked."

He kisses Ren on the cheek and walks past him toward the desk. "Did you know one of your key cards doesn't work? I must have grabbed a different one this morning, because the other card worked fine last night."

Shit.

"I, uh—"

"You didn't know?" Paul asks, fishing the other key card out of Ren's wallet and slipping it into his pocket.

Shit. Shit. Shit.

Ren shakes his head.

"You were hoping I would be able to join you, weren't you? That's why you asked for two," Paul asks, eyes gleaming.

"We didn't plan on it, so—"

"Oh," Paul says, disappointed. "Did they automatically give two cards when you checked in?"

Ren could say easily say, "Yes." He could nod in agreement and that would be that.

"You can't be a liar, too, Ren." His dad's warning rings in his ears and he can feel Cole urging him on from two floors below. He can do this. He can. He will.

"No, they didn't."

Paul is unfazed. "Next time tell Deidre not to leave her key card at the bottom of that cesspool she calls a purse. She didn't actually stay in the room with you, did she?"

"No."

"I'll just take this one down to the desk and switch it out while you finish getting ready," Paul says, holding up the other card.

Paul looks up at Ren, then, and frowns. "What's wrong? You look as though you've seen a ghost. Are you not feeling well after last night?"

Ren looks at the key card in Paul's hand. He swallows, wills the words to come out of his mouth—*I can't marry you because I love someone else; I've been lying to myself, to everyone; please forgive me*—but he can't stop staring at the card.

Paul follows Ren's eyes to the card in his hand. He looks back at Ren, expectant.

"Paul..." The words stick in his throat as he looks at Paul's gorgeous face, tense with confusion.

"Fuck, this is hard," Ren exhales. He runs his fingers through his hair, still damp from the shower.

Paul looks at Ren, eyes widening. His face heats up as he palms the card and squeezes around it, hard.

"Paul, I need to tell you something—"

Before Ren can finish, Paul walks past him and out the door. Ren runs after Paul, opens the door wide and realizes he can't follow because he's not dressed.

"Paul, wait!" Ren shouts down the hallway, but Paul ignores him.

He rushes back into the room. *Shit. Shit. Shit!* Heart pounding, he opens a drawer, pulls out a clean pair of jeans and a T-shirt and dresses as fast as he can. By the time he makes it out the door and down the hall, Paul is getting on the elevator. Paul turns to face the doors, his face like stone.

"Paul! Please!"

The elevator doors shut and just like that, Ren's heart is in his throat. Feeling around in his pockets, he realizes he left his phone in the room and has no key card to get back in. He spots the red EXIT sign and flies down the stairs, barefoot, heart beating out of his chest. His mind races with images, the worst, the absolute *worst* possible ending, the soundtrack one refrain: *Cole, Cole, Cole, Cole.*

Bursting through the second floor stairwell entrance, Ren scans the hallway leading to Cole's room. Paul is there, moving from door to door like a robot, swiping the key card twice at each room, just to make sure. Room 201, Room 202, Room 203...

Ren runs to him, grabs him by the arm. "Paul, stop!"

Paul yanks his arm away and moves on to the next door, his face the picture of steely determination. He's only three doors away from Cole's room, just moments from unlocking the door and discovering the truth. Hoping Paul will assume the next door is Cole's, Ren crosses to the other side and blocks Room 205 with his body. He says, "Someone will call security! You can't be arrested—it will be all over the news."

"Move."

"Paul, please. It's not what you think—"

Paul scoffs, turns around to face Room 206 and swipes. The little dot above the handle lights up green and the door unlocks, a soft click that echoes in Ren's heart like a life painted on glass, falling onto concrete.

Paul turns the handle on Cole's door and opens it wide, the door banging on the inside wall. Ren can't move, can't speak; he can't even scream.

From inside, Cole calls out: "Ren? You didn't call. Are you okay, baby?"

Paul winces and looks back at Ren, his eyes filled with rage. He takes his hand off the door and walks inside. The heavy door swings to close and Ren bolts for it, catching it just before he's shut out of the room.

He finds his voice. "Paul, don't—"

"Ren—oh *fuck*," Cole says, running right into Paul, who stops short at the entrance to the main room.

Cole backs up toward his bed, eyes on Ren. Paul follows, sizing up the room. Shaking, Ren grounds himself by positioning himself against the wall. He takes in Cole, his sleepy eyes full of concern, his hair messy and his chest bare. He wants to go to him, wrap an arm around him, sink into his space. But the tension in the air is like a chain around his ankles; it keeps them apart. Cole says nothing, and Ren knows they're both waiting for Paul to light into them, to attack and prod and blame, because they deserve it; it's their due.

Paul looks at Cole, who somehow manages to own the room despite Paul's height advantage and the trouble at hand.

"Those are my pajama pants," Paul says, his voice flat.

Oh, shit.

"I thought they were Ren's."

"He borrowed them from me," Paul explains, staring at the dove-gray cotton pooling around Cole's feet.

"It's not what you think..." Ren starts, searching for words.

"You said that." Paul sits down in the corner chair.

Paul stretches out, extending his long legs. He plays with Cole's key card, twirling it with thumb and forefinger in both hands. Only yesterday morning Ren climbed into Cole's lap on that chair and played with the hair at the back of his neck. He can still feel Cole's strong hand on his thigh, holding him there as they exchanged soft kisses and planned their day.

"Let's find out if it is what I think," Paul begins, hands stilling as he looks over at Ren. "I think you're fucking your friend. Am I wrong? Are you fucking him, or have you just been having slumber parties and sharing each other's clothes?"

Ren looks down at his own clothing and realizes he's wearing Cole's Berklee T-shirt again. *Shit. It just keeps getting better.* When he looks back at Paul he's met with the disdainful look Paul reserves for his most hated detractors. He had hoped it would be better—not easier, but better. Different. He had hoped he wouldn't ever be on the receiving end of that Paul James stare.

"I'm in love with him," Ren says.

And that's it. He'll tend to Paul's heart as best he can, but there's no going back, now.

Paul's eyes darken as he stretches the moment way past awkward. For a moment it looks as if he might cry, but just as quickly he pulls himself together, sits up taller in the chair and tosses the key card at Cole's feet.

Paul looks at Ren and asks, "Were you safe?"

"What?"

"Am I going to have to get tested?"

Ren moves to Cole's side. "Did you hear me? I said I'm in love with Cole."

"I heard you."

"What does it matter, we're not—wait. You think I'm—you want to take me back?"

"Take you back? Since when did we break up?" Paul asks, getting to his feet. "You're lonely. You fucked around. I'm pissed, and I'm quite sure that underneath this anger some part of me is shattered, but... this doesn't change anything."

Cole moves closer to Ren, folds his arms in a protective stance. They are inches from the edge of Cole's bed, the same spot where Ren declared his love for Cole just days before. Though he knows Paul deserves this moment to say his piece, Ren can't help looking at him like an interloper, invading a sacred space.

"No, I... I'm in love with him," Ren says.

Cole says, "For what it's worth, I'm sorry, Paul. I can't imagine what you must be thinking—"

"*You* do not talk. You don't say anything!" Paul shouts.

Ren says, "You deserve to be happy—"

"I *am* happy!"

"I just told you I cheated on you and you're happy? We're kidding ourselves, Paul. We tried. We both tried—"

"It's cold feet, that's all. People have flings. The distance and my schedule—it happens. We just need to spend more time together. We need—I'll take two weeks off. After the vote, we'll go away together. We'll forget this ever happened and plan the wedding and—"

"Paul!" Ren interrupts. "It's not a fling. It's *not*."

Cole unfolds his arms and reaches for Ren's hand. It seems like too much, lacing his fingers with Cole's in front of Paul, but words are not working. And it is too much. At the sight of their joined hands, Paul reels back as if he's been punched.

Again, Ren hears his father's voice. *"Whatever happens, you owe it to him to tell him the truth. All of it."*

"I've been lying to myself and—I didn't know, when I met you—I wanted to get over him, but I... it's not possible," Ren says, squeezing Cole's hand. "I've always been in love with Cole. And I always will be."

"So you've been fucking him all these years?"

"No."

Paul leans back against the dresser, his body blocking the mirror. He sighs. "How long?"

"Just... just this week."

Ren looks at the window, at a thin patch of light shining through the curtains. In the uncomfortable pause, he is transported to the morning after that first night, when he left the bed in his own room to pull back the curtains and let in the day. He felt no guilt that morning as they watched the brilliant sunrise, clutching each other, holding off goodbye. There was no hope of requited love, no promise of a future, of destiny fulfilled. There was only searing grief, tempered by the tender touch of the man he thought would never be his, a love he was sure he could not keep.

"We didn't plan it," Cole says, breaking into the silence.

Ren shoots a warning look at Cole. He looks as if he wants to say more, but instead he snaps his mouth shut, his eyes on Paul. Ren follows his eyes and gasps. Before him Paul is crumbling; somehow he looks smaller, stripped of his veneer and hurting, hurting so badly. This is a side of Paul he does not know.

He lets go of Cole's hand. "I owe you an explanation," Ren begins, moving closer to Paul while still giving him space. "I wanted—I take full responsibility for this. I thought I could love you knowing it wasn't enough. I thought I could *make* it enough. I tried. I really did.

"We were so young when this started and we didn't know how to handle our feelings... so many missed opportunities and bad choices. I think we were both waiting for the other person to figure it out, and then we just gave up. And I'm so sorry, Paul. If I had ever thought there was a possibility that Cole would return my feelings, I never would have said yes—"

"I'm your Plan B? Is that what you're saying? You couldn't have him so you settled for me?"

"No, I... I didn't know I had a chance—"

"And that's better?"

"I genuinely thought I wanted the life we made," Ren says, inching closer. "If it was going to be anyone else but Cole, it would—"

"Don't you say it. Don't you fucking say it," Paul whispers, shoulders shaking.

Ren's eyes well with tears and he pushes the heels of his hands onto closed eyelids to make it stop. It's not his moment to cry. "I'm so sorry—"

"We should have told each other, long ago," Cole interjects. "It would have saved everyone so much heartache."

Paul scoffs, glaring at Cole. "You should probably shut up."

"You deserve someone who loves you completely," Ren says, reaching out to touch Paul's arm. When he doesn't flinch, Ren squeezes gently, steps a little closer.

Paul says, "You never answered my question."

"What question?"

"Were. You. Safe?"

Ren panics, remembers the last time, the feel of Cole's bare cock inside him, the way they forgot themselves, the way they didn't care and didn't talk about it and didn't regret it for one minute. It had felt so right, so deserved. And yet now, standing before this man who loves him, this man who trusted him, it's clear that it was *not* right, or deserved. It was an act of selfishness.

"Ren, just tell me," Paul presses. "Were you safe?"

Ren squares his shoulders and steps back a bit. "No. Not every time."

Paul tilts his head a bit and looks at Ren as though he's a stranger, as though he's someone to fear. He looks down for a moment, then back up at Ren, this time with wet eyes to match Ren's, the mask gone. On instinct Ren moves to comfort him, but before he can lift his arms Paul pushes off the dresser and lunges for Cole, knocking him to the ground. Ren hears the thud of Paul's fist connecting with Cole's face and rushes to pull them apart. Before he can get to them, Paul throws another punch, but Cole turns his head away. Paul cries out in pain when his fist hits the floor and then he's on Cole again, trying to pin him.

"Paul, no! Stop!" Ren yells, as he tries to get between the two of them. He pushes Paul back enough for Cole to get two hands up on Paul's chest and hold him away. Ren holds on to one of Paul's arms, but he can't seem to get him off of Cole.

Paul breaks free from Ren and lifts his arm, ready to do damage.

"Paul! Stop!" Ren shouts. He jumps on Paul and tries to yank him off of Cole. He manages to pull Paul back enough for Cole to get out from under him and scooch back toward the wall; he sits up against it, wincing in pain.

Ren goes to Cole, crouches down to his level. Hand on Cole's chin, he turns his face from side to side to assess the damage: an eye that will surely be bruised the next day and a tiny cut above his right eyebrow, most likely from Paul's ring.

"I'm fine," Cole says, tilting his head away from Ren's hand.

"What the hell, Paul?" Ren says, looking back at him.

Paul is breathing heavily now, clearly shaken. He sits on the edge of the bed and stares at his own hands; he says nothing.

"Let me get something for that cut," Ren says, moving to stand.

Cole grabs hold of his hand and pulls him down to sit next to him, then brings their joined hands into his lap. "I'm *fine*," Cole assures him.

Ren leans back against the wall and surveys the room. Aside from the two of them on the floor, one bleeding, and the dejected man on the bed, nothing looks out of the ordinary. No furniture overturned. No clothes strewn about. No evidence of that which has been broken, of three hearts beating off rhythm and much too fast.

Suddenly he's looking down on the scene, feeling that familiar yet absurd wonderment. "*It's an aerial moment,*" Cole had said that first night in this magical, weird city, sitting on Deidre's kitchen floor. Cole had held his hand then, too, as he had so many times before, his thumb on Ren's wrist. There was something different about that night—possibility, a dormant connection woken by fate, a chance, terrifying.

Now, in this moment, there is a similar sense of danger, the unknown laid out before him like an empty desert highway, endless, the horizon not a destination but a thin line where sky meets clay.

Paul slumps over, stares at the floor, his hands on the back of his neck.

"We fucked up," Cole says to Paul, his tone strong but apologetic. "Ren is everything to me, and I'm not giving him up. This is bigger than us. This is true love. But I know we made a mess of things, and I apologize for that.

"And I'm sorry you had to find out this way," Cole continues. "I'm sorry you were dragged into this at all, but it's meant to be. What are the odds we would run into each other, here of all places? It was inevitable."

Paul looks up then, flexes his fingers and then shakes out his right hand. Then he turns and says, "You're both full of shit. Fucking cowards."

He stands, picks Cole's key card off the floor and pockets it.

"True love. Please. You say this is true love, and yet you let fate handle it? Bullshit," Paul says. "Do you think we'd have national marriage equality if I waited around until the time was right? If I didn't push and push and push for it? The time was ALWAYS right, and I wasn't going to stand around waiting for a bunch of narrow-minded closeted cocksuckers to give me the green light.

"You think this is real? That this is meant to be? Fuck that," Paul continues. "If this were some epic, 'inevitable' love, you would have fought for each other. You didn't even TELL EACH OTHER how you felt, let alone fight for what you wanted. Pining after each other while you fuck other people? While you promise *your future* to OTHER PEOPLE? That's love? That's meant to be? Don't kid yourselves. That's not love. That's a fantasy, that's—if you wanted each other, you would have done something about it. You really want something in life? You go get it."

Ren is in shock. Paul is rattling off some version of their truth as if it's the most obvious thing in the world. As if they're not idiots, but deluded. *Cowards. Deluded, cheating, asshole cowards.*

The old fears creep up like a bad dream, pushing at the soft corners of his mind, blanketing his short-lived happiness with age-old shadows.

Cole squeezes Ren's hand as if he knows, as if he can read his mind and feel his fears. Paul steps forward, towers over them, and Ren is acutely aware of how vulnerable they are. He feels small, and young, and... caught.

"What were you doing with me, huh?" Paul looks off to the side, eyes fixed on Cole's bed. "I would have swum the ocean to get to you, Ren."

Ren gasps. Next to him, he can feel Cole tense; the hold on their intertwined hands loosens, and he's not sure which of them initiated it.

Whatever he expected from Paul, it wasn't this. It never occurred to him that he would find their story ridiculous—unbelievable, even. Ask him to stay, yes. Call him a cheater and tell him to get out, yes. He could have dealt with most outcomes. But Ren never expected Paul to hold a mirror up to Ren's own face—close, too close, like the unforgiving makeup mirror his mother kept on her vanity that revealed every line, every blemish, every scar not visible in plain sight.

Without another word, Paul walks out, the door slamming loudly behind him. The sound is like a gunshot, snapping Ren to attention. He slips his hand out of Cole's grasp and stands up, starts pacing around the room. The guilt, once blissfully absent from his psyche, rears up like a giant bear woken from hibernation a month too soon. It will crush him, this guilt. It will tear him apart. He can feel it coming down hard; there is no escape.

"I'm such an asshole, oh my God," Ren says.

From the floor, Cole says, "Then we're both assholes."

"I can't believe I—Cole, this isn't me. I'm not a liar. I don't cheat. I don't hurt people with my reckless behavior—"

"We couldn't help ourselves, we love each other—"

"That's bullshit. Are you listening to yourself?"

"Ren, we handled this badly, yes, but please don't make it sound like we're some reality show rejects, here. That's not what this is, and you know it."

"We cheated, Cole," Ren says, voice resigned as he sits on the bed.

"I'm aware of that."

"We didn't use a *condom*."

"I know. That was—"

"I don't do that, Cole. I *don't*. I think somehow I lost myself, I forgot—but it didn't feel that way. It felt like I was finally waking up, like I was actually remembering something, something I needed—"

"Ren, stop. Don't you realize what's just happened?"

"I think I do, Cole—"

"Paul knows. He knows, now, and we can finally be together," Cole says, pulling himself up. He sits down on the edge of the bed next to Ren, one leg up so they can face each other.

Ren looks at him, touches his cheek, a barely-there brush over his sore eye. "Your face."

"I'm okay. I deserved it."

Dropping his hand, Ren says softly, "I'm not sure *who* I am anymore."

"Baby, why? I know this was awful, and intense, but—"

"I always use a condom."

"Why are you stuck on that? Yes, it was unsafe, and that's not like you, or me. But I'm clean, you're clean. We're okay."

"Because he's right."

"About what? Ren, no—"

"What would you have done if we hadn't run into each other?"

"Ren—"

"Because I would have married Paul. I would have loved you and missed you and when it was safe to do so I would have cried for you. But I had no plans to tell you. And you might want to tell me that you would have come for me eventually, but those are just words," Ren says, shoulders slumped in resignation.

"Baby, you know how sorry I am that I didn't—"

"Why didn't you tell me? Why *didn't* you come for me? Why didn't you tell me everything?"

"I told you—I didn't know how and then I thought you were lost to me."

"But it shouldn't have mattered," Ren presses. He's done it now. He's cracked the one box they were afraid to open, the one brimming with difficult questions, and bitterness, and pain.

"I did try to tell you. I sang a song for you, but you didn't listen," Cole says, his brow furrowed.

"You fucked Adam while I was in the next room!"

"Ren! Seriously?"

"Yes! Do you have any idea how much that hurt—"

"You were with Caleb—"

"And every other time? Wasn't I worth fighting for?"

"Of course!" Cole says, voice raised. "But Ren, why didn't *you* try harder?"

Ren looks at the floor. "I told you how I felt."

"We were sixteen! Are you telling me I blew my chance with you at sixteen and that was it?"

"Clearly not. I did just cheat on my fiancé with you."

"Stop. Wait. What is happening here?"

Ren stands and starts pacing again. He's distraught, the words and memories swirling in a frenzy. He's panicked now, the weight of their indiscretion and the old fears pressing down on every inch of him. "I don't know. I just—vacation is not reality. This place is—maybe we've been kidding ourselves."

"Are you saying you've changed your mind about us?" Cole asks, his voice strained.

"No, I just—could I breathe for a minute? I feel... out of my body and—I just don't think the issues we had are going to disappear just because we finally admitted we had—"

"Issues? What fucking issues, Ren?"

"We had every opportunity, Cole. Why didn't we take just one?"

Cole stands, arms crossed. "I thought we just did."

Ren is wild, now, as he lets it all back in; the old hurts stack up like bricks between them. "You're saying I'm worth it now? Why not two weeks ago? Or ten years ago?"

"You moved on! You pushed me away and—I tried. I tried to get you to come with me—"

"Where? To London?"

"Yes! That day, I told you how I wished I could take you with me—"

"And is that what I'm supposed to do now? Hmm? Drop everything and move to London to follow you?"

"Whoa. Fucking hell, Ren. These aren't our issues you're worried about. These are *your* issues."

Ren stops pacing. He takes in Cole's red, angry face, the hurt in his eyes. He shouldn't say it, the last thing. It could shatter them forever, but he has to do it. Because it's real, and it can't be avoided.

"I may be a mess about this, but Cole, you spent years jerking me around, confusing me with your innuendo and charm. You were oblivious to my feelings and I can't help but wonder now..."

"What? Just say it, Ren."

Ren sighs, slips his hands into his pockets. "I can't help but wonder how you could love me so much and still not see me."

Cole's eyes go wide, as if he's seen a ghost.

"Well, looks like you two are off to a good start."

Ren turns to see Paul leaning against the wall near the bathroom, a bucket of ice under one arm.

"Paul, I... I didn't hear you come in," Ren stammers.

"Here," he says, looking at Cole as he drops the bucket on the dresser. "For your face."

Cole forces out a "thank you" and then folds his arms again; this time he is the one sizing up Paul.

"I'm going home," Paul says to Ren. "I think you should come with me and sort this out. I think you owe me that."

Paul turns on his heels and leaves, the door slamming shut behind him. Ren falls into the chair, head in hands.

"I don't even know who I am anymore. I don't—I would never do these things to another human being. Why was it so easy?"

"There's nothing easy about this."

It's his own damn fault. Paul has done nothing but love him, and move them forward while Ren remained passive and agreeable. How could he complain about Paul's shortcomings and compare him to Cole when he had gone along with all of it, without question? If he'd lost some part of himself it was his own doing, and splitting up with Paul wouldn't mean getting that part back. Running off into the sunset with Cole wouldn't give him that part back either, for that matter. That was his job, and his alone.

His tone is sad and wistful when he says, "In the beginning I thought we'd end up together eventually, like in that movie, *When Harry Met Sally*. I kept thinking we were just caught in the second act, that soon you'd realize you loved me and come for me. But you never did."

"Why did you leave it all up to me, huh? I was a kid."

Ren looks up at his love, this man he has adored for so long. They've done so much damage—to themselves, to each other, to the men they recruited as substitutes. A tear falls down his cheek. He wipes it away, but more soon follow. He says, "If we were supposed to grow up together, how can we be sure we grew up at all?"

Cole steps back, lands on the bed as if someone has pushed him. "I don't know."

Ren crosses to Cole, stands before him and takes his face in both hands. He smiles at him through watery eyes. He knows what he has to do.

"Do you know what I wrote down on my paper, the one I dropped in the box for Zozobra? I wrote that I was afraid this wasn't real. I was afraid that we wouldn't last outside of this place..."

Cole is crying now, too, tears in lines down both cheeks. Ren wipes them away with his thumbs, but they just keep coming.

"I need to go, love."

"Ren—"

"I don't recognize myself. I haven't for a long time. I need time. I need to breathe, figure out what I want to do."

"You're going back with him."

"I'm going back to New York, yes. But not with him. There's no one else for me but you. I just—I need to face what I've done and make some decisions outside of this..."

"This what?"

"Us. This *us*."

Cole reaches up and pulls Ren's hands off of his face, holds them in his own. "How long?"

"I don't know."

"I'm not giving up."

"I hope not."

Ren leans in, presses his lips to Cole's. The kiss is soft, barely there, a sharp contrast to the feel of Cole's hands on his hips, fingers digging in, sure to leave marks. Pulling back, he sees the question in Cole's eyes, and the disappointment. He wants to soothe his worries with definite promises of where and when, but he won't do that. Not while there is still so much for him to face.

"Go, then," Cole says, his voice flat.

Ren kisses his forehead. And then he's walking away from him, his heart. As he leaves he slows the closing door with one hand so it will shut quietly; he's not looking for an ending.

Bare feet sinking into soft carpet, he walks to the elevator, his own heart numbing from the inside out. When the doors close, he pulls

Cole's T-shirt up and uses it to wipe his face. He will not cry in front of Paul.

Back on the fourth floor, he knocks on the door to his room and waits. Paul opens it almost instantly, then retreats into the room, clearly on a mission. He has all of their suitcases open on the bed, the curtains pulled wide and CNN on the television. "Our flight leaves in four hours. I called for a car. It will be here in an hour."

Ren nods and gets to work; there's no point in correcting Paul's audacious expectations. He may be going back with him, but he is not going home.

He's on autopilot as he packs—shoes in bags, pants on hangers, jeans rolled up, toiletries secured. He stashes away his treasures, trinkets he bought for Sean and his girls, for his parents, for himself, leaving one box out next to his carry-on. He texts Antonio and Deidre with promises to explain later and packs his carry-on with files, his sketchbook, his laptop and chargers.

When the front desk calls to inform them that the car has arrived, Ren is ready. As he leaves he does not look back at the room, the bed, that place near the door where he hugged Cole, held him close, reveled in the wonderment of *finally, finally, yes please, finally.*

In the lobby, he separates from Paul and walks quickly to the reception desk. He goes through the motions of checking out like a robot, his answers monosyllabic, his face a mask of polite response. Once finished, he takes out the small wrapped box, slides it across the counter and says, "Please see that Cole McKnight gets this."

Outside, he slips on his sunglasses, walks down the steps and meets Paul, waiting for him near the Town Car.

"After you," Paul says, holding the door for him.

Ren slides into the backseat and situates himself behind the driver, as close to the door as possible. He stares out the window, his body rigid and unwelcoming. This may be the longest "walk of shame" ever known to man, but that doesn't mean he has to give in to Paul's silent demands. That he's not sure how to sort out the last ten days, or the past fourteen years, or tomorrow and the day after that, is beside the point. Right or wrong, Ren has always made his own choices and he will not be swayed.

It seems only a moment has passed, and they're already approaching the exit for I-25. On earlier trips, he never paid attention to the signs and markers; he was always focused on getting back to New York, on gossiping with Antonio, on his phone, his schedule, his plan, his project. Now, with miles of highway in front of them and this strange, beautiful city behind him, he is struck with a sense of loss so profound, so all-consuming, he is once again that boy on a bus bound for Chinatown, willing himself not to cry. When he left Cole's apartment in Boston that day, he'd been so sure that any chance he had to be with Cole was lost, the sound of Cole and Adam's careless one-night stand a near-constant refrain the entire ride back to New York. But this is not that day; he is not that boy.

He lets the people, and sounds, and moments and colors of his Santa Fe heart fill him as he stares at the car's immaculate floor. Antonio's arm around his shoulder; a bowl of green chile; the smell of ash and burning paper; Sarah's infectious smile. The boots, and the promises and the ancient rites. The sweet honey on *sopapillas*, hot from the oven. Alegra's laughter. Kisses—for the first time, on a dance floor, compelled by a song; in a bed, trying for too much; quick coffee-flavored pecks they'd ducked into Burro Alley for; and one more, the last, the one he hoped would carry them, keep them, help them find their way.

Just before La Bajada, the tall hill that will obscure any view of Santa Fe, he turns for one last glimpse out the back window. Somehow, the picture soothes him. Somehow, the landscape is different: the endless sky, the slope of desert rolling into mountains capped with snow even in late summer. Somehow, it's no longer just a place; it's a beginning.

"You'll see," Paul starts, breaking into Ren's thoughts.

Ren turns, expecting to find Paul staring at him with hopeful eyes, but instead he's met with a profile as Paul stares out his own window. *Does he know I found my heart here? Does he know the dirt is magic, that it heals? Or is it just a place to him? Another campaign stop, another ally on the map?*

Perhaps sensing Ren's eyes on him, Paul turns, his expression guarded behind sunglasses and well-practiced neutrality.

"I'm going to forgive you," Paul says.

"I'm... I'm so glad. I hoped you would."

By the time either of them speaks again they've passed two casinos, sprawling oases in the desert. Ren isn't ready for the big conversation, the one in which they strategize announcements, divide up furniture and friends. So instead he says, "I'll stay with Harper until you head back to D.C."

"He's a mess. And a gossip," Paul says. "He'll have told everyone by tomorrow morning."

"Not if I ask him not to say anything."

Paul grunts. He maintains disdain for Ren's friend Harper Abbott's life of leisure, despite the fact that Harper had helped raise millions for President Landry's presidential bid.

"He will tell even *more* people if you do that," Paul warns.

Ren shrugs. "So I'll get a room at the W."

"I wish you'd let me manage the situation. Just come home. I'll stay in the guest room. It's only two nights."

He looks at Paul, a sad smile on his face, and thinks about how easy it would be to just fall back into it. The life, the work, the friends, the promise. He could pretend that the last few days were just a dream—a beautiful, life-defining dream—and get back to the world he built with Paul. It was a good life. It *is* a good life.

But it's no longer home.

The outskirts of Albuquerque are upon them when Paul takes hold of Ren's hand and says, "I don't mind, you know. Being second best."

It's heartbreaking and suffocating, watching Paul hold onto him for dear life. He loves him too much to let him beg.

"It's not about that," Ren says, letting Paul keep hold of his hand. "It's what I've always wanted, and I can't turn my back on it now. I'm sorry."

Paul gives his hand a tight squeeze and then lets it fall back into Ren's lap. "You'll see," he says, eyes looking out the window again. "Sometimes we have to let go of the life we hoped for in order to live another life. Just because you can be sure of me doesn't mean I'm not worthy of your consideration."

"You think I'm crazy, don't you?"

Paul is quiet for a moment, and it's too long—long enough to make Ren shift in his seat. They're turning off the highway toward the airport exit when Paul finally says, "I don't think you're crazy."

Seconds later Paul mutters, not softly enough, "I think you're a fool."

It's like a punch to the gut, his own deepest fears on the lips of the man he wronged. Paul is astute—you don't climb to his position without keen instincts and the ability to size up people and situations. He knows in his heart that Paul is wrong, but the old nagging worry keeps creeping in, blurring the edges of what he knows to be true.

The driver pulls up to the departures drop-off, and Ren is out of the car, hauling his own bags from the spacious trunk. Paul tips the driver and they walk into the airport and up to the first class check-in single file, as if on some fashionable death march.

One couple is ahead of them, so Ren turns away from Paul and glances around the airport; anything to distract him from the tension between them. In the main hall vintage planes hang from the ceiling, including an orange wonder right out of the Wright brothers' "impossible" fantasies. It reminds him of summer days, his back on the grass and his eyes on the clouds as the Blue Angels danced along a powder blue sky.

Stepping up to the counter, Paul hands his ID to the agent and nudges Ren to do the same. Ren slides his ID toward her, hoists his larger bag onto the scale and then glances back at the plane. It looks like a sculpture, like it couldn't possibly fly. But it did fly, once upon a time. It *did*.

"Have a good flight," the agent says as she hands him his boarding pass. He looks down at it—ABQ to ATL to JFK—and then hands it back to her.

"Ren?" Paul asks.

"I'd like to change my ticket. One ticket to Minneapolis, please."

⊞ Chapter 17 ⊞

The thing about driving in the heartland is, there are vast expanses of road and not much else—billboards offering free breakfasts with hotel stays and the occasional sign citing dubious science about fetal beating hearts. And when there is nothing else, there is no way to avoid thinking that one thing you *don't* want to think about.

Mile after mile, the memories enveloped him—from the moment he first set eyes on Cole McKnight, eyes shining, brimming with confidence, to the very last look on Cole's face just before Ren left: sad, resigned, maybe a little hopeful. On the long road home, the memories slid together and apart like scrims on a stage, transparent, painted in watercolor, a love in pictures.

Ren sips his mocha, stares out at the vast expanse of dark nothingness and contemplates his next move. He's not even sure what town he's in, just that the green Starbucks sign had beckoned him off Highway 94 and now he's sitting in a rented Toyota in Nowheresville, Minnesota, wondering how the hell he made such a mess of his life.

Did I really walk away from him, just moments after I got him?

Yes, Ren Warner. Yes you did.

The ground had been shifting beneath his feet for days; he was not the same man who arrived at the Albuquerque airport nearly two weeks ago. Half a lifetime rising above and making the most of things, and suddenly there was no need; suddenly the secret wish he had tucked away under layers of well-intentioned living was fulfilled. *Real.* Telling the truth about what he wanted, taking it, feeling no shame, turning toward the beautiful scary thing, it rattled him; like an earthquake of the soul.

He hated leaving Cole, but it was the right thing to do. Changing his plans last minute in favor of going home to Minnesota was also the right decision, no matter how important it was for him to sort things out with his now-ex-fiancé. Sure, Paul would have to deal with the reporters' questions on his own, but Ren was quite sure he preferred that anyway. Besides, it was Paul's own fault, issuing a press release without discussing it with Ren.

Paul was incredulous at first, but in the end he opted not to make a scene. He simply picked up his carry-on and marched off to his gate. Now, Ren has an hour of highway behind him and he's only ten minutes outside of St. Cloud. Time to make a decision.

He should call his parents, he really should. But he hasn't so far and with every Midwestern mile before him he dreads it more and more. It's not that he doesn't want to face Dad; he'll have to see him, and explain everything, and hope he isn't judged too harshly. It's just that he's not ready yet. He needs a soft landing with someone who will simply be thrilled to see him, no matter what he's done or how long it's been since they've talked about more than routine updates require; someone who just wants Ren to be happy, simple as that. Someone who will get him drunk and not ask too many questions about why. Someone who knew him before Paul, before Cole, before all of it.

Ren thumbs through his contacts and presses the number he's ignored for far too long.

"Ren?"

"Hey, Sean. Is this a bad time?"

"Nah. Just catching up on some grading, watching the game," Sean says. "What's up?"

"I'm not far from you, actually. I can be there in fifteen minutes. May I come over?"

It's after nine o'clock when Ren hits the outskirts of St. Cloud, and just a few minutes later he's parked on a quiet street in front of Sean and Erin's small yellow colonial. He smiles when he notices that Sean has left the porch light on for him. As he walks up to the door he's hit by the sweltering humidity, a sharp contrast to the bone-dry heat of Santa Fe's high desert.

Sean swings the door wide not ten seconds after Ren rings the bell and immediately grabs Ren in a giant bear hug. He smells like soap and freshly mown grass; like home.

Once inside, Sean carries Ren's bag to the first floor guest room and then ushers him into the kitchen. His blond hair, the same as Ren's, is cut military short, his skin freckled from a summer spent working on his lawn.

"I shouldn't have rung the doorbell," Ren says, glancing around the newly remodeled "country chic" kitchen. He helped Erin come up with the color scheme over email and is pleased now to see that she followed his suggestions and nixed the blue in favor of tangerine.

"S'okay. Meg can sleep through anything and Erin passed out in bed while she was reading to her. She'll only wake up if she has to pee or eat."

"How's she feeling? Everything okay with the baby?"

"Other than the fact that he's kicking Erin's ass, everything's fine, yeah." Sean is digging through the refrigerator. "I have pop, and orange juice and beer. Take your pick."

"Beer's fine," Ren says, ignoring Sean's look of surprise. "When is she due again?"

Sean smiles. "Thanksgiving, just about."

"Wow. Are you ready?"

"You're never really ready," Sean says, motioning for Ren to follow him into the living room. "But you know, the baby comes whether you're ready or not. You just deal."

Ren sits on one end of the sofa, Sean on the other, the muted television turned to ESPN. Sean leans across and clinks his bottle with Ren's. "I thought Dad said you were in Arizona, or something."

"New Mexico."

"Right. That's the place with the aliens, right?"

"What aliens?"

"In Roswell. Aliens landed there I think," Sean says, glancing at the scores running along the bottom of the television screen.

Ren laughs. "Yeah, well, I didn't go there. I was in Santa Fe, primarily."

"Awesome. Would I like it?"

Ren imagines Sean gobbling down plate after plate of green chile, traipsing through the artsy Santa Fe Railyard, looking for treasures, trying to hold his robe closed waiting for treatments at Ten Thousand Waves. "Yeah. I think you would."

"You on your way to Mom and Dad's?"

"Yes."

"They didn't say you were coming."

Ren looks at Sean, shrugs. He plays with the label on his beer bottle, softening from condensation. He can tell Sean wants to ask: *What's up; why are you here; are you okay*? And while he's grateful his brother has grown into a man of decorum and patience, he wishes Sean would just drag it out of him.

"Did you know?" Ren asks.

"Did I know what?"

"That I was in love with Cole when we were kids?"

Sean turns to him, eyebrows raised. "Pretty sure everyone knew. I thought you were dating the entire time, until you started going out with the Cable guy."

"Caleb."

"Right. What a douchebag."

"You really thought Cole and I were dating?"

"You were with each other *all the time*. And you were always touching each other and, you know, you'd get happy whenever he was around."

"Yeah."

Sean looks at him as if he's trying to figure something out and says, "What brought this on? You getting cold feet?"

"I ran into Cole in Santa Fe. We were staying at the same hotel."

"By accident?"

"Yes."

"Wow."

"Yeah. Wow."

Sean takes a swig of his beer, then another. "Dude, that's—I mean that is *really*... you don't think that's kind of like a giant sign?"

"How so?"

Sean looks at his beer, then abruptly stands up and leaves the room, throwing a "hang on a sec" over his shoulder. He returns moments later with a bottle of Wild Turkey and two shot glasses.

Ren scooches forward on the couch so he's closer to the coffee table. "When did you graduate to this stuff?"

"Believe it or not, Erin turned me on to it."

"Innocent little Erin?" Ren asks, as he accepts the shot from Sean.

Sean laughs, then leans in to whisper, "She's not so innocent."

"Do tell."

"She'd smack me for telling you this—and don't tell Mom like, ever—but we didn't meet at the library. We met when I helped her down off of the roof of her ex-boyfriend's truck. We were at the same house party. Erin was half-dressed and drunk out of her *mind,* singing a made-up song made up mostly of curse words. She looked like she was gonna fall, so I—"

"Came to her rescue?"

"Sort of. She wasn't happy about it. She wanted to finish her song."

Sean smiles, caught in his memories, then shifts his attention back to Ren. "So look, I like Paul. He's real smart and he seems to think you're amazing, so I can't fault the guy just for being, I don't know, a little *much*—"

"Erin's words?"

"Yeah. But I don't care about him. I care about you. And—it's okay that I'm saying this now, right? Like, if you're going to end up marrying the guy I don't want it to be weird at Christmas, you know?"

Ren laughs. "Not happening. Just say it."

"You just weren't yourself with Paul. I mean, it's not like you were a completely different person, like *Invasion of the Body Snatchers* or something. You were just... less you."

"It's okay. I know."

"Good, I don't want to piss you off. It was definitely worse with Paul, but that had been happening for a while. Like, we were all growing into ourselves and you were just, I don't know—doing something else."

Ren sits up taller. "What do you mean?"

"I don't know, it's like—hanging out with you was like hanging with Ren, but on dimmer."

"Why didn't you say anything?"

Sean settles back into the couch, "I don't know. We only see each other once a year. I didn't want to mess up your time at home. And honestly, I didn't think about it too much. I figured you said you were happy, so you must be happy. Was that wrong? Should I have, I don't know, staged some sort of Ren-intervention?"

Ren smiles. "A Rentervention?"

"Dude, no. Even I think that's bad."

Ren laughs. He looks at Sean—earnest, well-meaning, loyal-and-true Sean, Sean who labels songs "gay" but drives to Minneapolis every June to take his family to Pride, Sean who is a good brother and a decent friend—and laughs. He laughs so hard he falls back on the couch, belly heaving, legs splayed. He laughs and laughs, and then he's laughing *because* he's laughing.

Sean pours bourbon into two shot glasses and hands one to Ren. He clinks his glass against Ren's and says, "Rock on."

"Cheers," Ren says as they both take their shots.

Sean flops back against the couch; Ren follows. They stare at the television for a few moments, quiet, and then Sean says, "So how is Cole, anyway?"

Ren smiles, eyes still on the screen. He wants to say, *He loves me, and he's amazing, and I left him because it felt like too much, but he loves me. He loves me.*

But all that comes out is, "He's good."

Surprisingly, Mitch's old black leather couch is quite comfortable for sleeping. After two days and nights camped out in the studio, Cole is ready for some sunshine. He's made it up to the guesthouse twice to shower and change clothes and over to the main house a few times to shovel home-cooked food into his mouth and thank Mitch profusely for his hospitality, but other than that, he's mainly been stuck in these two rooms.

Stepping out into the courtyard, Cole squints up at the stunning azure blue sky. He's heard Sarah call it "Pecos blue"—something about a memorable camping trip she and Antonio took in the Pecos National Forest, farther north of Santa Fe than Galisteo. Out here where the horizon stretches on forever and every hour brings a new picture postcard, it's easy to feel as if you've been dropped into an epic movie, one you can only appreciate on the big screen.

Cole slips two fingers into his pocket and pulls out the small folded-up piece of paper he's been transferring from one pair of jeans to another since Ren left. That day he slept for hours, and when he woke he knew—he had to get out of there. The hotel held too many memories for him, so he packed up and checked out, intent on taking Mitch up on his invitation to crash at his guesthouse.

As he turned away from the reception desk, Amy had called after him. "Mr. McKnight, I almost forgot. Mr. Warner left this package for you."

The box was small, no bigger than a postcard, wrapped in purple paper with gold stars. He tore off the paper and into the box as if he'd find all of the answers inside, but instead he found a large chocolate sacred heart *milagro*, covered in what looked like hand-painted silver foil. Stunned, Cole traced the edges of the heart. How had Ren known about the *milagros* he had offered up in the Santuario? Had Antonio told him?

Inspecting the box further, he noticed a folded-up piece of paper stuck to the inside of the lid. On it, Ren had copied the poem "I carry your heart" by e.e. cummings by hand. Cole read the poem twice, mouthing the words as he stood there in the lobby of the Eldorado with no concern for who might be watching him. It was when he read *"i fear no fate (for you are my fate, my sweet)"* that he knew whatever this separation was about, it was only temporary.

Driving out to Galisteo later that day, the cut on his face was a stinging reminder of Paul's accusation that their love was a joke, that if they really wanted each other they would have fought for each other, or at least tried harder. Cole couldn't get his wits about him at the time, but he wanted to say so much to Ren about that, about why:

Maybe we couldn't be together, then. Maybe we'd like to think we should have been, but maybe we would have broken up. Maybe this is our time, and everything is perfect, and we shouldn't regret the missed chances because we took the only one that mattered.

By the time he had the presence of mind to say these things, Ren was gone, and all that was left to do was write about it.

When the sun came up on Sunday he had two songs written—one simple piece with a catchy melody that he showed to Mitch and the other a melancholy song he decided to keep for himself—and a good start on a third. It felt like cramming for an exam, each song an answer to one of Ren's questions, or one of his own.

And it wasn't just his own music he worked on while he practically lived in Mitch's studio—somehow, in the midst of his creative purge, he had figured out how to make "Forever Man" work.

Stuffing the poem back in his pocket, Cole takes off in search of more of the relentless New Mexico sun and a little exercise. Right off the back gate a trail runs parallel to the main house over to the stables, so he follows it. In his mind he hears Alegra singing the song they've tried so hard to get right. It was a good song, maybe even a great song. But both Cole and Alegra knew it could be a phenomenal song, on par with "How We Loved," so they kept at it. Now, Cole is sure of the song. He'll wait for Alegra to show up this afternoon and confirm it with her miraculous voice, but that's only a formality.

Rounding a corner, the main house in view, Cole notices the front door open and is surprised to see Deidre walking out. She, too, squints into the sun. When her eyes adjust, she spots him on the trail. She marches toward him, her oddly normal ponytail bouncing behind her as she walks. He meets her halfway.

"This is not what it fucking looks like."

Cole chuckles. "Okay."

Two weeks ago he would have scoffed and thought, "Yeah, right." But he's been on the other side of the looking glass now and he knows that, while the old adage "where there's smoke, there's fire" is true, in situations like this, things are rarely what they seem.

"Nothing happened," Deidre stresses.

"Okay."

"Would you stop looking at me like that?"

"Like what?"

"I didn't fuck him, okay?"

"Okay."

"Stop saying that!" Deidre shouts, her voice loud enough to wake the dead.

Cole raises both hands in the air as though she's holding a gun to him. "Ok—sorry. Want to take a walk with me?"

"A walk? Why?"

Cole shrugs. "Don't know. Just thought I'd offer."

Deidre looks back at the house, at her expensive rental parked in Mitch's circular driveway. On her feet she wears simple pink flats—not great for hiking, but they will get her to the stables and back.

It's the most awkward walk he's ever shared with anyone. He tries to talk to her, but she only offers mumbled responses. Music still in his head, he hums, then sings softly, trying out the lyrics for one of his new songs.

He stops when they reach the paddock next to the stables. Deidre is so tense even the horses seem to sense it, staying far away from the fence. Hands on her hips, she looks out at the horses, at the vast landscape; her mask of indifference falls away in the quiet between them. Face turned toward the sun, at last she says, "He's not in New York, by the way. He's in Minnesota."

"What? Why?"

"Fuck if I know," Deidre replies. "Paul wouldn't tell me more than that, just that Ren didn't go back with him after all, that he went to Minnesota instead."

Cole can't help himself—he grabs Deidre, lifts her up and spins her around. She seems surprised and even giggles a bit, her cheeks flushed when he puts her down.

She comes back to herself quickly. "Aww, were you worried he would go back to the most handsome, eligible bachelor in all of New York?"

He waves a finger at her and starts back toward the studio, a new spring in his step. "Uh-uh, lady. I'm not falling for your drama."

He's walking fast, and she's tiny; it takes her a few seconds to catch up to him. "I can be—I know I should apologize, but I won't, because I really hate doing that... but I'm... thinking it."

Cole laughs. "Don't worry about it."

He hadn't let himself think too much about the possibility that Ren would decide to go back to Paul; he hadn't let himself think about much of anything at all, pouring everything into his music, instead. Yet, now that he knows that Ren never even made it back to New York, that he went home, back to where their story began, back to where he has family who love him, Cole is overcome with relief.

They'd had so little time together before it all blew up in their faces, and there was so much left to repair, and decide; thinking about any of it would have sent him into a tailspin. He realizes now that his worries and emotions were there all the time, he had left them on page after page of sheet music—where they belong.

As they reach the place where Deidre joined him in the walk, Cole sees Alegra walking from the main house to the studio.

"I have to get back. See you later? Maybe? Or not. Either way, thanks for the walk."

He's almost to the studio when Deidre catches up with him again, dust covering her shoes. She taps him on the back. "What if it's worse?"

He raises one eyebrow in question, waits impatiently for clarity.

"What if it's worse than an affair?" Deidre says, looking him straight in the eyes. "What if I like myself around him? A lot? What if talking with him makes me feel like I could be different or... more?"

Cole looks at her, this hard-edged, tiny woman who seems to be waking up, and holds out his hand. "We're recording a song I wrote today. Will you stay and let me know what you think?"

Deidre offers him a half smile, and then takes his hand.

Ren pulls into Warner Boat Charters at the edge of town late Monday morning nursing a three-day hangover.

He spent Sunday with Sean and the girls, Meg squealing with delight when she realized her Uncle Ren had come for a surprise visit. She tugged him around with her like a pet, showing him every doll, every LEGO set, every sticker book in her playroom and then forced him to sit through two hours of her favorite YouTube videos, most of which made no sense to him. He loved every minute of it.

In the afternoon he sat on the porch with Erin and watched Meg ride bikes with her neighborhood friends. Now seven, she was growing like a weed; she towered over her friends of the same age.

Later that night, after a backyard barbeque reminiscent of every summer Sunday in the Warner household, the adults stayed up late talking. Sean and Ren managed to kill the Wild Turkey and the rest of the beer, thus marking the third night in a row that Ren had been drunk out of his mind.

The three-hour drive to Two Harbors seemed to take forever. Now, as he steps out of his rental, his head feels as if it's caught in a vise, his body is sore and heavy. "Never again," he mumbles, walking toward the main office.

It's quiet in the shop for a Monday, just two guys working on a Craftsman boat. He spots Jim, his dad's must trusted employee, and waves. Jim smiles back. "Hey, big city. Whaddya know?"

"I know you need a haircut," Ren shouts back. Jim laughs, and Ren carries the familiar feeling of camaraderie into his dad's office, for a moment forgetting that he's about to face the firing squad.

He finds his dad crouched down, searching through his old, beat-up four-drawer filing cabinet. He looks the same, maybe a few pounds heavier. With a full head of hair just beginning to gray and a strong, lean frame credited to genetics and the manual labor of hoisting sails and anchors nearly every day of his adult life, Erik Warner barely looks fifty, let alone sixty-two.

"Hey, Dad," Ren says.

His dad turns toward him and stands up, using the file cabinet for leverage. He's got Ren in a tight hug before he says, "Good to see ya, kid. You hit much traffic?"

A few minutes later Ren follows Erik out of the office into the parking lot, carrying two cups of coffee and a bag of donuts. As Erik passes Ren's rental he says, "They all out of American cars?"

Ren laughs, shakes his head. "Come on, Dad. You know Toyota makes cars for Chevy."

"The whole damn world is turned upside down," Erik mutters, climbing into the back of Henrietta.

A beat-up old row boat Erik got for his sons to play in when they came to work with him, Henrietta had become the shop's mascot. Just as he's done dozens of times before, Ren climbs over the side and sits on a bench. He looks in the bag and fishes out a glazed donut for his dad, a chocolate cake donut for himself.

"So, did you do the right thing?" Erik asks, taking a sip of his coffee.

"You get right to it, don't you?"

"Saw your name in the paper yesterday. Something about a January wedding?"

Ren sighs. He knew there was no way to stop the press release. He also knew that Paul would not want to be the source of any gossip or controversy that could possibly cast a negative light on equal marriage so close to the vote. So he wasn't entirely surprised to see the brief article in *USA Today* announcing their marriage in the context of exploring the viability of the forthcoming bill.

"So did you tell him or not?"

"I did, just... not before he had already approved the press release," Ren explains. "There isn't going to be a wedding."

As Erik eats his donut, Ren gives his dad the abbreviated, cleaned-up version of the last couple of weeks. He watches his face closely, looking for any signs of disappointment, but Erik's neutral expression gives nothing away.

When he's finished, the giant "to be continued" hanging in the air, they sit in silence for a few moments, looking out at the sunflower field behind the shop. They'd first planted the rows and rows of flowers when Ren was just four years old, his mother's idea for brightening up the overgrown lot. How many days had they sat out here in Henrietta, staring out at his mother's sunflowers while they ate a quick lunch or finished off ice cream cones from the Dairy Queen down the street?

Finally Ren can't wait anymore. "I'm so sorry, Dad. I know I should have told Paul right away, before I did anything with Cole. I should have told him a long time ago that—"

"That you don't love him?"

"No, I do love him. Just not... not the way you should love someone you want to spend the rest of your life with. Anyway, I'm sorry that—"

"Ren, stop. You're a grown man. You don't owe me an apology for a mistake you made that doesn't affect me."

"I know, but I feel just awful about—"

"*Ren*," Erik interrupts, his large, strong hand gripping Ren's shoulder. "Don't you think it's time you forgave yourself?"

"I hardly think a couple of days is enough time to forgive myself for cheating on Paul, Dad."

"No, son. When are you going to forgive yourself for giving up? You were just a kid. You thought you had a bucketful of chances left, all the time in the world, and you were *supposed* to feel that way. Don't keep punishing yourself just because you weren't ready for the real thing."

Ren looks out at the sunflowers, row after row of golden faces, taller than him. He lets silent tears fall as his father's grip on his shoulder strengthens. He says, "Warners never give up."

"Yeah, well, don't be so hard on yourself. Pretty sure you had something to prove."

Ren turns to look at his dad. "What do you mean?"

"I think that, sometime when I wasn't looking, you decided life would be better if you didn't need anyone or anything. If I *had* been looking when you made that choice I sure as shit would have told you what a foolish move it was. But you were already on your way, so..."

"I'm just so... ashamed. I've always thought of myself as strong, a go-getter, someone who goes after what he wants, and I've been a total coward all this time—"

"Don't bother with that."

"But—"

"Kid, just do better, okay? Just do better."

The moon is rising later that evening as Ren walks out onto his parents' dock and sits down, lets his feet dangle over the side, his toes in the water. Lake Superior, with its tides and endless horizon, is a world away from the lake in Wisconsin where he first learned the bitter taste of regret. And yet it seems as if he's there now, staring into a young Cole's expectant eyes, trying to understand.

His father may be right—there's no sense dwelling on the past—but that doesn't do much to rid him of the shame, the shame that surely pushed him out the door, away from Cole, again.

It's not just that he walked away from Cole; it's that he walked away from himself. When you give up on one great love, it's easier to give up on the rest, and that is a shame he'll need time to deal with.

You can build back up strong from disappointment; you can build something livable, even beautiful, from broken pieces. But when you build an entire life on a lie, on something you forgot or refused to do, it's hollow to the core. Now, he'll build something new, something entirely his own, something he needs.

The cloying heat tempered by the setting sun, Ren swishes his feet in the still water. He loves the lake when it's quiet like this, when the water says, "Hush, listen, all will be well."

Ren pulls out his phone and finds the only name that matters. He pushes the text button next to the name and taps out a message.

Ren: Hey, love.

Chapter 18

When the plane starts its descent into JFK airport, Cole packs his headphones away and lifts the window shade to watch the lights of the city come into view. They've taken over the entire first class cabin; Alegra, Gretchen and the band. He's managed to keep himself occupied for most of the flight, but the last hour or so he's been floating around in what ifs, trying to decide how to handle the next few days.

He's grateful for the semblance of a relationship he still has with Ren, despite the distance and their perpetual limbo. He wants to hold him, God how he wants to hold him. But that day in Chimayó he promised himself he would wait for Ren for as long as needed; he'd wait forever. Which is why he hasn't told Ren that he'll be in New York for several days.

Cole opens his wallet and pulls out a small piece of paper, now worn from his daily practice of reading the poem Ren wrote out by hand.

He hasn't seen Ren, or even heard his voice, in months. They've stayed in touch through daily texts—confessions, indulgent reminiscing, shared worries, little nothings and musings they feel compelled to share. Ren has set the pace and made the rules; all Cole can do is wait.

A change in cabin pressure rouses Alegra, and when she opens her eyes she's looking right at Cole.

When her stare becomes uncomfortable, Cole says, "What?"

"Don't worry so much."

"I'm not worried, I'm just... impatient."

"Tell me another one." Alegra stretches her arms over her head.

"It's not a *lie*."

"It's just me, you know. Nothing wrong with having one person you can fess up to."

Cole looks out the window, the lights of New York City in full view. Somewhere down there his love is walking home, or catching up with his dad on the phone, or stopping in a little bookstore to find something to read. He's deciding what he'll have for dinner, or shopping for a gift. He's living; he's living without him.

"It's just—what if 'more time' stretches on into years, into all the days? Are we ever going to be able to just... start?"

Alegra rests her head on his shoulder, tries to catch a glimpse of his view from her aisle seat. After a moment she squeezes his arm and says, "Fear not, my lovely."

"So, are we allowed to talk about it yet, or are you still engaged to the most eligible gay man in all the land?"

Deidre smirks and takes a sip of her Bloody Mary, bright red lipstick smudging her glass. Ren likes her new look—longer hair, now a light brown, probably her natural color, less eye makeup and simple hoop earrings. She seems softer somehow, less angry.

As is typical during the lunch rush, Coffee Shop on Union Square is packed with beautiful people eating twenty-dollar salads and drinking local beer. It's their regular hangout, or was, but they haven't seen each other since just before Thanksgiving, when she hand-delivered his final payment for the Santa Fe house project.

"I was never engaged," Ren replies, readying his burger with ketchup and pickles.

"Whatever. Are you done keeping up appearances, then?"

"If you're asking if, after five months, I can finally I tell people I broke up with Paul, the answer is yes. He announced our 'amicable parting of ways' just before Christmas, actually."

After a week in Minnesota with his family, Ren had returned to New York to find his life packed up in boxes and a fat envelope of legal documents pertaining to the "dissolution of domestic partnership." Paul had ensconced himself in his D.C. apartment and left everything to a team of assistants and attorneys and professional movers, all of whom looked at Ren with disdain.

It hurt to see their relationship dismembered, packed up and secured with packing tape, but Ren knew he deserved whatever ending Paul saw fit to give them. He left his ring on the dining room table with a note that simply said, "I'm sorry. I hope you find him." It was such a Paul thing to say; he hoped it would appease him somewhat.

The bulk of his belongings in storage, Ren sublet his sometime-design-assistant's one-bedroom on the Upper East Side and immediately set about finding a new workshop. Determined to "follow his bliss," as suggested by one June Merryfeather, he had cancelled every design job he could get out of without causing his clients undue stress and started assembling all he needed for his new venture—tools, equipment, ideas, interested buyers, curious retailers and supporters of any and every kind.

His social life was severely limited, due to his agreement with Paul that he would keep quiet about their breakup until President Landry signed the marriage equality bill into law. So Ren spent most days holed up in his studio, getting reacquainted with his first love. Every day he made something—a piece, a fragment, a possibility. And every night he sketched more ideas—retro dining chairs, a series of mirrors, abstract *milagro* wall art, a table from his dreams.

Slowly, calmly, over weeks and months, and with a steady confidence and newfound purpose, he had come back to himself.

"What's up with Mr. Sex Scandal?" Deidre asks.

"Are you referring to my one true love?" Ren teases, waiting for her inevitable gagging noises.

"Fuck off."

"You're so easy, Deidre."

"Not the first time I've heard that one," she replies, munching on a long pickle for effect.

"God, why are we friends again?"

"Hell if I know."

Ren winks at Deidre. She blushes, still not entirely comfortable with their legitimate friendship, no longer shaped by contracts or influenced by dollars.

"Cole is fine—good. I think. We text each other nearly every day, little things. Pictures. Updates. Silly stuff."

"Sexy silly stuff?"

"No, we—I asked him to give me time and he's been great about doing that. It's nice, actually. Before Santa Fe we had lost touch, and now it's like the old days, but better. We have our friendship back and I needed that. I think we both did."

Deidre looks at him as though he's speaking gibberish. "What the fuck are you talking about?"

"I told you wanted some time to myself to figure things out—"

"I know, but—damn, Ren. How much time do you need?"

"I'm not sure, it's just—"

"Wait. Stop. I don't want to hear your bullshit answer," Deidre interrupts. She fishes in her purse and pulls out an envelope, slides it across the table. "Here. It's from Alegra. She's doing a show at The Beacon tonight, some sort of album pre-release deal for her fans."

Ren opens the envelope to find a VIP ticket to tonight's concert and a backstage pass. "How did you get this?"

"Mitch. He asked me to give it to you."

Eyebrows raised, Ren asks, "You're still seeing him?"

Deidre blushes again, and shifts in her seat. "I like him, okay? And he seems to like me back. So just shut up already."

"The divorce, it's still happening?"

"So my idiot lawyers tell me."

Ren looks down at the envelope again, runs his finger over Alegra's name. He marvels at how much their lives have changed because of one amazing visit to that odd little jewel of a city.

When he pulls the ticket out to get a closer look, he sees it: *Opening Act—Cole McKnight.*

"Cole is in New York?"

Deidre shrugs. "Apparently."

"He didn't—why didn't he tell me?"

"I suppose because he's a goddamn gentleman and respects your wishes, or some such shit."

Ren thinks back over the last few weeks, trying to remember any mention of Alegra's concert, any hint that Cole would be coming to New York. They talked of Cole's album, now finished, and its March release date, just two months away. Ren shared pictures of Sean's new son, Charles Wallace (completing the pair from Erin's favorite book, *A*

Wrinkle in Time), all decked out in the clothes Ren sent for him. They said "I love you" at the end of every text. Twice, just before they hung up the phone Ren said, "Soon, love." But Cole had given him no indication that he would be here in just a few days.

He can barely finish his burger, the unsettling thoughts about Cole's intentions so insistent he's lost his appetite. He'd meant it when he said, "Soon." He was better, more sure of himself and of them. Old hurts had been healed over long distance, as they should have been ages ago, and he had stopped blaming Cole for his cowardice and berating himself for his own.

"Soon, love."

What was he waiting for?

"And you said this came from Alegra, not Cole?" Ren asks.

"Yeah." Deidre eyes him warily. *"What?"*

"Nothing."

"Don't do it."

"Don't do what?"

"That thing you do."

"What thing?"

"That thing where you over-analyze everything until you can't remember why you thought it was a good idea in the first place."

Ren slips the envelope in his wallet, flags the server down for the check. "And what good idea are you referring to, crazy girl?"

"The concert, dumbass."

Ren sighs. He's had enough of her tough love and relentless cursing. "Since when are you Team Cole, anyway?"

"Since you fucked up your entire life just for one chance with him."

Deidre offers him a small smile, the best she can do, and when the server drops the tab off at their table without so much as a "Thanks for coming," she slams her hand down on it before Ren can grab it. She pulls a credit card out from the pocket on her phone case and gets up, ready to move.

"Don't thank me for lunch. Don't thank me for bringing the ticket. Just go. *Go.*"

Hours later, Ren boards the #4 train bound for the Upper East Side, two grocery bags in tow. Somewhere between Coffee Shop and the frozen food aisle he'd decided not to go to Alegra's concert. If Cole had wanted Ren to attend, surely he would have told him, invited him himself. He doesn't want to miss Cole's debut, but still... he'll stay in instead and text Cole after the show.

The car is packed with people, so there's no place to sit. Ren shifts both bags to one hand and grips the nearest pole. Next to him a man is sitting with a large, skinny aspen sapling between his legs. It reaches all the way up to the top of the car. "New York, oh my God," Ren says, still mystified by the strange things he sees both above and below ground.

He's reminded of the aspen trees on the Sangre de Cristo Mountains, shimmering in the breeze. Suddenly he's overcome with an intense longing, once reserved for an elusive boy.

Can you fall in love with a city? Can you miss it like a friend?

It's an odd feeling, missing a place you don't really like and surely never wanted to visit in the first place. He speaks to Antonio a few times a month and sometimes Sarah, if she's home when he calls. But the calls never satisfy his desire to walk the dusty, narrow streets of downtown Santa Fe, the sunset at his back.

The train coming up on 86th Street, he prepares to get off and head home. He can hear it before the doors open, before a dozen people push past him to get off and on with their lives, before he falls in line behind them: the unmistakable sound of the song that changed everything.

The moment the doors slide open, Ren steps off to follow the sound of the busker singing Alegra's "How We Loved." Positioned near the stairs, beating a dirty white bucket for a drum, a dark-skinned man in gently worn attire, hat at his feet, sings beautifully, sings his heart out. He sings the song that seeped into Ren's bones, that moved his heart just enough, enough to try.

Suddenly he realizes he's been playing the same old game—testing Cole's patience, limiting contact and letting distance fuel new insecurities. He's been waiting for Cole to come find him away from the magic of Santa Fe, outside of their last best chance.

Dropping a five-dollar bill in the hat and his groceries next to it, Ren rushes for the stairs, taking them two at a time. Just as he had that horrible morning after Paul arrived, his mind races with one thought: *Cole, Cole, Cole, Cole.*

I'm such an idiot. I've been waiting for him all this time, just like before. Telling him I need space and time and secretly hoping he'll come for me, defy my reasons and come for me. I've telling him to wait while secretly waiting for him to show up.

On the street, he hails a cab and tries to remember to breathe as the driver cuts across Central Park on the byway. He looks at his phone; the concert has started by now. Once on Broadway the traffic slows, and by 80th Street Ren is out of the cab and running the remaining four blocks.

Inside the venue, the sound is deafening. The place is teeming with screaming girls (and some boys); they're screaming for Cole. Ren skirts the edge of the crowd looking for a decent view of the stage, avoiding the VIP section so as not to be spotted. He doesn't want to mess with Cole's performance by surprising him.

Gorgeous in a sweat-soaked plain white T-shirt and jeans, Cole is mesmerizing. He works the crowd with that same charisma he used to get them into bars, to convince Ren to stay up until dawn watching *Lord of the Rings*, to charm the monks into giving him a slightly higher grade.

Cole is singing a new song about his "baby, sweetheart, honey, love," and when Ren hears the rest of the lyrics he laughs out loud. It's for him, this song. *It's for him.*

He lets his heart swell and the music fill him. He screams with the girls, watches Cole's every move. It's exhilarating.

Three more songs and Cole thanks the audience, his band and Alegra, sweat pouring down his handsome face. Ren knows Cole will probably have to change for Alegra's set, but he can't wait. He has to see him now. Now that he understands, now that he's seen him, now that he knows, he can't wait one more minute.

Flashing his backstage pass, Ren winds around the darkened wings, looking for Cole. He finds him quickly, bending down over his guitar case as he fastens it shut. Ren watches as Cole stands up and moves toward the exit, a determined look on his face.

When Cole sees him standing there in the shadows he stops, lets his guitar case fall to the floor. Ren's heart beats so fast he wonders if Cole can hear it over the din of the crowd.

"Hi," Ren says, breaking the tension.

"Hi."

"Alegra invited me."

Cole smiles and looks off into the wings, where Ren assumes Alegra is getting ready to go on. "She's a romantic. What can I say?"

"Cole, I—I've been an idiot."

Cole takes a few steps closer. He laughs and says, "Again?"

"Yeah. At some point I stopped needing space and started needing you to show up on my doorstep with flowers and a well-written plea." Ren offers Cole a rueful smile.

"I can do that. You still love peonies, right?"

Ren laughs, takes a few steps closer. "I'm so sorry—"

"I think we're done being sorry. Okay? Can we be done?"

"I think so."

"Good. All I want is you, Ren. However I can get you."

Just a few feet between them now, all that's left of half a lifetime of divide. Just a few steps and he'll be in Cole's arms, press his lips to his skin, grip his damp shirt and hold on tightly, so tightly. Just a few seconds and he'll surrender to his forever man; he'll let it all unfold as it would, without his interference, without restraint. Just a moment now and he'll say *yes,* and *please,* and *won't you give me this,* and *aren't we perfect for each other,* and *I adore you, please come home with me.*

Ren notices Cole's leather jacket. "Were you going somewhere?"

"I was coming to find you."

Ren closes the distance between them, pulls Cole close. "I found you fir—"

Cole's mouth is on his before he can finish his sentence. The kiss is desperate, all of their patience gone. Around them, people rush to start Alegra's set as the crowd chants her name. Ren lets himself go, lets Cole pull him into this life he always wanted, lets him love him, lets him in.

Between kisses, Cole says, "Say it. Tell me again."

Ren speaks the words onto Cole's lips. "You are so in love with me. And I am so in love with you."

"Yes, baby. Yes. *Yes.*"

Cole hugs him, laughs into his ear. When he pulls back, he says, "You still owe me three days."

Ren laughs with him. "They're all yours."

⊞ Epilogue ⊞

Ren Warner is not a fan of New Mexico—all of that brown, and tan and more brown. And the snow. And too-fucking-slow sanding trucks and plows that would never make it through a Minnesota winter. And the blocks and blocks of tinsel-wrapped mailboxes. And tourists.

"At least it's not Texas," he mutters, glaring at a Toyota 4-Runner driving at a snail's pace down St. Francis Drive. In a raised voice he adds, "Why do they even bother buying these vehicles, when they drive like a grandma on Valium?"

"Calm down, kid. We'll get there."

Ren glances in his rearview mirror at his dad in the first backseat row next to Erin and Meg, then at Sean and little Charles, singing a silly tune. His mom, Linda, sitting in the passenger seat next to him, is wide-eyed, camera raised for photo opportunities. Round and "pleasantly plump," as she likes to call her ample curves, her hair dyed a shade lighter blonde than her natural color, she wears the first of several obnoxious Christmas sweaters she bought just for the trip. And somehow, Ren can't seem to make himself care. He's too happy.

Ren may not *like* New Mexico—he may find it frustrating, and too dry, and remote as hell; he may even finally understand why the locals refer to the "Land of Enchantment" as the "Land of Entrapment"—but he most definitely loves this city.

It took them two years to find a house they could afford and that Ren could stand to live in while they renovated it. They still kept Cole's flat in London and Ren's apartment in New York; their careers—Cole's music and Ren's furniture line—demand that they spend a great deal of time in both places. But deciding on Santa Fe as their permanent residence was easy for both of them. Here, they found each other again. Here, they were accepted and loved. Here, they became the men they always intended to be.

"Dad, see the mountain range there, at the edge of the city? Those are the Sangre de Cristo Mountains, the southern Rockies," he says. "If you look to your left you can see the summit, there, all covered in snow. We call it 'Baldy,' for obvious reasons, and you can see it from the Rio Grande."

"No kidding," Erik says, craning to look out the front window.

Cole is waiting in the gravel driveway when they pull up, wearing the heather sweater Ren bought him last Christmas, a pair of jeans and a smile brighter than the sun. He claps his hands as Meg hops out of the car. She runs right to him, shouting, "Uncle Cole!" and he scoops her up into a tight hug.

"Gosh, you're big," he says. "Stop growing!"

Her little crush on Cole still in full force, Meg giggles and hangs on to his neck. *I understand, little girl. Believe me.*

Ren smiles warmly at the pair and then helps his dad and Erin unload the trunk as Sean gathers Charles and his things.

"No jacket?" Linda asks Cole, kissing him on the cheek.

"Come on! I'm a Minnesota boy. This is nothing."

After everyone shuffles inside, after the family is situated and the house tour is complete, Cole steals Ren away to the kitchen to help him with dinner, and pulls him into the pantry. Once inside, he takes Ren's face in his hands and kisses him soundly, deeply, as though the only thing that matters is Ren's mouth, Ren's tongue, the swell of his bottom lip, still sore from last night's adventures.

Cole wraps Ren up in his arms, leans him back against the pantry door and says, "Hi, baby."

"Missed me? I was only gone three hours."

"I'm just happy."

"Yeah. So much."

More kissing, a little groping and still more kissing, until a knock on the door and a familiar voice interrupts them. "Ren, can you take your hands off your husband long enough to kiss your goddaughter?"

Ren turns in Cole's arms and opens the door to find Antonio standing in their kitchen, holding baby Cora. Not even six months old, she is the perfect combination of Antonio and Sarah—dark hair, a sweet face and, even at her young age, a wise expression. Like her father and great-grandmother before her, she will be able to spot soul-love, too.

Baby now in his arms, Ren says, "Where's Sarah?"

"She's bringing some of the kids over in the van. They'll meet us there."

Cole kisses Cora as he walks toward the stove. "I'll just start on the hot chocolate. Did you bring the extra thermoses, Antonio?"

"In the bag." Antonio points to a large paper shopping bag on the counter.

Ren squeezes Cora, takes her with him as he goes to explain the plan for the night to his family.

Cole fills a tin with homemade *bischitos*, traditional New Mexican Christmas cookies he'd made with Ren the night before. They'd cut the shortbread into the shapes of stars, and reindeer and bells, and when the cookie were baked, they dipped them in cinnamon and sugar, just as Sarah taught him.

They've been stocking up on cute customs, and silly anniversaries and other "couple" rituals ever since the week he spent in New York, holed up in Ren's sublet on the Upper East Side. They reasoned they had a lot of lost time to make up for, and therefore should get a pass on gag-inducing antics. It had started out genuine, but as was their way, quickly devolved into a game, another reason to laugh. All those years they'd spent longing for these moments and somehow poking fun at the cliché of it all released them from the burden of regret, of missing something they'd never had.

On his way to grab a few extra wool blankets for their excursion, Cole runs right into to his sister-in-law in the guest hallway, studying the row of framed, handwritten song lyrics. Ren had installed miniature spotlights above each piece, his own design, which made the narrow hallway seem bigger and gave it the feel of a tucked away space in an art gallery.

"Oops, didn't mean to run you over."

Cole opens the guest linen closet. He roots around looking for the new Hudson Bay blankets his mother sent from her last online shopping adventure.

"This one is my favorite." Erin points to a song he knows all too well. She leans in and stands on her tiptoes to get a closer look.

"You're not sick of it, then, I take it," he teases, finding the blankets on the bottom shelf. He shuts the closet door.

"Never. Like I said; it's my favorite. You won a Grammy for this, right?"

"Yup. I co-wrote it with Alegra."

"Why is most of the song in black ink, and this part in purple," she asks, pointing to toward the bottom of the page.

Cole moves to stand next to her, looking at the paper. A few coffee drip stains on the top left corner, a few lines crossed out in red, it's the verse in purple permanent marker—all he could find in the studio that day—that stands out.

"I wrote those lyrics the day after Ren left Santa Fe."

"Ah yes, the weekend of the surprise visit from Uncle Ren."

Erin turns to face Cole, leans one hip against the wall. Short in stature, Erin is curvy (or "stacked," as Sean likes to call his wife) and soft, with warm, patient eyes and, though tempered by marriage and motherhood, a hint of wildness about her.

"We'd been trying to get the song right for weeks, and then—well, you probably already know the story."

"I may have heard bits and pieces. Know what else I heard?"

"Oh no, I don't like that tone, Mrs. Warner," he teases, shifting the blankets to get a better grip on the blankets in his arms. "The last time you used that tone on me I ended up getting toasted at Meg's soccer game. That's the last time I trust you to make any drink for me, especially hot cider."

"No one knew, God," she says, with a good-natured eye-roll. "I *heard* that you like to serenade people. Sometimes in public places."

Cole laughs. "Erin, I perform in front of thousands of people—"

"Not the same thing! A serenade is personal."

"Are you asking me to sing to you?"

Erin bounces on the balls of her feet. "Come on—it's my favorite. Please? Consider it my Christmas present."

"So I can take back that turquoise choker we bought for you in Taos?"
"No way!"
Cole laughs again, sets the blankets on the floor. He leans back against the wall, facing the lyrics he knows by heart, and sings:

A girl like me
Don't have as many options as you see
At least, not the kind that means the world to me.

I was in a world of doubt
All my dreams, my moments going south
Until you took me by the hand, up, up, and out.

You're not a sometime thing, no
You're not my summer fling
You're not a line drawn in the sand.

You're not my maybe, baby
You're not my compromise
Darling, you're my everything, forever man.

A girl like me
Wants the stuff no Billboard rocket can buy
That look you give that always makes me sigh

It was always you
Though I held out to see it through
And it feels so right to tell you now that it's true

You're not a sometime thing, no
You're not my summer fling
You're not a line drawn in the sand.

You're not my maybe, baby
You're not my compromise
Darling, you're my everything, forever man.

If there is only this, if there is only you
Then I'll be happy until my dying day
There is nothing temporary about that thing you do
Or the way my heart asks to stay and stay.

You're not a sometime thing, no
You're not my summer fling
You're not a line drawn in the sand.

You're not my maybe, baby
You're not my compromise
Darling, you're my everything, forever man.

It's only a few blocks to Canyon Road from their house, and since it's a relatively warm winter night they decide to bundle up the kids and walk. The babies asleep in their strollers, the family joins other Santa Feans and tourists making their way to the iconic Christmas Eve Walk. Meg bounces with excitement; she's never been allowed to stay up this late before.

Farolitos, paper bag lanterns filled halfway with sand and lit by votives, line both sides of the sidewalks, and plastic replicas dot the roofline of nearly every adobe house and gallery along the walk. It's magical, like a winter fairyland, with bonfires on every other corner, carolers strolling along the winding street and art galleries open to share mulled wine, cider and cookies.

They find Sarah and the Alex Marin House kids halfway up the road, waiting for them next to a bonfire. After she checks on her baby, hugs everyone in the group and tucks her hand into the crook of Ren's arm, Sarah says, "See? Isn't this the most beautiful thing?"

Ren nods, kisses her on the forehead and watches as she and the others walk ahead. They're a motley crew, tall men with children and the tiny women they love. He smiles as his dad takes hold of the stroller for Antonio so he can slip into a gallery for whatever they're offering.

Ren is so full with the night, with his family, old and new, with the joy of standing on his true path, with this man he loves completely and the brilliant possibilities set before them, with the generous gift of...

"Grace," Cole says, breaking into Ren's thoughts.

"Hmm?"

"I've been thinking about our favorite argument." Cole slows to walk in step with Ren.

"The one where I say our impromptu meeting was random and you say it was fate?" Ren asks, a gentle tease in his tone.

"That's the one."

"And?"

"And I've come to believe that we were both wrong." Cole stops and turns to stand in front of Ren, his face illuminated by hundreds of votive candles and the soft light emanating from a nearby gallery.

"It wasn't fate, or chance. It was grace."

The mellow-sweet feeling Ren has come to know so well, the feeling that replaced all of his worries, and regrets and fears—that feeling washes over him now, ushering in perfect joy. He beams at Cole, wraps his right arm around him at the neck and pulls him in for a hard kiss that says: *Love, my love, how could I have doubted you for a moment?*

When the kiss ends, Cole laughs, steps back a bit and looks up ahead at their families. He holds his hand out to Ren. "Coming?"

Acknowledgments

I'd like to thank the Interlude Press team for their tireless efforts on behalf of this novel, specifically, Luther Huffman, for his unfailing kindness, even at three a.m.; CM Miller, for her confidence in this story; Becky Feldbush, for her vision; and Zoë Bird and Nicki Harper, for making this book better.

And thanks to my family, for getting me through and reminding me what's important—my parents, my son Jack, Polly, Patrick and Gregory, Jenny and Erik, Nikki and Francesco, Kameron, Erick, Emilia, Joey and G.

This book would not exist if it weren't for the steadfast support of my dear friend Mimsy. Thank you will never be enough.

I am indebted to the good and patient people who encouraged me when this novel was a different story, unfinished. There are too many of you to count, and I am grateful for every one of you.

interlude press

A Reader's Guide
to
Forever Man

Questions for Discussion

1. What is the role of spirituality in *Forever Man*? How does it influence characters and their actions, even those who do not consider themselves religious?

2. What roles do characters like Antonio, Deidre and June play in defining Cole and Ren, and their relationship?

3. *Milagros* are meant to represent prayers for miracles. At Chimayó, a place of pilgrimages for people seeking miracles, Cole purchases three sacred heart *milagros* and then he digs and saves a small cup of dirt. How are these actions tied to Cole's journey, and his decisions?

4. Cole defends his relationship with Ren as "an answered prayer." How do views of fidelity and morality shape Ren and Cole's evolving relationship?

5. Both Ren and Cole find themselves making changes to their professional lives by the end of the story. Do they both move forward? Do they both move in the direction they needed, or directions they were destined to follow? Did these changes need to occur before they could resolve their relationship?

6. At Santa Fe's Fiesta, the giant Zozobra is filled with slips of paper detailing the fears and regrets of participants, the things they want to let go of. Does the cleansing ritual of the burning of the Zozobra represent any transition for Ren and Cole, and does their participation in the ritual help the let go of their past issues?

7. The story of the death of Jimmy Padilla also serves as the foundation for Antonio and Sarah's love story. How does this parallel or compare to other relationships in the book, including Ren and Paul, Ren and Cole, Deidre and her husband and Cole and Liam?

8. A song from their youth first brings Ren and Cole together in Santa Fe. Music is an undercurrent throughout *Forever Man*. How does it act as a catalyst in the story?

9. How do cities serve as characters in *Forever Man*? How do locations such as The Santa Fe Opera, the Pink Adobe, Chimayó and the Alex Marin House contribute to these characterizations of the communities?

10. When Paul learns of Ren and Cole's relationship, he accuses them of being cowards. When two people have had a strong attraction for so many years without having acting on it, is it possible that the relationship was never meant to be? Does fate play a role?

interlude press

One Story Can Change Everything.

interludepress.com

Twitter: @interludepress · Facebook: Interlude Press
Google+: +interludepress · Pinterest: interludepress
Instagram: InterludePress

CPSIA information can be obtained
at www.ICGtesting.com
Printed in the USA
FSOW02n2305110417
32997FS